STONE SOBER

A HAWKE FAMILY NOVEL

BILLIONAIRES OF NEW ORLEANS: THE HAWKE
FAMILY
BOOK 3

GWYN MCNAMEE

Stone Sober
by
Gwyn McNamee © 2017

Cover Design: Michelle Johnson at Blue Sky Designs
Cover Model: Assad Shalhoub
Photographer: Christopher Correia at CJC Photography
Editing: Kathleen Payne

To anyone struggling with the demons of their past...sometimes confronting them and bringing them out into the light is the only path to true freedom.

ACKNOWLEDGMENTS

I, once again, have to start with the most important people in my life—my husband and my daughter. *Stone Sober* was a brutal book for me to write. So many things come to a head in this book that have been building since *Savage Collision*, and some of things I had to do to my characters broke me. I never could have finished without my husband's support and daddy skills.

I also owe another tremendous debt of gratitude to my beta readers—Dawn, Jennifer W., Renee S., Diane E., Audra F., Paula F., and my super-beta Christy. You ladies always ensure I'm on the right path and doing my own story justice.

And finally, I owe the biggest thank you in the WORLD to Crystal Perkins. She not only beta read *Stone Sober,* but she also helped me format the ARC and final book. She is such an amazing friend (and fellow author). I couldn't have finished on time without her assistance.

I love you all!

1

STONE

𝒴ou can't truly know what the phrase "sex on a stick" means unless you've seen Nora Eriksson wrapped around the fucking pole at The Hawkeye Club.

This woman was built for sin but still manages to look like a fucking angel.

The way her long, pale limbs bend and drape around the pole center stage should be illegal. She moves with a fluidity and grace that belies her profession and hints at her former life as a pre-med student. So many of the dancers are vulgar. But not her. No, Nora is exquisite and refined. Her stage name fits her. Cashmere.

The Hawkeye Club doesn't deserve her.

And that's a real dick thing for me to be thinking considering Savage owns the fucking place.

I would say I feel like a creep sitting in the dark corner of the main room and watching her in secret, but I'd be lying. The other patrons gawk at her openly and sit as close to the stage as possible, hoping to get a closer look or even to be touched by her.

Not me.

I much prefer waiting in the shadows and lusting after her in private.

Just like the club doesn't deserve her, neither do I.

She's a pristine diamond—shiny and new and full of hope despite her current job—and I'm a dirty, damaged, dangerous, rabid dog ready to bite. I would chew her up and spit her out and leave her broken without so much as a glance back. I can't do that to her, no matter how attracted to her I am.

Plus, it would be weird. Her sister is married to my brother, so that makes her...what? My sort-of-but-not-quite-sister-in-law?

It's awkward enough dealing with the fallout of Skye and Gabe finally getting together—things are just starting to get back to normal. I could only imagine how Savage and the rest of the family would react if I pursued Nora. It would not be a welcomed development. That much is obvious.

But I can't seem to stay away from her. Every time I'm in town, I find myself here, hiding in the corner like some demented stalker and watching her with a hard cock. I've been coming to the club for years, and *no* one on the stage has ever done this to me.

This isn't about how she looks or how amazing she is on the pole either; this is about *her*. And that makes it a hundred times worse. Maybe in another world, another life, another time, things could be different. Maybe I could be what a girl like Nora deserves. But I don't have the luxury of daydreams.

Thank God, I'm going home tomorrow.

I'm not sure how much more I can handle being in Nora's orbit, or even the same city. Dom's been begging me to move back. But putting myself so close to her on a continuous basis spells disaster in any language. My control can only last for so long when it comes to this woman.

The buzz of my phone on the table draws my attention away from the goddess on stage.

Shit. Skye.

> Are you coming back tonight? Why the hell did you bail? I don't like vague explanations. We need to talk before you leave tomorrow. Don't try to blow me off. <

At the word *blow*, my knee starts bobbing uncontrollably for the hundredth time today. Why is it so fucking hard to find any good coke in this city? This is fucking New Orleans, not some Amish town in Pennsylvania. All my regular sources here seem to be short at the moment, even Dom's guys. Which is...concerning.

He's been dealing with encroachments on his territory and supply lines for months. That it's resulting in an actual shortage means things will come to a head soon. And that's always messy when Dom is involved.

It's not like I *need* it anyway. Hell, it's already been almost two weeks since that party. But it certainly helps me clear my head of unwanted images and voices—bloody, beautiful, or otherwise. I'll just have to find something else to assist with stress relief tonight. Too bad it can't be Nora.

I set my phone back down on the table and scrub my hands over my face. The final notes of "Kashmir" wind down and Nora sashays off stage, that damn perfect ass flexing and rolling and torturing me with every step she takes in those mile-high heels. My cock swells even more, pressing against my boxers and bulging in my dress pants that hide nothing.

Fuck.

This is my chance to get out of here without her seeing me. If I wait too long, she'll come out from backstage, and my chances of a clean getaway are nil. I've managed to keep her from seeing me for this long, and I'd like to keep it that way. Just thinking of having to come face to face with her right now has my stomach churning.

I slide out from the corner booth and move down the back hallway to slip out the side entrance when a small, warm hand grabs my bicep.

Please don't be her.

With trepidation turning my already sour stomach into a roiling mess, I turn to find Renee—aka Scarlett—not Nora, staring up at me with a calculating smile on her too-red lips.

"Stone, I didn't even know you were here. Why didn't you come back and say hi?"

I smile at her and cover her hand with mine. She's a beautiful woman with many talents, and I always try to say hello if I'm in town. But there's no way I'm telling her the real reason for this visit. That would be...unwise. "I just stopped in to drop off something for Savage."

Lie.

Savage, and everyone else, is probably still at Mom's house enjoying Sunday dinner and fawning over the baby. I love them, I really do, but more than a couple hours with the family in full force usually means a pounding headache and frayed nerves.

I was almost relieved to get Dom's call. Even though I really didn't want to get involved in any more of his drama this trip, at least it gave me an excuse to slip out of there.

And once I had taken care of my business for Dom, there was only one place I wanted to be.

Wherever Nora was.

I ducked in here to catch a glimpse of her before I have to fly back to Cali tomorrow instead of going back for more family fun.

But now that I'm looking at Renee, a whole other kind of fun has entered my mind.

It wouldn't be the first time I've hooked up with one of the dancers, and not even the first time I've hooked up with Renee. That's how I know it will help me take my mind off everything going on and relieve the pent-up tension in my body.

"I'm on my way back to my hotel. Are you off soon?"

She grins and squeezes my bicep with her long-nailed fingers. My cock twitches in anticipation of having them wrapped around it. "In less than an hour, and I have a babysitter all night, so I don't need to be home right away."

Shit.

The mention of her kid has me momentarily rethinking my invitation. Taking her away from her child so I can get laid seems a little low, even for me. But then again, she's the one making a mother of the year choice, not me. She could just say no.

Who am I to police her morality?

I lean in and wrap my free arm around her back, pulling her against me. She presses into me and the scent of something over-whelmingly fruity swirls in my nostrils. What cheap perfume she wears doesn't concern me. She's gorgeous, warm, and very willing to do anything I want. It's just what I need tonight.

Brushing her auburn hair back over her shoulder, I kiss her cheek, then let my mouth linger against her ear. "The Windsor Court. I'm on the club level, so call me when you get there, and I'll come down and get you."

Her body practically vibrates against mine, doing absolutely nothing to tame the raging hard-on I've had since Nora wiggled her ass off the stage.

I would love to drag her outside and bend her over the hood of my rental car for a hot, quick fuck, but I need more than that tonight. We are going to need a room for what I have in mind.

A room, and some very sturdy bed posts.

NORA

I drop down into the chair in front of the row of lit mirrors and try to calm my racing heart and labored breathing.

It's not from the dance I just did.

He was here again.

Even though I couldn't see him, I felt his eyes on me from the back corner booth my entire time on stage.

His stare strips me bare and makes me feel vulnerable up there, when usually, the stage is the one place I feel somewhat safe and free.

Dang.

I wish I knew who he was.

He's been here before, at least a half dozen times since I started dancing. Whoever he is, he's careful to always sit in a dark corner. I've never seen his face, only a glimpse of a large, strong hand curled around a tumbler of amber liquid, sporting a watch that looks like it costs more than my car.

The waitresses would probably tell me who he is if I asked, but I'm always too flustered after feeling his heated gaze on my every move. Plus, asking about customers is a big no-no here. Byron would get wind of my questioning and then it would get back to Savage and Gabe, and I'd be stuck having a very uncomfortable conversation with my brother-in-law/boss and his bestie.

There are rules at The Hawkeye Club, rules that don't bend and certainly don't break without you being tossed out to the curb on your ass. Savage runs a tight ship; it's one of the things I appreciate about him and Gabe. They don't tolerate trashy stuff going on at the club, and at the top of that list is sleeping with customers.

Not that I would sleep with the mystery man.

No...definitely not.

If he can do that with simply his eyes, I couldn't imagine how he could break me down and tear me apart if he had his hands on me and his dick inside me.

I've been broken down enough for a thousand lifetimes.

The only reason I'm even functioning after what happened, after what I did, is because I found my place here, on the stage. It's offered freedom from what my life had become. This is exactly what I deserve and where I belong.

I was kidding myself to think I was cut out to be a doctor.

Paging Dr. Eriksson to the pole.

Looking at myself in the mirror, I know the me from two years ago wouldn't even recognize the me today. Heavy, dark eye makeup and thick lipstick weigh on the face that was once clean and makeup free. I never spent any time on trying to impress anyone with my appearance before. It was never important. School, books, studying, repeat, that was my life. Well, that and mountains of stress, anxiety, and pressure.

How thoroughly things have changed.

Scarlett strolls into the room with a smirk on her lips and a flush on her cheeks and exposed cleavage.

Her smile fades when her eyes meet mine in the mirror. "What's wrong, honey?"

I force a tight smile and lean forward to rummage in my makeup bag to avoid having to make direct eye contact with her while I lie through my teeth. Lying makes my stomach turn, and I've been doing it way too much for almost two years.

"I'm fine, just tired. Wishing I was on my way home instead of just starting my shift." That's not a lie. This is the last place I want to be tonight, and not just because *he* was here.

Sundays are always slow, and it makes the night drag.

With a sigh, Scarlett drops into the chair next to me, and I relax, giving up the charade of my makeup search. "Well, I'm almost done. One more dance, and I'm out of here."

That grin returns.

"What has you smiling like that? Big plans with Kade after work?" Although, I don't know what she would be doing with a five-year-old at eight o'clock at night.

She shakes her head. "Nah, I have *much* better plans than just hanging out with the kid tonight. His grandma has him until she heads into work tomorrow."

I see where she's going with this. "Ah, so there's a guy in these plans, then? One who is going to keep you occupied until the wee morning hours?"

A laugh tumbles from her, and she leans forward to examine herself in the mirror. "I sure as shit hope so. I haven't been fucked well in months."

Months? Try years.

I keep my sad sexual history to myself and smile at her. "Sounds like you have some major making up to do."

She nods and opens the mascara tube in her hand, then leans forward and reapplies it. "I do. That whole thing with my ex last year really fucked with my social life. I couldn't go anywhere without him following me and harassing anyone who dared try to show me any attention."

All the drama with her son's father last year had affected everyone. He even came in and confronted her while she was on stage one night. Thank God, Gabe talked to him and made him understand the ramifications of his actions. Gabe is one man I never want to be on the wrong side of—I value my life too much to get in his cross-hairs.

Scarlett deserves to have some fun and live a little. She hasn't had it easy. Working here has definitely taught me to appreciate what I've had my whole life—caring parents, a loving, although sometimes annoying and overbearing, sister, a nice house, food on my plate, and an education. Most of the girls here never got any of that, or if they had, it never lasted long. It's an all too common thread with these girls. So, if Scarlett has found someone who can make her smile like this, I'm happy for her.

I pop up from my chair and head to my locker to grab the outfit for my next dance. "Well, I hope you have a great time tonight." Scarlett is a good person, I genuinely do hope she can find happiness. She deserves it.

"Oh, I will. This isn't my first time with St—" She catches herself in the middle of saying something, and I look at her over my shoulder absently.

"With who?"

Her eyes don't meet mine. "Uh, Steve, his name is Steve. Anyway, he's really something else in the sack. Kinky as fuck and hot as hell."

"Kinky, huh?" I turn back to my locker and tug out my school-girl outfit. The plaid skirt and tiny white crop top always make me cringe. All I can see is Britney Spears with the pigtails. I refuse to go there, but I wear the ridiculous uniform because, for some sick reason, men dig it and my tips are huge. "Can't say I have any experience with that, other than the weird stuff some of our customers are into."

Scarlett's eyes gleam when I meet her gaze again. "Girl, you are missing out. You wouldn't believe what this man can do with some handcuffs and a little rope."

Handcuffs? Rope?

No thanks.

Hot, sweaty sex is one thing. But being tied up is another. Scarlett can have Steve. I'll take a hard pass.

2

STONE

"Mr. Hawke, here's your espresso." I look up from my computer screen and smile at my secretary, Heidi, as she sets the small, porcelain cup down on my desk. It's my seventh shot today, and my body is practically buzzing from all the caffeine.

"Thank you, Heidi."

She pushes her brown, greying hair behind her ears and returns my smile. "No problem, sir. Is there anything else I can do for you?"

Fuck, she just doesn't get it.

"You can stop calling me *sir*." Heidi has been working for me since I started at Leibmann, Marshall, and Spano right after graduation. Normally, having a woman call me *sir* goes straight to my dick. But having a woman old enough to be my mother constantly calling me *sir* is a whole different ballgame. I only play ball in the bedroom, not in my office, and certainly not with my employees. "I've told you to call me Mr. Hawke or Stone."

Her lips press together, and her head tilts to the side, studying me for a moment. Eventually, she nods. "Right, Stone." A tight laugh escapes her, and she brushes her hands down the front of her skirt. "Sorry, it's just unusual around here."

No doubt.

Heidi is old school, just like the firm. The partners here are past geriatric and closer to one foot in the grave, and they like things done the way they have been done since the practice opened in the 1950s. It's one of the many reasons I've never completely fit in here. Following orders or a delineated structure was never really my strong suit. If I'm not the one in charge, I tend to not play well with others.

I think the only reason they keep me around is that I'm young and handsome and juries and judges love me. The fact that I'm also smarter than most, if not all, of the other twenty attorneys in the firm doesn't hurt either.

And that's not just ego talking. Those are the cold, hard facts. I'm their go-to guy when they're struggling with difficult legal arguments and maneuverings. I can see things in a way no one else can, and it usually allows me to save their asses when they'd otherwise be shit outta luck.

They've let my slip-ups and missed deadlines fly because they need me. I stay because I like the money and what the money allows me to do. Like fly back and forth to New Orleans on a moment's notice to put out fires for Dom.

Not that I actually *like* doing that, but being back home has its benefits, and I owe Dom. Big. I'll never forget what he did for me or what happened, even though I've tried for years. I owe him everything. He put me on the path that got me where I am today, so even if I may have a few reservations about his tactics, I keep them to myself.

If the firm knew about my involvement with him, or what I've been doing in NOLA, they would can me in a heartbeat.

But maybe that wouldn't be such a bad thing.

I'm still fucking exhausted from this weekend. When I landed back in San Diego late last night, all I wanted to do was drive home and crash—hard. But before I had even set foot in the door of my condo, my phone had rung, and I had to spend three hours talking Dom out of doing something really fucking stupid. Again. He's a smart man, but lately, his decision making has been a bit...questionable.

Now, I'm running on two hours of sleep and epic amounts of caffeine just trying to make it through the day so I can crawl into bed and get some much needed sleep.

"It's fine, Heidi. Thank you for the coffee. I don't need anything else."

She moves to walk out the door but turns back to me when she reaches the jamb. "Oh, I almost forgot. You told me to remind you that the motion on the Ramirez case has to be filed first thing tomorrow morning."

Fuck. Fuck. Fuck.

Fucking Ramirez.

I had intended to get the motion done before I left for NOLA, but a beautiful blonde had distracted me the night before I left. Then, instead of working on it on the plane, I had two stiff drinks and passed out. Every single minute of my time home was so jam-packed with either family obligations or Dom obligations, I didn't even have time to think about it. And when things finally calmed down my last night there, I spent it ogling Nora and fucking Renee instead of working.

Fuck. Fuck. Fuck.

This is a deadline I can't miss. Or move.

No amount of flirting with the clerk is going to get me an extension.

It looks like another all-nighter.

"Thanks for reminding me, Heidi. Are you taking off for the evening?"

She nods. "Unless you need something?"

I shoo her away with my hand. "Go. Have a good night." There's nothing she can do to help me anyway, other than maybe grab me some more coffee.

"You too, sir."

I grit my teeth to keep from correcting her again. There's only one woman I want calling me *sir* right now. And she's back in New Orleans, wrapped around a pole. But I don't have time to be distracted by fantasies about the angel of the Hawkeye Club. There's too much work to be done to let my dick steal any blood from my brain right now.

The door to my office shuts behind Heidi, and I drop my face into my hands.

Christ, I really fucked this up.

Instead of driving home and climbing into my crisp white sheets, I'm going to be stuck here all night staring at my white computer screen and wishing I hadn't blown this off until the last minute.

I'll get it done. I always do. I work better under pressure, anyway. There were many nights during law school I stayed up straight through to finish an assignment last minute or to study for an exam I should have been preparing for all semester. And I still managed to finish top five in the class. There's nothing like procrastination to bring out the best, at least in me.

Still, I'm going to need more espresso, or maybe even something stronger.

I open the Ramirez case file on my computer and hunker down to dive into my long night's work. Two sentences barely hit the page before my cell rings.

Shit.

It's Dom.

Ignoring it isn't an option.

"Hello?"

"Stone, I'm glad I was able to reach you."

Like I'm hard to get ahold of?

I'm basically at his beck and call.

I've barely been gone from town twenty-four hours, and we've already spoken once.

What could he possibly need now?

I down my espresso in one gulp and prepare myself for whatever crisis required this call.

"What's up, Dom?"

He lets out a long sigh. "The shit is really starting to hit the fan here, Stone. What we discussed last night, well, things have gotten worse. I need you back here. Permanently."

I scrub my hand over my face. We've had this conversation before. Pretty much every time I go to NOLA, Dom tells me he needs me to stay. He's not wrong. Things are getting messy for him. He needs *someone* to help him weed through all the bullshit and put out the fires. I just don't know why it has to be me.

"Dom, we've talked about this. I have a job and a life here." The stable of women I have available to me in San Diego ensures I never go without, and there's always a willing partner up for anything. If I'm in NOLA, in such close proximity to Nora, I'm going to end up spending every night at the club. And I'm not confident I'll be able to stay away from her any more. That will lead nowhere good. It also means dealing with the rest of the Hawke clan on a daily basis. That's more stress than I care to have to deal with.

"You're the only one I trust anymore, Stone. Please come home. I need you."

～

NORA

"We're not having this conversation again." I glare across the table at Dani, and she feigns innocence while moving a sleeping Kennedy from one shoulder to the other.

Seriously, you would think she could take a hint and drop it, already.

"What? All I said was you should consider going back to school."

I guess it was too much to hope that after almost two years, she would finally let it go and accept the fact that I'm not returning to the pre-med program.

"And I've told you a hundred times, I'm happy working for Savage."

She narrows her eyes at me. He's her husband, and I know she loves him, but I don't think she'll ever be one hundred percent on board with his business. At least, not as long as I am working there. It's one thing if it's strangers, but when it's your sister, withholding judgment can be tough. Especially for someone like Dani who doesn't withhold *anything*. I don't think she was born with a filter.

"She does have a point, Nora."

I turn to Caroline and narrow my eyes. "Oh yeah, what point is that?"

She shrugs. "Well, you are young and beautiful now, but you won't always be. What are you going to do when your metabolism drops along with your tits and ass?"

Dani barks out a laugh, but I just scowl. "I'm twenty-one, almost twenty-two, I have time to figure it out."

Plenty of time.

It's not that they don't have a point. I'm just sick of hearing people tell me I should be doing more with my life. There's nothing wrong with stripping, and it's not like anything seedy goes down at the club. Savage and Gabe are pretty clear on the fact that shit doesn't fly. And from what I've heard about the manager over at TWO—the new club location they opened a while back—he's just as strict. I don't mind it. Having controlled and disciplined employees is necessary to achieve the type of success the Hawkeye brand has and respect the name carries.

Caroline laughs and rolls her eyes at me. "You say that now, but don't you ever want what Dani has?" She points to Dani and waits for my response.

"I guess."

I honestly hadn't really thought about it yet. Just trying to keep up with school took everything out of me. I didn't have time to date or consider what my future would look like after I graduated. By the time I finished med school and residency, I would have been thirty and working so much, I wouldn't have had time for a family anyway.

"Even if you did keep your body in shape, you're never gonna meet the man of your dreams at a goddamn strip club." As soon as the words leave her mouth, her eyes dart over to Dani, who scowls at her.

I lean back in my chair and cross my arms over my chest. "That's a little judgmental. You don't think decent guys ever go to the club just to blow off a little steam? What does that say about Savage and Gabe? They own the place."

Most of the patrons of the club aren't totally bad guys, they just aren't exactly white knight, happily-ever-after material either. Although the mystery man who sits in the dark corner booth always manages to get my heart racing and me imagining things I would normally *never* consider with a customer.

Dani throws up her free hand to stop the conversation. "Look, I didn't want to get into all that, and I don't want to start an argument. Let's just forget it. I'm just happy to be here with my two favorite girls. I just could *not* handle being cooped up in the condo anymore. Savage is home so much more now, which is great, but now that Kennedy is here, I'm going stir crazy. I thought after she was born, maybe I would go back to work part-time, because I can do pretty much everything from home, but he doesn't want me to. He doesn't understand that I go crazy not having adult conversations all day. He's the only one I have to talk to, unless I go across the hall to see Gabe and Skye, but they both work so much. We really need to start doing once a week lunches or something just so that I know I can look forward to a day out of the house."

I understand Dani's plight. Not working and being at home all day is so out of the norm for her. When she quit the paper, it was to stay home with Kennedy, but she never intended for that to be permanent. Knowing Savage, I'm sure the reason he doesn't want her returning even part-time is the potential need to put Kennedy in daycare or hire a babysitter. Savage doesn't like anything he can't control, and leaving his only daughter in someone else's hands is definitely out of his comfort zone.

I'm not sure how Dani can stand it, being married to such a control freak. Savage is a wonderful boss and a fantastic husband. I know he treats her like a queen and loves her to death, but there's no way I would be able to handle that. I'm sure the only reason it works is because she stands up to him and calls him out on his bullcrap.

Caroline picks up her glass of wine and drains half of it. "Girl, you know I'm down for that. I really miss having you at the office. Dealing with Doug's temper tantrums was always a lot easier when I had you to bitch to."

They devolve into a conversation about Dani's former employer while I turn back to my lunch.

The burger in front of me isn't as delicious-looking as it had been when it first arrived. I've suddenly lost my appetite.

It's always the same conversation with Dani, and more recently, our mother. It was only a matter of time before she found out I dropped out of school and have been stripping. When I moved out of my campus apartment once the school realized I was no longer a student, I had my mail forwarded to her place while I had been searching for new digs and staying on a friend's couch. Apparently, she thought it was perfectly acceptable to commit a federal offense by opening my mail, including the letter from Tulane confirming the cancellation of my scholarship.

You'd be surprised how red a human face can get when someone's really angry. I swear, she turned a shade so dark, it was almost purple as her rage overtook her.

Her reaction was precisely why I hid it from her for so long. I knew she wouldn't understand, just like Dani never will. She pretends to be okay with it, yet she continuously brings up me returning to school at every opportunity, even spurring our mother to continue to harass me about it as well.

"How will you explain to people what you do?...What will you do when you can't use your body anymore?...You won't have any career or education to fall back on ...What were you thinking?...How will you ever find a nice man to settle down with?"

The questions are always the same, and I always give the same answer. I have time to figure it out. I'm in no rush to decide my entire life. Taking the reins isn't exactly something I excel at, so I'm perfectly content to let others take the lead right now. I made the only decision I could at the time, and I'm confident it was the right one. I wasn't cut out for med school. I couldn't even handle pre-med. I wouldn't have survived if I'd stayed there under the suffocating mountain of stress.

I do want to get married and have babies eventually, and working the pole probably isn't the best place to find my soulmate, but I'm not about to let them know that I agree on that. Right now, I just want to enjoy the freedom that dancing gives me—freedom from the stress of school, freedom from having to think about what I did and why I left, freedom to just be, well, free.

Dani found her happily ever after, and I'm thrilled for her. But I never want anything to tie me down again—not school, not a job, not a person, not life.

3

SAVAGE AND DANI'S REHEARSAL DINNER LAST WINTER

STONE

I can't take any more of this. Time to make my getaway. Maybe if I casually move away from Mom and this conversation, no one will notice.

My back slams into something hard and something wet splashes down the skin exposed by the open back of my dress.

"Oh crap!" I turn toward the poor soul I just slammed into. "I'm so sorry, sir. I didn't see you there." I survey the damage to his shirt and let my gaze trail up.

The blue eyes staring back at me can only belong to a Hawke.

Even if those tell-tale blues weren't there, it would still be obvious who this is. He's almost a carbon copy of Savage. The same broad shoulders and straining muscles are encased in a crisp, white dress shirt and sport coat, and the same devastating smile touches his lips.

He glances down at the wet spot on the front of his shirt and his now half-empty glass of what I can only assume is whiskey given the amber color. A smile tugs at the corner of his lips.

"No harm done."

Dangit, Nora. You're such an idiot sometimes.

I should've watched where I was going instead of just backing up, but I had to get away from the conversation with Mom.

As if this whole rehearsal dinner isn't awkward and overwhelming enough, she had to bring up, yet again, in front of a large group of people that I'm pre-med at Tulane. I still haven't mustered up the nerve to tell her I quit school and am stripping. I'm sure my reprieve is only brief. She'll find out soon enough, and I would prefer it come from me, but in the meantime, having to listen to her gush and go on and on about how smart I am and how incredibly proud I make her is way too much to handle.

Guilt churns in my stomach over lying to her, and now for smashing into Stone and ruining his shirt. I peek up at him from under my lashes and try my best to calm my racing heart.

"You must be Nora." His deep voice rumbles with the statement, sending a shiver down my spine.

What the heck was that?

I can't even find my voice to respond. He watches me expectantly. I shift uncomfortably under his intense scrutiny.

Speak, Nora.

"Oh, yeah, and you're Stone?"

He flashes me a perfectly straight set of white teeth. "That's a pretty fair deduction."

I chuckle and glance down at the floor. Looking him in the eye after I just ruined his shirt and spilled his drink is way too overwhelming. I'm such a klutz sometimes. "Look, I'm really sorry about your drink and your shirt."

And acting like a total moron.

His large palm lands on my shoulder, and he gives it a gentle squeeze. The heat from his hand sends a wave of electricity across my exposed skin. "Don't worry about it. It'll dry."

I'm rendered speechless, yet again. His hand moves over to

my chin, and he tilts my head up until I'm forced to look him in the eye again. "Did you hear me, Nora?"

Somehow, I manage to snap out of my Stone-induced haze. "Yes, I know, but I should have watched where I was going. I'm just...I'm sorry."

His hand falls away, and he chuckles. "You already apologized, Nora. Several times. It's fine."

I never expected Stone to be gracious. Given the few things my sister and Savage have told me about him, it always made him sound like he was kind of an arrogant jerk.

"It's nice to finally meet you." His eyes roll down my body, and a rush of heat floats across my skin. I get naked in front of hundreds of men a week for a living, but this one checking me out in the sun dress I'm wearing has me blushing like a school girl.

Geez, Nora, get a grip.

"It's nice to meet you, too."

Actually, a lot nicer than I had anticipated. And I certainly never thought I'd find him so attractive. But there's just something about him...

He tosses back the remainder of his drink. "Are you having a good time?"

I shrug and glance at Mom over my shoulder. "I guess that depends on what you mean by good?"

It would be a lot better if she kept her mouth shut, but I'm not about to tell Stone that. It would open the door to more talk about school. And that topic is firmly off-limits.

He grins and follows my line of sight. "Yes, I met your mother. I understand exactly what you're saying. These things can be a little bit overwhelming, as can family in general."

I laugh and run a hand through my hair, pushing it back off my face. "That's an understatement. I thought my family was bad, but your family is very...what's the word?"

He leans in and sets his lips next to my ear in a far too familiar manner. "Passionate?"

When he pulls back, he offers me a conspiratorial wink that goes straight to a part of my body I haven't felt much from in almost two years.

Jesus...

I clear my throat and look anywhere but at him. "That's one way of putting it. My sister fits right in, I guess."

Stone tosses his head back and laughs loudly, drawing the attention of the people milling about around us. "Yes, Dani can certainly hold her own. She's good for Savage. He needs somebody like that in his life."

I don't disagree with him, but I'm a little surprised by his insight. From what Dani tells me, he doesn't exactly spend a lot of time or share a lot of love with Savage. And it sounds like it goes beyond the typical brotherly angst.

The strange dichotomy between what I've heard and how Stone's acting right now makes me want to know more. *Why does everyone think he's such a d-bag?*

"So... Dani tells me you're a lawyer?"

His eyes narrow slightly, as if he's searching for something in my question. "If I confirm that, will you hold it against me?"

I smile at him and shake my head. "Not as long as you don't hold my profession against me."

I'm assuming he knows I dance. Mom seems to be the only one who I've managed to keep in the dark about it. Bless her heart, the woman is not very observant. I'm sure if she paid enough attention, she would have realized something major has changed in the last year.

That wicked grin makes another appearance. "Fair enough."

"What kind of law do you do?"

He shrugs as if his work isn't important. "Mostly criminal defense, high-profile stuff, but I do some civil work too."

"Oh, high-profile, huh?" I'm not sure if it's meant to impress me or not. It's hard to gauge whether Stone is just being friendly and answering my questions or if he's trying to get in my pants. He could just be naturally charming and flirtatious. Or he could be the dog Dani warned me he is.

"Yeah, most of it. The firm I work for has been around for quite a long time. It's one of the largest criminal defense firms in the nation, but I also do a lot of pro bono work for clients who can't afford to hire lawyers."

Wow. I certainly wasn't expecting that. I didn't think Stone was the pro bono type, more the I-only-do-something-that-bene-fits-myself type. At least, that's the impression I got from what I've been told.

Why in the world does everyone have an issue with this guy?

I mean, I guess I can see how some people might think that he's arrogant. In most cases, arrogance isn't warranted. Like with all the guys I knew in school.

But with Stone, just the way he carries himself and talks makes you believe every word out of his mouth is true and that any problems that arise, he can fix. I can't put my finger on the right word to describe his presence. It's like he fills up the entire space and swallows you into him. I can see how it makes him great at his job. Juries must love him.

But there's a difference between being arrogant and sucking your own dick. Stone might be confident, but in his case, I don't think it's unwarranted or to stroke his own ego. He's just a man who gets what he wants and always succeeds. I can see that after three minutes talking to him.

Yet he has a heart under all that bravado.

Imagine that.

NORA

She can't hide her surprise when I tell her about my pro bono work nor has she been able to cover up the way she's been reacting to my flirting with her the last few minutes. The flush over her alabaster skin, and the way she's chewing on her bottom lip, makes my dress pants suddenly feel a little confining.

Jesus.

Who would have thought I'd find something so interesting and unexpected tonight? Weddings and everything about them are a pain in the ass. Courthouse, justice of the peace, I do...that's the way I'll do it if I ever fall down that rabbit hole. This whole horse and pony show is a bit over the top, if you ask me.

I was just about to write off this dinner and slip out to find something more entertaining when Nora backed into me and surprised the fuck out of me. Never in my wildest dreams could I have imagined my first time meeting Nora would be like this. From the little I know about her, I guess I always envisioned her as a younger version of Dani. And while they certainly look alike —the same blonde hair and intriguing blue eyes, same long legs and pale skin—Nora seems to be absolutely nothing like the older Eriksson.

How can she be so incredibly different from her sister?

Nora is a born submissive. That much was clear almost immediately—from her calling me sir, apologizing repeatedly, avoiding eye-contact, and fidgeting under my assessment. She senses what I am and is responding naturally. It's also just as clear she has no idea *what* she is.

Everything about her screams innocent. There's no way she's ever been with a Dom or even explored her submissive tendencies. I have a hard time even believing she actually works for Savage and Gabe at the club.

Dani seems the more likely candidate to work the pole than Nora, but Dani is about as far from submissive as anyone I've ever met in my life. I don't know how Savage does it considering he's almost as much of a control freak as me. But what I said to Nora is true, Dani *is* good for him. I've never seen him this happy, and I truly am thrilled for them. What they have would never work for me, though. Dani is demanding and pushy, and that works for them, but it's far from what I'm looking for.

But Nora...she's...perfect.

Well, she would be, if not for the fact that she's off-limits. Dani already told me, in no uncertain terms, that I need to keep my eyes and hands off her before I even met her. And now I see why. She's magnificent. I can't even imagine what she looks like on stage.

My cock swells with that visual, and I have to shift my stance to avoid having a massive boner pointed right at Nora. That's very ungentlemanly. Not to mention, her mother is standing right there, too.

Down boy.

Even if she weren't in the no-fly zone, it would never work anyway, at least, not any longer than a night or two. Not only do we live on opposite sides of the country, but the flack we would get from both our families wouldn't be worth the trouble. Plus, I don't have time for anything. Between work at the firm and Dom suddenly needing me for every little thing now that I'm done with school, it's been a never-ending cycle of phone calls, court appearances, briefs, little sleep, and lots of late nights the last six months or so.

The only thing keeping me going sometimes, is the fact that I can unwind and de-stress at one of the clubs with any number of willing and beautiful women. Or lately, maybe go to a party and do a little of the white stuff. I never thought I'd be that guy who did coke. It was for supermodels and drug addicts who can't handle their shit. But it's pretty common in legal circles these days. It seems like at least half the lawyers I know use it, at least recreationally, though some have a major issue. Every once in a while, the high it provides is the only thing that can clear my mind and set me free from the bullshit cluttered there.

I'd love to lose myself in Nora tonight, but that's not wise, so maybe the little vial in my pocket is the way to go. I palm it with my free hand and work it between my fingers. It's been a couple weeks. I deserve the release.

But Christ, I wish it could be with her instead of a drug.

A loud round of laughter explodes from a group to our left that includes a slew of Hawke cousins, and Nora tosses them a slightly dirty look over her shoulder. "How do you handle this all the time?"

She doesn't need to explain her meaning. I laugh and twist my empty glass in my hand. "Well, first, I tune out about ninety percent of what gets said by anyone with the last name Hawke..." The corner of her mouth ticks up into a tiny grin. "Second, I drink..." I hold up my empty glass, and she opens her mouth, no doubt to offer another apology, but I stop her with a raised hand. "And third, I like to find other ways to enjoy the situation and make use of my time." Like finding a dark closet somewhere to engage in some cardio.

I'm not totally sure she catches my meaning immediately. Just another thing that convinces me she's more innocent than many may believe given her job. But after a few seconds, that sexy blush spreads over her cheeks again, and she returns to finding something very interesting about her shoes.

She ponders them for a second before looking back up at me with a grin.

It's a terrible idea. I know it before the words are even out of my mouth. But I can't stop myself. This may be my only opportunity with Nora and the only way to redeem this day and maybe make the rest of the party more bearable.

"Perhaps you'd like to join me?"

The warmth in her eyes disappears, and the look she gives

flashes from interest to confusion to something almost resembling anger in a split-second.

Shit.

"I think I'll pass. It was nice to meet you, Stone. This has certainly been enlightening."

She turns on her heels and stalks from the room toward the hall. I can practically feel her fuming even as she retreats.

Note to self: you were right. Stay away from Nora Eriksson.

4

PRESENT DAY

NORA

Stone Hawke is an ass. There's nothing else I can say about him without digging out a bunch of four letter words I, unlike my curse-like-a-sailor sister, refuse to use.

I've never met someone so self-centered in my life, and that's really saying something considering I spent time in the pre-med program. Even future doctors have egos too big for their own heads.

Like Stone.

He's been sitting across from me at the Hawke Sunday family dinner for the last several minutes, practically undressing me with his eyes and acting like a king on his throne while the family fawns over him.

At least, some of the family. Savage and Dani toss each other occasional looks that give me the distinct impression they aren't very happy with Stone about something. And every once in a while, Skye will reach over and grip Gabe's shoulder as if to warn and stop him from commenting.

Storm, Ben, and Mrs. Hawke seem completely oblivious, though. She's been prattling on about how happy she is Stone was able to come for a visit so soon. Apparently, he was here about three weeks ago, and no one had expected him back so soon. He's barely been able to get a word in over his mother's gushing.

"I'm just so glad you're here. I feel like I barely saw you last time."

Stone smiles at her and reclines back in his chair. "You were more focused on the baby, Mom, and that's totally understandable. She's your grandchild."

Mrs. Hawke smiles and nods. "Yes, but you are *my* baby."

Everyone chuckles. Such a mom thing to say, for sure. Mom says the same thing about me when she manages to get me in the same room. I admit, I've been avoiding her. I just can't handle the inquisition anymore. She just doesn't understand that I'm an adult now and perfectly capable of making my own decisions, ones she may never agree with.

"Mom, I'm twenty-six years old." Stone's comment holds no bitterness, just a hint of amusement.

"Doesn't matter. You will *always* be my baby. Now, everyone, dig in!" She pushes back from the table, which is piled high with a dozen delicious-looking items. "Does anyone need a refill on their drinks?"

Stone reaches forward with his right hand and grabs the empty wine glass by his plate. "I'll take another glass, Mom."

She smiles sweetly as she makes her way around the table to him and drops a kiss on his forehead before removing the glass from his hand.

When she retreats, his attention returns to the table. Or more specifically, to me.

Ass.

I hate the way he looks at me like he owns me. As if that would ever happen. Of course, he's beautiful. I would be lying if I said he wasn't one of the most physically attractive men I've ever met, but the ego that radiates from him is something I could never look past. I can't believe I didn't see it immediately when we met the first time.

His blue eyes don't leave mine until his mother returns with his drink. "Here you go, sweetheart."

"Thank you, Mom." He tips the glass to his lips, opening them to let the wine slip between them. His eyes slide closed momentarily, and a sexy groan of appreciation sounds from deep in his throat. That shouldn't be so hot, but I find myself having to look away. "This is delicious."

Despite my best efforts, I can't keep my gaze diverted long. It's like my eyes are drawn to him.

He opens his eyes, and they meet mine again. The twinkle there heats my skin, and I'm pretty sure I'm blushing. "A flavor this incredible should be enjoyed *all* night long." His clear innuendo thrown my way seems to blow past everyone else as they dig in to the meal Mrs. Hawke prepared.

I shouldn't have come here tonight. I've managed to avoid all the other invites to the Hawke family gatherings, feigning work or family time with Mom. But, Dani requested my presence, saying she needed another "buffer" at the table since Stone was going to be there.

She didn't elaborate. But she didn't have to. Stone and Savage have always had a tense relationship, according to her. I know it has something to do with Dom Abello, but Dani has never really gone into details.

There's no reason to. Stone has never really been on my radar. I've only met him twice—once at the rehearsal dinner and then again at the wedding. And yes, at first, I thought he was charming and gracious, and I couldn't understand why Dani had issued me a warning about him. But it wasn't long before his clear sexual interest in me led to some not so subtle innuendos that showed me his true colors. And then I saw him sneak away with a girl during the wedding reception and return looking rumpled and with a satisfied grin on his face.

Jerk.

Stone Hawke is the kind of man women either avoided or flocked to, depending on whether they wanted a white picket fence or just a good lay. There was no way he would provide the former, but I had no doubts the latter was well within his wheelhouse. He oozes sex and dirty, nasty things. His eyes promise debauchery and depravity, and his lips speak of scandal.

Staying far away from Stone has been my plan since the moment I saw his true colors. He's bad news, and I put anything bad behind me. But that doesn't mean the sexual pull he emits isn't trying to suck me into his orbit.

Dani leans over to me. "Why is Stone looking at you like he wants to eat you instead of this meal?"

I jerk and turn my head toward her to meet her eyes. "I have no clue."

"You two never..." She wiggles her eyebrows suggestively, and I smack her shoulder.

"No!" The word comes out louder than I had intended, and every single pair of eyes at the table land on me.

Heat spreads up my neck and across my face with my blush. "Sorry."

Stone chuckles and smirks at me as if he somehow knows he's the cause of my fluster.

"Well, on that note." He pushes his chair back and stands—his black dress pants and white button-down shirt straining to contain the obvious muscles in his legs, arms, and chest—and holds up his wine glass. "I have an announcement to make."

Everyone turns to watch him—some of the gazes holding interest, others harboring unease—and he grins. "I'm not just back for another visit. As of today, I am officially back, permanently."

"What?" Mrs. Hawke leaps from her chair while jaws drop on

everyone else in the room. "Are you joking? What about your job?"

He shrugs. "I quit."

Savage scoffs. "Did you quit, or did they just finally fire you?"

"Savage!" His mother's censure has him biting back whatever he was about to say next as he raises his hands in surrender.

"No, Savage." Stone takes a sip of his wine and places his free hand on the back of his chair. "I did not get fired. I quit because I wanted to come home. Everything that happened with Gabe, and now having Kennedy here, I just felt it was time."

My eyes flit over to Gabe. It wasn't that long ago he was in the hospital and in really bad shape. He almost died, and that, combined with his relationship with Skye, created more tension than I care to remember. Savage wasn't even talking to him for weeks. Talk about awkward. But things have finally seemed to have settled between them, which makes being at work with those two a whole lot easier.

Mrs. Hawke makes her way around the table until she's standing beside Stone. "What are you going to do? You don't have a job here, you aren't even licensed in Louisiana."

He wraps his arm around her and kisses the top of her head. "Don't worry, Mom. I took the bar in February."

She jerks away from him. "What? I don't even remember you being here in February."

"I know, I didn't tell anyone, other than Dom, that I was doing it. I'm going to set up my own firm. Dom is already sending some business my way."

A growl sounds from my left. I look over at Savage, and his fists clench on top of the table. "You're going to work for Dom?"

Stone's eyes harden, and his lips press into a firm line. "Look, I know you've always thought you were too good for Dom, even after he helped you after college, but I don't want to hear a word from you about this."

Yikes.

The tension in the room as the brothers stare each other down is so thick, you could cut it with a knife. Storm breaks it by rising and raising her glass in the air. "Well, I think this news calls for a toast. To having baby brother back in the fold."

Mrs. Hawke returns to her seat and grabs her glass. Everyone has a smile on their face, although at least half of them are clearly fake.

What the deuce is up with this family?

I'm so glad I don't have to deal with them on a regular basis, outside of work. My own family is enough to handle; I don't need their family drama piled on.

I raise my glass, intending to down the rest of my wine, but then everyone begins leaning forward to clink their glasses against one another. Following suit, I stand and lean forward to meet all the glasses.

When Stone gets to me, a devilish smirk crosses his perfect lips as he reaches across the table with his glass and tinks it against mine.

The sleeve of his shirt rides up with his movement, and my breath stalls in my chest.

A gleaming and very familiar watch sits on his wrist.

Holy mother of God.

It's him.

∾

STONE

Nora freezes, her eyes locked on our touching glasses.

I'm about to ask her if she's okay when the glass in her hand falls from her fingers onto the table. Red wine splatters across the white linen table runner and runs across the tabletop.

Someone gasps and says her name.

"Oh, crap!" She seems to snap out of whatever the momentary lapse was as everyone scrambles to throw napkins on the spreading liquid.

Everyone but me.

What the fuck was that about?

And did she just say crap? Who the fuck says crap?

I watch her as she fumbles with the glass, trying to right it and mop up the wine.

"I'm so sorry." Her voice wavers slightly, and her hand shakes as she presses her napkin over the wine closest to her. A dark flush spreads up her neck and over her pale cheeks.

Christ, I fucking love skin like hers and the way a flush or mark stands out in such sharp contrast.

I will my dick to remain at heel so I don't embarrass myself in front of the entire Hawke clan.

Nervous eyes flit over just about everyone—except me. She makes a concerted effort not to glance my way. It simultaneously makes the corner of my mouth quirk up, knowing I am somehow affecting her, and makes my stomach churn with unease wondering what set her off. The last thing I want to do is scare her, especially now that I'm back home.

It wasn't an easy decision. But the workload at the firm, coupled with what Dom was asking of me, meant something had to give. Coming back to NOLA took a lot of convincing, but I think it's ultimately for the best. I'll have to work directly for Dom, and he's referring me a lot of clients, plus I want to take on a few *pro bono* cases. I have so many more options here.

I'll also have Nora within reach. A moral conundrum if there ever was one. Seeing her, just being around her, seems to ease the ache in my chest, but I can never have her, which only creates more frustration.

Being home will mean balancing a tight-rope between my

attraction to her and my desire to do the right thing and keep her away from me.

My mother appears at Nora's side with a roll of paper towels. "It's okay, dear. Spills happen."

I tip my glass back and down the remainder of my wine while I watch Nora become more and more frantic.

What the hell is going on with her? She looks like she's just seen a ghost.

The wail of a very angry newborn cuts through the chaos. Dani turns to go attend to her in the bedroom, but Nora puts a hand on her arm to stop her. "It's all right, I'll go."

Confusion flits across Dani's face for a moment, then her eyes flick over to me before returning to her sister. "Okay, thanks."

Nora scurries out of the room like her ass is on fire, and Dani and Savage both cast disapproving gazes at me. "What?"

Mom finishes cleaning the table and disappears into the kitchen. Dani rolls her eyes at me and returns to her seat. "Stop making sexy eyes at my sister, Stone. You're making her uncomfortable."

I bark out a laugh and drop back into my chair to finish my dinner. "I am not making sexy eyes at her. If she's uncomfortable, that's all on her."

Dani narrows her gaze on me and presses her lips together tightly but doesn't utter another word. The baby's cries stop, and she seems to relax a little as Savage places a hand on her forearm and rubs it gently.

Shit.

I didn't mean to upset her. Even though Savage and I tend to butt heads, pretty much all the time, Dani is good for him, and I never want to hurt her, even unintentionally.

Besides, it's not like anything can ever happen with Nora. Shamelessly flirting with her and watching her from the shadows is going to have to be the extent of my contact with her. My dick practically weeps at that thought, but it's the way it has to be.

I hold my hands up in resignation. "Danika, there's nothing to worry about. I promise I'll be good."

Savage snorts and the corner of his mouth ticks up. "You? Good? That'll be the fucking day…"

He's not wrong.

Everything base and animal in me is screaming to grab Nora and show her what I really want from her. But she's far too innocent to be stained and corrupted by me. If she weren't a stripper, I would probably think she's a virgin the way she flushes and reacts to mere glances from me.

But the way she moves on stage tells me she's used that body for more than just dancing.

And I want it. I want *her*.

Control your shit, Stone.

Giving in would only prove Savage's point.

I glare at him but withhold the retort burning on the tip of my tongue.

While his comment may be true, it doesn't mean I appreciate him constantly reminding me how disappointed and embarrassed he is by me.

His clear distain for my decision to work with and for Dom grates especially hard on my nerves. Dom has been nothing but good to our family. He took care of Mom when Dad died and was the only father figure I ever had. I think Savage sometimes forgets that while he had ten years with Dad, I was only five when he died. Dom stepped up and stepped in for him. Dom saved me.

What he does isn't always ethical or legal, but he's good to us.

Savage needs to give him some fucking credit.

He also needs to realize I'm not his baby brother anymore, no matter *what* Mom says. I haven't been for a very long time. I'm perfectly capable of making my own decisions about who and how I fuck and who I work for.

Being back in New Orleans permanently is certainly going to mean more conflict and confrontations with Savage. But he's going to learn very soon that I'm not the same person I was when I left for college eight years ago.

He has no idea who he's fucking with. He can't intimidate me anymore. The role of master and commander isn't his anymore, and he's just going to have to learn to accept that.

5

NORA

*F*rom backstage, I peek around the corner of the wall and out beyond the main stage to the darkened area where the customers sit.

I can't see into the far corner, but that's the whole point, isn't it?

It's precisely why he chooses that seat every single time. The shadows conceal his identity, or at least, they did.

It's been two weeks since the awkward and disastrous dinner at the Hawkes' where Stone inadvertently outed himself as the shadow man, and I made a fool of myself before scampering out early without making eye contact with him again.

Crap.

Just thinking about that night makes me cringe.

Why couldn't I have just been cool and masked my reaction when I saw the watch? Instead, I was a total bumbling idiot.

Real smooth, Nora, real smooth.

I haven't seen him—or the hand and watch, rather—since

that night, but before every time I step onto the stage, I sneak a look out to the infamous corner to see if he's there. I'm never sure if I *want* him to be there or not.

Dancing with his eyes on me made me feel more exposed than I have in my entire life. It's like he could see through the carefully crafted façade I created for Cashmere and saw all my secrets.

Anyone knowing is scary, but a man like Stone Hawke knowing me intimately terrifies me. And we've barely spoken and only touched briefly when we first met at the rehearsal dinner.

Honestly, if he were to get those big hands on me, I would probably shatter into a million pieces.

So...

Survival mode.

Avoidance is always the best answer.

"What are you doing?"

I jump and whirl around. "Nothing." Gabe eyes me suspiciously as I brush past him back toward the mirrors to touch up my makeup.

He follows me over and leans against the counter. "I'm not blind. Every night, you've been looking for someone. Who is it?"

"No one." My answer probably came a little too quickly and with a little bit of a she-doth-protest-too-much vibe.

Gabe scoffs and crosses his arms over his chest. "Remember when you called me out on the Skye thing? Well, now it's my turn. Something is going on. Are you involved with a customer?"

"What?" I whip my head sideways and meet his questioning gaze, but only briefly. I'm a bad liar, and Gabe is too perceptive. Plus, he's my boss. Lying to him just feels wrong. But I guess it's not a lie really, because we aren't dating. We aren't anything. "No, of course not. I'm not that stupid."

He raises an eyebrow. "Then, what's up?"

Geez, I wish I knew.

I release a sigh and drop into the chair. It's not like I can be honest with him. Gabe knows Stone way too well. They're practically brothers, and given how close he is to Savage, I imagine his feelings about Stone mirror the oldest Hawke's.

So I need to tread carefully. "There's a guy who's been coming to watch me dance..." I trail off, not really sure how to explain what's been happening.

Gabe stiffens, and his eyes narrow on me. "Who is he? Did he do something out of line?"

I shake my head and run my hands back through my curler-created spirals. "No, nothing like that. And, I'm not sure who he is. He always sits in that corner booth, where I can't see him." Tiny lie. I *have* never seen him...here.

"So what's the problem?"

The words to describe what I feel when Stone watches me are hard to find without sounding totally crazy. I search for them while Gabe eyes me and waits. "I guess he makes me feel...exposed."

Gabe barks out a laugh and grins at me. "That's really something, I guess, considering you're about to bare it all for total strangers."

I can't help but chuckle with him. "Believe me, I know how crazy it sounds."

His head shakes. "Not crazy at all. That's exactly how I felt with Skye."

"Whoa! Back up a second, this is completely different. You've known Skye your entire life. I don't even know who this guy is."

He shrugs and pushes off from the counter. "Sometimes, it doesn't matter. You can't help who you fall in love with or who gets under your skin. It just happens. Just remember the rules. No special treatment just because you are Savage's sister-in-law." With a parting wink, he disappears out toward the bar area and leaves me even more confused than before.

Criminy...

I don't have time to worry about Stone.

This job is supposed to be an escape. I'm not going to let him ruin that for me.

Ignore him.

Ignore how he makes you feel.

Concentrate on forgetting everything that led you here.

I return to the edge of the stage to get ready for my routine. Scarlett's music winds down, and she saunters off stage toward me with a grin and a bunch of bills tucked into the garter on her left thigh.

"Good crowd tonight. The guy in the first row on the left is a good tipper, and an ass man."

I smile at her. "Thanks."

She pauses next to me. "Did anyone tell you they are looking for some girls to take a couple shifts over at TWO? Apparently, they have a couple people out with the flu or something."

Huh?

"No. I just spoke with Gabe, and he didn't mention anything."

Why didn't he tell me about this?

"Well, you should ask him. I may go over a couple nights. I hear things are hot over there."

Getting out of here, even for a just a little while, would be good. I love working for Savage and Gabe, and Byron and the rest of the staff here is great, but working for your brother-in-law while his brother is secretly watching you from dark corners is causing me way too much anxiety right now.

This job was supposed to be stress-free. I want and need to keep it that way. The last time I gave in to the crushing pressure of stress in my life, bad things happened.

And I won't allow myself to fall into that situation again.

My music cues up, and I take one more quick peek out at the corner. It still appears to be deserted, but I guess I can't know for sure until I step out onto the stage and feel the heat of his eyes on me.

How is it possible to dread and crave something so much at the same time?

STONE

If Dom doesn't stop talking, I'm going to kick him in the fucking nuts. Or maybe throw the paper weight on his desk at his skull. Something to shut him the hell up.

I should've known this meeting was going to be endless. Dom can never seem to get shit together so we can deal with it all at once. It's always one disaster after another...on and on and on.

My bouncing foot shakes the whiskey in my glass resting on my knee. I scratch idly at the skin on my exposed forearm.

Christ.

I'm not usually this wound up. But the move was one giant time-suck, and I haven't been able to give myself any time to relax and enjoy myself. And, by the looks of how this meeting is going, I won't have much now that I'm finally getting settled in here, either.

I need a fucking release...sexual and otherwise.

It would be nice to just do a line right now, just to relax—but Dom refuses to allow drugs in his office.

Not that I blame him.

He's managed to stay out of the slammer thus far by keeping his hands relatively clean and leaving the dirty work to his underlings.

Of course, he'd never have something as incriminating as blow in the same room as he is. Especially not after what happened all those years ago.

Still, a little would be nice. The euphoria it produces can't be rivaled. And the way it washes away all my worries for a while is something I desperately need right now.

Dom is exhausting, but I knew what I was getting into when I agreed to move back here and essentially become his fixer.

I don't know what went down with the attorney who was handling his shit prior to me graduating law school, but somehow, I've become the "only one he can trust," with just about everything.

It isn't exactly my first career choice—I mean, who goes to law school to become counsel for the mob? But I owe him.

He's gotten me out of some serious jams over the years, the least I can do is the same for him now that I'm qualified. If it weren't for Dom, I'd probably have spent most of my time in juvie or jail and then probably would've made my way to prison.

A mob boss being my saving grace sounds insane. But two things he always taught were respect and discipline. He made sure I got myself in control, and control became my entire life.

"Stone?" I jerk my head up to look at Dom, and he narrows his eyes at me. "You okay, son?"

"Yeah, sorry just thinking there for a moment."

He leans back in his chair and takes a sip of the 50 year Macallan he has sitting in his tumbler. "I was saying that I really need you to go talk to Castillo for me."

Shit.

"What is it this time?"

The corner of his mouth quirks up and he shrugs. "Well... they seem to have gotten it into their heads that they can take over the area." He snorts and takes another sip. "We both know that's not happening."

"No, it's not. What would you like me to do?"

"Reason with them."

I bark out a laugh. "Why can't you do that?"

He leans forward and rests his elbows on the desk. "I *may* have accidentally insulted Castillo the last time we met in person. I don't think he likes me very much right now."

"Dom, nobody likes you very much."

His head falls back as he roars with laughter. Most people would probably be terrified to insult a man like Dom, but I know he's not as bad as everybody thinks he is. Plus, he would never, ever do anything to hurt me. I'm more of a son than his own damn kid.

When his wife left him, and took Luca with her when he was only four years old, Dom didn't do anything to stop her. I was too young to really question it. I know Dom still supports them, but she doesn't want him to have anything to do with his son.

I can't say I blame her. We grew up with Dom around, and Mom has always turned a blind eye to his shady dealings, but there's a very real danger there. And as his son, Luca would have been a prime target. From what I understand, Patricia fled back to her parents somewhere in New Jersey, and I haven't seen her or Luca since. I'm sure Dom watches them. It's strange that he hasn't tried to bring Luca into the fold. I can only assume it's to keep him safe. But I'm sure Dom has eyes on them to assure that.

"Very true, Stone, very true. I wouldn't say I have a lot of friends."

Savoring the burn of the whiskey down my throat, I take a moment to consider the situation. Castillo is ruthless. Dom's been battling his desire to expand their territory for years. It doesn't surprise me they are making another push. It does surprise me Dom would be dumb enough to insult the man to his face. There's no way that didn't aggravate an already touchy situation.

"I'll contact Castillo and ask for a meeting tomorrow."

Dom nods and drains the last of his drink. "Good. One less thing for me to worry about."

I check my watch.

12:30.

Nora should be going on stage right about now with her second dance. That damn little schoolgirl outfit. Not normally my style, but on her?

Fuck.

I need to remember not to think about her while sitting in business meetings. My swelling cock is bound to get noticed one of these times. With as much discretion as possible, I adjust my poor, neglected dick and finish my drink.

"If there's nothing else...I'm going to take off."

His brow shoots up. "Got somewhere else to be?"

You could say that.

"Kind of. I'll let you know what I get arranged tomorrow."

Dom heaves his bulky frame up from his chair and meets me on the side of the desk. He grasps my hand and claps me on the shoulder. "You're a good kid. If I haven't mentioned it, I'm glad you're home."

He has mentioned it. Many times.

And repeatedly told me that the continued success of his empire is essentially in my hands from now on.

But I'm not going to remind him of that. Right now, there are only two things on my mind. Getting out of here fast enough to catch Nora's last dance of the night...and getting some blow.

6

NORA

*W*orking at TWO today is going to provide three things I desperately need: money, peace of mind that Stone won't be watching me from the dark recesses, and space from Savage and Gabe. The last is especially needed after my blow up with Gabe last night when I confronted him about not offering me the opportunity like he did the other girls.

Criminy!

Who the fudge does he think he is, anyway?

He wouldn't admit it, but I know, without a doubt, that he and Savage didn't tell me because they want to be able to keep an eye on me, and that's easier to do at the main club. They dramatically underestimate my ability to take care of myself. Even after I helped Savage when that fight broke out, back when he started dating Dani, he still sees me as a princess, not Xena Warrior Princess like he should. Okay, that's probably an overstatement. I'm much more likely to back away from a fight than start one, but I don't like knowing he feels like I need protecting.

TWO has only been open for about a year, but it already appears to have a pretty decent crowd from what I can see when I push through the front door. It's barely four in the afternoon, but the place is already packed. The bouncer gives me a once-over and approaches.

"You Cashmere?"

I crane my neck up to look him in the eye.

Dang. This guy is a giant.

"Yeah."

He grins, extends a massive hand, and crushes mine with a vise-like grip. "Solomon. But people call me Big S, or Saint."

Ouch! You certainly are big.

No, big isn't even the right word. Enormous is close. Maybe ginormous?

"Nice to meet you."

"You too." He tosses his head toward the bar area behind him. "Vance is over there. You can check in with him. Let me know if you need anything."

I nod and wander off toward the bar, taking stock of the crowded main floor on my way. A rowdy group of college age guys surround the main stage. The pile of bills at the feet of the girl on the pole gives me hope for the evening. A small table in the corner holds a duo of older men in suits who are more interested in whatever they're discussing than what's happening on stage. And there's another group of men who look like mini-van dads sitting off to the side and watching everything from a safe distance.

From the bar, a tall, thin, and incredibly handsome blond guy watches my approach and offers me a grin when I finally reach him. "Hey, you must be Cashmere."

"I am. Are you Vance?"

He nods and makes his way around the bar to meet me on the other side. "Follow me to the back. I'll introduce you to the girls."

A short hall leads back to a changing room very similar to the one at the main club. Rows of vanity mirrors line two walls and lockers take up the one across from where we enter. Three women in various stages of undress glance over at us before returning their attention to their preparations.

"Cherry, Rose, Carmen, this is Cashmere. She's going to be helping fill in until Michaela and Jasmine are back."

Mumbled hellos and waves over their shoulders are the only welcome I get. Not that I expected much different. This is their domain. I'm an outsider.

Crap. I hope they don't know who I am.

If they knew I was Savage's sister-in-law, that could make this even worse. Given their lack of interest, though, I'm pretty sure I'm safe...at least for now. I'm sure Vance knows, no doubt Savage or Gabe mentioned it to him as soon as I told Gabe I wanted to come over here. But everyone at the club is pretty good about keeping real names and anything else personal private.

Vance leads me to an empty vanity station and motions toward it. "You can get ready here. There are open lockers for your stuff." He glances down at his watch. "You go on in about an hour. I need you on the floor until then. Let me or one of the girls know if you need anything. Thanks again for helping out."

"No problem." Really, he's the one doing *me* the favor. Dancing was supposed to be a way to escape from the shitty choices I made—something mindless and easy and fun. It's turned into a giant complicated pile of crap since Dani married Savage and Stone started watching me.

Maybe here, I can get some relief.

My ass barely hits the chair before a young blonde woman with breasts the size of basketballs appears in the mirror behind me. She smiles and leans down, resting her elbow on the back of the chair. "So, how long you been dancin' for?"

"About a year and a half, almost two."

Her eyes widen. "Wow, that long? I just started a couple months ago."

If I didn't know the law required her to be twenty-one to dance, I would be sure she was barely eighteen. But Savage and Gabe would never risk having someone underage working for them. The only reason I was allowed to keep dancing when the new law upping the age passed was because I turned twenty-one a month before the grandfather clause expired.

"What did you do before this?"

The question is innocent enough, but my gut clenches, and I bite the inside of my cheek to stop myself from snapping at her to mind her own business. "Uh, I was in school."

"For what?"

I sigh. My answer is bound to create an issue, and if I don't answer, she's going to think I'm anti-social or uppity. I'm screwed either way, so I might as well just be honest. "Pre-med."

She jerks up, and her eyes narrow on me. "Oh, one of those smart girls who thinks she's better than all of us, huh?"

Exactly why I didn't want to answer your question.

I turn to her and try to do some damage control by telling her the God's honest truth. "Not at all. I never should have even been there. This is where I belong."

Her pale blue, heavily-makeuped eyes consider me for a moment before they soften slightly. "If you say so." She turns away from me, and I slump down further in the chair.

Well, the night can only get better from here...*right?*

STONE

Godfuckingdammit!

Not only did I miss Nora last night at the club because of how long Dom kept me in the meeting, now she's not here at all when she would normally work tonight. Just my fucking luck.

"Where is Nora?"

Byron quirks a dark eyebrow at me and leans against the bar. "Why do you care?"

A growl forms deep in my throat, but I doubt he can hear it over the thumping bass of the music.

"I have some business with her."

He chuckles and runs a hand back through his hair as he straightens. "I bet you do..."

I slam my palms down on the bar top. "What the fuck is that supposed to mean?"

Byron doesn't even flinch, just crosses his arms over his chest and watches me with a knowing glint in his eyes. "Do you honestly think I haven't noticed you sneaking in and out the back door and sitting in the corner booth watching her over the last couple months? I'm not blind, you know. It's my job to know what happens around here. I'd be surprised if your brother doesn't already know too, considering the way he watches those cameras with an eagle eye."

Shit.

The fucking cameras.

But...no...no way Savage has noticed. I would have had my ass reamed out a long time ago if he saw any correlation between me being here and Nora. He must be too wrapped up in being a dad and the new construction on THREE happening to be watching as closely as he used to. Which is probably the only reason he hasn't tried to skin my hide.

Savage may not be on my case, but Byron has apparently made it his business to question my interest in Nora.

"Are you going to tell me where she is, or what?"

He considers me for a moment before dropping his arms and reaching for a glass. "She's over at TWO. They had a few girls get sick and needed some people to fill in for a couple days."

A band tightens around my chest.

Shit.

The thought of her at TWO makes my skin crawl. Not

because of anything specific, but mostly because I've never set foot in there, and the unfamiliarity of it equals unsafe in my fucked up mind. Working so much with Dom over the last several months has shown me the real seedy side of NOLA. It's not that I didn't know it existed. I've represented some pretty shitty people in California and they are everywhere. But NOLA's crime and underworld is something else entirely. And it's something Nora doesn't need to be within a hundred miles of.

At least here, I know she's safe. Byron, Savage, Gabe, and the bouncers ensure that. I don't know the guys at TWO. And that means I don't trust them.

Byron slides a tumbler full of a dark liquid across the bar to me.

"Have a drink."

I reach out and grab the glass, raising it to my lips for a sip of the warm, spicy bourbon he poured.

Chill, Stone.

There's no point in freaking out or flying off the handle about this. Especially not at Byron. The guy's been a loyal employee and everyone loves him.

He watches me for a moment before he leans against the bar and sighs. "Can I make a suggestion?"

My glass clinks against the bar a little harder than I intended when I bring it back down. I grit my teeth. "Sure."

"Nora is a good girl. I still don't know how she ever ended up in this place. When she started, she told me she just liked dancing, but I know there's more to it than that. There's a lot to that girl, and she doesn't need your kind of trouble in her life. And *you* don't need the kind of trouble it would cause you with Savage and Dani if you pursued anything with her. So, keep skulking in the corner and watching her if you want to, but I would recommend keeping your hands to yourself when it comes to Nora."

Visions of my fist smashing into Byron's face flash in my head, but I manage to contain my rage long enough to drain my drink and take a step back from the bar. The last thing I need is to beat the shit out of Savage's bar manager. Ending up in jail and even further on my brother's bad side are two things I'd rather avoid.

"Thanks for the advice."

He nods, but we both know I'm not going to take it.

I'm drawn to her like a fucking moth to a flame. Or more like a hungry wolf circling an injured lamb. The whole innocent thing has never done anything for me before. I prefer women who let me give them what they need, even if they don't know they need it. Women who are open and willing are my usual fare. Nora will run screaming if I try to do what I really want to.

The drizzle falling when I step outside cools my temper but not my desire for her. The engine on my Aston Martin Vanquish roars to life, and I peel out of the parking lot onto the rain-dampened street.

Fucking shit.

My bone-crushing grip on the steering wheel turns my knuckles white.

Why can't I stay away from this girl?

It's not like me to do stupid and reckless things, at least, not anymore. I went off the rails a bit during my formative years, but control is my life now. I crave it, I need it more than I need oxygen most days. And this woman makes me want to throw all that carefully honed control out the window.

I can't have her.

I know that.

That fact had been accepted the moment I met her and took her small, cool hand in my huge warm one to shake it. Her cornflower eyes had flickered up to meet mine, and a flush had spread over her pale skin instantly before she lowered her gaze to the floor and pulled her hand from mine.

Our first encounter told me all I needed to know. She was polite and surprisingly shy and soft-spoken. And it was clear she's a born submissive.

Under normal circumstances, that fact would have me practically coming in my pants. But when the girl was so tangled in my already fucked up family dynamics, and clearly a good girl, that fact instead gave me the worst case of blue-balls I've had in my life.

Fuck. Just FUCK.

And now, I'm driving across town for this girl.

Why?

We've barely spoken to each other and when we have, the vibes rolling off her certainly weren't *take me back to your place and have your way with me.* They were more *if you even think about touching me, you're going to lose your balls.*

She's attracted to me, that's one thing she can't hide. But attraction isn't enough, not for what a girl like Nora wants and deserves. For a girl I'll spend a night or two with, sure. But not Nora.

The sign for The Hawkeye Club II appears and I veer into the lot, barely touching the brake.

An unstoppable need to see her drives me across the pavement. Night fell hours ago, and the lot is packed with cars. Despite my desire to get in to see her, there's no way I'm parking my baby anywhere near the vehicles of the drunk revelers, especially when it's raining.

I pull around the back of the club toward the rear door. A flash of white blonde hair draws my attention to the corner of the lot and I slow.

Nora.

She jogs toward a car parked under a lamp. A dark blue truck three spots over slowly inches out of the space...without its headlights on. A shiver rolls through my body. Whatever the driver is up to, it's no good.

Why the fuck isn't someone escorting her out?

My foot moves from the brake to the gas almost involuntarily, and I crank the wheel and gun it. Eating up the pavement, the car shoots across the lot toward her.

She pauses next to her car and rummages through her purse, seemingly oblivious to the fact there is someone in the truck watching her. It creeps forward out of its spot toward her.

It only takes a few seconds for me to reach her, but it feels like hours. My car skids to a stop next to her. At the squeal of tires on the wet pavement, her head jerks up and wide eyes search the dark tinted windows.

Grasping something in her hand, she turns and lunges for her car door just as I throw mine open.

"Nora!"

The truck tears off without me ever seeing who was driving

"Nora!"

My hand lands on her shoulder, and before I even know what's happening, my arm twists sideways.

Fuck!

And something smashes into my balls.

7

NORA

"You kneed Stone in the balls?" Caroline's incredulous tone matches my feelings about what went down last night perfectly. I still can't believe it happened.

I sigh and drop my face into my hands. "Yes. *Hard* too. He dropped so fast, I thought I'd ruptured something." I look back up at her to gauge her reaction.

Caroline scoots forward to the edge of her chair, her eyes wide and begging for more. She's practically salivating. "Oh, my God, what did you do then?"

"As soon as he collapsed, I jumped in my car and got the heck out of there."

She jerks back. "You just *left* him there? With potentially damaged nuts?"

Fudge!

The look she's giving me right now does nothing to alleviate my guilt. I barely slept last night thinking about what happened.

He just came out of nowhere. I didn't know it was him. What was I supposed to do?

"I didn't know it was him until *after* the damage was done. It all happened so quickly. All I saw was this silver sports car barreling across the parking lot toward me, and I panicked. I tried to get in my car, but then someone grabbed my arm. I guess my self-defense training paid off because I just reacted and twisted his arm back and threw my knee into him. I didn't even see who my attacker was until I had pulled out of the spot and turned the car around. My headlights landed on his face. At that point, I was so flustered...I didn't know what to do, so yeah, I left."

"Whew. Girl, kicking a man in the nuts is no small thing. Are you sure he's all right?"

I reach out for my water and gulp it down, trying to soothe my dry throat. The thought I may have seriously hurt him has been weighing on me. I still can't believe I actually kneed him in the junk. Poor Stone...

But seriously, what was he thinking? Charging at me like that and then grabbing me? He's lucky I wasn't carrying a gun.

"No, I'm not sure he's all right, but what can I do now?"

Caroline chuckles and grabs her glass of wine. "You could at least check on the poor guy." She takes a sip, eyeing me over the rim of the glass.

Crap.

I probably *should* call or something to make sure he didn't end up in the hospital with a ruptured nut. "Wouldn't Dani have heard something if Stone was seriously injured?"

Caroline raises and lowers one shoulder. "Maybe, but it's not like Savage and Stone are close. So it's possible Savage wouldn't even know."

I chew on my bottom lip.

Should I call him?

Go over to his place?

Or just leave it alone?

My phone ringing pulls me from my thoughts of Stone's junk. I wrestle it out of my purse. It's Dani.

"Hey, are you on your way?"

An exasperated sigh greets me. "No, I'm not going to make it. Kennedy had a rough night last night and didn't sleep much, and she's passed out now. I thought maybe she'd wake up before I had to come meet you guys, but she's still out cold, and I don't want to wake her."

Guilt pokes at me when I realize I'm actually glad Dani isn't going to make our lunch date.

Having to explain the whole Stone fiasco to her would have been awkward and probably would have led to a lot of questions I can't answer.

Why was Stone there? Why the heck did he charge over to me like that?

I'd love to know the answers myself, but the only person who has them is probably still doubled-over in pain and wanting to kill me right now.

"Oh, that sucks. I guess I'll talk to you later then." I try to keep the relief out of my voice.

"Yeah, we'll figure something out. Maybe I can sneak out for dinner later this week or something and leave Kennedy with Savage." She can't hide the desperation in her voice. Her need for some adult only time must be driving her insane.

"Sounds good. Just let me know what you can swing."

Caroline quirks an eyebrow. "Dani?"

"Yeah, she's not gonna make it."

"Shit." Her eyes drift over to the glass of wine sitting at Dani's spot. "Well, I guess that just means another glass for me." She drains what's left in hers and then grabs the other.

I chuckle. "Aren't you worried about going back to work drunk?"

She grins. "First of all, two glasses of wine does *not* get me drunk. I'm practically a professional wine drinker. Second, Doug is pretty much useless as a boss. He doesn't give a shit what we do, so even if I did go to work drunk, as long as my pieces are ready when it's time to publish, he wouldn't care."

"You're lucky then."

She shrugs. "I guess so. But, back to Stone...what are you going to do?"

I haven't told anyone about Stone or that I know he's been watching me. I'm not even sure how I feel about it, so explaining it to someone else is impossible. He's not doing anything illegal, or really anything creepy, considering it's a strip club. Men come to watch naked women. It's the fact that he's always lurking in the shadows, clearly intent on remaining anonymous, that throws me for a loop.

Stone doesn't strike me as the type of guy who sits back and watches. He's definitely more of a see, take, destroy kind of guy.

So why hasn't he made any moves on me?

Other than the innuendoes and flirting at dinner the other night, he's gone out of his way to make sure I *didn't* know he was interested.

"I'm not sure what to do, Care. I mean, I barely know the guy. Maybe I should leave it be?"

She snort-laughs and takes a sip of the new full glass of wine. "I've met Stone, Nora. Do you really think he's going to just *leave it be*? He's probably nursing his wounds right now, but I bet you a million dollars, this is not the last you will see of Stone Hawke."

I'm sure it's not, and I'm at a complete loss over what to do about it.

~

STONE

I never imagined I would ever be voluntarily putting ice on my nuts. But *Fucking A*, they hurt...still, even though Nora waylaid me almost fifteen hours ago.

This is the kind of pain I wouldn't wish upon my worst enemy, and she did it to me when all I was trying to do was protect her from whatever the creep in the truck had in mind.

The ache between my legs reminds me that underestimating her was a huge mistake. She clearly knows how to defend herself.

At the cost of my poor junk.

And now, I have to try to move again.

With a groan, I grit my teeth and roll up to a sitting position before dropping my legs off the side of the bed. The ice pack that's been chilling my sac ends up on the nightstand before I gingerly rise to my feet.

Fuck.

Every little movement sends searing pain through my groin. She really did a fucking number on me.

I'm almost proud. Most women wouldn't have the first clue what to do if someone approached them aggressively in a dark parking lot like that. Granted, I wasn't being aggressive, but she didn't know the difference. Her split-second reaction was exactly how I would want any of the women in my life to respond. So while my body screams at her, I know she did the right thing.

I shuffle to the bathroom and run my hands over my unshaven face. I look as bad as I feel. The whiskey and blow I did last night to try to ease the pain has done nothing but leave me a fucking mess.

The only reason I'm even getting out of bed today is the meeting with Castillo. That's not something I can just blow off, even if I still feel like my nuts were crushed in a vise.

Meeting with the head of one of the most dangerous crime syndicates in NOLA while I'm not at the top of my game probably isn't the best idea, but skipping or trying to reschedule the meeting would be insulting and would end up putting Dom in an even worse position than he's already in. I know he doesn't want to start a war, but drugs are a big part of his business and so are the docks. He can't just stand by and let Castillo run him over.

And he's relying on me to broker some sort of peace.

Pull yourself together.

A long, scalding hot shower should do the trick. I hope. I don't want to have to resort to my other pick me up. Not when so much is at stake. Dom is trusting me to get the job done, and the last person in the world I want to disappoint is him. Not after what he did for me...

Despite my best efforts, the image of the gun in my hand flashes before my eyes and the deafening crack of it firing resounds in my ears. No matter how many years pass, I can't keep myself from reliving that moment over and over again. The blood. The fear. The promise Dom made to me...

I shake my head to clear the memory and step into the hot spray.

There isn't any time to dwell on the past now. I have to look to the future.

A future I wish could include Nora. Her unusual mix of sexy and innocent drew me to her, and after seeing her last night, I know there's more to her than any sleazeball at the Club could possibly know. To them, she's Cashmere. To me, she's a weakness I can't afford to have.

The water washes the remnants of the dirt and grime the wet pavement left from my hair but does nothing to ease the ache in my balls.

Shit.

I wonder how long this will last. I had hoped to finally get a chance to enjoy the pleasure of a willing piece of ass tonight, to both relieve the tension and try to get Nora out of my head, but by the feel of my boys, that's not in the cards.

Drying off and slipping into my suit pants takes more time than usual. I am moving ridiculously slow to avoid any unneeded tweaking of my groin.

I button up my shirt and grab my jacket. My hand is on the doorknob to leave when the doorbell rings.

What the fuck?

No one has this address. Well, no one but Dom, Skye, Storm, and Mom. And any of them know to call before they just stop over.

I pull my hand away and lean in to check the peephole.

I'm not sure what your heart stopping should feel like, but I'm pretty sure it just happened.

Nora.

Nora fucking Eriksson, at my door.

What the hell is she doing here?

A huge part of me wants to leave her standing on the porch shifting nervously from foot to foot. She would deserve it after what she did to me last night. But the more rational part of me realizes she was just defending herself from a perceived threat, and leaving her twisting in the wind would be a real dick move.

I slide the deadbolt to the side and crack the door open. Her head jerks up, and wide, uncertain blue eyes meet mine.

"Oh, hi. I wasn't sure you would be home." Her voice is high and lyrical, with a slight waver I've never noticed before.

I make her nervous.

I stifle the grin threatening to spread across my face and keep my eyes locked on hers.

She glances away and twists her hand on the strap of her purse for a minute before her eyes return to mine.

"Did you come here to finish what you started last night? 'Cause I'm not sure my balls can handle another blow like that."

A flush spreads up her neck and across her cheeks, and those soft blue eyes widen. "What? No...I, uh, came to apologize."

As much fun as fucking with her further would be, I take pity and open the door fully so she can enter. The scent of almonds and sugar swirl around her as she brushes past me into the house.

Damn, she smells good. Was she baking cookies?

She stops and turns in a circle, taking in the extravagant and intricately carved woodwork in the foyer. It was one of the things that originally drew me to this property. Even after only seeing pictures online, I could tell the craftsmanship was top-notch. They just built things better in the early 1900s than they do today. They took pride in their work. I appreciate the beauty of their craft. So even though I'll never need the five bedrooms, I bought this massive Victorian without ever setting foot inside.

"Wow, this is gorgeous."

I'm tempted to tell her she is too, but considering the last time I tried to talk to her, she kicked me in the nuts and tried to rip my arm off, I bite back the words.

Shit.

Since when do I not tell a beautiful woman what I think? Holding back is so not my style, and it's making my already tender balls ache to have this woman in my orbit without acting on it.

"Thank you. I'm very lucky to have found it."

She offers me a small smile, and I usher her through the doorway into the living room.

After a cursory glance around, she turns her attention to me and meets my eyes again. "About last night..."

8

NORA

Stone holds up a hand to stop me, giving me a second to take a deep breath.

While I'm grateful for the momentary reprieve and time to think, I also know him halting me may prevent me from ever getting the words out.

I wasn't expecting my reaction when he opened the door.

Guilt, sure. I did knee him in the junk.

Attraction, maybe. Because God knows, Stone Hawke is sexy as sin.

But the physical draw, as if I was the Earth and he the Sun was unexpected. It's left me incapable of forming coherent thoughts or full sentences. Maybe it's the suit he's wearing. Because, *dang*, now I understand what women mean when they say suit porn.

It's hardly fair to the fairer sex that he can look that good just by slipping on a dark suit.

Crapola.

"You don't have to explain. You were just defending yourself."

My eyes cut back up to his and find them full of understanding and something else...

"I swear, I didn't know it was you."

He smirks, and that slight curve of his perfect lips makes my legs quiver more than after a ten hour shift in my heels.

I need to get out of here.

He takes a step toward me, and I instinctively move back a step. "I yelled your name...twice. Your *real* name."

He did?

"I didn't hear you. As soon as I saw a car careening toward me in the lot, I think I kind of blocked out everything but my need to get in the car. What were you doing there anyway?"

The muscle in his jaw ticks, and he takes a deep breath as he seems to contemplate something.

Stone Hawke unsure? I never thought I'd see the day.

"What if I told you I was there for you?"

He takes another step toward me, but his words have frozen me in place. Of course, I know he's been watching me, but going so far as to follow me to the other club is a whole different story.

I'm not sure if I should be flattered or terrified.

Before I can muster up a response, he's so close, his body heat radiates around me. His arms move out on either side of me. I move to step back but meet the resistance of the wall. His scent envelops me—leather and something dark and spicy, like black pepper.

God, he smells so good.

There's probably never been a women caged between Stone Hawke and a wall who wasn't immediately ready to jump him, but I can't let myself give in.

No more bad decisions, Nora.

His blue eyes burn.

Fire on water.

I gasp in a breath and shake my head to clear the fog that's formed. "I would ask why, if I didn't already know the answer."

Surprise flares in his eyes, and he leans back slightly, never removing his palms from the wall on either side of my head.

"And just what is it you think you know?"

I look to the right, to where the very distinct gold watch sits on his wrist, and smile. "Next time you want to anonymously stalk a girl, you might not want to wear such a distinct watch."

His eyes fly to his wrist, and he pulls back, releasing me from the confines of his arms.

Why isn't he saying anything?

I expected a smart-ass response or some effort to defend himself. But instead, he takes a step back and watches me like he's searching for some explanation on my face.

Finally, after suffering under his withering stare for what feels like ten minutes, he clears his throat.

"How long have you known?"

I shrug and try to appear nonchalant when, in truth, my heart is practically beating out of my chest. "Since the dinner at your mom's house. I saw the watch."

He clenches his teeth and adjusts the watch with his right hand. "I wasn't stalking you."

"Really? What do you call coming to watch me from the shadows for months and then showing up in the middle of the night in the parking lot at a place you wouldn't normally just run into me? Don't tell me it was a coincidence you were there last night."

His lips press together in a tight, thin line, and his eyes narrow on me. "No, it wasn't a coincidence. I stopped by the main club, and you weren't there. I asked Byron why you weren't working and he told me you were over at TWO."

Dangit.

I'll be having a little talk with Byron next shift. If Savage and Gabe find out he told Stone where I was, he'll be fired on the spot, regardless of the fact Stone's family. He never should have given that information to *anyone*. I'm sure he thought it was fine, given it was Stone asking, but I need to make sure something like that will never happen again. I love Byron and would never rat him out, but the misstep could have led to something much worse than a knee to the balls.

"So why the ambush in the parking lot? Typically, you're more of a shadows guy."

He cracks a smile, but it vanishes almost as quickly. His eyes darken, and he steps closer, caging me in once again. "Jesus, you have no fucking clue how close you came to being in real fucking trouble, do you?"

What the heck is he talking about?

"I'm not following you."

Having him this close again is making thinking clearly impossible.

One hand leaves the wall just long enough for him to rub it over his face before it returns to the side of my head. "The truck parked a few spaces over from you. You didn't notice someone sitting in it, or it rolling forward, with no headlights on, when you were walking to your car?"

I shake my head and envision the parking lot last night. My car was parked under the lamp post. I always find a lit area to park. A mental image of each and every car near mine pops into my head, but I don't remember any moving or anything suspicious. "What? No. I would have seen that, I'm careful."

His head drops back, and he barks out a laugh. "I learned first-hand last night that you can defend yourself, but you were clearly *not* paying attention to your surroundings. Why wasn't someone escorting you to your car?"

Because I was stupid.

The night ended with a clash with another dancer, and I was flustered, racing out the back door without even thinking about securing an escort from Saint or one of the other bouncers.

Apparently, Lucky felt the fact I had been pre-med meant that I was a rich bitch no matter what I said or did. I had to get out of there or I was probably going to have a meltdown in front of everyone. They could never understand what I went through, what happened...

STONE

Her eyes glaze over like she's a million miles away, and her body goes rigid.

She's lost in some memory. Maybe of last night, maybe of something else.

I don't want to scare her, but she needs to understand how dangerous the situation was last night, what could have happened if I hadn't shown up.

Christ.

Just the thought of something happening to her...of some scumbag pervert getting their hands on her...

It makes me want to throw that carefully maintained control to the wayside, kiss the fuck out of her, and tell her she's mine. But seeing how fragile she looks right now ensures me I'm making the right decision not pursuing her. My life is messy and dirty. I'm messy and dirty. She needs and deserves someone who can give her white picket fences, kids, and total security. I can't offer that, even if it's what I really want, deep down.

My loyalty is to the man who saved my life, the man who is my father, for all intents and purposes. And that brings things with it that make it impossible to ever have Nora with me. Even if I could overlook the danger to her, even if we could get past the inevitable judgement from our families, there would still be the issue of what *I* am, what I *need* to be. And that's not anything she's ready for.

That doesn't mean I have to stop worrying, though. Things happened too fast for me to grab the license plate of that truck, and given where we were in the parking lot, I doubt the cameras will have picked up anything useful. Still, I'll go back and talk to Vance and the other staff so they understand what went down. They need to know there may be someone sketchy hanging out and waiting for the girls when they are alone.

It isn't just about Nora's safety; it's about the safety of every single woman who works there.

And now, even though she's here and safe with me, Nora's still a million miles away. That won't do at all.

"Where'd you go?"

It takes a minute, but her eyes finally refocus on mine, and the fear I find there chills my blood. Fear is something that doesn't belong tarnishing such a beautiful face. It's one of the reasons I'll continue to deny myself what I want. Because she would fear me too, eventually.

What are you so scared of?

"Nowhere." She shakes her head and forces a tight smile, trying to make light of whatever just happened in her head. But I know something more is going on than just realizing what danger she was in last night. She was scared when I appeared, but she reacted quickly and struck accurately, debilitating me almost instantly. I don't believe for a second she was frightened enough to cause the distress I just saw in her eyes, even after learning about the sketchy truck being there. No, there's something else going on. And even if we can't be together, I'm going to figure out what it is so I can do everything in my power to see that she never gets that look in her eyes again.

I focus on her and hold her gaze, waiting for her to come clean about where she really disappeared to.

That bottom lip of hers disappears under her teeth again momentarily and her eyes flick down to the floor before she straightens. "Thank you, for trying to help me. I'm sorry I—"

"Almost made me a eunuch?"

She finally cracks a smile, and the way it lights up her face has me leaning in closer. Closer than I should. Closer than is wise when I'm barely clinging to restraint right now.

My lips hover mere inches from hers...so close, I can see the bottom one quivering slightly.

Her small hands land on my chest, but I don't have time to wonder whether it's to push me away or draw me closer, because the shrill ring of my phone breaks the spell she has cast over me.

Whoever the douchebag calling me is, he's about to lose his fucking balls.

I draw back from her and reach into my pocket for the offending device.

Dom.

I turn my back to her and step away a few feet before answering. Nora undoubtedly knows who Dom is. Pretty much everyone does in this town. Between his drug business, the girls he runs on Bourbon Street, and all the other things he has his hands in, he's basically a household name. Plus, she was there to see Savage's less than positive reaction when I announced I was moving back and going to work for him. That probably means she also knows what he does, or at least has heard rumors. She doesn't need to get wrapped up in the kind of business I do with him.

"Yeah?"

"Are you on your way?"

Fuck.

I check my watch. My meeting is in less than half an hour, and all the way across town.

"Leaving now." I don't give him time to ask why I'm cutting it so close before I hang up.

He would never understand letting a woman interfere with business. In his world, which I guess is mine now too, women are, for the most part, expendable. You have your wife, and you have your side piece, or pieces. The wife stays home and remains either oblivious or turns a blind eye while raising your kids while you're free to fuck your way through town. I never, in a million years, would have expected a man like Dom to let his wife walk away from him, especially with his son. Women are expendable, but not wives and families. I suspect he loved her more than he ever dared let anyone know and thought living apart would keep his family safe. But I haven't had the balls to ask him about it, and he never brings it up.

Regardless of his situation, letting Nora delay me for this meeting would not be explainable or well received.

I can't believe I forgot about the meeting. Five minutes later, I would have been late and would have put us in an even worse position by strolling in there, apparently not caring about making him wait. It's just one of the hundred reasons I need to stay away from her. No distractions.

When I return my attention to her, she's back to avoiding my gaze. Her eyes land anywhere else in the room but on me, and she has her bottom lip pulled between her teeth.

Fuck, I want to bite that lip.

"I have to go."

Really, I need to get the hell away from this girl.

"Oh, okay."

Was that disappointment in her voice? Or is that just hopeful thinking?

She moves to step around me but I grip her bicep as she passes, stopping her with the side of my body pressed against hers. That damn sugar cookie scent invades my nose again, and I try and fail in not taking a deep breath to bring it all the way into my lungs. Those blue eyes cut up to mine.

I bring my free hand up to grip her chin, ensuring she can't look away from me. It's important she understand what I'm about to say.

"This can't happen."

She doesn't move, doesn't flinch, doesn't even blink. Nor does she take any time to consider her response. "I know."

The words linger in the thick air between us for a moment before I slowly uncurl my fingers from her arm and let my other hand fall from her face.

Releasing her and letting her walk out of my house is like having the air sucked out of my lungs. I can't see her anymore, even at the club. It's becoming an addiction, a way for me to relax and destress from the pressure of working in Dom's world. Those eight minutes and thirty-seven seconds I see her on stage have become my oxygen, and I don't know how to breathe without it. But I have to learn.

9

STONE

*T*he word *tense* doesn't even begin to describe the atmosphere in the room, sitting across from Eduardo Castillo. Whatever Dom said to him, anger is a weak term for what the leader of the largest up-and-coming crime syndicate is throwing at me.

No less than seven armed guards stand at the ready around the room, probably with at least two dozen guns at their disposal, either on their persons or within arm's reach.

I came alone and unarmed.

That's the way I prefer it.

A show of force does no good from my perspective. Castillo's beef isn't with me personally, and he knows what Dom would do if any harm befalls me.

Still, that doesn't make the churning in my stomach lessen. Keeping my cool, at least outwardly, while my blood is thrumming in my veins and pounding in my ears is something I forced myself to learn. It's essential in the courtroom and in meetings like this.

Keep it calm and cool, Stone.

After several moments of silence, and a harsh stare down, no doubt intended to make me quiver in fear, Castillo finally nods at me. "So, Mr. Hawke, what is it I can do for you?"

I grin and cross my ankle over my knee, trying to demonstrate I'm as relaxed as if we were old friends. "Let's not play that game. I don't have time for bullshit. You know why I'm here."

One bushy eyebrow slowly raises. "Do I?"

Fucking prick.

I give him my best don't-fuck-with-me stare and wait.

Another tense minute passes before he chuckles and reclines back in his over-stuffed leather chair. "What is it you expect to accomplish by coming here, Mr. Hawke? I think I made myself pretty clear when I met with your employer last month."

I scoff and sit up straighter, using my full size to reinforce the confidence I'm trying to put out. "Telling Dom you have no involvement with his missing shipments, when we all know it's been you, doesn't get us anywhere. We need to be honest with each other to ensure other steps don't need to be taken."

My words elicit a grunt from one of the goons behind me, and they all shift a step closer to us.

"Do you really think coming into my place of business and issuing threats is the way to keep things amenable?"

The smile I give him is anything but friendly. "That wasn't a threat. That was an observation of the situation and anticipation of the likely result if the channels of free and open communication are not opened. If I were making a threat, you would know it."

He steeples his fingers in front of his mouth and considers me for a moment. "I appreciate your directness, Mr. Hawke. I agree that avoiding any...conflict...is probably in everyone's best interests. But I wonder what it is you expect me to do here."

"I expect you to show some respect for Mr. Abello and his business. I expect you to back off the attacks on his shipments and stop interfering with the docking of his boats in Barataria Bay. Any further actions taken against the organization will result in swift reprisals."

A sly smile spreads across his face. "Now that was a threat."

Damn right, motherfucker.

One that should have been issued a long time ago, before it even got to this point.

"It certainly was. And I suggest you take it to heart and reconsider your current course of business."

Castillo appeared during the massive influx of people after Katrina. It didn't take him long to stake his claim in several areas of the city during the period of unrest. And his rumored ties to the Madrigal Cartel meant there wasn't much of a fight to him invading territory and setting up shop.

Until he was stupid enough to mess with Dom. Dom has let it go on far too long, thinking it would never affect him. And now, Castillo has an ego the size of Texas because he's gotten away with so much for so long without resistance.

"You can tell Dom I am sympathetic to his concerns, but obviously, I deny any involvement in any unfortunate incidents that may have befallen any of his businesses. If he has a problem, I suggest he look within and clean up his own house before making accusations that could result in war."

I rise from my chair and re-button my suit jacket. "If that's the way you want to play this, just remember, I gave you a friendly warning."

Castillo smiles, but it doesn't touch his eyes.

This is going to get bloody.

No way Dom is going to let this guy get away with continuing to fuck with him. Things are out of my hands now. I stay out of the enforcement side of the business. I don't want to know what goes on. Out of sight, out of mind. Plausible deniability.

Being the voice of reason is one thing, getting my hands dirty is another.

They are dirty enough to last me a lifetime already.

It's easy to walk out and not look back. He doesn't deserve my time or any more of my attention. This hard stance he's taking will only end up with him in a body bag. And frankly, I don't give a shit one way or the other.

That's part of how I'm able to justify what I do for Dom. The people who get hurt always have it coming. He's ruthless, but he's not stupid or cruel. He makes decisions based on logic, not rash judgments. It's the only reason Castillo wasn't dead the moment Dom's first shipment disappeared.

I slide into my car and rev the engine. A light rain hits the windshield as I head back toward Dom's. He's not going to like the news I have for him. Thankfully, he's not one to shoot the messenger.

My phone rings just as I pull up outside Dom's building.

Shit.

The last twenty-four hours have been full of surprises already. First the nut shot, then Nora showing up, now Savage is calling?

What the fuck does he want?

"Hello?"

"Stone?" Savage's voice is gruff and laced with the ever-present exasperation that's there when he talks to me.

"Who the hell else would it be?"

He sighs loud enough for me to hear it through the line. "Don't be a smartass."

"What do you want, Savage? I'm about to step into a meeting."

"With Dom?"

Like that's any of your business.

"Yes, with Dom. Why?"

"Look, I really need to talk to you. There are some things you need to know now that you're back permanently. Things you should have known a long time ago."

The last thing I want to do right now is have a chat with my brother. Whatever Savage has to tell me can wait...indefinitely for all I care.

"Not now. I need to go."

"Fine, but can you come over to the club after you're done? Gabe and I will be here all night, and it's probably best if we're both here when we talk."

I'm not going to be able to deal with Savage after the day I've had already, let alone when I'm done meeting with Dom. And I need to steer clear of the club for a while if I'm going to stay away from Nora.

"Not tonight. If you want to talk, we can do it tomorrow night."

He lets out an annoyed sigh. "Fine. But be here tomorrow night."

I hang up and slam my hand on the steering wheel. Why does my brother always have to be such a demanding asshole?

I step out into the drizzle. I'm going to need something stronger than a drink before I meet with Savage and Gabe. I sure as fuck hope Dom's guys have found some shit for me.

NORA

"How did it go over at TWO last night?"

Gabe's voice makes me jump. I hadn't even heard him approaching me at the bar. The bass bumping through the club and the loud partiers tend to make it a little difficult to know when someone sidles up next to you.

H. E. Double Hockey Sticks.

No way I'm telling him about what happened in the parking lot. Even if he might get a kick out of hearing that I maimed Stone, he would ream me out for not having an escort.

Byron eyes me warily across the bar. I've already had my talk with him, and he's apologized profusely, assuring me he would never give that information to a patron. It was only because it was Stone. I can understand that, somewhat, and I know he's worried I'm going to tell Gabe. I offer him a reassuring smile and turn to my boss.

"It was okay. Good money. But I prefer working with the girls here who I already know. I'll still fill in there when needed. I think I have two more nights this week I'm already scheduled."

Despite getting some time away from Gabe and Savage...and Stone...working at TWO left a bad taste in my mouth. It wasn't that there is anything inherently bad there, it just has a different feel and the girls don't know me. I'm just someone who came in and is taking money from their wallets. I'm comfortable here, where I know the people and the lay of the land. Even if it means having the Hawke boys watching over me like big brothers.

"I didn't think you'd like it much. That's why I didn't mention it to you originally."

I narrow my eyes on him, ensuring he knows I know he's full of crap.

He chuckles and winks at me. "Just finish your scheduled nights there and we'll keep you here unless you tell us otherwise in the future, okay?"

"Sure."

Byron lines up the drinks I ordered, and I pile them on my tray before meandering over to the table that ordered them. These three have been here all night. They must have dropped at least a grand already between drinks and tipping the girls. So far, they've been relatively easy to please, but that tends to change as the alcohol content of their blood increases.

"Here you go, boys." I smile and set the drinks in front of them.

The blond with the quick smile and wad of cash sitting on the table in front of him grins at me. "Thanks, Cashmere. Now, when will we get to see your fine ass on stage again tonight?"

Jerkface.

I bite back the initial response on the tip of my tongue.

Don't insult a customer for saying the same crap everyone does.

I don't always work the floor, but we were short a waitress tonight and it means more tips. Calling this guy a d-bag would probably cut me off from their cash-flow.

"In about half an hour." I practically run away from their table after snatching up the ten they give me.

Why am I so testy today?

It's like my temper fuse got cut in half. I'm usually so even-keeled, but tonight, everything is agitating me.

Who am I kidding? I know exactly why I'm so on-edge.

Stone Hawke.

Going to his place was a bad, bad idea. I should have left it alone and avoided any confrontation until it was absolutely impossible not to. Undoubtedly, I would have run into him at a Hawke family event, or even at the club eventually, but I could have put it off and ensured it happened in a public forum instead of his personal space.

I gave him the upper hand, and then I let my mouth run away with me.

I really hadn't intended to tell him I knew. It just slipped out. And once it was out there, hanging in the air between us, there was no going back.

Him caging me in against that wall should have felt restricting. I should have wanted to push him away and escape the confines of his arms, but it felt so darn good. Better than anything I've felt in almost two years. And he wasn't even *touching* me.

Shoot.

I haven't been attracted to a man in so dang long. Why does it have to be the bad-boy Hawke?

Maybe now that things are out in the open, we'll be able to avoid each other. He said this can't happen, and he's absolutely right. It can't.

No more bad decisions.

It's the mantra I repeat a thousand times a day. One I know will keep me from ever falling into the abyss again. I'm sure my sister thinks deciding to strip was the worst decision I ever made, but it's the right place for me right now. It's the only place there isn't any pressure to be brilliant and perfect all the time. Here, I can pretend to be a blonde bimbo with a great body. That's all they want, anyway. It's probably all Stone wants.

Byron waves me back over to the bar, and I bee-line for it, offering smiles to some guys at the other tables as I pass. One reaches out and smacks my ass, making me yelp.

Tubbs, one of the bouncers, immediately makes his way toward us from the side of the room. His eyes never leave the offending man, and I don't hang around to watch the lecture he's about to receive. A lot of things fly in here, but touching one of the girls like that isn't one of them.

When I reach Byron, he quirks an eyebrow at me. "You okay?"

I wave him off. "Yeah, I'm fine. That's the most action I've seen in a long time, though."

He chuckles and leans against the bar. "I find that hard to believe."

I guess it is kind of crazy. Almost two years is a long time to not be touched by anyone. And people expect strippers to be without morals and common sense.

The morals, I have. The common sense...that's debatable. Looking back at what brought me to where I am today, any sane person would say every single choice I've made has been worse than the last. At this point, I'm starting to wonder if I'm even capable of doing anything right anymore.

10

STONE

*a*fter last night, the coffee I'm about to get won't be near enough to wake me up and get me on track this morning. My confrontation with Nora affected me more than I care to admit. A half-bottle of Lagavulin and a few grams of coke haven't erased her almond sweet scent from my nose.

Fuck.

Maybe the smell of coffee will help. Something needs to because Nora, coupled with the meetings with Castillo and Dom, have left me completely off-balance. I don't even remember feeling this much stress in law school or studying for the damn bar.

All it takes is a fucking woman to get under your skin, apparently.

I yank open the door to Crescent Coffee and freeze halfway through the jamb.

You have got to be fucking kidding me...

I would know that ass anywhere, even encased in skin-tight spandex instead of bare on the stage.

Of all the coffee shops in NOLA, fate had to lead her here this morning. What did I ever do to piss off that fickle bitch?

The prudent choice would be to turn around and run back to my car at the curb. But doing the prudent thing has never been my forte.

I slide into line behind her and peek over her shoulder. Her focus is on the cell phone in her hand and not on the creeper leering at her. This close, that goddamn scent works its way into my nostrils despite the overwhelming coffee smell this place has.

Why are you torturing yourself?

I never thought I was a masochist until now.

Instead of moving back, I lean in closer, until I'm confident my breath will fan her neck when I speak.

"You must have been put on this Earth to torture me. It's the only explanation for how your ass can look so amazing in those pants."

She doesn't jerk away. She doesn't look back. She simply shuts down her phone and slips it in her purse.

"Are you following me, Stone? I thought we already discussed that stalking is frowned upon by law enforcement."

The words are spoken so evenly and without malice, I can't help but smile.

"Aww, if I didn't know better, I would think I'm starting to grow on you."

Nora snorts out a laugh and finally glances over her shoulder at me.

"I'm not following you. My new office is just two blocks over, and I haven't managed to locate my coffee maker at the house yet."

"Likely story." She rolls her blue eyes before moving forward with the line.

I wish I were joking. Not having coffee immediately ready for me has made for some rough mornings the last couple weeks. Thank God, I found this place. If I can't get an IV drip of caffeine, I can at least get a quad shot to get me through the a.m. Today, I have three court appearances for various clients—two of Dom's men who got caught with some stolen goods, and one pro bono disorderly conduct case for the parish. It will be good to be back in the courtroom. Those four walls always felt like home to me and working for Dom has meant I haven't been in one in far too long.

Nora reaches the counter and orders while I dig out my wallet. I catch the attention of the barista and wave a twenty at her. "I've got this."

"No, he doesn't." Nora shoots daggers at me and shoves a ten across the counter. When she gets her change, she practically races to the end of the counter to wait for her drink.

Her self-preservation skills are clearly better than mine. I order and pay for my drink then move to where she stands, purposely avoiding looking in my direction.

"You could have let me buy you a cup of coffee, you know. It's not like it's an agreement to give me your soul."

Although, I wouldn't mind having that.

Those damn hypnotizing blue eyes meet mine, and she scowls. "You buying me coffee is a date. And we aren't going there, remember?"

I chuckle and lean against the counter. "We can't have a cup of coffee together as totally platonic friends?"

She scoffs. "I highly doubt you have platonic friends."

Got me there.

"Look, just sit and have your coffee with me. I promise I won't bite, unless you ask."

A low noise that sounds an awful lot like a growl emanates from her throat. I manage to hide my grin by turning to check on our drinks. A young guy, who can't be much older than Nora, brings them both over and smiles at her. "Hey Nora, how are you?"

My spine stiffens and a feeling a lot like jealousy has me taking my cup from him a little too violently.

"Hey Jamie, I'm good. It's nice to see you. Call me so we can get that dinner we've been talking about." Before she can take her drink from him, I snatch it, offering him a scowl.

He narrows his eyes on me before smiling at Nora. "Sure thing. See you later."

When I turn to hand Nora her drink, she eyes me and chews her bottom lip. "If I agree to sit with you for a totally platonic cup of coffee, you have to stop with the sexual innuendos."

Might as well be asking me to stop breathing.

I toss her a sly grin. "I'll be on my best behavior."

She grabs her drink from my outstretched hand, careful not to touch my fingers. "Somehow, I highly doubt that."

That damn ass squeezed into the yoga pants taunts me as I follow her to an open table near the back of the café. I swear, a woman created yoga pants just to fuck with men on a daily basis and keep us in a perpetual state of semi-boner.

Nora drops into a chair across from me and takes a drink from her cup, watching me intently over the rim.

I've never struggled to find something to talk about with a beautiful woman, but remove flirting and sexual innuendo, and my vast conversation skills are somewhat limited.

"Are you dating that guy?"

Well, that came out a little more bluntly than I intended.

She looks over her shoulder toward the counter then back at me. "What? Who? Jamie?"

I nod, trying to keep my annoyance out of my features but probably failing.

A laugh bubbles up. "Not that it's any of your business, but no, we went to high school together."

"Oh."

Oh? Really, Stone? That's the best you have?

She sets her cup onto the table and clears her throat. "How are you liking being back?"

While I'd much rather be talking about her, at least she saved us from any more uncomfortable silence. No doubt, I would have said something to offend her, one way or the other, if she hadn't jumped in with her question.

I sip my espresso and consider my answer before replying. Being home has been strange. Things have always been a bit tense with Savage, but since I've returned, that tension has quadrupled. I get he doesn't want me to work for Dom, but his unwarranted disdain for him, after everything he's done to help our family, really grates on me. He needs to drop his holier than thou attitude and accept that Dom is going to be a part of my life, all of our lives really, forever.

And that tension makes it awkward for the rest of the family. They don't want to choose sides. I can't really blame them for that. But if I could tell them everything, what he did for me, I know they'd see things my way.

"It's been interesting."

A slim brow raises. "I couldn't help but notice a bit of...well... tension between you and Savage."

"Yes, it would have been hard to miss." It makes me wonder what else she's caught on to.

She takes another drink, then turns the cup in her hands. "Does that have anything to do with you working for Dom Abello?"

The question lacks any malice and seems genuine. Maybe she doesn't have the preconceived notions about him that others seem unable to shake.

I nod and take another swig of my much-needed caffeine. "It's hard for some people to understand my loyalty to him."

"So explain it to me."

～

NORA

My request seems to shock him. He stops twisting the cup in his hand and watches me for a moment. Those familiar blue Hawke eyes assess me, and I turn my attention out the window instead. One can only withstand that kind of scrutiny for so long.

"I never really knew my father. He died when I was five. Savage kind of took over the role of man of the house, more out of a sense of duty than any real necessity. My mother was well taken care of, by Dom."

Over the last almost two years working for Savage and Gabe, I've heard bits and pieces of Dom's involvement with the Hawke family, but the whole story remains somewhat elusive. Dani says he was basically a father to Stone, but she made it very clear he's a scumbag and Savage hates him. Something happened, when she went to cover the story about his men getting killed, but she doesn't ever want to talk about it. And eventually, I stopped pressing. Dani doesn't do anything she doesn't want to, so unless she wants to talk, I'll never get it out of her anyway.

"Was he in love with your mom?"

Stone tosses his head back and laughs. "No, nothing like that. It's more like he's an older brother. She was best friends with his younger sister growing up, and my dad and Dom were close when he was still alive. I think he felt a sense of duty to my dad to ensure the family was okay. And it's something my mom and the rest of us have always appreciated."

"Except Savage?"

His head rocks side to side as if he's considering his answer. "Savage has a bit of a problem with his ego. He thinks he can do no wrong and that he knows what's best for everyone else. He borrowed some money from Dom after college to start up his first bar, but after that, he distanced himself and started lecturing us about how dangerous Dom was."

Well, he's right.

It's no secret what Dom Abello does or what he stands for. But Stone doesn't seem like some idiot who would blindly follow someone with no redeeming qualities. His loyalty intrigues me.

"It seems Savage's feelings haven't affected your relationship with Dom, though."

He shakes his head but doesn't respond right away, instead taking another drink from his cup. "No. Because Dom has done things for me that Savage will never truly comprehend."

I wait for him to expound, but the silence between us lingers into an almost uncomfortable length. This may be a good time to end this "platonic coffee."

Stone sighs and runs a hand back through his thick black hair. "I was really messed up as a kid. Maybe I was trying to compete against four siblings for my mother's attention, or maybe I was just a little punk. Either way, I got into a lot of trouble. Petty shit mostly—shoplifting, fights with kids at school, shit like that. And then something major happened. Dom stepped in to try to get me back on track. He helped me gain control of my life. If it wasn't for him, I would probably have spent most of my teen years in jail, and I certainly would never have gotten where I am today."

The clear love and respect Stone holds for Dom is actually quite endearing. Even though it's created a rift between him and Savage, he's not willing to cave on his sense of duty.

Fudge.

Why does he have to be so darn charming and clearly passionate about the people he cares about? It makes pretending to hate him even harder.

"Have you told that to Savage? Maybe it would help him understand?"

He barks out a laugh. "It wouldn't matter. Even if I could tell him everything that happened, which I can't, he's too stubborn to ever admit he's been wrong all this time. It's better if I just leave it alone and let him think whatever he wants. We can play nice when we're with our mother. We've been doing it for a long time already."

Huh.

The mention of things he can't tell Savage certainly has my interest piqued, but if he can't tell his own brother, he's certainly not going to tell me. And that's probably for the best anyway. Revealing deep, dark secrets isn't something platonic friends who barely know each other do. It would definitely be a step in the wrong direction for us trying to ignore the attraction simmering between us.

He studies me for a moment, and it's like being put under a microscope. "What about you?"

"What about me?"

A smile tugs at the corner of his mouth. "Do you like working for my brother and Gabe?"

"Of course I do, why else would I still be there?"

My answer may have come a little too quickly. It's true though...mostly. Savage and Gabe are great bosses really, the best I've ever had anyway. I could do without the leering and groping patrons, but that's just part of the job, and compared to other clubs, The Hawkeye Club is basically a palace where we are treated like queens. All I have to do is take my clothes off and dance a little. I really can't complain about anything.

Stone smirks and leans forward, resting his forearms on the table between us. "The money?"

I narrow my eyes at him and take another sip of my latte to prevent myself from saying something stupid.

Does he really think that's why I do it?

Am I nothing more than some money-grubbing skank to him?

"It's not about the money. Yes, I make a decent living dancing, but it's more about the freedom of it." I give him the same line I've regurgitated to Byron, Gabe, Savage, Dani, my mom, and anyone else who has asked since I started working at The Hawkeye Club.

It's not a total lie, and it's always easier when there's at least a half-truth to what you tell people.

His dark brows furrow, and he narrows his eyes at me. "You really think people believe that?"

"What the heck is that supposed to mean?"

He leans back in his chair, giving me space to breathe. Or at least try to.

"Stone, what's that supposed to mean?"

A nonchalant shrug is the only response he offers. And a small smile tugging at the corner of his mouth. He's so darn smug, like he knows exactly what I'm thinking.

I guarantee he has no clue why I'm really stripping, even if he can see through my sort-of lie.

Anger simmers just below the surface, something completely foreign to me. I don't get mad. Not really. I get frustrated. I get annoyed. I get irritated. But to get me angry...that's a real feat.

Yet Stone Hawke has managed it more than once already.

11

STONE

I'm being a total asshole. I know that.

But I've learned that letting someone sit and stew with a question or observation is more likely to illicit a truthful response than bombarding them with questions.

The way Nora is fidgeting in her seat assures me I've struck a chord.

She finally cracks. "Answer me, or I walk out of here right now."

As much as I would *love* to watch her walk away in those damn yoga pants...I'd much rather get her to talk. I need to learn more about her to figure out how to maintain this "friendship" thing we're shooting for.

I hold up my hands in surrender and offer her an apologetic smile. "I was simply making an observation, Nora."

"An observation of what?"

"Of you. You put on a good show while you're center stage,

but there's something in your eyes that tells me in your heart, that's not where you want to be."

She scowls and crosses her arms over her chest. "I don't think anyone grows up *wanting* to be a stripper, Stone."

Touché.

"True, but I also doubt most of the women who end up dancing have the kind of intelligence and options *you* have available to you."

Her jaw drops. "Wow, could you be any more insulting toward girls who dance?"

"It wasn't meant as an insult, just an observation. Yes, there are girls who dance to pay for law school or medical school, and there are probably some who truly enjoy doing it, but the vast majority of dancers do it because they have a lack of job options that will earn them that kind of money, many don't even have high school diplomas. Tell me I'm wrong."

The press of her lips into a tight, thin line would be adorable if she wasn't so mad at me for being correct.

I don't want her mad. What I do want is to push her to open up to me. She's so guarded around me and presumably around everyone else. She needs a push or she'll drown in whatever is weighing on her so heavily. Nora is struggling, whether she wants to admit it or not. I understand why Savage and Dani are so protective of her. She has a pure, kind soul, and it would be easy for someone to take advantage of that. In her profession, there's no shortage of creeps. What happened at TWO the other night only demonstrates that. For her to be doing this, exposing herself to this lifestyle when she has a hundred other options, something must have really shaken her. And she clearly hasn't worked through it yet.

Maybe it's not my place to try to help her. Hell, not probably. It *isn't* my place. But no one seems to be getting through to her, and she's floundering. She needs direction, and that, I can do. It's just going to take some pressure.

"I know you were pre-med at Tulane. What I don't know is why you dropped out to strip for my brother."

Anger flares in her eyes, and her hands clench around her coffee cup. "Why is that any business of yours, anyway?"

Damn. She's feisty when she's mad.

That's not good for my libido. Vivid mental pictures of her simmering while trussed up in my playroom flit through my head and are nearly impossible to shake.

She may be submissive, but she's got fire just below the surface. When a match is lit, she will ignite.

But this isn't the time or the place. It's never going to be the time and place with Nora. It can't be.

Keep it platonic.

"Aren't we having a friendly get-to-know-you conversation? Did you ask me about working for Dom? I answered your questions, even if they weren't totally comfortable for me."

That was likely admitting too much. I can't ever tell her, or anyone else for that matter, what happened to indebt me to Dom. It's not that I don't want to tell her. Honestly, there are times I feel like talking about it instead of burying it as deeply as possible, all these years would have been a lot healthier mentally. Plus, it would help her, and Savage, understand why I owe Dom so much. But opening up about it isn't an option. And I don't want to encourage her to pry. So hopefully, she lets the fact I didn't really reveal anything in depth slide. I need her to open up to me even if I can't fully to her. *She* needs it.

Her eyes close momentarily before they return to mine. She offers a tight smile. "You're right. You did. I'm sorry. I just..."

I wait for her to finish her thought, but instead, she tosses back what's left of her drink and sits fiddling with the cup.

Whatever happened to make her leave school, it's obviously still weighing on her heavily. It's not in my nature to back down from a challenge, but maybe Nora Eriksson is weaker than I initially thought.

That mix of submissive and spitfire I've seen had me convinced she could stand up to me and hold her ground when pushed. Maybe I was wrong. She's not ready for me to push her. She's not ready for any of this.

"Look, you don't have to—"

She shakes her head. "No, it's fine. I just wasn't cut out for the pre-med program. It was more work than I was able to handle, and I got overwhelmed. It's as simple as that."

Somehow, I highly doubt that. She doesn't strike me as the type to give up easily, and from what I've heard through the family grapevine, Nora was the valedictorian of her high school class. Someone capable of that kind of achievement doesn't just quit. Something happened. Something specific. Something she doesn't want to talk about.

Which only makes me want to press her more.

I lean forward again, putting myself closer to her personal space. Her eyes widen slightly, but she's otherwise unflinching. There's the strength I know is buried underneath her fear. "There's more to it than that, Nora, and we both know it. If you don't want to tell me, fine. But don't lie to me or give me half-truths. That's not what *friends* do."

Her nostrils flare. The empty paper cup crinkles and finally caves between her clenched hands. "I'm not lying. You're an A-hole for saying that. Pre-med was just too much for me. Do you have any idea what that class schedule is like? How much studying and homework it takes to not fall hopelessly behind? I couldn't hack it. End of story."

"Bull. Shit." She may talk a good game, but the slight waver in her voice and tremble in her bottom lip give her away. "Don't talk to me like I don't understand, Nora. I went to law school, remember? And then studied for and took a bar exam in two different states. I understand what working hard means. And I don't believe for one fucking second that you just said, 'fuck it, I can't hack it' and gave up."

Her blue eyes blaze, and she shoves back from the table, taking her crushed cup with her. "You are a real jerk, Stone."

Before I can formulate an apology, she turns and storms out of the coffee shop.

Well, shit. That did not go as planned.

∾

NORA

Stone Hawke is the single most infuriating person on this planet. I'm one hundred percent convinced of that fact.

I mean, come on! Where does he get off accusing me of lying?

Yes, he's right. I wasn't telling him the whole story. But the last person I'm going to tell the truth to is that man. He wouldn't understand. He made it through law school and two bar exams, apparently, easily. The stress and pressure of it didn't cripple him, it didn't make him do things that will haunt him the rest of his life. Stone is a powerhouse. He doesn't break; he doesn't cave; he doesn't back down from anything. The continuous pressing, probing, pushing...I just couldn't take it anymore.

How can he see right through me so easily? I never thought I was transparent. I've managed to make it through almost two years without having to explain myself to anyone more than telling them I wasn't cut out for school and I wanted to dance. Why can't he just leave it at that?

His need to know more, to delve into the depths of my soul to find the truth, is unnerving. No one has ever pushed me before, not like this. Of course, Mom and my teachers wanted me to succeed academically, but that was never a problem. Not until I hit Tulane. But this is different. It's like he's dismantling my carefully constructed world one piece at a time and trying to draw me out into the world I left behind intentionally. One where I make terrible decisions. And I can't let Stone Hawke become another one, no matter how much I may be drawn to him.

If I had my way, I would never see his handsome, arrogant face again. That would make things so much easier.

Too bad that's virtually impossible. There's no doubt he'll be at the club, and I likely can't avoid Hawke family gatherings forever. This was so much easier when he was living across the country and hadn't weaseled his way under my skin. Men don't usually look beneath the surface. They see a beautiful blonde dancer with a nice body and that's all they care about. Not Stone. He *sees* me. He sees things I don't want anyone to notice. And that's thrown me more than I care to admit.

Instead of heading back to my apartment like I had planned, my run-in with Stone has left me needing a little one-on-one time with Kennedy and Dani. Maybe it's time she knew what's been going on. She could help me run interference with him when we're forced into "family" events together in the future.

Then again, revealing why I'm so pissed off would only encourage her to press me more about returning to school. And that's the last thing I need.

Crap.

The elevator ride to the top of Savage and Gabe's building gives me some time to formulate a plan. The plan is...wing it. I can fudge what really happened with Stone and avoid opening the door to yet another conversation with her that's going to lead nowhere.

I knock lightly before pushing the door open. They never lock the place since you need a code for the elevator to get up here, but I learned my lesson the hard way that not, at least, knocking can lead to seeing my sister and my boss in very compromising positions. By this time, Savage should be at the club, and the coast should be clear. Still, better safe than sorry.

"Dani?"

A sharp cry draws me down the hallway toward the bedrooms.

"Dani?"

She sticks her head out of the nursery and smiles. "Hey, come on in. I'm just getting her dressed."

I follow her into the pale pink room and grin at my niece on the floor. At only a few months old, she already has everyone wrapped around her tiny fingers. Dani finishes buttoning up her adorable outfit and hands her off to me before rising to her feet.

"So what's up? I wasn't expecting to see you today." Sudden panic flashes in her eyes. "We didn't have plans, did we? Shit, I knew I was forgetting something."

Laughing at her would be bad form, but she's been so spacy since having the baby, it's almost comical. "No, we didn't. I just wanted to stop by to say hi."

Dani pins me with a knowing look and ushers me out of the room and down the hall to the kitchen. "You want some coffee?"

Ick.

Under normal circumstances, I would take her up on that, but after what just went down with Stone, even the thought of coffee puts a sour taste in my mouth. "No thanks, I just had some."

Kennedy grabs a fistful of my hair and tugs at it playfully.

"Come put her down in the highchair. I haven't fed her breakfast yet." Dani moves around the kitchen while I settle Kennedy in her chair and strap her in.

Seeing Dani in mom-mode is still a little weird for me. Dani from two years ago would have already been at the office or out chasing down a lead on some ground-breaking story. Mom-Dani is one hundred percent focused on her daughter, at least right now. She goes stir-crazy and wants to go back to work, but I know she will always choose what's best for her child, even at her own expense.

She drops down into a chair next to Kennedy with a bowl of

baby cereal and motions for me to take a seat across from her. "So, you want to tell me why you're here. You don't just drop by."

Got me there.

And I really need to talk to someone. I suppose I *could* call Caroline, but knowing her, Dani would find out about it anyway. Might as well cut out the middle-man.

"Do you promise not to say anything to Savage?"

It would be an epic disaster if he found out. Talk about awkward. He would definitely tell Gabe and probably confront Stone. Work would be unbearable.

Her head jerks in my direction with narrowed eyes. "Why? What's going on?"

"I'm serious. Promise me you won't say a word."

She rolls her eyes and turns her attention back to feeding the baby. "Fine, I promise."

Where do I even start?

There's no way I can tell her everything. She would freak out if she knew Stone has been watching me at the club, and that I kicked him in the nuts, and that we almost kissed, and that I had an almost-date with him today.

"It's Stone..."

She chuckles and glances over at me. "What did he do now?"

Just pushed every damn button I have.

I shrug and try to sound nonchalant about the whole thing. "Nothing specific. I ran into him grabbing coffee this morning, and we sat down for a while to chat."

A blonde eyebrow arches at me. "Chat? Stone Hawke does not chat."

Poor choice of words on my part. It's only piqued her interest more. With a sigh, I slump forward onto the table. "No, I guess not."

"So what happened?"

He stripped me with barely more than a look and then tried to dismantle me with questions designed to open my soul to him.

I watch her continue to feed Kennedy while I try to come up with an answer that won't give too much away. "I don't even know how to explain it. He's just so..."

What's the right word here?

Dani jumps in to fill the void before I can get anything else out. "Douchey?"

I scowl at her and shake my head. "No, I was going to say intense."

She nods and smiles at the baby. "Yes, that's certainly true too. But if you hadn't already noticed, it's kind of a Hawke trait. Hell, even Gabe has that same intensity going on."

Her observation isn't anything I don't already know. I must make some sort of noise in response because she looks over at me with concern etched on her face and narrows her eyes at me. "Is he still hitting on you? I can have Savage talk to him, or hell, I can talk to him again and get him to back off."

Was he hitting on me?

When he first came up to me at the coffee shop, yes. But once we sat down and started talking, it moved into something much deeper than simple flirting. It felt...intimate.

"No, nothing like that. I guess I'm just not sure what I should be doing when I run into him. I mean, Savage seems to have some real issues with him and he's my boss, and your husband. I don't want to step in the middle of some family drama."

She sighs and sets the bowl down before giving Kennedy the spoon to play with. "Look, Savage's issues with Stone shouldn't affect your feelings about him. I'm sorry if I pushed you to feel or think a certain way about the whole situation. The only thing I'm going to say is this...be very careful around that man and the company he keeps. There are things you don't know about Abello, things that would make you run the other way as fast as your feet could carry you, things I'm not even sure Stone knows about. At least, I hope he doesn't. Because him continuing to work for that man would be a thousand times worse than it is now if he did know."

"What the heck are you talking about? Does this have to do with what went down before you guys got married?"

Dani shakes her head and pushes up out of her chair. "Shit, I'm sorry. I shouldn't have said that. Just be careful. Even without his connection to Abello, Stone is not the kind of guy you want to get tangled with."

The cryptic stuff is starting to get on my nerves, but I know better than to press her for more information. It hasn't worked in the past and only manages to strain our relationship. Even without his connections to the mob boss, I know Stone is dangerous. He's dangerous to my heart. With his uncanny ability to read me like an open book, I know I can't spend time with him and retain my sanity.

"Well, you have nothing to worry about there. There is no way, under any circumstances, that I am getting involved with Stone Hawke."

12

STONE

"Thanks again, Mr. Hawke."

I pause in the hallway outside the courtroom and turn back to my client. Michael Figueroa is far too young to be facing this many felonies. The laundry list read by the commissioner today at the initial appearance made me cringe. Maybe because I could have been exactly where he's standing if things had gone differently...if Dom hadn't stepped in, set me straight, and covered my ass, I would have been toast.

It's ironic that working for Dom is what put Michael here. His men know the risks they take when they sell their souls to him. But he also takes care of them if one of them goes down.

Michael won't pay me a dime, and his parents and pregnant girlfriend will never want for anything if he's sent away. I'll do everything in my power to keep that from happening, but *shit,* getting caught with ten kilos isn't something you just walk away from most of the time. If I can't find some decent motion issues to get the case tossed, he's going to be spending a huge chunk of his life behind bars.

Fuck.

"Don't thank me yet."

"But you got me out on bond."

I didn't do shit. Dom's vast network got him out on bond before he even made his initial appearance. All I did was prevent the commissioner from raising the amount by pointing out that he hadn't fled in the twenty-four hours between his release and his court appearance.

If he didn't have his connection to Dom, he would have been sitting on a massive cash bail for the entire time the case is pending. And he certainly wouldn't have me as a lawyer, unless I took him on as a pro bono client. I've been waiting for the court to call with some appointments to cases for indigent clients, but thus far, I've mostly been working for Dom and his friends and employees. It's good money, but it doesn't feed my soul the way helping the truly needy does. I can only imagine where I would be without what Dom did. That's all I see every time I see an indigent client in court with some bumbling lawyer who doesn't know his ass from his elbow.

Getting a lawyer who actually knows what they are doing and is willing to fight for you is like hitting the fucking lottery. And Michael gets it just because he was willing to do Dom's dirty work.

"Just don't blow it. You know the terms of your release. Stay out of trouble, make your court appearances. We have the prelim in a couple days. Given the evidence they have, we'll likely waive it but I want to talk to the district attorney first. We'll get the discovery after that and then we'll sit down and go through everything together. Any questions?"

He shakes his head. "No, man. Just thanks."

Watching him walk down the hallway, I can't ignore the twinge of guilt in my gut.

Don't, Stone.

He's an adult. He made his choice. He wasn't blind to this possibility.

Just like I'm not blind to what I'm doing for Dom.

But I also know what it's like to grow up without a father. And there's a pretty good chance Michael won't get out until his son is the same age he is now. There's no telling what that will do to the poor kid. I was lucky. I had Dom, and as much as I may complain about it, I also had Savage who did everything he could to step in as man of the house. That's a lot for a ten year old to take on, but he stepped up and helped Mom with everything and anything he could. Michael's son...who knows.

Shit.

I scrub my hand down my face and make my way out to my car in the parking lot.

It's been a long fucking day.

And it's only going to get worse. I still have to touch base with Dom before I go meet Savage and Gabe tonight.

That's two meetings I am *not* looking forward to. As expected, Dom was less than pleased with the outcome of my sit-down with Castillo. Things are going to get very messy soon. And that means more work for me dealing with aftermath.

Today, we talk strategy, and it will get heated. But at least with Dom, I know where I stand.

The same can't be said for Savage.

Fucking douche.

I don't know exactly where things took the turn between us but working for Dom has clearly put extra strain on an already tenuous relationship. Whatever he wants to discuss, it must be important. Or at least, *he* thinks it is. That doesn't always equate to important for anyone else. But I can't deny the fact that he said Gabe should be there for this conversation has been sitting uneasily in my gut since last night.

Gabe has always been the buffer between us, the third Hawke

brother for all intents and purposes. His ability to rein Savage in when he gets out of hand has prevented many fights over the years. So if he is joining the meeting, that either means he agrees it's important enough to require his presence, or he doesn't trust Savage to remain objective during the conversation. Either way, it doesn't bode well.

Two shit meetings, back to back. What a fucking wonderful evening. The only thing that could make it worse is if Nora's working tonight.

I haven't been able to stop thinking about our conversation over coffee. Her reaction to my pressing her about school and stripping surprised me. Given how deferential and timid she usually is, I assumed she'd crumble under my pressure and answer anything I asked. Clearly, I've underestimated the effect whatever happened to her in school had on her. The intensity of her reaction to my questions ensures me there's more to that story.

I'd be tempted to delve deeper to find out, but being in the same vicinity as Nora is bad for my control, and my libido. I wanted to chase after her when she left in a huff. Whether to apologize or push her more, I'm not sure. Either way, I had to force myself to let her go. She needed the space, and I'm not one to force someone to do something they aren't ready for. It's evident she needs some time before she'll be ready to talk. I want to help her, but I also know being near her is dangerous. For both of us.

Yet, instead of staying away from Nora, I'm going to be heading right for her. Although, she may be at TWO tonight...if fate is on my side.

Yeah fucking right.

Fate has never been on my side. If anything, that bitch hates me.

She took my father, she led me down the dark path that brought me to the worst moment of my life, and then when I finally get my shit together and figure out what I'm going to do with my future, she tosses Nora in my path.

That woman is pure temptation.

My own goddamn kryptonite.

And I haven't even kissed her yet.

No, Stone.

Just like you told her, that can't happen.

NORA

Something's definitely up tonight. Savage and Gabe have been wandering around the club, almost like they're waiting for something or someone. Savage usually stays in his office, and Gabe is so laid-back most of the time, so seeing them like this is putting all the employees on edge.

I'm sure it's nothing, but in the back of my mind, I worry it could have something to do with Dani.

I grab the drinks off the bar and place them on my tray. "Do you know what's up with them?"

Byron shrugs. "Nah, they've been like that since last night. I don't know what's going on. Don't worry too much, they get like this sometimes when personal shit gets in their heads. They'll chill out eventually."

There really isn't anything I can do other than trust him. He's been here forever and knows them better than anyone here. And if it were about Dani, I'm sure I would have either received a call from her, or Savage would have told me what I need to know by now.

Of course, my instinct is to run to the back and grab my phone to call and check in on her. But it's after eleven, and Dani is probably passed out after dealing with Kennedy all day.

I just need to get back to work and stop worrying about other people's headaches. I have enough of my own as it is.

But even now, I can't get what Stone said out of my head.

You put on a good show while you're center stage, but there's something in your eyes that tells me, in your heart, that's not where you want to be.

His words shook me more than I'd like to admit.

Others have voiced their concerns—primarily Dani and Mom—but no one has ever hit so close to the truth before.

Crap.

I don't know what to do with him. Things were going so well here, and now, Stone has me second-guessing everything I've decided is best for my life with one dang observation.

I'm so distracted, I almost walk past the table I'm carrying drinks for. "Hey y'all, I have your drinks here."

"Thanks, darlin'. What time do you get off tonight?"

I usually don't mind helping out on the floor when we are really busy. It usually keeps me from thinking too much because I'm running all over the place. But tonight, I kind of wish I had said no and could just sit in the back. I don't have the energy to deal with these guys tonight and remain perky and friendly like I need to.

"Too late for you, hon." I plaster a smile on my face and lean against the table, giving him a good view of my mostly-exposed breasts.

He chuckles, and I give him a wink before Byron waving me over to the bar catches my attention. "I gotta go, boys. Does anyone else need anything?"

Casanova grins at me and waggles his eyebrows suggestively. Real charming. "Just your number."

A round of laughs follows me across the room until it's drowned out by the music. Thank God I only have twenty minutes before I need to be back on stage. At least there, I can lose myself in the music and forget everything around me, including Stone and those yahoos.

I lean toward Byron over the bar so he can hear me. "What's up?"

He grins. "I need you to settle a bet between those two guys." He tosses his head to the other end of the bar where two men are in a heated debate.

"What's the bet?"

"Genius number one was saying one of his friends almost died from carbon dioxide poisoning from his AC unit going out and his buddy keeps telling him it's carbon *monoxide,* not dioxide. They have been arguing about it for twenty minutes. Why the fuck one of them doesn't just pull out their cell phones and Google it is beyond me. But I told them I had someone who could settle it once and for all."

Great.

Now I'm a sideshow act? The stripper who knows her chemistry. I'm sure Byron didn't think asking me to help would offend me. And really, it doesn't, I just can already anticipate the reaction from these guys when I school them. One thing I learned pretty early in life, that's only been reinforced working here, is that most men want their women pretty and silent. I'm not much of a talker, so while misogynist mentality bothers me, in general, I don't put up much of a stink. But men who think women should be pretty and silent tend to not respond well to a woman who is pretty and smarter than them. The macho pride prevents them from just accepting the fact they aren't the smartest one in the room. So I already know this likely won't end well.

Still, Byron wants my help, so I force a smile and make my way over to the end of the bar. As I approach, their bickering cuts through the loud music. When I step up behind them, they turn and stop mid-sentence.

"I heard you boys need a little science education."

The tiny guy on my left barks out a laugh and rolls his eyes. "Yeah, right. A fucking stripper is going to teach me anything."

After plastering on an even brighter smile, I clear my throat. "Actually, I was valedictorian of my high school and pre-med at Tulane on a full scholarship.."

Funny man's smile disappears quickly, and his friend freezes, mouth agape.

"Which one of you thinks it's Carbon Monoxide?"

The guy on the right tips his beer toward me with a small grin on his face.

I turn to the smartass on my left. "Carbon Monoxide, or CO, does not occur naturally in the atmosphere. It's the result of oxygen-starved combustion in improperly ventilated fuel-burning appliances such as oil and gas furnaces, gas water heaters, gas ovens, gas or kerosene space heaters, fire places and wood stoves, and is also produced by gasoline engines that don't use a catalytic converter. Carbon dioxide, or CO_2, on the other hand, occurs naturally in the atmosphere. It's a natural byproduct of human and animal respiration, fermentation, chemical reactions, and combustion of fossil fuels and wood. Some cars do produce it, if they have a catalytic converter. However, if your friend was in his house when he was poisoned, it was Carbon *Monoxide*, not Dioxide. Your buddy is right."

Without waiting for their responses, I turn on my heels and make my way back stage to get ready for my dance.

Take that, pompous d-bag.

13

STONE

*W*hen I pull into the parking lot of the club, I'm tempted to turn right around and drive home or maybe down to Bourbon Street.

The meeting with Dom was tense. He wasn't happy with my inability to resolve the issue with Castillo.

Like it's my fucking fault the asshole is an arrogant prick who has balls the size of Texas.

What was I supposed to do? Put a gun to his head and demand he call off his guys? That's not my style and Dom knows it. But now he's had time to stew since I talked to Castillo, and he's pissed.

I got out of there when Dom called in his muscle. Their plans are none of my business. I prevent the messes where possible and clean them up afterward. The middle is out of my hands.

Having a showdown with my brother is the last thing I want to do right now, especially if there's a chance I'll run into Nora. I need to be completely on my game when dealing with Savage, and seeing her will throw me off in a way that's not fixable. Even if she's not here, I just don't have it in me to deal with him tonight.

Shit.

I don't have a choice. Savage is relentless and won't stop until he says whatever he needs to get off his chest. It's a trait I can't really fault him for considering I'm the same way. It's why not getting Nora to open up has been eating away at me so much. Maybe I'll figure out a way to get through to her without putting myself in a too-tempting situation with her, but I don't hold out much hope for that.

Besides, right now, I need to concentrate on getting whatever this is with Savage done fast so I can go home and crash.

With a resigned sigh, I shove open my door and trudge up to the front door of the club through the drizzle. There's no need to sneak in the back this time.

Flashing lights and thumping bass assault me as I step inside. Rocky nods to me and lets me pass and Tubbs gives me a quick wave from his spot near the bar. The plan is to head straight upstairs to get whatever shit show Savage has planned over with as soon as possible, but the moment my eyes wander over to the stage, I'm frozen in place mid-stride and any plans fly out the window.

Fucking of course.

Nora twines her legs around the top of the pole and slides down it slowly, letting her hair and breasts fall back on her way to the stage.

My cock swells, thankfully still working after the other night, and my breath catches in my throat. This isn't one of her usual dances. This is something...different. Strong. Sensual. Seductive. And yet...ethereal.

I can picture how beautiful she would be trussed up and suspended from the ceiling. I know exactly what binding I would use on her too.

Angel wings.

I've been working on it for years with my rope models, when I was still in San Diego, but I've yet to use my perfected version. I haven't found the right person.

Until now.

When she reaches the stage, her legs fall open, releasing the pole from their tight grip, and she spins to the side, sprawling flat with her face down.

Jesus H. Christ.

I need to get the fuck upstairs before I come just watching this.

The elevator doesn't arrive fast enough to save me from the sight of Nora running her palms over her breasts and tugging her own nipples. I'm tempted to turn around and climb in my car to relieve some pressure before the meeting when there's a ding and the doors finally slide open.

Savage's door is ajar and Gabe's voice filters out into the hallway as I approach.

"How much are you going to tell him?"

"All of it. He needs to know the truth."

Truth about what?

I push the door open and Gabe turns and nods at me. Savage just motions for me to close the door and points to the empty chair next to Gabe.

Instead, I stand behind it and rest my hands on the back. "What's so important you had to see me tonight?"

A nervous glance passes between them.

"Jesus guys, out with it."

Savage leans back in his chair and crosses his arms over his chest. "It's about Dom."

Motherfuckingsonofabitch.

I take a step back. "Oh hell no, I am *not* going to listen to another 'Dom is a bad guy' speech from you, Savage. You've made your feelings about him very clear. But I'm a big boy, and I'm more than capable of making my own life decisions."

He slams his palm on his desk and practically growls at me. "Will you quit being a fucking litigator for two fucking seconds, Stone? You don't need to plead your case, just fucking listen. There are things you don't know, at least, I pray you don't know them, because if you are still willing to work for that fucker after finding out what he did, then you and I are *really* going to have a problem."

The look in his eyes, ones so goddamn similar to mine, gives me pause and has me biting back the retort on the tip of my tongue. What could possibly be so bad?

I know just about everything about Dom, and it hasn't stopped me from trusting him, loving him, and bending over backward to help him in any way I can. I highly doubt there's anything serious enough to get me to rethink my relationship with him—personal or working.

"Stone, just listen, please." Gabe is generally a pretty easy-going guy. So when he sounds this serious, I know it's time to pay attention.

"Fine, what's so terrible that makes you think it will change my mind about working for Dom? You do know I'm not clueless about what he does."

Gabe stands and moves to the end of Savage's desk, leaning forward with his palms flat on the surface. He looks from Savage to me with a firm set to his jaw. "But you don't know what he did to us...what he did to Dani."

Dani?

"What do you mean what he did to Dani?"

Savage motions to the chair again. "You might want to sit for this."

～

NORA

His eyes were on me.

There's nothing else in the world that can cause my body to heat and respond like having Stone Hawke watching me dance.

I felt it the moment he walked in the club.

It made me wish I wasn't going all out and flaunting myself just to stick it to those turds from earlier.

At the time, it seemed like a good idea—to show them what I can do after leaving them speechless with their jaws on the floor.

But with Stone there, it felt like every move I made was one step closer to me ending up in his bed.

I didn't dare look over at him, but now that I'm sure he's gone, I lift my head from the stage just as my song ends and glance over at the elevator bay. The numbers light up indicating it's stopped on the second floor.

He must be meeting with Savage and Gabe about something. Maybe that's why they've been antsy all night. For Stone to willingly sit down with his brother somewhere other than at their mom's table, something pretty serious must be going on. But at least it means he's not down here watching me, or worse trying to get me alone again.

Whew.

I'm glad he's going to be tied up upstairs. I can go on my break and hide out in back until I'm sure he's gone.

When I reach backstage, Dawn gives me a weird look in the mirror as I pass.

"What?"

She spins around on her chair and eyes me up and down. "Why are you all flustered?"

I examine myself in the mirror in front of me. "I'm not flustered." Sure, my chest is a little pink, and so are my neck and cheeks, but I just got done dancing my butt off. At least, that's what I tell myself it's from and what I hope she'll believe.

Candy laughs from next to me. "Dawn's right, you are most definitely flustered."

Crap on a cracker.

Apparently, I completely suck at hiding my reaction to Stone. Even his mere presence has thrown me enough for Candy and Dawn to notice. This from a man I've barely even touched. If I ever let him get his hands on me, I'll probably spontaneously combust and engulf him in the inferno.

There's no use trying to lie to the girls.

"Fine, maybe I'm a little flustered."

Candy leans toward me. "Because of those guys at the bar you stuck it to?"

I look over at her to assess whether she's being genuine or snooty. Her wide green eyes seem curious. "Who told you about that?"

She shrugs and spins her chair in a circle before stopping to face me. "Byron. He was wicked impressed with you, you know. I swear, if he wasn't gay, I would think he has a little crush on you and that big brain of yours."

I bite back a laugh and turn and rest my butt on the vanity. "No, it wasn't those guys. The one was a jerk, for sure, but I try not to let stuff like that get to me." Besides, I just stuck it to them both on and off the stage.

Dawn crosses the room and leans next to me. "Then what's up?"

Darn it.

I would really love to tell them about Stone. It's not like I can discuss it with Dani or Caroline, at least not any more than what I already told them. And I don't really talk to any of the girls I was friends with in college anymore. But I can't really tell them. The whole "no getting involved with patrons" rule is pretty steadfast, and I doubt the fact that he's Savage's brother would make a difference on that. In fact, it would probably make things worse if the bosses found out.

Keep it vague.

"It's this guy..."

Candy's eyes light up, and she leans forward in her chair. "Ooh, do tell."

I shrug and kick off my heels, stretching my ankles and calves. "There's not much to tell. Nothing's happened with him, we haven't even kissed. But every single time I see him, it's like...I don't even know how to describe it...the world stands still and I'm stripped bare."

Dawn bursts out laughing. "Stripped bare? Honey, you do know what you do for a living, right?"

Duh.

I roll my eyes at her. "Yes, that's not what I mean. Haven't either of you ever met someone and just had an instant connection with them? Like they can see through you? And even though they have tons of faults, you can't seem to stay away?"

Candy stands and pats me on the shoulder. "The only instant connection I've ever had with a man was a quickie in the bathroom. There's a reason I'm still single."

Dawn nods and chimes in. "Ditto."

I snort-laugh and nod as Candy makes her way over to the stage. Once Cherry is done, she's taking the main stage. Dawn taps me on the shoulder. "I do get the whole overlooking faults thing, though. My ex could be a real fucking jerk, but when he wasn't drunk and an idiot, he was sweet, caring, a powerhouse in bed, and treated me like a queen. I forgave him his faults to a point, but I eventually had to draw the line at banging other girls. Cheating is an absolute deal breaker for me. Just make sure you don't let the guy walk all over you and have some limits."

It's good advice but really, it's unneeded. I don't have any plans to act on this weird attraction between me and Stone. Why did I expect them to understand the pull between us when I don't even get it? It's just one more thing to remind me that my supposed high I.Q. doesn't mean anything in the real world, just like it didn't after I got out of high school.

I'm twenty-one years old. I'm a stripper. And I have absolutely no clue what I'm going to do with the rest of my life. Stone is just another wrench I don't need thrown in right now. Telling myself I'm happy doing what I'm doing has kept me going for a while now, and I'm not about to let it stop because a handsome guy shows me some interest and gets my heart racing. And I'm going to try to forget the way he seems to know me at my core unlike anyone ever has before.

Stone will just have to find some other woman to flatter with his sexy grins and dreamy, lustful looks.

I'm fine where I am and how I am.

For now.

14

STONE

I don't know whether I want to hurl or kill someone...mainly Dom.

How the fuck could he threaten to kill Savage and Gabe? They are practically his family. Fuck that, we *are* his only family. His own wife and kid didn't stay, but Mom treats him like a brother and we've always stood by him even though his lifestyle has never been exactly upstanding. Yet, he did it.

The anger roils my stomach and heats the blood in my veins. I don't even bother waiting for the elevator, instead I charge down the stairs and into the back hallway of the club.

My chest tightens, and I heave in deep breaths to no avail.

Air. I need air.

Thank God the back door is right here. I don't think I'd make it through the club to the front.

The door slams against the outside brick wall when I throw it open.

The drizzle has turned into a full-fledge downpour, but I couldn't fucking care less.

Let the cold rain cool my temper.

Or at least try.

I step out into the alley behind the club and pace, because I can't think of a single other thing to do right now. Everything is such a jumbled mess. None of it makes sense.

What the fuck was Dom thinking?

I just can't wrap my head around what Savage and Gabe told me. Dani wasn't a real threat to him. The information she gathered would never have been enough to take Dom down legally. She may have caused some waves with a newspaper article, and it may have sent the Feds, and even the local P.D., sniffing around in places they had never thought to look before, but there was no definitive evidence of any direct wrongdoing on Dom's part.

He would have walked away, with barely a scratch and maybe a dent to his network.

But instead of talking to her, reasoning with her, he tried to kill her...

Fuck. Fuck. Fuck.

Of course, I heard about Matteo and Dom's other guys getting killed, but fuck if Savage and Gabe didn't do an amazing job covering up their involvement in that shit. To be honest, I wasn't really aware of what was happening back here when it occurred. I was too wrapped up in studying for the bar and starting work at the firm. Maybe if I had been paying attention, I wouldn't have been blindsided tonight.

Now I get it...the animosity Savage, Gabe, Dani, and even Skye have thrown my way with regard to me working for Dom. As far as they're concerned, I've sold my soul to the Devil himself.

And this peace they've brokered...there's no way that shit's gonna hold. Not if they keep telling people about it.

Jesus FUCKING Christ.

All they had to do was stay quiet, but they've already told me and Skye. Who's next? Storm and Ben? Mom?

If she finds out...

I shove my hands back through my wet hair and drop my forehead against the damp bricks. She won't survive this, losing him. He's her best friend and the only one who stood by her after Dad died. I was only five. All my memories of Dad can probably be counted on one hand. But Dom, he was there. Always. For whatever any of us needed. He rescued me from some pretty shitty stuff more times than I can count. He paid for my fucking law school, for fuck's sake.

And now, I'm indebted to him, and so fucking intertwined, there's no way to get out even if I tried. You don't walk away from Dom Abello. You leave in a body bag.

"*ARGH!*" I bellow out my frustration and pound my forehead into the wall.

There's no fucking way I can let this go. I have to talk to Dom. But if I go now, I'll do or say something I'll regret, something that could get me in an even worse situation. Something that would likely get me and the rest of those I love killed.

"Stone?"

Her voice barely registers over the now driving rain and the blood rushing in my ears. If it were anyone else, I probably wouldn't have even noticed.

Nora though...all she has to do is say my name and it's like a fucking lightning bolt straight to my cock.

"What are you doing out here in the rain?"

I turn to her and run my hands over my wet face. "Trying to find my sanity."

She cocks her head, and rain drips down off the side of her face. Her body trembles in the cool air.

"Shit Nora, get inside out of the rain."

Instead of following my order, she narrows her eyes at me and steps closer, glancing briefly at the door hanging awkwardly on its hinges.

Fuck, I hope I didn't break it.

"What's going on? I know you were upstairs meeting with Savage and Gabe. Is something wrong?"

I've never wanted to laugh and cry so much at the same fucking time. What *isn't* wrong is a better question.

In less than two months, I've gone from practicing at one of the largest and most esteemed firms in California to becoming the fixer for a mob boss who tried to kill several members of my fucking family.

And I couldn't tell Nora about it even if I wanted to. Which I don't. It would only drag her into an already deadly situation.

I close the distance between us, until there's less than six inches separating our wet bodies.

"Nothing you need to worry about, Nora. Go back inside. You're going to get sick standing out in the rain in this."

Like I could miss the way the flimsy gown she's wearing turned even *more* transparent in the rain. My fingers tingle wanting to trace every damn curve the dress is clinging to. Through the dark storm swirling in my head, she's a beacon of light.

She shivers and licks water away from her lips.

Fuck, she's beautiful.

And freezing.

I'm cold out here in a full suit; she's basically naked. I glance up at the video camera attached near the back door.

Please let Savage and Gabe be too busy to be watching.

"Come with me."

~

NORA

He reaches out and wraps his arm around my shoulders so quickly, I barely realize what's happening.

It's absolutely freezing out here, so when he tugs me to his side and walks us back to the open door of the club, I don't offer any protest. The heat of his body warms me even through his soaked clothing, and I huddle closer to him as we approach the door.

This is bad.

When I heard the door slam and a scream and came out to investigate, the *last* thing I expected was to find Stone having a meltdown in the rain.

He's always so controlled and stoic, except when he's making sexual innuendos and giving me panty-melting smirks. Finding him on the edge of an apparent breakdown has my stomach twisted in knots.

What could Savage and Gabe have said to him that would have set him off?

There's tension there, that much was obvious the few times I've seen them all together, but I've never seen Stone like this.

It's almost like he's...lost.

With his hand on the small of my back, he ushers me into the back hallway and down toward the dressing room. I glance back to the still-open back door but don't have time to mention it to Stone before he's pushing me into one of the bathrooms.

The door clicking shut behind us echoes in the small space.

My eyes meet his in the mirror above the sink. I'm suddenly very aware his hand is still pressed against my back and how close he is to me. Heat radiates off him and warms my chilled skin.

Why are we in here?

I hope he's going to tell me what's going on, but this is an odd place to have a chat.

"What are you doing?"

He stills behind me, his eyes darkening and swirling with something—not uncertainty, it's more like...resignation?

One step has him pressing his hard body against mine. His lips find the sensitive skin of my neck, and a shudder rolls through me with the hot breath that floats over my skin. The hand at my back slides around to grip my left hip while the other skims over the thin, see-through, wet fabric barely covering my stomach. His fingers creep up under the hem of the wholly obsolete slip of lace, and he cups my core.

Goddangit.

"Warming you up."

The words are like a lightning bolt straight to my clit, and I can't help my body from arching into him, seeking more of his touch.

His eyes hold mine in the mirror, almost daring me to look away, while he slips his fingers into my barely there thong and brush against my now wet flesh.

He sucks in a breath, and his hand tightens on my hip before he slips the tip of his finger inside me.

"Oh...God..."

I barely recognize my own voice. His growl in response vibrates against my back and through my ears.

The finger presses into me slowly. My body quivers, and I clench around it, grasping for more. He groans and adds another finger, eliciting a strangled gasp from me. I close my eyes and drop my head back against his shoulder.

His ministrations still.

"No, eyes on me."

It's not a request. It's a command. One I don't consider resisting for even a second.

I snap them open and meet his commanding gaze again in the mirror. He glances down to where his hand is moving under the see-through material, and my eyes follow his.

God, that's so hot.

He adds his thumb to the mix, and my eyes snap up to connect with his again. My hips move in time with his pumping fingers, rolling and arching despite the firm grip he maintains on me.

A very hard, very prominent bulge presses into my lower back, just above my ass.

My fingers itch to touch him, to hold that hot flesh in my hands, but he's maintaining such a tight grip on me, I can't move away enough to get my hand in between us.

Instead, his pumping, driving rhythm has me clawing at his arms. If it weren't for this dang suit, the evidence of my wild thrashing would be all over his skin.

I should be questioning this, fighting this, telling him to back away and leave me the heck alone, but my body demands what he's giving me. His touch ignites a deep, burning need in me long forgotten, or at least, pushed aside.

"Stone...please..."

My words don't have the desired effect. Instead of pushing me over the edge and giving me what I crave, his hand stills, and he shoves his hard dick against my back forcefully.

I plead with my eyes, begging him to resume his expert touch, but he just stares at me. It's impossible not to squirm under his intense scrutiny. My core clenches around his fingers almost of its own accord, silently imploring him to finish what he started.

He finally grins and begins again in earnest.

H. E. Double Hockey Sticks...

I'm going to come, and I'm going to come hard.

This isn't a gentle, loving touch. Not at all. This is rough and almost angry. Though I don't know if it's at me or whatever situation sent him out into the rainy alley in the first place.

And frankly, right now, with my orgasm hovering just on the periphery, I don't really care.

His fingers pump and stretch while his thumb swirls and

presses in an expert pattern that sends wildfire raging through every fiber of my being. My legs quiver, and my arms shake. Keeping my eyes open and trained on his becomes a nearly impossible task when all they want to do is roll up in my head. But, somehow, I know if I let that happen, he's going to stop.

I wouldn't survive that.

Wildfire becomes a violent inferno—all centered where his hand is probing my body. He presses his lips to the side of my neck, just under my ear. His panting breaths match mine.

The wave of the fire storm crests, and I can't fight it. My eyes roll closed and fireworks ignite against my lids as pleasure ripples through my body.

Those magnificent fingers don't stop moving until I release a heavy breath and sag back against him. When his hand finally stills, I open my eyes, and through the post-orgasmic haze, meet his in the mirror.

Dang. That was...

His gaze darkens and hardens. He pulls free of my body and takes a step back before scrubbing his left hand over his face.

"Shit."

One word.

Then he's out the door before I can even react.

What the Devil just happened?

15

_____

STONE

*T*he pounding of my feet on the pavement does nothing to relieve the tension still permeating my body. After last night, a ten mile run seemed like the only potential way to clear my head and maybe alleviate the pressure and anxiety building since I saw Nora...since I touched her.

What the fuck was I thinking?

I wasn't.

That's precisely the problem.

After learning about what Dom did, all rational thought went out the window. All I wanted was to forget...all I wanted was her.

I don't know how I managed to stop myself from yanking my pants down and pumping into her over that damn bathroom counter. That had to be the most restraint I've ever had. Her warm, wet heat clasping around my fingers almost made me come in my pants.

And now, my damn cock stirs to life just thinking about it.

Jesus. Is it even possible to think about her without getting hard?

I pause and lean against a lamppost to catch my breath and give my dick time to deflate before I finish my run. Sweat pours down my face and over my bare chest and back. Even at ten in the morning, and with the cooler fall temperatures, I'm drenched.

Several heaving breaths later, I resume the incessant *thump thump thump* against the street and make my way back into my neighborhood. Riverbend is exactly where I always wanted to live growing up, and busting my ass has allowed me to afford a house here. The mix of Tulane and Loyola students and other young professionals makes for eclectic neighbors and the restaurants around here can't be beaten. Plus, the houses are gorgeous.

By the time my house comes into view, my breathing is nothing more than gasping pants. I sag down onto the top step of my porch and drop my face into my hands.

That can't happen again.

I can't lose control around her.

There can't be any reason to give her false hope that this can happen between us.

It's not fair to her to let her believe we can ever be together.

The honk of a horn draws my head up, and I wave at the neighbor from across the street.

What's his name? Billy? Bob? Billy Bob?

I should probably know that. But frankly, in the handful of weeks I've been in this house, I've been so busy unpacking, straightening out Dom's cluster fucks, and dealing with my family shit, I haven't bothered to spend much time getting to know anyone living around me.

It's not like I can give them a tour of the house anyway. Well, at least not without locking the door of the master bedroom.

Too much explaining I don't want to have to do.

I heave out a sigh and drag my ass inside to chug a bottle of water and then head straight into the shower.

Cold water is the only option.

I'm too hot to tolerate even a luke-warm stream.

The water cools my skin, but the image of Nora bent over in my shower fills my head and brings my cock to full attention. By the time I made it home last night, I was such an emotional mess, I finished off a bottle of Balvenie and crashed.

Christ...

What kind of fucking perv jerks off at my age? But Nora's gasps and moans last night echoing in my head don't leave me much choice. I need the release, the relief from the pressure that's been building and threatening to explode.

I fist my hard cock and squeeze it until it's almost painful before stroking it slowly root to tip. My palm glides over the head, and my hips buck in response. The cool water doesn't tame my libido, it just stings against my heated skin.

That damn sugar cookie scent fills my nostrils and brings with it the breathy sounds she made last night. My hand strokes fast...harder. Every brush of my palm over the aching head of my cock sends a zing of heat straight to my throbbing balls. I slap my other hand against the wall to hold myself up.

Remembering the way her pussy clenched and rippled around my fingers when she came is all I need to send an orgasm racing through me. My legs shake, and my hand stutters in its rhythm as I shoot my load against the tile of the shower.

"Jesus fucking Christ..." I pant under the icy water until the quivering and tingling in my limbs subsides.

How the hell did I get myself into this mess?

I've done everything I can to stay away from her, to keep her away from me. Yet, I still ended up fist deep in her pussy last night. She was there when I was weak and reeling from what Savage told me, it's the only explanation for my behavior, and I can't fall into that trap again. I can't let my desire for Nora over-ride what I know is right...staying away from her.

Even if it won't be easy.

I soap up and relish my time in the cool water.

Now, all I want to do is towel off and collapse into bed. I'm beat. The lack of sleep—which can be directly blamed on Dom and Nora—is wreaking havoc on me. My ten mile run felt like a full marathon. And since I don't have anywhere I need to be today, I plan on taking advantage by crashing for a few hours.

I'm not dumb enough to think I'll be able to stop thinking about what Dom did, or wondering how I'm going to confront him about it without revealing Savage and Gabe told me what happened. But maybe with enough booze, I can at least make the attempt for the evening.

Maybe a drink before I hit the sack would help me get a few solid hours of sleep. I step out of the shower and grab a towel off the rack when an incessant pounding noise drifts up the stairs.

What the fuck is that?

I sling the towel around my waist and make my way downstairs. There better be a fire or a damn gas leak, otherwise the asshole beating on the front door better be able to take a punch.

Water drips off me and onto the wood floor as I cross to the door.

I yank it open without bothering to check the peephole and freeze.

NORA

I should have taken a moment to gather myself before pounding on his door like a lunatic, but there's no way I could have anticipated he would open the door dripping wet and with nothing but a small towel wrapped precariously around his trim hips.

Shitake mushrooms.

I'm in so much trouble.

The speech I've run through my head a hundred times in the last twelve hours disappears the moment I take in the water trickling over his toned pecs and down through the peaks and valleys of his perfect six pack.

Why God?

When I manage to tear my eyes away from his hard, wet flesh and back up to his face, all I get is a dark eyebrow quirked at me.

"You...you...you can't..."

Fart knocker! Where has my ability to speak gone?

"I can't what?" His deep voice floats across the space between us and reverberates in my chest. He leans against the jamb, the towel shifting and exposing more of his muscular thigh.

Gulp.

"You can't just...you know..." He's not going to make me say it, is he?

His blue eyes search mine for a second, and there's no humor in his gaze. He looks...angry. Maybe coming here and expecting to talk it out with him was a huge miscalculation on my part. But it's not like I can let what happened last night just go. "No, I don't know. Why are you here, Nora? To tell me what I can and can't do? Because I stopped taking orders from people a long time ago."

Grrrr.

Why is he so dang infuriating?

"No, that's not why I'm here..." Not completely, at least. "Look, can I come in?"

He glances over his shoulder into the house, as if considering whether to grant my request. Then he shrugs and pushes off the door, stepping to the side to permit me entry. He moves down the hallway.

This time, I'm not distracted by the beauty of the old home, it's the bunch and curl of the magnificent muscles under the damp, tanned skin stretched over his back that has me banging my shoulder against the archway into his living room.

"Ouch!" I grab my shoulder and rub at it. Another klutz move I only seem to make around Stone.

He pauses and looks back at me. "You okay?"

"Yeah, I'm fine." No way I'm admitting to him I just maimed myself because I was too distracted by his beauty to watch where I was walking.

With an odd look tossed my way, he proceeds to the bar across the room and pours himself a drink. I stop in the middle of the room, unsure what I'm supposed to do or say. He wasn't wrong, I did come here to yell at him and tear him a new one for getting me off and then walking away with nothing more than an uttered curse. But now that I'm here, and he's leaning against the bar staring at me expectantly, I can't seem to muster up the courage to go through with it.

Come on, Nora, grow a pair.

But I know that won't happen. It's not that I'm a pushover, I just tend to prefer not to stir the waters if it can be avoided. Confrontation isn't my thing. Or at least, it wasn't. But ever since Stone Hawke stormed into my life, things seem to be a lot less clear.

The silence blooms between us like a mushroom cloud, sucking the oxygen from the room. Under his scrutinizing gaze, my skin heats, and I run a hand back through my hair while I pace.

"Nora, tell me why you're here."

Not a question. A command.

One I'm pretty much incapable of resisting.

"I came to yell at you."

He raises the glass to his lips and takes a sip, but I catch the slight curve at the corner of his mouth.

Pompous pig. How can he think this is funny? How can he think what he did was okay? People don't just *do* that and walk away. At least, not normal people. Now, I've always known Stone wasn't like everyone else, but I would think he has basic decency. Last night makes me question that belief.

"You can't just...do...that to someone and walk away, Stone."

His eyebrow raises, and he downs the rest of his drink.

"Should you really be drinking at ten in the morning?"

With a chuckle, he pushes off the bar and stands to his full height so I have to look up at him. "Is that why you're here, Nora? To yell at me, tell me what I *can't* do, and lecture me about my drinking? If so, I suggest you leave before I stop thinking it's kind of cute and you end up pissing me off."

This time, my growl isn't internal. "Fudge, Stone, you are so dang frustrating."

"Am I?" That damn smirk returns, and he crosses his arms over his chest, only drawing my attention back to the bulging, flexing muscles there.

"For the love of...are you *trying* to make me crazy?"

He shakes his head and takes a step toward me, that damn towel shifting slightly and opening to reveal even more of his thigh. Two more inches to the right, and he'll be hanging out in all his glory.

I really haven't thought this out very well. Staying across the room, maintaining a safe distance, would have been prudent. He's too close for me to think clearly. The crisp smell of his soap and shampoo mingling with his natural spicy scent overwhelms me and makes my head swim.

Survival instinct kicks in, and I force myself to take a step back. My knees hit the couch, and I almost buckle backward onto it but manage to catch myself.

"You think *I* make *you* crazy?" He shoves a hand back through his wet hair, sending drops of water falling onto his shoulders and down his chest. "Jesus, Nora, you couldn't have things more backward."

What?

"Then...why did you leave like that and say...you know, what you said?" I can't say I've ever had someone get me off then curse and disappear. I think I was rendered mute and immobile for a good ten minutes after he fled. Thank God no one came looking for me, they probably would have thought I was having a stroke or something.

He pinches the bridge of his nose and releases a heavy sigh. "Last night was a mistake. One I won't be repeating."

The blood in my veins turns to ice. My head swims and I wobble slightly on my feet. I know us together is a bad idea, but to say it's a mistake?

Whatever is going on with Stone, it has to do with whatever Savage and Gabe said to him. He was not himself, that much is readily apparent. That has to be what's behind this. Given what happened, I don't believe for a second this is all about *us*. "What happened last night?"

Hard eyes meet mine. "You were there, Nora."

"That's not what I mean. What happened with Savage and Gabe? I know you met with them, and you were a mess when I found you in the alley."

Those blue eyes flare. Maybe pointing out his weakness last night isn't the best course of action. Stone isn't one to allow a chink in his armor. That I could so easily see it is probably a huge blow to his ego.

"It doesn't matter what they said. I shouldn't have lost control like that with you."

The regret in his voice shatters me more than I would have thought possible. We didn't even sleep together. He didn't even *kiss* me. Yet his rejection feels like having a white hot poker shoved through my heart.

When did what Stone Hawke thinks become so dang important to me?

The attraction has always been there, but somehow, in the short time we've known each other, he's managed to totally unravel me. And there's no doubt I affect him.

"Don't act like it wouldn't have happened at some point, Stone. No matter what we may tell ourselves, the whole 'friends' thing was never going to work."

He considers me for a moment before scrubbing his hands over his face. "You're probably right, but it can't happen again."

"Why not?"

I know the answer, but I need to hear it from *him*. Because as much as I agree he's bad news, and I'll probably regret this, I'm drawn to him like a moth to a flame. Even though I know I'll get burned, the heat is too much to resist.

16

NORA

Stone pauses for a moment and fists his hands at his sides. His eyes track up and down my body, finally settling on my face. "Because you don't know me, Nora. You don't know what I would do to you, physically and mentally. You don't know what being with me would mean."

Huh? Why is he speaking in riddles? I get that his boss is dangerous and Stone doesn't seem to be the hearts and flowers type, but his words don't make any sense.

"What's that supposed to mean?"

He turns his back to me and goes to pour himself another drink. I don't dare comment on it this time.

Is he going to answer me? Am I supposed to leave?

Stone Hawke is, without a doubt, the most exasperating man I've ever met. If he's not going to respond, I'm getting out of here. There's no point waiting around for an answer from him if he doesn't want to talk. I can't force Stone to do anything. That is abundantly clear.

"Well?"

The glass hitting the marble top of the bar resonates in the room, and I'm surprised it didn't shatter with the force he used to slam it down. He splays his hands out and drops his head. His shoulders bunch and flex with every little move.

I want to go to him. I want to wrap my arms around him and press my lips to his damp skin. I want to know what he tastes like.

But something tells me to stay back...that going over there would only push him deeper into wherever he is in his head.

Whether it's really about me or about whatever went down with the guys last night, there's something eating away at him.

Coming here was a mistake.

My need to confront him and get how I felt off my chest outweighed the potential of hurting him and dragging up whatever upset him so much. I didn't even consider that when I stormed over here.

"I'm...just going to go. I'm sorry..." I turn toward the front door but don't make it three steps before his hand wraps around my bicep. His fingers dig into my skin, and when he spins me around, and his eyes meet mine, they tighten like a vise.

"My life is not normal, Nora. Not even fucking close. I'm not like the boys you were with in school. And things just got a hell of a lot more complicated last night."

I shake my head and stare up at him, trying to find an explanation. "I don't understand."

His lips press into a tight line, and he grasps my other arm firmly. "And you won't. My life isn't the right place for a girl like you."

Whoa...what? A girl like me?

Things are suddenly crystal clear. Acid churns in my stomach and works its way up my throat. I swallow it down and struggle against his grip. He releases me, letting me take a step back from him.

I refuse to let the tears burning in my eyes fall. I won't give him the pleasure of seeing me cry. "Wow. I get it now. This is because I'm a stripper."

His eyes flare open, and he reaches for me again, but I retreat another step. With his palms up, he backs away. "What? Jesus, Nora, no...how can you think that?"

"What am I supposed to think? You come and watch me dance, you're clearly attracted to me, but you won't be with me?" He steps forward and opens his mouth, but I halt him with a raised hand. "And before you even start, don't give me the B.S. about Savage not being happy, because you aren't even close to him, and I think Gabe and Skye proved that even *that* doesn't have to be an issue. You don't want to be with me because you think you're better than me. You're a lawyer, and I just shake my jiggly bits for perverts."

By the time I'm done, my chest is heaving and warmth has spread over up my neck and cheeks. I can't remember the last time I was this mad. Well, yes I can. It always seems to happen around Stone.

He smirks and arches an eyebrow.

Jerkface thinks this is amusing?

One step brings him closer to me. "Are you done?"

Crossing my arms over my chest, I stand my ground. There's nothing left to say, but I refuse to cut and run now. I want to know what lame excuse he's going to use.

"For someone who is so damn smart, you are being really fucking stupid right now."

I gasp and clench my fists at my sides.

Grrrr.

I'm not an aggressive person by nature, but he's certainly causing me to reassess my stance on physical violence.

He closes the distance between us so fast, I don't have time to react or prepare any of my defenses. One hand threads into my hair while the other grips my hip and tugs me against him. His lips find mine in a punishing kiss. Hard and wet, our mouths clash, and our tongues dual.

There's no doubt what he's doing. He's staking a claim.

And I'm letting him.

Just as quickly as he descended on me, he pulls back, still gripping my hair firmly in his hand. He tugs on it hard, sending sharp stabs of pain across my scalp and forcing me to look up at him.

"This has nothing to do with who *you* are, or what *you* do, Nora. This is about *me*. You may not like what you find if I let myself go with you."

"Isn't that for me to decide?"

A wry grin tilts his mouth. "And I thought you were going to be easy. But it's okay, I like a challenge."

Did he just call me easy?

I don't get the chance to voice the question. He kisses me again and shoves his hips against me, pressing his very hard, very hot, very large erection against my stomach. Warmth floods my body, centering at the aching, needy spot between my legs. His strong fingers hold me in place. There's a very real chance he's leaving bruises on my hip, and I should care considering how exposed my body is every day, but I can't bring myself to muster up any opposition.

He pulls away, leaving me gasping for air, and any humor that had been present quickly drains from his face. "It's time you learn what being with me really means."

~

STONE

Nora's mouth opens and that hot pink tongue slips out and over her lips.

Fucking hell...

She doesn't even realize she's doing it or that it's driving me absolutely insane. The image of those plump wet lips wrapped around my cock invades my brain, washing out any rational thought. Then all the things I want to do to her join the party, and I'm basically a quivering mass of barely contained lust.

It would be so damn easy to take her. Only the thin towel and her yoga pants are preventing me from shoving her onto the couch and pounding into her.

But she needs to know who I really am...*what* I really am... and that means we need to at least make it upstairs before I put my hands on her.

I step back and release her hair. Before she can question what I'm doing, I drop my shoulder into her and flip her over with a startled yelp so she's dangling down my back.

"Cheese and crackers, Stone, what are you doing?" Her hands grip at the towel, seeking something to cling to, but all she manages to do is yank it right off my hips. It falls to my feet, exposing my ass in all its glory to her.

Her sharp intake of breath spreads a smile across my face.

Yeah, check it out, sweetheart.

I smack her ass, eliciting another yelp, and head toward the stairs.

"Stone, put me down."

That earns her another smack and me another sharp cry from her.

"You'll stop talking and squirming, if you know what's good for you."

I make it to the top of the stairs before she huffs out a long sigh, her warm breath skating across the bare skin of my ass.

Resignation.

About fucking time.

"You can kiss it, if you want to, sweetheart."

She growls and digs her nails into my thighs.

Ouch.

But *fuck* is that hot. The fire in Nora wars with her naturally submissive tendencies, but when she lets it out, *Christ*, it's sexy as fuck.

The lights are still on in my room and the bathroom from when I raced out to answer the door.

Good. It will give her a clear view of exactly what's in store if she really wants to play this game with me.

When I reach the bed, I flip her off my shoulder and onto the mattress. Her startled yelp makes me grin. She's so damn adorable. And she's clearly never had anyone handle her the way I just did. Knowing that makes my cock swell even more. For all intents and purposes, she's a virgin. At least to my world.

She glares up at me from where she lies sprawled across the grey comforter. Her chest rises and falls as she takes in heaving breaths. The tank top she wears barely contains the swell of her breasts. There's definitely anger flashing in her blue eyes, but that's not the only thing there. That turned her on. Big time.

It's a good start.

But it's barely the tip of the iceberg, and I need to know she can handle it before we go any further. Things are already too complicated to throw her into the mix unless she *really* wants to be here.

"Was that really necessary?" The words come out slow, almost as if she's trying to control the shaking in her voice, but she's failing miserably.

I smirk and nod. "Yes."

That's all she's getting. I reach down and grasp my throbbing cock.

Her eyes track the movement and widen slightly before she sucks in a deep breath and audibly gulps.

My cock twitches in my hand. With her gaze still very much focused on my cock, I slide my hand up the shaft—once, twice, three times.

The shudder that rolls through her body continues straight through mine.

Fuck. I didn't think I could want her any more than I already do, but she's killing me.

I stifle a chuckle when she finally jerks her stare away from me stroking myself and focuses her attention to one of the large beams of the four-poster bed.

Reluctantly, I release my dick and take a step closer to the bed. I don't need to look to know what she's seeing, but I want to gauge her reaction up close.

The metal eye ring protruding from the wood glints under the room lights. Her eyes jerk over to the opposite side of the bed to the matching ring. Then they flit to the two beams at the head of the bed before finally coming back to meet mine. Thin blonde eyebrows furrow her forehead.

"Are those..."

She trails off, apparently unwilling or unable to voice what she knows to be true.

I don't answer her. Nora needs to learn she won't always receive answers from me, and that *I* am in charge here.

The half-voiced question lingers in the air between us while my cock continues to throb. Having her on my bed while I'm buck fucking naked is pure torture.

"Kneel."

At first, it appears she may defy my command. Her eyes narrow briefly, and her fists clench at her sides. But then something softens in her gaze, and she slides up until she's kneeling in front of me.

"Good girl." She doesn't even realize what she's doing yet. Her desire to comply with my commands is innate.

I offer her my hand. When she accepts it, I don't miss the way her eyes dart down to my cock briefly before returning to my face as she climbs from the bed to stand before me.

"What are you doing?"

Excellent question.

"Showing you who I really am."

Her eyes widen, and she sucks that lip under her teeth again.

Fuck, that's so hot.

"You better release that lip. You're going to need your mouth wide open for this."

The gulp she takes is audible and makes me smile.

"Kneel."

There's a hesitation, but it's only momentary before she lowers herself to her knees in front of me. The wood floor is going to be uncomfortable. But she'll survive. It's just giving her a taste of what she's in store for if she really wants to do this with me.

"You sure you want to do this, Nora?"

She nods her head. I reach down and grasp her chin. "No nodding. 'Yes, sir,' is the appropriate response."

Her lips tremble before the words I've been dying to hear from her finally tumble out. "Yes, sir. I want this."

Fuck yes!

I release her chin and drop my hand to my side. My cock bobs in front of her face, and she reaches out for it. I catch her wrist before she can wrap her small fingers around it.

"Mouth only. Hands behind your back." I drop her wrist, and she complies.

If she starts twisting that hand around me too, I'll blow in a fucking second. Besides, seeing her on her knees, hands back, with my cock buried down her throat is pretty much my dream come true.

She peers up at me from under her long lashes and leans forward. Her hot, pink tongue darts out and swipes across the tip of my cock.

Holy hell!

Before I can even catch my breath, she sucks me into her mouth, swirling that sweet tongue around my length the entire way in.

17

NORA

"Jesus, Nora." His fingers catch in my hair, and he tugs me forward, pushing himself further into my mouth. The slightly salty taste of his pre-cum dances across my tongue.

My lips stretch to accommodate him.

Christ, he's big.

I moan around his cock, and his hips buck, driving him even deeper.

I'd give just about anything to be able to grab him. But that's not what he wants or needs.

Blue fire blazes in his eyes as he stares down at me. I pull back, swirling my tongue across the bottom of his dick along the way, then move back down until the head hits the back of my throat.

"Fucking Christ!" He yanks on my hair and reaches down to grasp my chin. "I'm going to fuck your mouth, Nora. But I'm not going to come. Your sweet pussy is going to milk that from me."

Heat floods my core. By the time he finally touches me, I'm going to be drenched.

Who would have thought Stone's filthy mouth would rev me higher than any sweet words ever have?

He releases my jaw and pulls his dick from my mouth.

"You ready?"

There's no question what my answer is. "Yes, sir."

"Good girl."

The head of his cock presses against my lips, then he shoves forward, all the way to the back of my throat, almost gagging me while his hands tighten in my hair, holding me in place. I groan, and it seems to spur him into action. His hips snap back and slam forward, thrust after thrust, doing to my mouth what he's promised to do to other places.

The muscle in his clenched jaw throbs, and he squeezes his eyes shut, then jerks himself free of my mouth.

He doesn't say anything. But his heaving chest and wild eyes tell me what I need to know.

His control was slipping. He was going to come.

I can't stop the smile from forming.

He raises an eyebrow. "Proud of yourself?"

I nod and try not to appear too smug.

There's no humor in his look. "Did you just nod, Nora?"

Crap.

"Sorry, sir. Yes, I am proud of myself."

A smile plays at his lips. He holds out his hand and waits for me to take it.

Stone's hand clasps around mine, and he tugs me until I'm pressed up against him, his arousal straining between us.

Geez, there's no way that's gonna fit.

Almost as if he's reading my mind, he chuckles and grinds his hips against mine, pushing the rock hard flesh into my lower abdomen.

"You should be proud, Nora. Pushing me to the edge like that isn't easy to do."

My heart swells in my chest.

He releases my hand, letting it fall to my side. "Turn around."

His deep, gravelly voice goes straight to my aching core, and I squeeze my thighs together as I follow his order. If I didn't already have an inkling, seeing those eye hooks screwed into his massive bed confirmed Stone is definitely into some kinky stuff.

I'm not entirely sure how I feel about that. I've never been with anyone who did more than stick it in, get off, and pull out. Experimenting wasn't really an option. But something tells me that with Stone, it wouldn't be experimenting at all.

*Oh no...*This man knows *exactly* what he's doing in the bedroom.

And I trust him. *Mostly.*

When my back is to him, he reaches over my shoulders and threads his arms through mine, pinning me in place with his chest pressed to me and my arms immobile.

What the...

His warm breath flutters against my neck before a barely-there kiss is brushed against my skin. I shudder against his strong hold but it isn't uncomfortable or an unpleasant feeling. No, being pinned against Stone is definitely somewhere I want to be.

"Move."

He tugs lightly on my arms, urging me to step back with him. Then he turns us until I'm facing the far wall of the room. Three large black lacquered wardrobes line the wall, almost reaching the ceiling.

Stone must have a lot of clothes.

With a nudge, he urges me to walk forward across the wood floors until the cabinets tower over me. His arms tighten around mine, pulling my shoulders back almost painfully and leaving no space whatsoever between my back and his hard chest and very large erection.

"Open it."

His command and the heat of his breath against my neck render me mute. I couldn't form a response even if I wanted to.

I tug my arms out from his loosened hold and step forward tentatively.

Why do I feel like I'm not going to like what I find in here?

My hand quivers when I raise it to the shiny silver knob. After a deep breath, I tug on the right side door, and it pops open, swinging into the room.

I gulp through the knot suddenly in my throat.

Two rows of coiled rope hang on the door, varying in widths, textures, sizes, and colors.

"Open the other one."

When my shaking hand manages to open the other door, I can't help the audible, sharp intake of breath.

Holy...

Mother...

Flashes of shiny metal and dark leather flood my vision. I can't focus on just one item.

Either he keeps his kitchen implements in a very strange place, or he's into some seriously twisted stuff. These look like torture devices.

The giant thing that looks like a meat hook with a ball on the end of it sends a shiver down my spine, and I step back, directly into Stone's hard, warm body.

His large hands land on my biceps, and he squeezes them gently. "Say something."

I would, if I had any freakin' clue what words were. My ability to string letters together seems to have flown the coop along with any willingness I may have had to explore Stone's kinky side. This...this is something else entirely.

"Nora?" A gentle shake snaps me from the dark hole of morbid images I was drowning in.

How do I phrase this question without sounding judgmental?

"What is all this stuff for?"

A soft chuckle floats from behind me, and he presses his lips to the skin right behind my ear. "Fun."

Fun?

I'm not exactly seeing how a giant meat hook, leather straps, whips, and all the other insane-looking devices hanging within the bureau could possibly be for *fun*. At least, not fun for me...

"Even that giant meat hook with the weird ball thing on it? What's that for, anyway?"

His right hand reaches around and clasps my jaw, urging until I look up at the ceiling. Smack dab in the middle of the large open area of the room, several large ring hooks are screwed into the ceiling.

"That's an anal hook, and it's for your pleasure. Up there," he draws my face back down until I'm looking at the chest again, and then slides his other hand down between my ass cheeks, pressing firmly against the tight fabric of my yoga pants, "and down here."

Oh no...

I clench my cheeks against his probing fingers and try to put some physical distance between us, but he doesn't relent. He holds steadfast, keeping me prone against his body.

"Are you starting to understand what I was trying to explain to you?"

What else can I do but nod?

I'm literally speechless. And I'm not sure if I should be screaming and running as far and as fast from Stone as possible, or turning around and jumping him right now. It would be fruitless to deny my attraction to Stone, what he does to me every time he's in the same room. But I'm not naïve enough to think Stone isn't a dangerous man. He is. The life he leads—working for Dom Abello and this dark, sexual side—are so far and beyond what could be considered safe or normal.

Dangit.

Space.

That's what I need.

Somewhere out of Stone's orbit, where I can think and process all this.

Because there's no way I can think clearly with a very hot, very horny Stone pressing himself against me.

STONE

The way Nora clenched her ass around my hand and tried to wiggle free of me should give me pause. She's uneasy. But...she hasn't said she wants to leave. And she hasn't struggled. She's followed every order I've given her without question and responded to me when I've asked if she wants to continue.

There's a submissive in there somewhere, she just doesn't want to acknowledge it.

Of course, she's bound to be curious, and probably a little— or a lot—shocked by what she's seeing. But I don't want to give her too much time to dwell on all the awful things she's probably picturing in her mind. She needs to experience what it's like to be with me, before she lets unfounded, uneducated fears ruin the potential for something amazing between us.

"Stop."

She flinches slightly in my arms, and I pause and let her settle before turning her to face me. It kills me she's averting her eyes, but I understand it.

I wrap one arm around her waist and tug her to me while I tip her chin up with a finger until those baby blues meet mine. Drowning in their depths is a very real possibility. I've never wanted to lose myself so completely in someone else, to push the entire world away and just *be* with them. It's terrifying and thrilling at the same time.

Her bottom lip quivers slightly. "Stop what?"

"Stop thinking I'm going to mutilate and torture you."

The look on her face is fucking priceless. She has the balls to pretend to be shocked by my statement, when we both know that's *exactly* what she was thinking.

She wouldn't be the first girl to see my bag of tricks and go running. But most women crave a sexual dominant, even if they don't know it. And when they've opened their minds and their legs to me, I've never heard any complaints.

Nora won't have any either.

Her eyes drift to the side, refusing to meet mine despite the fact that I'm still holding her chin up. "I don't think that. I just...I mean...what am I *supposed* to think?"

"You're supposed to trust me and trust that I would never do anything to hurt you or anything you don't want me to do."

The silence that fills the room is deafening. I release her chin and step back, sure she's about to bolt and ready to give her room to do so without making her feel more uncomfortable.

But instead of racing toward the door, she moves over to the other two bureaus and stops in front of them.

What is she doing?

"What's in these?"

I chuckle and step up next to her. "The one on the left has my suits. This old house has a tiny closet. The one in the middle... well...why don't you look?"

Nora sucks at hiding her emotions. The trepidation in her eyes when she glances over her shoulder at me is crystal clear. But so is the curiosity.

When she returns her attention to the cabinet, I close the little distance between us until I'm a mere inch away from her. The doors open, exposing ten drawers. She reaches out and pulls one open, and her breath audibly catches.

Vibrators fill the drawer, varying in sizes and shapes. With strangled noise, she shoves it closed and opens the next one, revealing thirty different butt plugs. Her body visibly trembles as she tugs on another one. This one gives her pause. I doubt she's seen half of what lies on the velvet bottom of the drawer before.

Good.

The thought of surprising her with some of the things in there makes my cock harden even more.

"Still think I'm going to torture you?"

She chuckles and turns to face me. "Oh, I'm sure of it now."

The gleam in her eye and tilt of her mouth assures me it was said in jest. But she's right, I probably will torture her...in a way... but she'll enjoy it.

I capture her face between my palms and angle it up to me fully. "Are you going to bolt?"

Uncertainty flashes briefly before she shakes her head. "No."

"Is there anything you don't want to do? Anything you don't want *me* to do? Anything that's a hard limit?"

Her brow furrows, and she glances over her shoulder at the open bureaus. She turns back to me with her lip pulled between her teeth. "I'm not sure. I've never tried anything."

I take her face in my hand and brush my thumb across the soft, delicate skin of her cheek. "Are you open to trying things? To trusting me to know what you'll enjoy? I promise if you ever want me to stop, you just say the word. You're in control."

There isn't any hesitation this time. She nods. "Yes, but I do need you to explain what *that* is." She points to the side of the room under the window without tearing her eyes from mine.

There's no need for me to look. I know exactly what she's pointing at, and a grin spreads across my face.

God, she's so fucking adorable.

Her innocence is like fucking gasoline being thrown on the fire of my libido. The smart thing would be to show her the door before we both do something that's only going to complicate our lives more, but I can't find the strength to push her away. Not while I'm buck naked and have her in my domain.

That probably makes me a fucking dick. A selfish one.

She doesn't need to be exposed to the crud and filth in my life, especially after what I found out last night. But her sweetness seems to quell the burning rage that's been simmering since I learned the truth, and it always has. Until the day she showed up in my house, I hadn't realized how I'd been using her as a balm to soothe my soul since the first time I met her. Going to the club to watch her whenever I came into town became a ritual. And once I moved back, leaving her be was physically impossible for me.

I can't stay away from Nora Eriksson.

It may be both our undoing.

But it will be *so* fucking worth it to finally have her in the hundreds of ways I've been imagining for so long. To finally watch her unravel in my arms. To have her lose herself in me. To give her the release and direction I know she needs. To set her free from whatever has her tangled up in her own head.

And I know the perfect place to start.

"Nora, I'm not going to tell you what that is. It's best explained by demonstration."

Her responding moan and shudder is the only invitation I need, and I descend on her mouth, intent on finally giving her *all* of me.

18

NORA

The moment his lips hit mine, I sag into him, pressing my body against his and granting him entrance to my mouth.

His tongue slips along my lips and tangles with mine. Heat floods between my legs, and I wrap my arms around his neck, tugging him closer. Even pressed against me, he's not close enough. I need him on top of me, inside me, I need it all.

He growls and reaches for my thighs, urging me to wrap my legs around his trim waist.

Sweet Lord...his dick is enormous.

And it's rubbing in all the right places. How the heck did I get that thing in my mouth?

Tearing off my yoga pants and sliding down on it sounds like Heaven right now.

Every step he takes toward the contraption at the side of the room grinds his hard, hot flesh against me, and I can't contain the moan that slips from my lips and into his mouth. He tastes of whiskey and all things forbidden. And I want to devour him.

I can't believe we're doing this...that I'm letting *him do this to me.*

We've danced around whatever this is between us for so long, I thought it would never happen. And after the way he left things last night, this is the last place I figured we would be. But, despite everything, it feels *right.*

When he reaches the window, he sets me on my feet and pulls back slightly before looking at the red leather piece of furniture I can only describe as some weird form of chaise. I knew the moment I saw it, it was anything but an ordinary place to rest. And now, after exploring all of Stone's gadgets and gizmos, I'm more confident than ever that whatever this is, it's something designed for some sort of sexual play.

A large hand slides to the hem of my tank top, and he tugs it up and over my head in one smooth motion.

The brush of his warm palm along my skin sends a bolt of electricity straight to my core.

It feels like I've been waiting forever to have his hands on me. He deftly unhooks my bra, and he skims his fingertips over my skin lightly when he drags the straps down and off my arms.

My nipples pebble in the cool air of the bedroom, and Stone groans before reaching out and pinching them roughly.

"Ouch!"

His eyes narrow on me, and he bends down and sucks one into his mouth then repeats the process on the other.

Oh, my God...

Those things I call legs become obsolete, and I practically collapse against his supportive arms. That zing shooting through me is unlike anything I've ever experienced. Every flick of his tongue and tug of his lips cascades pleasure through my body.

"Sometimes a little pain enhances the pleasure, Nora. Trust that I will never *truly* hurt you. Everything I do is for *your* pleasure. You can tell me to stop at any time, but we are going to need a different word, because I guarantee, you will be begging me to stop when you don't really mean it."

I do trust him, or maybe I'm just shoving any uncertainty to the back of my mind, behind my raging lust.

Either way, I don't give a darn right now, as long as he keeps touching me.

Even the mention of a need for a "safe word" can't break the spell he's cast around me or quiet the raging inferno coursing through my body.

His fingers work their way into the waistband of my pants, and he kneels and rolls them down and off my legs, tossing them over his shoulder when they're finally free.

Only a tiny thong separates Stone from the place I need him most.

A tiny, soaked thong.

He lingers on his knees in front of me, his mouth mere inches from my flesh. The warm flutter of his labored breaths fans over my stomach and makes me quiver again.

Dang...

I brace my hands on his shoulders, and he slides the thong down. When I shift my weight to step out of them, it brings his face even closer to my wet center, earning me another appreciative groan and a glazed look in his eyes.

Instead of rising when I'm finally naked, he grips my hips and leans forward, burying his mouth and tongue into me with no prelude.

Jesus, Mary, and Joseph...

My legs buckle, and I dig my nails into his shoulders to keep my balance as he goes to town on my most intimate place. Rough day-old scruff rubs against my thighs, but it's the furthest thing from my mind. He just keeps going...

Swirling...

Sucking...

Probing...

Unrelenting...

The room spins.

Then two fingers are pushed inside me, spreading me open and pressing in all the right places.

He curls them into my G-spot and pulses them in time with his oral ministrations.

Holy...

I'm going to come...already.

Of their own accord, my hips thrust in rhythm with his penetrating fingers and swirling tongue. I'm humping Stone's face, and I don't care at all. I need this.

My body tightens as heat slowly spreads out from my core.

"Oh, God...Stone!"

Wave after wave of exquisite pleasure roll through my body. My legs buckle. Strong, gripping hands hold me steady while he continues to devour me.

He moans against me and laps at my overly sensitive, wet flesh. I try to shove him away when it becomes too much, but he holds firm, forcing me to take whatever he's offering.

And I do. Every flick of his tongue. Every push and pull of his fingers. Every tug of his lips.

Until he bites down on my clit and sends me spinning off into orbit again.

"Holy..."

I bite down on my lip and finally collapse against him. He relents and moves away from me, rising and wrapping his arms around me to support my weight.

His lips find mine. The taste of my release lingers there, and *dang* that is hot. Far sexier than I ever thought it would be. But maybe it's just because it's Stone. The way he devoured me like a starving man makes my heart practically beat out of my chest.

"That was nothing, Nora. You better be prepared for what's about to happen. What's your safe word?"

STONE

She swallows and looks up at me with that glazed post-orgasmic haze clouding her eyes.

Fuck, she is beautiful...

"Um...cupcake?"

I bark out a laugh and squeeze her against me. "Cupcake?"

Her cheeks flush, and she glances down at the floor. "Yeah, isn't it supposed to be a word I wouldn't normally use during... you know..."

There's no question what she's getting at, but I want to hear her say it. I give her a second to finish her thought, and when it's clear she won't, I fill in the blank for her. "While we're fucking?"

That sure got her attention back on me. Her head snaps back up, and wide eyes meet mine. "No...no...I didn't...I wouldn't..."

Seeing her this flustered is such a turn-on. She's so confident on stage, it's like she's a completely different person there. This is the real Nora. This is the Nora I want to know and experience fully. That Nora is a façade, someone she created to wall herself off from whatever happened in her past. It was a way for her to keep living without being crushed under the weight of her mistakes. But *that* Nora can stay at The Hawkeye Club. *This* Nora is mine.

"You would never say *fucking*." I brush my thumb along her wet bottom lip. "Do you *ever* curse, Nora?"

She shakes her head and peers up at me from under her thick, black lashes. "Not since I was about five, and my dad washed my mouth out with soap for saying a four-letter word. My sister never had the same aversion to the taste of Dial."

I tip my head back and laugh. "Oh, sweetheart, I can guarantee you will be screaming four-letter words very, very soon."

The corners of her mouth curve up. "I highly doubt that."

"That sounds like a challenge." I lean down and brush my lips against hers briefly. "And I do love a good challenge."

And we are going to start right now.

"Stay."

I release her and move over to the cabinet where I grab a coil of jute rope. It's the perfect one to start with. It won't leave the nasty abrasion marks some of the rougher ropes will. Although she will certainly have some physical reminders of what we're going to do, I know I can't mark her too badly, not with the way she's completely exposed on stage almost every night. I also snatch a condom from one of the drawers and roll it on before I turn back to her.

She eyes me warily as I approach her, uncoiling the rope slowly with each step. Her eyes move down to my straining cock, and she sucks in a breath.

"I'm going to explain to you what I'm doing. Remember, cupcake, use your safe word if you need to." I wink at her, and it earns me a tentative smile.

Her nerves are adorable.

I can't wait to fuck them out of her.

When I reach her, I hold the rope up so she can examine it. "Have you ever been tied up before?"

She shakes her head no.

I narrow my eyes on her. "Nora…"

"Oh, sorry. No, sir."

I press my lips to her forehead. "Good girl." Her eyes drift back down to the rope. "I'm not just some asshole playing with ropes. I've trained under a shibari and kinbaku master in San Diego. It's an art form, not just something you do during sex."

The deer in headlights look she's giving makes me pause.

"Are you okay with me binding you?"

Her response isn't immediate, and her eyes darken slightly as if she's turning over her answer in her head. Binding is not only intimate, it's an ultimate trust. If she's not ready for it, I would understand that. But I hope she has enough faith in me to do this, because I know she'll love it.

"Yes, sir."

The words are barely audible, but they are there. I smirk and sidle up to her. "Turn around and place your wrists together behind your back."

She complies. As soon as her hands are in position, I loop the rope around her wrists and bind my way up her forearms, tugging them together tightly. When I reach her elbows, I tie off the binding and tug on it, jerking her back against me.

She releases a small yelp, and I tilt her head back until she's looking up at me. "Does that hurt?"

"No, sir. It's a little uncomfortable, though."

I can't help the grin that spreads across my face. "I know. I can't wait to see the marks on your delicate skin. So fucking sexy."

Christ, that lip quiver is so damn hot.

Images of my dick disappearing between those plump lips race through my mind. It was fucking bliss. But I want to be buried inside her pussy right now. Her mouth can wait 'til later.

I return her face-forward until she's looking at one of my favorite pieces of equipment...if you can call it that.

"That is a Tantrachair." She inhales a sharp breath, squirming slightly in my arms. "It's exactly what you think it is. It's a chair for fucking. It allows me to force you into hundreds of different positions with very little effort."

She moans, causing my cock to jump between us.

"Go." I urge her forward and assist her to straddle the chaise. When she's steady on her feet, I swing my leg over and sidle up behind her, then I push between her shoulder blades, urging her down until her breasts are pressed flat against the highest red leather peak of the chair. She squirms slightly, adjusting herself, and shoving her ass against my cock even harder in the process.

I bend over and whisper in her ear. "Don't move. This is going to be hard and fast."

The responding groan is slightly muffled by her face being dropped over the edge of the chair. I run a finger through her folds, making sure she's still wet from her orgasm, and I find her absolutely drenched.

She's getting off on this. Thank fuck.

Gripping the ropes in front of me with one hand, I position my cock at her entrance with the other. One swirl of my hips with the head at her opening has her bucking against me. As much as I would truly enjoy toying with her, I've been hard for way too fucking long and thought about fucking Nora far too many times to hold off any longer.

Without preamble, I shove into her in one hard thrust, rocking her forward against the leather.

"Oh...God..."

"Sweet fuck!"

Our words mingle together. Her tight, wet cunt contracts and stretches around my cock, sending ripples of pleasure straight up my spine.

I pause for a moment, not only to give her time to adjust to my size, but also to give me a second to try to control myself so I don't blow my load in three seconds.

But the reprieve doesn't last, once I've pushed my orgasm back, I pull back and plunge back into her with a snap of my hips.

She cries out and clenches around me, but I don't relent. I pound into her, tugging on the rope to angle her exactly where I want her and keep her prone. Her hands flex and squeeze together at the base of her spine, and fuck if that isn't the hottest thing I've ever seen. My bindings against her pale skin.

The pink marks it's going to leave are going to have me wanting to fuck her all over again.

Jesus.

Just thinking about unwrapping her and seeing them has me almost coming on the spot. I plow into her...harder...faster...

Sweat trickles down my temple and drops onto her back.

She squirms and moans beneath me, desperate to move and gain some control. But I keep her down, tightening my grip on the rope and her hip, and continue my relentless rhythm.

This isn't about long, drawn-out pleasure. This is fucking... pure and simple. This is pounding into her and hopefully driving out some of the relentless need I constantly feel for her.

Her pussy clamps down tightly around my cock on every thrust, squeezing my flesh like a vise. The tingle in my balls tells me I won't last much longer, and I know she's close too. I slide my hand from her hip and down across her stomach until I find her clit.

The moment my finger swirls around it, she bucks on my cock and tightens again.

"Crap...Stone...*please!*"

Now it's a race to the finish line, and I'm determined to ensure she makes it over before I do. My fingers flick and swirl while I drill into her, holding off my own release.

"Come for me, Nora."

My words come out strangled through my clenched teeth.

Her pussy quivers around me, and she throws her head back toward the ceiling. "Oh, God...I'm gonna come!" I slam into her three more times, then twist her clit between my fingers, and she detonates.

Her arms tug at the binding as she bucks against me. I hold her steady and pound into her until my orgasm is finally ripped from my body by her clenching cunt.

I collapse on top of her limp body, careful to support my weight and not crush her arms pinned between us.

Our panting breaths are the only sound in the room. After giving both of us a minute, I stand and tug her upright. Her head drops back against my shoulder, and her half-lidded eyes meet mine.

"That was...wow."

Wow?

It's as good a word as any other to describe that, but it's not enough...not nearly enough.

I press my lips to her ear and flick my tongue out along the shell. "Don't think I didn't notice your word choice. I'm just going to have to try harder next time."

Her responding whimper goes straight to my cock and ensures me she's willing to continue to play my games.

Christ, playing with Nora is going to be so much damn fun.

STONE

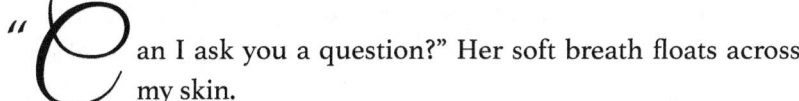an I ask you a question?" Her soft breath floats across my skin.

I tug her closer into my side. It's been a long time since I snuggled with a woman like this, and having Nora pressed against me is pure bliss. "What? Of course, you can ask me anything."

Doesn't mean I'll answer it, though.

Who knows where she's going with this. There are things I can't discuss, no matter how much I may want to tell her. And then there are things I would never utter a word about and don't want her, or anyone else, to know.

She sighs and runs her hand down my chest, stopping just above my stirring cock. "I'm just wondering where you learned all this. I mean, it's not exactly stuff they teach in high school sex-ed."

I chuckle and kiss the top of her head. Discussing how I've gained my sexual experience with the woman I'm currently fucking isn't usually on the top of my list. However, talking about it now doesn't seem like such a bad idea because not only do I *want* Nora to know, it also gets my mind off what I learned about Dom.

And it's not like I have anything to hide, at least about this.

"Well, I was always kind of intrigued by the lifestyle but never knew anyone who was involved until I got to college. My senior year, one of my friends invited me to go to a club with him. I just didn't know it was a sex club."

Her head jerks up and wide eyes meet mine. "A sex club?"

Surely, Nora can't be so naïve as to *not* know sex clubs exist.

"You've never been to one?"

Instead of laughing at my joke, she smacks my chest, narrows her eyes on me, and tries to appear pissed.

Unsuccessfully.

"I'd be lying if I said I wasn't shocked a little when I walked in there, but truthfully, I was more intrigued than anything. It was almost like walking in somewhere and instantly knowing you're home. That probably sounds crazy, but I don't know how else to describe it."

She shakes her head. "That doesn't sound crazy at all."

How can she understand so easily?

Most people would wonder what kind of fucked-up deviant I am to feel at home in a sex club. But Nora, she just inherently gets it. A strange tingling sensation starts in my chest.

What is it about this girl?

"So, did you dive right in, or...?"

A laugh rumbles in my chest, shaking her slightly. "The first couple times I went, I just observed, taking it all in and learning the names and uses of all the different implements. After going for about six weeks, I met the man who basically changed my life."

She stills in my arms, and I realize how that might've sounded and chuckle. "No, not like that, I'm definitely straight. Although, I was never opposed to a threesome if someone suggested it."

The silence I'm met with lingers a little too long. I know Nora hasn't experienced a lot of the things I have, but I don't see any reason to hide any of it from her. If she wants to do...whatever the hell it is we're doing, she needs to be okay with my past. At least, that part of it.

Rather than wait for her to respond, I figure it's better to just plow ahead.

"At that point in my life, I was just about to graduate, and I was heading on to law school. I was looking for any way to unwind, destress, and kind of ground myself, I guess. Even with my life and future planned out, I felt...adrift. When I went to the club that night, there was a demonstration from a shibari and kinbaku master. I'd heard him mentioned in the club before, but I hadn't ever seen a live demonstration. There wasn't any sex involved, but it was one of the most sexual and sensual things I've ever experienced in my life."

Trying to put this into words is difficult. No one has ever asked me about it before. But I want Nora to know.

I need her to understand.

"Watching him bind her into a beautiful piece of art...it was more erotic than anything I'd seen in the club with people outright fucking, and something about it just spoke to me and my soul."

She smiles against my chest and presses a kiss there.

"I approached him after the demonstration and asked him if he would teach me. At first, he said no, but as you may have discovered, I'm persistent when I want something."

Her responding chuckle vibrates against my chest. "Really? I hadn't noticed."

I smack her ass, earning me a playful yelp.

"I eventually got him to agree to at least meet with me once."

"What happened?"

I shrug. "I guess I must've said or done something right

because when we were done with our session, he told me to be there at the same time next week."

Christ...it feels like such a long time ago.

"How long did you train with him?"

"Once a week for almost two years. I'm not a master nor even close to being one. That takes a lifetime of dedication. But something about creating the bindings just...I don't know...it calms me and makes me feel like I'm in control of something so important and beautiful. The other stuff..."

I chuckle and squeeze her ass. "Well, that's just for fun. Being in control and having someone place that much trust in you is very heady, and the rush I get from it is indescribable. And it is a trust. If I didn't know what I was doing, I could seriously hurt you or me."

She's quiet for a few moments, no doubt running through her head every possible way I can maim her with what she saw hanging in those cabinets.

"You just have to remember that this isn't about pain or sex. It's about the ultimate pleasure through dominance and submission. For both of us."

She nods and stretches out languidly, letting out a deep sigh. I'm thrilled she's open to exploring this with me, but she needs to do a little research to fully understand what this all means.

"I want you to look at something when you get home."

"What?"

I brush my hand across her abdomen. "I have a good friend who is a Domme. She has an online column called Dear Mistress. It's part of the Shameless Book Club. People can send in questions about the lifestyle or really anything BDSM related, and she answers there. I think you would find it very informative."

She considers me for a moment. "Okay, I can do that. But..." Her eyes flit over to the wall of cabinets, and a blush spreads on her cheeks. She pulls her bottom lip between her teeth and then looks back at me. "Um...you want to show me what all those whips and things are for?"

I raise an eyebrow.

Whips and things?

The chuckle slips out before I can stop it, and her blush darkens and she buries herself deeper against the pillows, trying to hide her face.

"Don't be embarrassed, Nora. I'll show you whatever you want."

It just surprised the fuck out of me. It's the last thing I expected her to ask about because they're probably the most sinister looking items in my cabinet next to the anal hook and Wartenberg wheels.

"Just remember...you asked for it."

NORA

Stone climbs from the bed in his full naked glory and saunters over to the cabinets. A soft creak sounds when he pushes the door open all the way. The floggers, paddles, and something I'm not sure about all sway against the wood. He runs his hand over the line of options, seemingly considering the different possibilities.

Crap. What was I thinking?

He stops on a black leather flogger with a red braided handle and long, thick strips. A drawer opens, and something long, black, and silky looking gets pulled out. He wraps it around his right hand and then grabs the flogger. Then he moves over to the ropes and grabs several coils and loops them in his elbow. When he turns back to me, he offers me a sly smile.

"This is deer skin leather." With each step he takes toward the bed, he smacks the flogger against the palm of his hand, sending my heart thudding harder against my rib cage every inch closer he comes. "It's thin, light, and soft as silk. A lot of the other ones are quite brutal. But since this is your first time, I'll take it easy on you."

Take it easy on me?

Something tells me Stone doesn't go easy on *anyone*. He's far too formidable and driven to not go all out in everything he does. So he's either lying to me, or he's going against his own nature.

"Lay flat on the bed and spread your arms and legs."

My eyes automatically move to the eye rings on the bed posts.

He chuckles. "I'm going to tie you now. It's your first time, and I want you to experience it fully. If you aren't tied, you're going to instinctively move and try to cover your body. Don't worry, I just want to give you a little taste."

Well, heck, I just had a taste of him. And it wasn't nearly enough.

I spread out on his bed, the cool, crisp sheets against my back. He stands at the side of the bed, staring down at me with appreciation and lust burning in his eyes.

"Remember, the anticipation is worse than any pain you may experience."

The word *pain* alone makes me cringe. And he hasn't even touched me yet.

He pulls the silky strip of fabric from his hand and dangles it over me. "I'm going to blindfold you. Sensory deprivation will make the feelings strong, more intense. It will also stop you from watching what I'm doing and overthinking things."

Yikes.

I'm not sure not being able to see what's happening is a good thing. But I trust Stone when it comes to this. Plus, if it's too much, I can always scream *cupcake* at the top of my lungs. He leans over and ties the blindfold around my head then he tugs it down to make sure I can't see. The rope wraps around my wrist, and he pulls it to the side until I can't move it. The process is repeated on my other arm and legs until I'm held prone by the ropes.

My blood rushes in my ears. The *thud, thud, thud* of my heartbeat sounds like a banging drum. I brace myself for the impact of the flogger.

Geez, this is going to hurt.

I've never been hit by anything in my life, except Dani when we were kids.

But instead of the sharp bite and sting of a strike, soft, featherlight strands tickle over the skin of my abdomen. My body bows and arches into it. The restraints tighten around my wrists and ankles, and I force myself to drop back down to the mattress.

Stone drags the flogger lower, dipping it between my legs, over my wet center. The drag of the leather against my clit has my hips arching again. The inability to clench my thighs together against the onslaught of sensations there is overwhelming.

A low whimper falls from my lips. Stone's chuckle in response only makes my body thrum more.

The leather leaves my skin briefly before a sharp sting hits my chest. I jerk against the bindings.

Ouch.

A dull throb radiates out from the point of contact, almost as if I've been slapped. But really, it doesn't hurt, just tingles and warms.

Was that it?

Warm, wet lips pressed against the spot interrupt my analysis.

"That wasn't so bad, was it, baby?"

I shake my head no then remember... "No, sir." It wasn't bad. Like at all. In fact, I'm pretty sure I like it.

But I'm withholding judgement. Because something tells me, Stone is far from finished with me. His hand scalds a trail over my belly and down between my legs.

Fingers delve into my slick center, and he gives an appreciate groan.

"I think you're liking this, baby."

I clasp around his fingers, my body craving something to fill me.

But he retreats, leaving me panting and bereft.

No!

Before I can beg him to come back, another sharp sting smacks across my abdomen.

"Ahh!" I cry out, more out of surprise than the sting rippling across my skin. Another strike lands almost immediately, this time right across my left breast, followed closely by one on my right.

My entire body vibrates and burns, like napalm rolling over my skin.

"Stone!" He catches his name in his mouth, sliding his tongue along mine while his hand brushes my overly-sensitive nipple then moves to the other one.

Something presses against my clit...but it's not his hand.

It's...

Oh Lord...

It's the handle of the flogger. I can't stop my hips from arching against it. The hard leather-wrapped handle moves lower, and he drags it through my wetness then returns to gently probe at my opening.

He's not gonna...

The tip slips in, just barely hovering inside me. "Christ, you're wet, baby."

A groan is the only response I can muster to his words. He laughs against my lips and pushes the handle into me further.

I was right, Stone Hawke is everything dark, dirty, and depraved. And I love all of it.

What does that say about me?

20

STONE

"How's the temperature?"

"Perfection." Nora sighs and slides even deeper into the bath water like a siren slipping into the ocean waves. Seeing Nora so at peace and relaxed makes my dead heart beat a little faster. I never imagined I'd have her naked and sated in my clawfoot tub.

I glance down at the tray in my hands.

"So, I know I promised to feed you, but I don't really cook other than reheating leftovers my mom sends home on Sundays, and I've already devoured all those, so our options were slim."

She peeks an eye open at me. "What did you bring?"

I hold up the bottle of water and hand it to her. She giggles. "All you have in the house is water?"

Smartass.

"I'm not that bad. I also brought us Pop Tarts."

She bursts out laughing. "Seriously, Pop Tarts? What are you? Ten?"

I scowl at her and set the plate and my bottle of water on the small table next to the tub. "No, twenty-six, but that's beside the point. Pop Tarts are nutritious. They have fruit."

Nora twists open the bottle of water and takes a sip while giving me an incredulous look. "That logic seems flawed to me."

"Well, I do logic for a living, and I can tell you, it's rock solid."

Her lips turn up and her eyes slide closed again. "Whatever you say, counselor."

A laugh bursts from me as I reach down and nudge her shoulder. "Scoot forward." She opens her eyes and considers me for a moment before straightening and inching forward in the tub until there's enough room for me to slip in behind her. I guess she wasn't expecting me to join her. Maybe I should've asked, but I thought it would be a given. We both need a nice long, relaxing bath after what we just did. But especially her.

I'm so damn proud of her and the way she placed her trust in me. She's a fucking beautiful submissive.

I'm selfish to have acted on my feelings for her though. She's going to get dragged into my life no matter how hard we try to keep this quiet.

But for right now, I'm going to enjoy this.

The warm water envelops me, and I slide my legs along the outside of hers and settle behind her.

"Now, I do have to apologize because the Pop Tarts are cold. I haven't quite found my toaster oven yet. It's in one of these boxes piled up downstairs. I only unpacked absolute necessities first."

"Like all your toys."

I wrap my arms around her waist and drag her back against me, then press a kiss to the back of her head. "Yes, exactly." She laughs and takes another sip of her water then eyes the plate of Pop Tarts. I press my lips to her ear. "You should really eat something."

"I will. Just let me relax in this awesome water for a little bit."

That sounds absolutely heavenly to me too. I am spent, and

she has to be utterly exhausted too after spending the whole day and part of the night fucking. I grab her water and place it on the table then reach over and grab a bottle of shampoo sitting on the side of the tub.

"Drop your head back in the water."

She looks over her shoulder at me and then sees the shampoo bottle. "You're gonna wash my hair?"

"Yeah. Why not?"

There's a brief moment of consideration before she shrugs. "I don't know. No one's ever done it before except a beauty salon or when I was a kid."

I grin at her and squirt shampoo onto my palm. "Well, that's about to change then."

Nora deserves to be taken care of. She should be treated like the fucking queen she is. I know I can't give her everything she wants and needs, but I can do this.

She moves forward a bit and then tilts her head back until her hair is drenched before she sits back up. The shampoo slips through my fingers and I delve them into her thick blonde hair. She moans and turns into my touch. I lightly scratch her scalp as I work the shampoo into her hair, kneading and massaging my way across her head.

"God, that feels good."

"Good." I lean forward and kiss her temple. She relaxes back against me as I continue to work.

"How do you know how to do this so well?"

I bark out a laugh. "I grew up with three older sisters who had no qualms about making their little brother play hairdresser with them."

Her laughter fills the bathroom, and I imagine she is picturing me as a small boy with my sisters gathered around me, putting me in dresses and makeup. She's not far off. That was basically my childhood until I got old enough to realize what they were doing.

She shakes against me. "Oh, my God, I can't believe you let your sisters *abuse* you like that."

I grin to myself. "Yes, it was truly awful child abuse." I fucking love my sisters more than anything, but they definitely took advantage of their little brother. At that age, I was willing to do just about anything to get to play with the big kids, so it didn't matter if I was put in a pink dress or forced to wash their hair. I played along.

Savage was too busy being the man of the house to really pay me much attention, and when he did have time, he was with Gabe doing things he insisted I was far too young to participate in.

"What was that like, growing up with three older sisters? I mean, I know you and Savage never really got along, but it seems like maybe you and your sisters had a better relationship?"

"Oh yeah. I was definitely closer with them than I ever was Savage. Maybe because they were girls and I wasn't constantly fighting for control with them like I was my brother. They were fairly easygoing and playful, but Savage was always so serious and strict."

She nods and glances up at me. "I can see that. Obviously, I've met Storm and Skye, but what was Star like?"

NORA

Stone stills behind me and his hands stop moving in my hair.

Crap. Way to ruin the mood with that question.

"I'm sorry. I shouldn't have..."

His lips find the back of my neck and his hands resume the wonderful scalp massage. "No, it's fine. Losing her was probably the single hardest thing in my life. Star was the most singularly good, real, and most caring person I've ever known."

It's a little hard for me to picture. I don't doubt Skye is a wonderful person, Gabe wouldn't have fallen head over heels in love with her if she weren't, but she's a little abrasive. Considering her and Star were identical twins, I would think they shared some of those qualities.

"I know what you're thinking. You've only ever known Skye after we lost Star. I'm not gonna lie and say she wasn't always a little bit difficult, but losing her twin sister definitely changed her dramatically. They always balanced each other out. It was like a yin and yang thing with those two. Once Star was gone, Skye kind of became an angry, bitter person, and she's only just starting to come out of it. I think finally getting together with Gabe and having someone else to worry about and take care of was what helped her work through some of her shit."

Of course.

That totally makes sense. I shouldn't judge Skye. I have no idea what she's been through, what any of the Hawkes have, for that matter. I lost Dad when I was young, just like they lost their father, but they also lost a sibling. They've had to endure more than any one family should. The fact that Stone turned out so well is a true testament to how his mother raised him, and apparently, the intervention of Dom.

"I wish I could've met Star."

His hands move from my head and wrap around my waist. He tugs me against him tightly. "Me too, babe. You would've liked her a lot. I have no doubt that you'd been friends with Star. She had a way of getting people to open up about whatever was eating at them. Everyone just felt comfortable around her and trusted her implicitly with their deepest darkest secrets."

The thought of opening up to someone, anyone about what happened creates a war inside me. I don't want anyone to know my shame, but sometimes talking makes things better. Although, in this case, I'm not sure that's true. Who knows, maybe Star would have been the one I felt comfortable enough with to tell all to. I guess I'll never know.

"What about you? What was it like growing up with Dani as an older sister?"

I laugh at his question because he's no-doubt imagining a tiny blonde dictator cracking her whip. He nudges me forward. "Rinse."

So demanding...

"Yes, sir." I glance over my shoulder to see his reaction, and a smug smile spreads across his lips as I tilt my head back into the water.

When I come back up, he's still grinning. "I know what you're thinking but she really wasn't that bad."

He scoffs and grabs his bottle of water. "I find that hard to believe, knowing what I do about your sister."

I can't say I blame him. Dani is not the easiest person in the world to get along with. "I know what you mean. My sister can be...well...a handful."

His chest rumbles behind me. "A handful? More like five or six handfuls from what I've seen of her. She pretty expressly forbade me from pursuing you when she barely knew me."

What the heck?

That's certainly news to me.

I turn between his legs until I'm halfway facing him. "What do you mean?"

"When I got to town before the rehearsal dinner, I saw her at my mother's house. We had only met once before that, and we really didn't talk much that time, so it kind of floored me when she walked right up to me and told me in no uncertain terms that I was to keep my hands off you at the wedding."

I release an annoyed sigh and return to reclining against his hard chest. "That does sound like Dani. She can be a little over-protective. I mean, that's how she met Savage in the first place."

"I know, and I laugh to myself every time I imagine what that meeting must've been like. My brother doesn't usually take well to people telling him what to do, and something tells me Dani didn't go in there being very diplomatic."

"Oh, I know she didn't. I spoke with Savage right after, and he was very clearly shaken by his meeting with my sister. Although, I didn't notice it at that time that apparently it was more than just the way she confronted him. He clearly had a thing for her from the beginning."

Stone's hands slide slowly up and down my arms. "Apparently."

A comfortable silence descends between us. This is pretty much perfect. Who would have thought Stone could be sweet?

"Well, for what it's worth, I'm glad you didn't listen to her about keeping your hands off me."

His lips press against the back of my neck, and I feel the smile on them. "Oh yeah, why is that?"

He's clearly fishing for compliments, and as much as I'd like to deny him one to prevent that big head from getting even bigger, he deserves it.

"You're pretty damn good with those hands. And everything you put in them."

I can practically feel his pride swelling around us in the tub as his cock hardens behind me. Slowly, I try to slip my hand between us but he catches my wrist and halts my progress.

"No. Don't. Just relax for a while."

Is he serious?

He's got another raging hard-on pressed into my back and I'm supposed to just leave it?

This guy really does love to torture me...in the best way possible.

21

STONE

I'm a fucking idiot.

Instead of relishing in the peaceful after effects of my time with Nora once she left to head home this morning, I had to flip on the fucking television. Images of police tape and blood splattered restaurant windows flood the screen.

"Good morning, I'm Edmond Ewing. Today's top story... three unknown gunmen entered the El Torro Blanco restaurant on Oretha Castle Haley Boulevard at midnight last evening and opened fire, killing all fifteen men inside. The police have no suspects at this time but are searching for a black SUV seen in the area immediately prior to the shooting..."

That's Castillo's place.

There's no doubt in my mind this was Dom's doing, and that it was meant to send a message.

The men he used will have already left town by now, and they probably won't be back soon, if ever. Dom's network ensures his goons are well taken care of, especially those who do a good job for him.

This was an excellent job, especially if Castillo was one of the men inside.

But I doubt it. I would have heard something if we had taken him out.

If Castillo had any doubt before about Dom's willingness to do what needed to be done to ensure the safety of his shipments and turf, I'm sure they're long gone now. That doesn't mean Castillo is no longer a threat, though. This could be the start of a very bloody, very dangerous war.

One I will be in the middle of as Dom's consigliere. One I will be dragging Nora into by getting involved with her.

And seeing the aftermath of crossing Dom only reminds me of what I've so desperately been trying to forget for the last thirty-six hours. He tried to kill my sister-in-law and threatened to kill Savage and Gabe.

No matter how many times I go over what they told me, I can't wrap my head around Dom's reaction. It's just not like him to do something so reckless, especially where family is involved. That's what concerns me. Maybe he's losing his grip. If that's true, and he's unpredictable, there's nothing stopping him from going after them again.

I'll never let that happen.

My alarm on my phone sounds.

Shit. Lunch with Mom.

I almost forgot I'm meeting her today.

But maybe it will be good. Perhaps she can offer some insight on the Dom situation. Although, I'll have to walk a fine line. There's no way she knows what's really going on. As much as she cares for him, I don't think she would willingly let him get away with the kind of stuff he's doing if she knew the full extent of his business and actions. And certainly not if she knew what went down with Savage and Dani. Dom may be *almost* family, but we *are* family. And Mom is one fierce momma bear when someone or something threatens one of us.

By the time I drag my ass to the restaurant where we're meeting, I have a pretty good idea how to broach the topic with her delicately. At least, I hope I do.

"Stone!" Mom waves me over to a small table in the corner. "I was getting worried. I'm so glad you made it." She stands and embraces me, giving me a kiss on the cheek and then wiping off the lipstick she left there.

"Hi Mom, sorry I'm late. I got tied up."

With a wave of the hand, she dismisses my apology and takes her seat. "No problem, honey. I've just so been looking forward to this. I feel like we haven't had any time alone since you got back."

True. And I feel bad about it, but between unpacking, putting out fires for Dom, and trying to feed my addiction for Nora, I haven't exactly been thinking about spending time with my mother.

"I've been busy."

She smiles at me over the menu. "Dom is keeping you on your toes, huh?"

To say the least.

Now is the time to be diplomatic. "He has a lot going on, hands in a lot of pies. My help is definitely needed."

"Oh, I'm sure. He's always so busy. Sometimes, I don't hear from him for a week or two, and I start to worry. He actually just called the other night."

"Oh yeah, what did he want?"

The menu drops again. "Oh, you know, just to chat. He was asking about how everyone was, Dani and Savage in particular. And of course, Gabe, because he was so worried when he was in the hospital."

It takes every ounce of will-power not to roll my eyes. Of course, Dom was worried when Gabe was in the hospital. He wants him gone. I'm sure Dom would have thrown some sort of party if Gabe hadn't made it. And his interest in Savage and Dani may seem innocuous to Mom, but I know better. He was feeling her out to see if they've mentioned anything to her about what he did and trying to learn anything that would benefit him and give him the upper hand.

"What'd you tell him?"

She narrows her eyes briefly and considers me. "I told him everyone was good, and we are happy to have you back and working for him."

I toss her a wry chuckle. "Well, not *everyone* is happy I'm working for him, Mom."

With a heavy sigh, she sets down her menu and clasps her hands together on the edge of the table. "I just don't understand why Savage is so hostile toward Dom, after everything he did for him, for us."

"Mom, come on, you know what Dom does for a living, what his business is. Savage doesn't want to be associated with him in any way, and he doesn't want anyone else being dragged into it either."

That's as close to telling her the truth as I can get. If I unloaded on her about what really happened, it would only stir up more shit...for everyone.

Life threatening shit.

Her mouth presses in a thin line, and she grabs her napkin off the plate and twists it between her fingers. "Dom may not be an angel, Stone, but he's a *good* man. Even as a child, he was always looking out for me and his sister, and he was a *great* friend to your father. You were too young to really understand, but when he died..." She pauses and takes a deep breath. "Dom was the only comfort I had. I was overwhelmed with you five, and I don't think I could have made it through without him. So, I let some things slide that I may not be totally okay with where his business dealings are involved. I won't apologize for that."

The strong defense of Dom doesn't surprise me. It's almost

word for word what I would have said to someone questioning why I could work for the man. But that's before I knew what he did to my family. He may be basically family, but they are my flesh and blood.

I reach across the table and still her nervous hands. "Mom, I get it. I really do."

Unfortunately.

It's really all I can say. I would give anything to be able to spill about everything that's gone on, to make her *see* him. But I can't. Even if I didn't give a shit about my law license and breaking client confidentiality, there's the very real issue of the threat to Savage, Dani, and Gabe. And Skye for that matter, if Dom finds out she knows everything.

He has to suspect. Given how well he knows us, and the Hawke dynamics, he can't believe Gabe wouldn't have told Skye once they got together. The fact that he probably knows and hasn't done anything yet is concerning, to say the least. He's either lying in wait for his chance to strike, or something is already in motion.

I don't believe his love for Mom or the Hawkes in general will be enough to stop him considering everything he's already done.

The waiter arrives, and I release her hands and offer her a reassuring smile. She hasn't told me much, but it's enough to have the acid in my stomach churning with dread.

Dom isn't a man you want to mess with.

But neither are the Hawkes.

I just need a plan.

NORA

I'm *not* fully prepared when I take Stone's advice and Google "Dear Mistress."

Good God!

It's not that I don't know this kind of stuff goes on. I mean, I've seen Stone's room and toys, and it's impossible not to have at least *heard* of some of this stuff in popular culture. But the things discussed in this column...

I'm in a state of permanent blush! I'll probably need to break out BOB before I head over to work tonight. Especially since I won't see Stone. I'm working a double, and there's no way I'm going to have the energy for him tonight. Saturdays are always insane.

I scroll through the questions and answers on the site until one particular post catches my attention.

Common BDSM Misconceptions (and yes, these piss me off)

1. BDSM must include sex.
Wrong. BDSM is not about sex. It is about pushing limits, psychological control, relinquishing control, and self-expression. It's a true power exchange.
2. Submissives are weak.
Wrong. Submissives are the definition of strength. It takes brass balls to willingly hand yourself over. If you don't think so, try it.
3. There is ONE TRUE WAY.
Wrong. Your kink lifestyle is what you make it. You mold it to fit your needs. Yes, there are guidelines, but it's up to you to make it your own.
4. Dominants are the only ones in control.
Wrong. A Dominant's job is to fulfill their submissive's needs, and in turn, satisfy their own needs. A Dominant must respect the submissive's needs, even when the submissive calls all activity to a halt. In terms of control, the Dominant must have extreme self-control, which allows them to not only take their submissive

on a journey, but to also be able to make responsible decisions and judgment calls when necessary.

5. BDSM is only about pain.

Wrong. BDSM is a power exchange between two willing people, which does not necessarily involve pain. Pain can certainly be a part of it, if that is your fetish. Pain gets adrenaline pumping through the veins, which increases sensation, which leads to pleasure.

6. Dominants are male; submissives are female.

WRONG. Your role in this lifestyle is NOT defined by your gender; it's defined by your personality and your desires. Don't believe me? Let me show you what this female is capable of.

7. BDSM is dangerous.

Wrong. The lifestyle motto is "Safe, Sane, Consensual," and it is not a suggestion — it's a hard rule.

Reading this particular post from Dear Mistress makes me feel like an idiot. Because basically, everything I thought is wrong.

What kind of a judgmental a-hole does that make me?

One night with Stone confirmed a lot of this. It wasn't about pain. Yes, some of it was a little uncomfortable. The rope marks around my wrists are proof of that. But there wasn't anything I would call *painful*. The only thing that came close was the flogger, but even that was...exhilarating. I know Stone said that wasn't nearly as harsh as some of the other things in his collection, but even so, I don't think Stone does it to cause me pain.

It's about the control for him and knowing I'm giving myself over to him. Well, that and seeing the marks and knots on my body.

And I can respect that. He won't ever make me do anything I don't want to. I know that implicitly. Stone's a pusher by nature. Just like he pushed me to talk that day at the coffee shop, he *will* push and encourage me to do new things, but he will always respect my wishes.

I just need to figure out what they are.

The problem is, I will probably let Stone do just about anything. He has that effect on me. And it's terrifying. Losing myself to *anything...anyone* is a mistake I won't make again. I need to maintain some semblance of control around him, no matter how impossible the task may seem.

Continuing to read this site isn't helping. I shut down my computer and head to the bathroom to shower before I head to work. Reading all this stuff has made another one very necessary. My phone rings just as I'm about to step in the spray.

When I grab it off the counter, I catch a glimpse of myself in the mirror.

Crap on a cracker.

How the heck am I going to hide these?

The rope burns around my wrists are even darker and more obvious in the lighting in here. They aren't horrible, but you can definitely tell something was there.

Continued rings echo in the bathroom. I don't even look who it is, just answer.

"Hello?"

"Nora! Do you have plans tomorrow night? I need you."

Dani.

I sigh and wipe at the fog starting to form on the mirror from the running shower. "For what?"

There's a momentary pause before she replies. "Well, I need you to come to the Hawke dinner with me again."

Geez, you've got to be kidding me.

Last time was awkward enough with Stone flirting with me and making sexual innuendos about everything. There's no way I can sit at a table with him now that I know what he looks like naked and what he feels like inside me. It will be impossible to keep it a secret.

Then again, maybe it wouldn't be so bad if everyone knew.

This doesn't feel like a casual thing to me. Maybe I'm reading too much into it, I mean, it's only been one night. But if this is something that's going to continue, why hide it? I understand there will be people displeased, to say the least. But we are adults. Who we choose to be with should be of no concern to anyone at that table.

In one night, Stone has made me happier than I've been in almost two years. I don't want to hide that or give that up because our families have ridiculous concerns.

"Nora? You there?"

I shake my head and pinch my eyes shut. "Yeah, sorry. Um, sure I'll come. You wanna tell me why you need me there so badly."

There's a momentary pause followed by a sigh. "Things are just...a little complicated and unsettled between Stone and Savage right now. Having a non-family member there helps because they're on their best behavior."

Best behavior?

I can't contain my chuckle. Stone doesn't behave.

Ever.

It's part of his charm.

"Look, I gotta jump in the shower before work. I'll be there tomorrow, but you owe me."

"Whatever you want."

If I said *Stone,* that might be a little awkward. Instead, I just hang up and clean off the mirror again so I can see my reflection. Tonight will be a long one at work when all I really want to do is see Stone. But tomorrow night is going to be even longer surrounded by the Hawkes with our secret. Maybe it's time we come clean, regardless of the fallout.

22

NORA

The bracelets I slapped on barely cover the red marks left by Stone's ropes last night. Not that I mind.

I never, in a million years, would have thought I would be so turned on by being tied up and ridden by an unbroken wild stallion.

There were so many times I was *this* close to screaming out a word I haven't uttered since I was five and imitating Dani. But I didn't want to give Stone the satisfaction of knowing he broke me in that respect. He may break me in other ways, but not that one.

But dang, when he was inside me...it was like being on another plane of existence. Sex has *never* been like that for me before. He gave me the first orgasm I've ever had that I didn't cause myself. Another thing I won't ever tell him. I can't let his head swell with that knowledge, it might explode. It's dangerous already.

"Cashmere!"

I jerk my head in the direction of Gabe's voice. He narrows his eyes on me and marches into the changing room, looking around, probably checking to make sure we're alone. Both he and Savage always make an effort not to show any favoritism or be overly familiar with me in front of any of the other girls. And they always use my stage name unless they know we are alone. "Where the hell were you? That's the third time I said your name, and you just stared at the mirror like you were lost in Narnia."

Not far off.

It's like I've been walking around in a trance since I left Stone's. And what I read online didn't help. My imagination has been running wild with all the things he can and probably will want to do. Things I didn't even know existed a day ago. Things I never thought I would *want* to try. But with Stone, it feels like anything and everything is possible, and a whole new world has been opened to me...kind of like walking through a wardrobe into a foreign land.

"Sorry!" I jump from my chair and offer an apologetic smile. "Just thinking."

He leans against the counter and raises an eyebrow. "You've been off lately, even more so tonight. Want to tell me what's going on?"

I shrug and try to brush past him, but he places a hand on my shoulder, effectively stopping me in my tracks.

"I'm fine."

"I don't buy that. You know we'll help you if something's wrong. You're family."

And therein lies the rub.

"Thank you for worrying, it's actually really sweet. But I'm fine, I promise. Just have a lot going on right now that I'm trying to sort through." Like sleeping with the man who's basically your little brother...who likes to tie women up and bang them senseless, who also works for a mafia don.

"Don't let it interfere with your work, and if there's a problem, come to me or Savage."

I nod my agreement, and he releases me.

"Robert's waiting for you in the Champagne Room."

Criminey, I'm too exhausted for a lap dance.

Stone really managed to wring every ounce of energy from me during our time on that devil chair. And then with the flogger...when he entered me after...it was like he was melding our bodies together. His lips and hands were all over me, and I couldn't do anything but accept every ounce of pleasure he gave me. And when he finally came and ripped the blindfold off, the look in his eyes was so feral, so raw, so...Stone. The bath was incredible and relaxing and certainly needed, but the shower this morning, together, was anything but relaxing. Who knew tile could be so dang cold against your back? I had to bolt this morning before he could pin me against the front door for round four.

Just thinking about it makes heat and moisture rush to my core.

Dangit.

This thong is way too tiny and too thin to hold up to the memories of being with Stone.

Robert's a regular though, so I can't turn him down. It would be bad for business. He's been coming by to see me several times a week for the last few months and seems like a decent guy.

I make my way to the Champagne Room and try to push what happened earlier today and last night to the back of my mind. It's the only way I'll get through this night.

Giving lap dances is just part of the gig, and I really don't mind it, as long as the guy keeps himself in check and follows the rules. Some of the girls let things go a little too far, but not me. I'm not afraid to do what it takes to get some perv's hands off me if he gets a little too friendly.

Unbidden, images of Stone's large, warm hands and memories of how they felt all over me fill my head. My body heats, and

I have to pause and lean against a wall briefly to gather myself together before entering the Champagne Room.

Do your job. Forget Stone. At least for now.

Easier said than done.

I pull back the curtain to the small, private room, and Robert sits waiting for me on one of the couches. He's older, probably in his forties, with dark hair and an olive complexion that reminds me of Stone.

Crap. Stop it, Nora.

Thankfully, Robert has never done anything out of control or that made me feel uncomfortable. I'm not sure I could handle dealing with that tonight. Stone has certainly thrown me off my game. Not that it's a surprise. He is a true force of nature.

"Hi Robert."

He scans me up and down and offers me the same gregarious smile. "Cashmere, it's so good to see you."

I nod and chuckle to myself when he says my stage name. He may be the only customer here right now old enough to actually get the joke. He's seen my spotlight dance, so I have no doubt he's figured it out.

He grins while I remove the sheer wrap I have covering me and let it fall to the floor. His eyes track my every movement as I make my way over to him, gyrating my hips in time with the music thumping through the room.

All I need to do to forget Stone is concentrate on this dance and making the customer happy. I've done this hundreds of times. It seemed right, fitting, where I was supposed to be and what I was supposed to be doing. But that was before Stone.

Here goes nothing.

~

STONE

My lunch with Mom earlier only confirmed my suspicions about Dom. The fact that he's fishing around for information tells me he's worried. It also pisses me the fuck off that he's using Mom that way after what he did, that he can maintain the façade of a friendship with her after trying to harm her children. But I need to know more before I can confront him.

There has to be a reason he went after Dani. Something more than just her digging around. Reporters, local police, the FBI, they've all been after him for years. And he never does anything so rash. He analyzes. He assesses. He waits for the right time to strike, and only when necessary. But none of what he did was necessary. It makes me wonder what he would have done if this had all gone down when I was already working for him. Would he have brought me into the fold? Asked me to *deal* with Dani? Give me an opportunity to sort things out? Or would he have gone behind my back and resorted to violence just the same?

I need to talk to Savage and Dani. She may be able to shed some light on what went down. When I met with Savage and Gabe, I wasn't exactly thinking clearly, and certainly wasn't in any shape to be asking them the questions I really need answers to, in order to understand the entire situation. And I can't know how to approach Dom without all the information and being one hundred percent on my game. That would be a *very* bad idea, one that could cause a lot of trouble for more than just me.

So instead of relaxing on the couch on my lazy Saturday night while Nora's at work—because God knows, if I went and watched her, I wouldn't be able to keep my hands off her—I'm jumping in my car and driving over to their condo building.

How the hell did things get so tangled and fucked?

Even the rumble of the Aston Martin engine doesn't soothe the discord roiling through me. A non-descript grey sedan parked across the street from the condo building catches my eye as I park in front. The driver has his face buried in a newspaper.

Weird place to park and read.

But I shrug it off and enter the building, intent on getting the information I need. The ride up in the elevator only adds to my unease about the situation. Gabe and Skye can take care of themselves, that much is readily apparent, but Savage and Dani have weaknesses, ones Dom can and will exploit if he needs to.

I hear the biggest one through the door. Kennedy's wails are hard to miss.

After a quick knock, I throw the door open and enter.

Savage appears in the archway to the kitchen. "Stone? What are you doing here? Is everything okay?"

"We need to talk."

His eyes narrow on me, and then he motions me to follow him toward the kitchen.

The scent of fried garlic, olive oil, anchovies, and red peppers hits my nose before I even make it to the archway. "Are you making *aglio e olio*?"

He stops in front of the stove and stirs something in a pan on the burner. "Yeah, it's just about ready. Stay and eat with us. Dani is just trying to get Kennedy down for the night."

I'm never one to turn down a good meal, especially since I don't cook. Savage and the girls were always the ones under Mom's foot in the kitchen. My time was spent mostly with Dom at that age. I'm just glad Nora likes Pop Tarts as much as I do and is willing to overlook my lack of domestic talents.

"Sounds good. Can I do anything to help?"

"Just grab a bottle of wine and some glasses. Otherwise, everything is almost done."

I wander over to the wine fridge and grab a bottle of Pinot Grigio. A dry white always goes well with this dish. By the time I have the bottle open and the glasses poured, a frazzled Dani appears in the kitchen and gives me an awkward smile.

"Oh, hey Stone. I didn't know you were joining us."

"Unplanned. Sorry I'm crashing."

She waves me off but tosses Savage a questioning look. "Are you two going to behave?"

Savage laughs and I offer a tight chuckle.

Dani grabs a giant bowl of pasta off the counter before joining me at the table, taking the seat across from me and adjacent to the head of the table where Savage always sits. "Kidding.. You're welcome any time. Is something up?"

I glance over at Savage when he settles. "Well, did Savage tell you we had a talk the other night?"

Her mouth presses into a thin line, and she nods. "Yeah. I'm sorry you had to find out like that. I mean, having that kept from you for so long, but the situation is delicate, as I'm sure you now understand."

No shit.

"I think that's an understatement. And that's why I'm here." Dani serves herself and passes the bowl to Savage, who then passes it on to me. After dropping a hefty helping onto my plate, I take a bite and savor the familiar flavors. "I need to know more about what you found out about Dom. I don't understand why he flew off the handle like that. Something doesn't sit right with me about the entire situation."

Savage pauses with his loaded fork halfway up to his mouth. "Really, Stone? It shouldn't surprise you that Dom tried to have Dani *killed*. He's a ruthless crime boss, not the warm, friendly uncle you seem to think he is."

A couple days ago, I probably would have gotten pissed and told Savage off for a crack like that against Dom but speaking in his defense now seem less...well...defensible.

"I know what he did was awful and unforgiveable. Believe me. But what I *don't* understand is why he would be worried about Dani digging into things she would never be able to prove enough to actually *mean* anything to him in terms of affecting his business or getting him thrown in jail." I look over to her. "I'm not trying to insult your work, Dani, it's just that, from a legal stand-point, most of what Savage told me you'd been investigating could never be proven enough to charge him, let alone beyond a reasonable doubt to convict him of anything."

She smiles and takes a sip of her wine. "No offense taken. I knew it was an uphill battle. I thought I'd finally made some headway when Paul agreed to get me information, but, we all know how *that* ended."

With a gunshot to his head and Gabe killing three of Dom's men. That goes unsaid. Kind of would have ruined the meal.

"Dom is smart. Smart enough to know he wasn't in any real danger. So why do you think he was so intent on getting rid of you?"

Savage offers a muffled cough, and I know he's holding back from whatever he really wants to say, but I let it slide and keep my focus on Dani. "My best guess? I was going deeper and deeper into his history, I'm talking *decades* back, looking for anything that might have been missed that would still be within the statute of limitations. Maybe there's something there he doesn't want found."

That would make sense, I guess. There are probably hundreds of things that could have gotten Dom thrown in the slammer, that happened before I was even born, and I have abso-lutely no clue about them. But still, it would have to be some-thing pretty damn major for him to have reacted that way.

I guess there's only one way to really find out.

"You know he's having us watched, right?"

Savage's words have me jerking my head in his direction. "What?"

He nods solemnly and reaches for his wine glass. Two long pulls later, he places it on the table and relaxes back. "We've always known he's kept eyes on us since it happened, but it's picked up. There's a rotation of five or six cars that are always outside the building, outside the club, or following one of us."

The grey sedan out front...

Motherfucker!

"Why is he watching you? And why more recently?"

Savage shrugs and leans forward, resting his elbows on the table. "Beats me. It seems to have become more noticeable since Gabe was released from the hospital, but that could just be coincidence. I do know it's *definitely* become more frequent since you moved home."

Son of a cocksucking bitch!

23

STONE

I managed to avoid Dom's texts and calls all day yesterday, all last night, and all day today. He keeps telling me we need to talk about our next step, and he needs me to call him or come in. But I just can't.

That bloodbath is still the lead story, and I can't stomach watching that video and then talking to the man I know is responsible for it. Dinner with Savage and Dani last night gave me some ideas about why things went to Hell in a handbasket so quickly between them and Dom, but I still have more questions than answers.

Which is a total motherfucking bitch.

It's crazy how quickly things have changed.

I still owe Dom my life, but I can't make excuses for his actions anymore, not when they're directly affecting me and my family. I also can't charge in there, guns blazing and demanding he back off and give me answers. That would never fly with him.

Even for *me*, he's not going to just lay it all out there and agree to stop what he's been doing. No way.

If Savage and Gabe being basically family hasn't stopped him so far, why would anything *I* have to say change that?

There needs to be a plan in place before I do *anything*. And right now, I have nothing. It feels like that night before my first trial when I had no fucking clue what to put in my opening statement. My mind is a complete blank.

Well, that's not entirely true. One very sexy blonde is occupying a lot of my brain right now.

I have so many plans, so many things I want her to experience. And I'm selfish. I want it all now.

Having someone so naïve to my world, who's willing to experiment, is rare indeed. When I was studying under Master Tadashi, I almost exclusively used experienced rope models. And the women at the two BDSM clubs I was a member at in San Diego were all more than willing to try just about anything outside of shibari.

Nora's innocence is like crack to me. I need to have my hands on her, see her bound, touch her, tease her, and drive her wild.

Fuck yes.

A plan starts to form, and I need to see her tonight. It would have been amazing to have her come over after her shift last night, but she got off at three, and I know she has to be utterly exhausted after working that long.

I glance at the clock. Ten a.m.

She should hopefully be awake by now.

Even if she's not, she'll get my message as soon as she gets up. I pull out my phone and shoot her a text.

< I'm sure you're just waking up, but you need to be here tonight. >

It's kinda stalkery that I know her schedule and that she has tonight off, but I'm sure she expects that by now. It takes a few moments before she replies.

> Yeah, I'm exhausted. Just getting up. Why do I need to come over there? <

Smartass.

< Because I told you to. >

There's a long wait before she finally replies.

> Am I going to need my safe word? <

I chuckle.

< Yes. Did you check out Dear Mistress? >

This time, her response takes long enough that I'm starting to get worried. Maybe I'm pushing her too hard. Maybe she looked at the articles and it freaked her out instead of having the opposite effect.

No.

Having her read it was the right thing to do. She needs to understand completely before I let things go any further.

> I looked at it before work yesterday. <

I wait for the three little dots that tell me she's writing more but they don't come. And I'm impatient. This thing between us is all kinds of wrong for a hundred different reasons, but it's also the only thing that seems to help me turn off my head besides the occasional line. I *want* her to *want* this. And I think deep down, she does too. She's just too afraid to admit it. Her interest in the flogger demonstrated her inquisitiveness and willingness to at least try. But I know Dear Mistress' column can be very eye-opening for someone who isn't very familiar with the lifestyle yet.

< AND? >

Another five minutes passes, and I'm confident I won't like what her reply is.

> Chill. My mom called. I found it very informative. It answered a lot of questions I had, and it definitely made me blush more than once. <

I bark out a laugh imagining her in front of her computer getting all hot and bothered by Dear Mistress' tales. It's a very good sign.

< So you aren't going to run away screaming? >

> No promises. <

The smile spreads across my lips. I can't fucking wait to see her tonight.

< Be here at 7. >

> I'm supposed to go to your mom's house for dinner with my sister. Not sure why she wants me there.<

Shit! Family dinner.

I had *not* anticipated her being invited again. It puts a minor kink in my plans, but it gives me an idea for something much more interesting.

< Be here at 5. Wear a black dress and no underwear. >

I'm confident she's going to ask why, but instead, she just sends a simple smiley emoji.

She may not be smiling when I initiate my plan tonight.

I relax back into my leather chair, trying not to dwell on the uncertainty and turmoil in my life right now. I'd much rather concentrate on planning my evening with Nora.

But the third glass of Scotch I'm currently draining doesn't seem to be helping me keep a clear head. All I see are those images from the news over and over again. And that damn grey sedan sitting outside the condo building.

As soon as Savage mentioned it, the hairs on the back of my neck had stood on end. And I know why. I've seen that car several times, across from my office, outside the courthouse, even outside the coffee shop where I ran into Nora. Savage, Dani, Gabe, and Skye aren't the only ones being followed. He has people on me too.

Though I have no fucking clue why.

I rise and make my way over to the bar to pour myself another glass.

Ah, fuck it, make it a double.

◞

NORA

I tug on the hem of my black dress, willing it to stay at least to the knee. Something tells me if I go into Stone's house with it riding up my thigh, there's no way we will make it out of there and to dinner on time. The dress had seemed Hawke dinner appropriate when I pulled it from my closet and put it on earlier, but now that I'm walking up the steps to his place, it's riding up at least half an inch with every step I take.

Crap.

His text from earlier has had my head spinning all day about what his plan might be.

The last Hawke family dinner I attended, he practically undressed me with his eyes. And he wasn't exactly subtle about it given the way that everyone reacted.

I don't think Stone has a subtle bone in his body. He's more the come-in-with-a-bang-and-a-crash type guy.

Which is actually really hot during sex, but it doesn't bode well for us remaining under the radar this evening. After giving it some more thought, it's not the right time to out ourselves. We've only been together one night, and even though I think there's more there, I hope there's more there, going public would make things very messy if we don't turn into anything more than a flash in the pan, get it out of our system type thing.

Double crap.

I barely have time to knock on the door before it's open, and he tugs me in. His lips descend on mine, and his hands clench my butt, hugging me against him.

Jesus, he's hard already?

I just walked in the door.

His hands slide under the hem of my dress until he's cupping in my bare ass. Heat floods my core. Fingers slip between my cheeks and brush against the sensitive flesh. I shudder against him as his tongue licks along mine and probes exactly like his cock did the other night, working me in and out.

My head swims.

It's physically impossible for me to be within ten feet of Stone Hawke without losing my mind. And I hate that. I hate that he can do this to me. It's hard to retain any semblance of control over myself when I'm complete mush around him.

I half expect him to pin me against the wall and do me right here. And that sounds pretty gosh darn good right now with the way his fingers and tongue are toying with me.

But instead, his mouth closes, and he pulls his head away and removes his fingers from where I so desperately want them.

Great, now that he's got me all hot and bothered, he's just gonna stop? What a turd.

He takes a step back from me then pulls on my dress until it bunches up around my hips, exposing me to him.

"I'm happy to see you followed my directions and came sans panties."

I raise an eyebrow at him. "Like you wouldn't have just taken them off yourself if I had worn them, *sir*."

A grin splits his face, and he chuckles. The sound vibrates through my chest like a freight train barreling down at me.

God, he's hot when he laughs.

He needs to do it more. I get that his job is important, and he's probably required to show some decorum around colleagues, but he's so stoic all the time...except when he's flirting or when I do something to amuse him. And it seems he likes when I talk back to him a little and call him out on his BS.

After another appreciative glance down my body, he checks his watch.

"Fair point. We don't have much time, and we shouldn't drive together. So let's get you ready."

Huh?

"Uh, Stone, aren't I already ready?"

That dang sexy chuckle surfaces again, and he shakes his head, a devious glint in his blue eyes.

"Oh no, darling, I've got something special planned for you for dinner."

He reaches into his inside coat pocket and pulls out a pair of black underwear. They aren't particularly sexy, just a basic black thong, so I'm not really sure what the purpose is. But then he drops them in my hand.

They're way heavier than they should be, and there's definitely something hard and firm inside.

What the what?

I reach out to open them to see what they are when they suddenly start buzzing and vibrating against my palm.

Jesus H. Christ!

My jerk back almost makes me drop them as Stone's laugh echoes in the entryway.

It's a dang vibrator.

I shake my head. "Oh no, Stone, this is so not happening. We're going to be sitting at a table surrounded by your entire family and my sister. It would be one thing if it were just the two of us, but you can't seriously expect this to be going on at a Hawke family dinner."

With a grin, he holds up a tiny electronic device and presses the button on it, sending the panties into convulsions on my hand again.

"That's what makes this game even more fun."

Game?

This doesn't sound like much of a game to me. It sounds more like Stone wanting to mess with me in front of everyone we know.

The panties stop quaking, and he drops the remote back into his pocket then reaches out and takes the panties from my hand.

His fingers slide deftly into the fabric, and he holds them open. "Step into them."

Crap.

I don't particularly feel like defying him today. The opposite, actually. Everything I've learned about Stone so far has convinced me that it's probably a pretty bad idea. Not that I think he would ever hurt me, physically at least, but that look I always thought promised debauchery was exactly right, and I know I've only seen the tip of the iceberg with him. It's fun to joke with him, but truly defying him is a whole different ball game.

So I take a deep breath and step into the panties. He slides them up, slowly, intentionally slowly, letting his fingertips graze my calves and thighs on the way to cover my wet core. When they're finally situated, he adjusts the vibrator until it's directly on my clit. Then he cups me and squeezes gently while leaning in and pressing his lips to my throat.

"This is going to be so much fun, Nora."

Yeah, a real freaking circus.

Only, I'm the one on full display in the center ring while he's the ring master, directing the entire performance as he sees fit.

A grin splits his face.

"I think we need to take this for a test drive before we get to my mom's house."

Test drive?

The question is on the tip of my tongue when the vibrator clicks on, sending an immediate jolt straight to my core and through my body. I have to grasp his shoulders to keep from falling to the floor.

Oh, my God. There's no way. My legs quiver as the hellish thing assaults my clit.

He leans in and chuckles against my neck, his warm breath against my skin only adding fuel to the fire the vibrator has already ignited within me. He frees one of his arms from my death grip and reaches into his pocket. The vibrator stops, and my panties are normal again.

"Jesus, Stone, no way. You can't do that while we're at dinner. I won't be able to handle that."

The evil grin that spreads across his face before he presses his lips to mine spells trouble, and when he pulls away, determination blazes in his eyes. "Oh, sweetheart, you need to give yourself more credit. I have faith in you."

That makes one of us.

He steps back and pulls my dress back down. "I've been meaning to ask why the black dress?"

"Harder to see panty lines." His grin makes me smile in return despite what I know I'm walking into.

Stone is such a bad decision. I knew it from the beginning, and his intention to humiliate me in front of his entire family and my sister just confirms it for me. He has no boundaries or sense of decorum, which is pretty funny considering he's a lawyer. But apparently, the only decorum he possesses is used in the court room, not with me.

He's a lion, and I'm a helpless gazelle with a broken leg sitting in the middle of the Sahara waiting to be eaten.

And Lord, can this man eat...

When he steps back, he surveys me up and down, his gaze burning my skin everywhere it lands.

He looks like he wants to dive in and devour me right now, and frankly, I wouldn't mind that. It will be a lot better than whatever is going to happen at the Hawke dinner, I can tell you that. A tug pulls me away from the wall, and he smacks me on the butt.

"You better get gone, love. You need to get there before I do. I'll be ten minutes behind you. I have something to work out." His erection rubs against my hip, and my mouth waters.

Maybe I can just skip this whole thing. I could just head home or go to the club and get in a few extra hours. However, I know if I attempted to escape, it would only be setting me up to face his wrath later. Stone knows what he wants, and what he wants is apparently to play with me tonight.

I'm all for fun and games, but if things get too out-of-control, I'll bail.

At least, that's a promise I make myself as I step outside into the light drizzle and head toward my car. The drive to the Hawke house gives me time to think and consider.

There's no way I can get away from Stone—not now, not ever. Even if I were physically able to do it, he's already wound his way into my heart in a way that terrifies me. The only thing that scares me more is the thought that he feels absolutely nothing toward me.

I'm beginning to think that might be the truth.

Maybe I'm just a toy, a plaything, something to be entertained by. At first, I was okay with that...sort of. We both needed to get whatever was going on between us out of our system, but it's become more than that to me, and I can't help but wonder where I stand with him.

Maybe tonight will help me get a grasp on it, but somehow, I think that's doubtful.

What's more likely is I'll leave dinner tonight either ready to kill him or jump his bones.

24

NORA

"*W*hose phone keeps buzzing?" Ben asks the question for the third time tonight. He's apparently missed the two dozen other times the sound has permeated the room despite my best efforts to keep my thighs pressed together to muffle it.

Someone kill me now and put me out of my misery.

I get why the bad guys use torture as a way to get what they want. It definitely works, and Stone is doing a bang up job on me right now. I've never been so horny and angry at the same time before, and that's saying a lot, considering how Stone's toyed with me. Horny and angry seem to go hand in hand with Stone.

Tonight is a whole other level, though.

Every time I get close to coming, he stops the vibrator, leaving me hanging, frustrated, and murderous. It's a good thing we aren't having steak tonight. A sharp knife would likely be in his eye right now.

But I could use this spoon...it hurts more anyway.

I chuckle to myself at the *Robin Hood* reference, and let out a soft sigh when the vibrator stops. Ben carries on despite not receiving an answer to his inquiry. "Caleb has been a huge help. I'm so glad you guys hired him to manage THREE. He really has a good eye for the interior design and layout. He mentioned something was slightly off about the bar design, and after going over everything with him, I think he's right. We need to adjust the bar depths along the back wall so that the girls with shorter arms will be able to reach all the bottles without having to call someone else over to help them."

Savage nods and glances to Gabe. "It's not a bad idea. I know Byron does that at the club for the girls, but it would save a lot of time if the girls could get everything themselves. We can just keep the extra bottles on the higher shelves and bring them down when needed."

Gabe seems to contemplate the suggestion. "I understand what you're saying, but I kind of want to look at it myself so I can see what we would be doing instead of what we have now. When are you and Caleb heading over there again?"

Before I can hear the answer, the dang vibrator starts up again, and I grit my teeth to keep from moaning.

"Seriously, whose phone is that?"

Stone smirks across the table while I try not to squirm in my chair or bite my darn tongue off. "I'm not sure."

The vibrations roll through my body, making my legs quiver and my core damp with need. I'd give anything right now to come, from the vibrator or Stone inside me. I'm not picky. Just no more of this godawful torment.

A moan threatens to move up my throat, but just in the nick of time, Stone stops the demon panties and smiles at me over the table.

Ben, Savage, and Gabe return to their conversation, but Stone also returns almost immediately to his infliction of absolute anguish on me.

Bits and pieces of voices and words break through the constant on and off buzzing of the vibrator and jerking of my body.

"...wish you could find more employees like Caleb and Vance..."

"...hard to find good workers..."

With an evil glint in his eye, Stone leans his elbows on the table, showing me he no longer has a hand on the remote, and the vibrator is on at full speed.

Evil, evil man.

"Well, it's *so hard* to find dedicated workers nowadays. People are always *buzzing* from here to there, quitting jobs left and right, working themselves up into a *vibrating frenzy* with their inability to remain still in one place."

Heat crawls up the back of my neck, and Stone leans back in his chair and drops his chin down, trying to hide his smile. The vibrations stop, and I suck in several deep breaths.

So. Dang. Close.

He is the Devil.

At least he's given me a reprieve.

The relief is short-lived though, because he cranks the vibrator again, and I gasp this time, unable to keep it from leaving my lips.

Jerk.

It stops, and I almost sigh with relief. "What's with you tonight, Nora? You're acting all weird...very jumpy?" Dani couldn't be more right. I glance over and offer her a reassuring smile.

"Nothing, I'm fine." Which is only true momentarily before Stone cranks up the dang vibrator again.

Holy Hannah!

My fingers grip the edge of my seat to keep me from bucking around like a cowboy on a dang wild bronco.

Stone grins at me from across the table, that sly, knowing

smile that makes me want to punch him in the face even though I know I could never do it. It's embarrassing enough I'm squirming and jerking around, but I'm probably also leaving a giant wet spot on this chair because...*oh, my God*...this thing has had me so close to coming a hundred times already in the last hour.

And that man knows exactly what he's doing to me.

I don't know how much more of this I can take. Maybe I can sneak over to the bathroom and relieve some of this tension. That might make the rest of the evening more bearable.

The vibrating ends, giving me a moment to create a game plan.

Good, because Lord knows I won't be able to walk with that thing going to town on my lady bits.

I close my eyes and take a deep breath before I push away from the table. "Excuse me, I need to use the restroom." I smile politely at everyone around the table, including Stone, who raises an eyebrow but doesn't say anything.

His reaction is troubling. It's almost as if I can see him calling me out on my lie. And I know I'll have to pay the price. But I don't care right now. I need to get off more than I'm afraid of the repercussions with Stone.

STONE

I'm a real bastard, and I know it. But I can't help myself from toying with her.

Watching her squirm in her chair as the flush spreads across her breasts, up her neck, and over her cheeks every time I turn on the vibrator has my dick throbbing in my pants. Thank God they're jeans and not some loose fabric where my raging hard-on would be standing out proudly.

I can't even stop myself from smiling while she's fuming at me from across the table. She could cut ice with the daggers she's shooting at me.

"Excuse me, I need to use the restroom."

Well, well, well, what do we have here?

She can't possibly think I'm going to let her sneak off to go masturbate.

But she offers everyone a smile, and I raise an eyebrow. That smile wavers slightly before she beelines for the hallway, almost as if she thinks if she moves fast enough, she can get away.

I need to be quick if I'm gonna catch her before she can lock the bathroom door on me.

Game on.

Trying to appear nonchalant, I push away from the table and point toward my wine glass. "Looks like we're running low on wine. Why don't I grab another bottle?"

Mom smiles at me. "Oh, thank you, dear. There should be a bottle of white in the fridge and a couple bottles of red on the counter."

I dodge into the kitchen as quickly as I can without being obvious and sneak out the other door into the hallway. Nora's shooting down the hallway toward the bathroom as fast as her heels can carry her.

A couple quick, jogging steps bring me to her—the benefits of long legs—and I wrap my arm around her waist and flatten my hand across her chest, halting her progress.

"Where do you think you're going?"

Her heart thunders underneath my palm, and her chest heaves. It might be from the constant vibrator action, but it could also be because she knows she's been caught red-handed.

I brush my lips against her ear. "Did you really think I was gonna let you slip away to go touch yourself?"

"What? That wasn't what I was—"

"Don't even bother, sweetheart. You're a really bad liar."

She shakes her head. "But Stone...please."

Christ.

The pleading and begging in her voice practically makes me cave and drag her in there to get her off. Practically.

"You think you're the only one this is hard for?" I grab one of her hands and shove it between us until she grasps my rock hard cock. "I have to sit there watching you squirm and flush, knowing you're wet and close to coming, and there's nothing I can do but watch."

She moans and squeezes my dick, turning her head back until her mouth is at my ear. "Oh, there's a lot you can do."

I chuckle and slide my tongue around the lobe of her ear. "Not right here, not right now, babe. It will be worth the wait, I promise you that."

For both of us.

Nora has absolutely no idea what I have in store for her when we get back to my place. I may be hearing *cupcake* for the first time from her tonight.

My aching cock gets another squeeze. "You better not break that promise."

"Oh, honey, I won't. You're going to pay for what you just tried to do."

A shudder rocks her body, and I grin against her neck. Nora better be prepared for what's coming.

"I want you in my bedroom, naked, waiting for me when I get home. Understand?"

She nods and starts to pull away.

"Where are you going?"

Her eyebrow pops up. "To the bathroom?"

"Do you actually have to go?"

She leans back toward me. "Well, no, but I need to splash some cold water on my face before I spontaneously combust, okay?"

I chuckle, then glance over my shoulder toward the dining

room to make sure no one heard me. "Fine. But if you aren't out in less than two minutes, I'm coming in after you."

"Stone, you bringing that wine?" Mom's voice carries down the hallway, and I shoo Nora toward the bathroom.

"Yeah, Mom, coming."

Hopefully...

I swing through the kitchen and grab a bottle off the counter on my way back to the table.

Mom greets me with a furrowed brow. "Everything okay?"

"Yeah, I just had to reply to an email quickly. Sorry."

She smiles and pats me on the arm before handing me the corkscrew. "No problem, dear. Thank you."

The minor shake in my hand while I open the bottle is hopefully not noticeable to anyone else at the table. Touching Nora like that with the entire Hawke clan seated so close has thrown my body into overdrive.

By the time I get home and finally get inside her, I'm going to come in about two fucking seconds.

I drop back into my seat and rejoin the conversation.

"...and she didn't think anything of just waltzing in and demanding we hire her." The incredulous look on Savage's face makes me smile. I don't even know who he's talking about, but I already feel sorry for the poor girl. She's probably some girl with huge tits who has been told she's beautiful her whole life and who is desperate for some cash. Too bad she doesn't know Savage. His standards are high...sky-fucking-high. That's why ninety-nine percent of the women who waltz in trying to work at The Hawkeye Club get rejected. Sometimes he'll send them over to one of the bars or restaurants and offer them hostess or waitressing gigs, but more often than not, they were kicked to the curb, as politely as possible.

Nora returns and slips back into her chair, purposely keeping her eyes on the table and off me.

Dani leans over to her. "Everything okay?" The question

carries over the table, and Nora shifts in her seat before offering her sister a smile.

"Fine. I'm just really tired. I think I need to head home soon."

I barely contain a snicker. She's trying to force my hand, to get me to leave now instead of when I want to.

She has no idea she's poking the sleeping bear.

"If you aren't feeling well, Nora, you should head out, get some sleep." Her blue eyes flash in my direction, a mix of heat and condemnation.

This woman is fucking *pissed* and begging for me to fuck her.

One of my favorite combinations.

Oh hell, this is going to be fun.

25

NORA

I shift my weight from one foot to the other and glance at the clock on the nightstand again.

Where the heck is he?

It's been over an hour, and I'm still standing here waiting. I'm ashamed to admit I raced back to Stone's house as fast as my car would go. I probably broke a hundred miles an hour getting here. Because if I don't come soon, I'm going to kill someone. Probably Stone.

What the H.E. Double Hockeysticks could he be doing that he's not here yet?

We left at almost the same time. He pulled out from the curb, and we passed going opposite directions, even though we were headed for the same place.

I hate to admit it, but the sneaking around is actually pretty dang hot. I was equally pissed and on fire having him almost get me off with the entire Hawke family watching.

He must be taking his sweet time getting here just to mess

with me more.

Sadistic prick.

What he's doing to me is absolutely the worst torture I've ever endured. And here I was worried about the whips and chains and all that crap in his cabinets.

The rumble of a car engine breaks through my internal rant.

Please be him. Please be him. Please be him.

A car door slams right below the window facing the front of the house.

Releasing a deep breath of relief, I straighten my back and wait for him...not so patiently.

Thank God, he's here.

My heart races in anticipation.

What will my punishment be?

I knew I shouldn't have tried to sneak off. I should have known I would never get away with it.

If tonight was just a game, I can only imagine what an actual punishment will be.

Oh God, what have I done to myself?

The front door bangs shut and the distinct sound of someone climbing up the stairs echoes into the room. Every footstep sends a shudder of anticipation and fear through my body. I want to face the door to watch him enter, but for some reason, waiting, standing at the end of the bed and facing the cabinets seemed like the right thing when I got here.

In my peripheral vision, he appears in the doorway. I turn my head to him, but he doesn't even look my direction when he enters the room.

What the heck?

I'm standing here naked, and he won't even look at me?

Instead of approaching me, he beelines for his closet in the corner.

I press my thighs together to try to tame the ache there.

Having him in the same room without him touching me is almost as bad as those devil panties.

He removes his sport coat and hangs it up. Then slowly... ever so deliberately...he removes his shirt one button at a time. With his back to me, all I can see is his arms bunching and flexing through the crisp fabric as his fingers move down the buttons.

Fudge, he's so darn sexy and strong. I know exactly what he can do with that body, and I want that. *Now.*

It falls backward off his shoulders onto the floor.

Nail marks still mar his back from when he took me in the shower the other night.

It was one of the only times my hands haven't been bound in some way, but honestly, I don't mind. Being bound and having Stone take control sets my mind free from all the stuff it's always littered with—mostly the crippling self-doubt. Seeing my marks on him is...indescribable. A sense of pride and longing, along with a surge of lust flows through me. I get it now...why he likes marking me.

Turn around!

I want to scream it, but something tells me that would only draw his ire more than my stunt at dinner.

He reaches down to his crotch.

Oh, Lord...

The clink of his belt buckle has me pressing my legs together to keep the throb there under control.

Then the telltale sound of the zipper hits my ears, and another shudder rolls through my body because I know exactly what's beneath those tines of metal—the thing I've been craving for going on three hours now.

His jeans slowly lower down his legs, exposing his amazingly toned thighs and butt.

Sweet Lord, he's not wearing any underwear.

He steps out of them and kicks them into the closet.

With his back still to me, he strolls over to the row of wall cabinets.

Oh crap, I'm in so much trouble.

I tense wondering what sort of torture device he's going to grab for me tonight. His hand lands on something leather I can't quite make out in the dimly lit room. Then he grabs several coils of rope and there are some flashes of metal that make me cringe.

How is it possible to want something so much and be so dang terrified of it at the exact same time? With Stone, it seems to be the typical dichotomy.

When he finally turns toward me and gives me a full frontal view of his massive erection and toned, lean body, all the air is sucked from my lungs. It really isn't fair for Stone to be this handsome.

He wanders over to the bed and sets the items he's selected on the end of it without looking at me.

Man, he must be really pissed. That does not bode well.

I tense and wait.

A thousand bloodcurdling scenarios run through my head. Then the heat of his body reaches me, and I know he's close. That familiar spicy, masculine scent wraps around me just before he moves in behind and presses his hard cock into my back.

One hand wraps across my abdomen while the other lifts my chin, tilting my head back to look up at him. When my eyes finally meet his, I find them cold and icy. But there's a heat shimmering just beneath the hard, crystal surface.

"You know you're in trouble."

It's a statement, not a question. I refuse to break eye contact despite every instinct telling me to run.

"Yes, sir."

"What did you do wrong?"

I don't need time to think about my answer because it's obvious. "I tried to sneak away to go get myself off."

"And why is that wrong?"

Again, the answer falls from my tongue before I even have a chance to consider the question. '"Because...You give me my orgasms now." I don't know where that came from. It just seemed like the correct answer.

He can't hide the slight twitch at the corner of his lips at my words.

"Good girl. But I still have to punish you since you clearly haven't learned your lesson about orgasm denial tonight...yet."

Oh God, I hope he's not planning on dragging this out any longer. I don't think I can take it.

"Climb up on the bed."

There's no question I'm going to follow the order.

Stone releases his hold on me and watches me walk to the head of the bed and climb on. With that look in his blue eyes that promises nothing short of debauchery, he reaches down to the end of the bed and grabs one of the coils of rope.

"Lay flat, head on the pillow."

I comply. The rope uncoils slowly, and he holds his hand out and waits. It takes me a moment to realize what he wants, but then I give him my hand.

He hooks the rope around my wrist and hand, his fingers flying so fast, I can barely keep up with what he's doing. Before I know what's happening, both of my arms are bound to the bedposts near my head.

Without a word, he moves down between my legs and grabs the leather strap. I shiver.

What the heck is he gonna do with that thing?

STONE

Nora eyes the thigh restraint with trepidation.

I can't say I blame her, given the fact I've made her wait this long and promised punishment. It just won't be what she thinks.

Smacking the leather straps against my open palm sends cracking sounds ricocheting around the room. She jumps and tugs against the wrist restraints.

"What is that?" Her voice is barely a whisper, and I'm seriously wondering if I'm about to hear "cupcake."

This woman tied up in my bed is a fucking wet dream made reality. Even her fear is sexy as hell. That she is still willing to play with me when this is so new to her is so damn heady. I don't ever remember wanting a woman this badly in my entire life. My cock throbs, reminding me of just how long it's been since I've been inside of her...

"Your punishment."

Her teeth slide out over her bottom lip, and she bites down so hard, it turns white.

I fight back a chuckle. "Have something to say?"

"No, sir."

Good, I don't want to have to gag her. At least, not until I get some four-letter words out of those sweet lips. Plus, she's nowhere near ready for that.

The mattress dips under my weight as I climb between her legs. "Spread them."

A moment of hesitation is the only indication I get that she may not be with me a hundred percent. But it's at least ninety percent, because the trepidation in her eyes has been replaced by a blazing lust, and they drop down to my cock bobbing between my legs.

When she opens her legs wide for me, the glistening of her pussy almost makes me come on the spot.

Holy fuck is she wet.

I guess two straight hours of vibrator action will do that. And I hope some of it has to do with me too.

Slowly, I trail my fingers up from her ankles, over her calves, and across her quaking thighs until I'm a hairsbreadth away from her cunt. I know what she wants, I can practically see her begging with her eyes, but she isn't going to get it.

My hand slides over her thigh as I wrap the strap around it. The heat of her gaze following my every move burns my skin and almost makes me rethink my plan momentarily. But only momentarily. I repeat the process on the other thigh, and she quirks an eyebrow at me, apparently wondering what they're for.

When I reach around her neck with the strap and hook it to both thighs, the look in her eyes tells me she's finally getting the picture. With a quick jerk, I tighten the strip of nylon through the neck padding, yanking her legs open even wider.

She yelps and tugs at the arm bindings. "What the—"

I grin down at her. "What the what, Nora? What the hell?"

Instead of admitting what she was about to say, she presses her lips together tightly and shifts awkwardly.

"I told you...you need a lesson on orgasm denial."

Before she can protest, I drop between her legs and lick her slit.

Sweet mother of God, she tastes so fucking good.

Her flavor on my tongue has my cock twitching. I reach between my legs and wrap my hand around my shaft. A moan falls from my lips, partly due to having my face buried in her pussy and partly because the feel of my fingers around my throbbing flesh is so damn good.

"Oh, God...Stone!"

She tries to buck her hips against my face, but the thigh restraints prevent her from moving even an inch. A frustrated groan rents the air and urges me forward.

I stroke my shaft, hard and slow, squeezing when I reach the head. My tongue slips along her, and I savor every fucking moan from her.

When her body begins to quake, signaling her impending orgasm, I pull back and blow over her wet flesh.

"No! Don't stop...God...please, Stone!"

She doesn't get it.

I would love nothing more than to bury myself inside her right now, to give us *both* what we want. But she needs to know who is in charge here. She needs to understand this dynamic fully.

Over and over, I bring her and myself to the brink, only to pull back just before falling over the edge into the bliss of orgasm.

Her strangled moans and begging increase exponentially each time I stop.

"God dangit, Stone. I can't...I can't take it anymore..."

I'm right there with her. Every drag of my palm along my raging cock brings me agonizingly close to coming. Even my iron will and stamina won't save me much longer.

Christ, this woman makes me feel like a teenager again.

I want to keep pushing her though, I want to know her limits. I want to know what it's going to take to get her to either drop an F-bomb or scream "cupcake" at the top of her lungs.

But she's been tortured enough...at least, with my tongue.

After one final swipe over her clit, I sit back on my heels. Her angry stare lands first on my eyes, then drops down to my cock in my fist.

Having Nora watch me stroke myself is almost as sexy as having her tied up in one of my bindings and completely at my mercy.

"You aren't going to let me come?"

I grin at her and shake my head. "No, but I'm going to let you watch me come."

She bucks against the restraints again and lets out a frustrated, strangled cry. "Arrrgggg! Stone, you can't do this to me!"

"I can, and I am. You know the word to make this all stop." But she doesn't want it to stop. Not really. I rise up onto my knees between her legs and stroke my cock. Slowly at first. But watching her watch me has me speeding up my movements and twisting my fist around my flesh harder.

A low moan rumbles from deep within her chest.

She fucking loves this.

Tingles shoot through my balls and up my spine. My pace increases, every stroke bringing me closer, and closer, and closer.

I force myself to keep my eyes open when I finally come.

"Fuck, Nora!" Hot spurts of my jizz shoot across her stomach and up over her tits and neck. But she doesn't recoil, she squirms and bucks, desperate to get to me. My head swims, and I continue to stroke my cock until every last drop falls against her alabaster skin. I finally lose control of my body, and my eyes close.

Several deep breaths later, I reopen them and meet Nora's gaze.

She's never looked sexier than with my cum all over her, bound to my bed and completely at my mercy. My plans for the evening have suddenly changed.

I can't wait all the time it will take to complete what I originally planned. With Nora, my will-power seems to be non-existent. I have much bigger plans for Nora Eriksson, but tonight, I need to be inside her more than I need to see her in one of the bindings I've been dreaming of.

26

STONE

"You okay?" My eyes move over the rope bound around her wrists and the leather across her thighs. She's been tugging on them enough, there will definitely be marks, ones that won't be so easy to cover on stage. But fuck if she isn't the most exquisite creature I've ever seen.

She nods and eyes my still-hard cock in my hand.

I reach behind me and grab a condom. Dragging the latex over my sensitive flesh has me gritting my teeth to keep from whimpering. This hasn't just been torture for her.

Nora's eyebrow wings up. "You don't need a few minutes?"

An amused chuckle slips from my lips as I lean over and brace myself up on my palms on either side of her splayed legs.

My lips graze hers briefly. "Hell no. Not with you spread out like a fucking buffet with my cum all over you. You should see the way it glistens in the moonlight from the window. It's the fucking hottest thing I've ever seen."

She moans slightly and shifts. Her desperation is palpable.

When I finally get inside her, she's going to explode like a fucking nuke.

"You uncomfortable?"

"Yes, sir." Her eyes plead with me to release her.

If I hadn't already given up on my detailed plans for the evening, that look surely would have thrown them to the wayside. She's been through enough today, and done surprisingly well, apart from the attempted masturbation situation. But she's new at this, and her submissive nature is warring constantly with her desire to find control over her own life. She hasn't yet grasped that I'm offering her a way to not worry about control anymore. It must be hard for her to obey me without question when she's never done this before, yet, for the most part, she does it.

That deserves respect and recognition.

"I'll give you a choice."

Her eyes widen, and she lifts her head slightly. "About what?"

I smirk and rock my cock against her wet pussy, eliciting another groan and shift from her as her eyes roll back in her head. "About how I'm going to fuck you."

She snort-laughs and grins at me. "Since when do I get a choice in that?"

Sassy mouth. There's my spitfire submissive.

"This is a one-time offer. Don't get used to it. I'm feeling generous, despite your behavior at dinner tonight."

The corners of her luscious mouth tip up. "What are my options?"

Christ, there are so many fucking things I want to do to her, ways I want to *do* her, but most would probably send her running to the hills, or they would take too long to set up. And my patience for waiting has worn thin.

"Well, I can leave you like this and fuck you so hard, you will most definitely have marks from the bindings for days."

Her eyebrow raises. "Or?"

"Or..." I lean back and stroke my cock, making sure she can see my hand rolling over every inch. "Or I can untie you, flip you over, and pound you into the mattress so hard, you'll leave a permanent indentation there."

I'm hoping she's going to take option two. But really, I won't complain either way, as long as I'm buried deep inside her in the next two minutes. There's just something about being with Nora that feels completely new and different each and every time, like I'm a goddamn virgin, getting my dick wet and getting my first taste of pussy.

Those soft blue eyes follow my movements as I languidly stroke my cock waiting for her response.

"Two."

Music to my fucking ears.

My cock slips from my hand, and I lean forward over Nora to unhook the leg restraints from behind her neck. She burrows her face into my chest and sharply bites my nipple.

Fucking A!

I jerk back and glare down at her. She gives me an innocent smile, but the devious pride is lurking just beneath.

"What was that for?"

She lifts one shoulder as much as the rope allows and smirks. "I don't know, it was just calling to me. I had to."

Well shit, I can totally understand that feeling. I've been there a thousand times with Nora already. So while I want to be mad, I can't muster up any anger at her actions.

I lean down and press my lips to her ear. "Just don't forget who's in charge here, Nora. You don't want me to have to renew your lessons, do you?" A bite punctuates my words and she yelps.

"No, definitely not, sir."

I growl in her ear and kiss her cheek. "Good girl."

With that confirmation, I finish releasing her legs, and she groans as she's finally able to lower them from the splayed position.

"Move them around to get the blood circulating again." She nods her understanding while I shift up and untie one wrist, then the other.

The angry red burn marks marring her pale skin make my cock throb. It's almost as hot as my cum still spread across her body.

I kneel between her legs and massage her wrists in my hands. Her eyes remain locked with mine the entire time.

"You all right?"

She sucks in a deep breath and shifts her legs on the outside of my thighs. "Yes, sir."

I continue to rub her wrists, my eyes moving between her face and these damn gorgeous marks.. "Feeling coming back?"

"Yes, sir." Her response this time is soft, and she goes silent again. The spark that makes an appearance when she's playful or angry seems to have disappeared.

Her silence is somewhat concerning. At this point, I'd expect her to be begging for my cock again or even using her safe word if this has been too much. Instead, she watches me with rapt attention, and the wheels churning in her head are practically visible in her eyes.

"What's wrong?" I release her hands and sit back on my heels.

She shakes her head. "Nothing, I just..."

Oh, shit, here it comes.

I've been expecting to hear *cupcake*, but I certainly wasn't anticipating it coming now, after releasing her. During dinner, sure. While I was eating her out like a fucking starving man at a buffet, definitely. Even when I was making her watch me stroke my cock...but now?

"Nora, talk to me. This doesn't work if you don't tell me what's going on in that head of yours."

I shift so her legs are between mine. She lifts a shaky hand and holds it up in between us. "I just never expected to like...*this* so much."

Holy fucking shit.

That was certainly not where I anticipated this going. Not at all.

Pride swells my heart and my cock.

I lean down, pushing her arm in between us, until I'm a mere inch from her face. "There's nothing to be ashamed of, baby."

"I know." She says the words, but the doubt is still there. It's written all over her face and in her eyes. She wants this. I know she does. It's in every moan and cry and the way she submits to me so willingly. She's just caught up in the mindset of the vast majority of society who believe what we're doing is somehow deviant.

No worries, I'll fuck any lingering reservations from her tonight. By this time tomorrow, she will know she belongs with me and won't be going anywhere, no matter what happens or what anyone says. I'll do whatever it takes to protect her, to protect my family, and what's mine. And she is mine.

Before she has time to think anymore, I lean back and admire my cum spread across her skin one last time. "Roll onto your stomach."

A flush instantly spreads across her breasts and up her neck to her cheeks. Her thighs press together. I can only imagine how badly she needs to get off right now. I, for one, could never tolerate that kind of orgasm denial.

Nora is one fucking tough girl.

One hard smack to her thigh gets her moving, and she turns over, sliding her legs outside mine where I kneel in the center of the bed.

Fuuuckkkkk...this ass!

There's no doubt in my mind no one else has ever been between these cheeks. And I plan on being the first. But not tonight. Tonight, her sweet fucking cunt is calling to me like a siren from the waves, urging me to plunge in. Images of her in the tub swirl through my head.

I smack her ass with my left hand while I stroke my dick with my right.

She moans into the pillow and shifts, pushing her ass into the air toward me.

That's all the invitation I need.

I align my cock with her wet core and shove into her with one hard thrust.

NORA

Holy mother fudger!

His massive dick spreads and stretches me. He buries himself to the hilt, his thighs smacking against my ass with enough force, I'm sure the skin there will be as red as that on my wrists.

I've never needed anything as much as I need him inside me like this right now. Everything he's done over the last four hours has been pure, agonizing torment. And he's been getting off on it.

I shift under him, trying to get him to move, but he remains still, buried deeply inside me.

Contracting my inner muscles around him doesn't get him moving, so I look over my shoulder.

As soon as my eyes meet his, he pulls back and then slams into me again, so hard, it squishes my breasts painfully into the unforgiving mattress. He plows into me, over and over.

Good Lord...

It's never felt this deep before. Every thrust fills me and every retreat feels like I'm losing a part of my soul.

Sweat drips onto my back, and his grunts mingle with my groans. I turn my face into the mattress to stifle a scream when he increases his pace and shifts back slightly.

His hands grip my hips, and he jerks me up and back, until

my ass is in the air and my knees are spread wide across the sheet.

My legs quiver, and his fingers inch between my butt cheeks. He retreats again, pausing with his cock barely inside me, and waits. I turn to look at him, and this time, when our eyes meet, instead of shoving his dick into me, he pushes his thumb into the place no one has ever dared venture before.

I cry out and bury my face into the pillow as my channels clasp his dick and his thumb.

"Fuck, Nora. I can't wait to be inside you, here."

He punctuates his words with a thrust of his hips timed with that damn thumb.

Oh, God.

There's no way I'm going to last with the probing he's doing. That dang thumb...it makes his dick feel even bigger. I can't even describe the sensations spreading through my body. Tingling... electric...blazing...

I need more.

"Stone..."

Every push and drag brings me higher and closer to Heaven. It's so close, I can almost taste it.

His left hand slides down from my hip, and his fingers find my clit.

Holy mother of God...

Swirling, rubbing, twisting joins the motions of his thumb and dick, and I detonate, my entire body convulsing around all the parts of him embedded inside me.

He bites out a curse and pumps into me harder, adding fuel to the fire blazing through me and drawing out my orgasm.

Intense, driving thrusts finally bring him over the edge, and he cries out my name as he empties himself inside me.

Sweet Lord...

I collapse to the bed, and he follows, dropping onto his side. The fact that the evidence of his earlier masturbation is now spread all over the sheet barely registers as he pulls me against him.

His warm, panting breaths float across my neck and tickle my ear. He interlaces the fingers of his left hand with mine and squeezes gently.

"Christ, Nora, that was incredible."

I manage to nod my agreement and shift back against him. His semi-hard cock is still inside me, and I know, as much as I want to, I can't let myself fall asleep right now.

He must realize the same thing, because he drops a kiss against my shoulder and turns me onto my back.

"I'll go start the shower for you. I'll change the sheets."

I nod and offer him a small smile as he slides from the bed. The sound of the water hitting the tile floats from the bathroom.

When he exits, he grins at me before disappearing out into the hallway, probably to grab new sheets. I shift back and look down at the evidence of what happened this evening, both on the sheets and on my wrists and thighs.

What am I doing? How can I like this?

Movement at the end of the bed draws my attention. Stone stands at the foot, assessing me. "Nora, are you all right?"

I nod and climb off the bed, making my way to the bathroom and shutting the door before he can question me further. I'll probably get punished for nodding and not responding *yes, sir* to him, but right now, I just need a little space to think and a shower sounds amazing.

When I finally drag myself from the steamy room, he's lying in bed, waiting for me with concern in his eyes.

He holds his arm out to me, and I walk over and drop my hand in his. I let him tug me onto the bed, and his strong, warm body surrounds me.

"Baby, we need to talk."

Bile churns in my stomach.

Oh, God, what did I do wrong?

"I saw that look in your eyes before you darted into the bathroom...the way you looked at the marks I left on you."

Crap.

"You want to know why you like this?"

I hesitate, unsure if I really want to hear what Stone has to say. He's been pretty spot-on with every observation he's ever made about me, and I'm not sure I'm ready to face the truth that's sitting on the tip of his tongue.

But a huge part of me wonders...if what happened in school is why I'm like this...why I enjoy what Stone does to me.

"Yes."

He squeezes me gently and places a kiss on the top of my head. "You don't have direction anymore. You've spent your entire life, or at least your adult one, thinking you were going to medical school. You busted your ass in high school to get the best grades with that goal in mind. And now, you've left that behind, for whatever reason."

I freeze at his words. It's not that he's wrong; quite the contrary. I just don't know if I can handle him pressuring me to talk about why I left school again. He needs to know eventually, but not tonight. I don't have the physical or mental energy for that right now.

"You don't have to tell me what happened, at least, not right now..."

A relieved breath leaves my lungs, and I relax against him.

"But you know I won't let it go. Because I want to know everything about you, everything that makes you who you are today."

Well, dang if that isn't the sweetest thing.

Stone is not one for mushy words, but I genuinely believe he means that. I could say the same. I want to know Stone, inside and out, but something tells me he'll never let me close enough to do that. Not with his job and the kind of life he lives. Not with his family harping on everything he does. He's closed off and only giving me glimpses into who he really is. But those glimpses tell me so much, prove he's so much more than everyone assumes.

I don't know if he's waiting for some kind of a response from me or not. I place a kiss against his chest and wait for him to continue.

"You enjoy this, the way I take control and what we do, because it means you don't have to search for control and direction in your life anymore. You don't have to think. I take control and make the decisions when we're together. You're naturally submissive, and being able to rely on me to care for you and make these decisions relieves you of a tremendous weight you've been carrying, probably without even knowing it. It allows you to free your mind of all the self-doubt and listlessness you've been drowning in."

Jesus.

My heart pounds in my chest.

Is he right? Is that why I love being with him so much? Because he takes control when I can't?

Something in his words rings true. Deep in my heart, I know he's right, even though I don't want to admit my life has become such a chaotic mess because I can't manage to get myself together.

I let one night change my plans for the future, my entire life. Maybe I'm not as strong as I always thought.

Stone slides his hand under my cheek and tips my face up to his. "Don't. I see what you're doing to yourself. Liking this... needing this...it has nothing to do with you being weak, Nora. It's the opposite. It takes a really fucking strong person to give themselves over completely to someone else, to let someone else take total control. And you've done it, basically without question, with me, even though you've never experienced this before and we barely knew each other. Never forget that *you* are the one with all the power in this relationship. You hold all the cards and decide what does or does not happen here. Not me."

Power.

That one little word holds so much meaning.

And now, after tonight, I realize that while I may hold the power between us, when it comes down to it, Stone truly holds the power to break my heart.

27

NORA

*W*hatever just happened with Stone was not normal. I know that.

The way he touched me, looked at me, the sensitivity in his every movement and word...he was truly taking care of me and giving me what I needed. Not a quick bang. Not a kinky one. It almost felt like he was making love to me this time. But I'm not dumb enough to believe Stone loves me. Men like Stone love women, they don't fall *in* love with one.

Still, I've never been so relaxed and exhausted in my entire life. I've also never been so content.

Who would have ever thought I would find release like this with a man like Stone...with the things Stone *does* to me.

His warm, hard chest rises and falls beneath me, and his heartbeat thumping next to my ear further lulls me into a blissful state.

It's been a constant struggle to keep my guard up with him. The need to protect myself and my heart from him has always been at the forefront, preventing me from truly opening up to him about anything.

Those walls came *crashing* down tonight in a way I never imagined possible.

And isn't that a doozy.

I want to know him, and I want him to know me. After what he said earlier, I know he understands me on a much deeper level than I even understand myself. The insight he had on my situation, without really knowing anything about what happened, was equally terrifying and relieving.

Not being able to talk to anyone has been crippling me. I need to talk to him. I need to give him something in return for what he's given me.

"You want to know why I wanted to become a doctor?"

My question shatters the comfortable silence in the room. He doesn't respond, but his hand shifts up and runs through my hair and then down my spine. I know he's awake and listening.

"Because of my father. He died when I was only seven, and at the time, I was too young to really understand it. But as I got older, I became bitter, thinking there was more the doctors could have done to save him. It became an obsession for me, to get my degree so I could help people and ensure no other little girls lost their fathers the way Dani and I did."

His fingers dance across my skin, and despite the topic of conversation, his touch quells the anger and distress that usually arises when I talk about Dad.

"How did your dad die?"

I release a sigh and spread my hand over Stone's chest. "He was a cop. Got shot in the line of duty."

He squeezes me tightly to him and presses a kiss to my head. "Shit, I'm sorry, Nora."

"It's okay. You don't have anything to apologize for. It's not your fault he died, and it was a long time ago. I know there was nothing anyone could have done to save him. Once I was old enough, I learned how bad it had really been. But that didn't change the burning desire to become a doctor and help people."

A silence lapses between us, and I know what's coming next. Dread pools in my chest.

"What changed? Why did you leave school?"

The same questions...over...and over...and over...from everyone I know. Stone is just as relentless as my mother and Dani. He gave me a reprieve earlier, so I probably owe him. I also opened the door to this conversation, but I just can't right now.

"Please don't. Not right now. I don't want to ruin the moment by talking about that."

I'll tell him the truth eventually. He deserves to know the truth so he can understand how I got where I am. If I don't reveal everything, there will always be that empty space between us filled by all the things left unsaid.

For a minute, I think he's going to fight me on this. Maybe tie me up and bang me senseless until I relent and spill my guts...but he doesn't. He relaxes under me and threads his fingers through my hair in a soothing rhythm.

"But you're happy? Dancing?"

"Yes." My answer comes too quick. Even I notice that.

He doesn't believe it. The heaving sigh he releases is a dead giveaway. I can't really blame him since even I don't believe me anymore.

But the need to explain and defend my choice burns my tongue.

"Really, it's not so bad. Yes, there are some jerks, but I have a lot of really nice customers and some great regulars. Like this one guy, Robert, he's older, and he just seems so...I don't know... lonely? He doesn't give off the creepy vibe at all, and he never touches me. It's almost like he's on the job more than there to enjoy himself."

Stone stills under me, and the air in the room thickens with tension.

What just happened?

I shift up onto one elbow to look down at him. Even in the dark of the bedroom, his blue eyes flashing with anger are clear as day. "What's wrong? Crap, I'm sorry, I shouldn't be talking about that right no—"

He shakes his head and shifts back until he's propped up against the headboard. "No, it's not that." An arm snakes out and tugs me to straddle his lap. "I need you to tell me *everything* about this Robert guy."

"What? Why?"

Crap, what if he's going to go beat him up or something even worse?

"Nora." His large warm palms cradle my cheeks, returning my attention to him. "This is important. I need to know what he looks like, what he wears, if you've ever heard him talk about his job or employer, literally *anything* you can remember."

Goose bumps pebble across my skin. "Stone, you're scaring me."

He pulls me to him, crushing me against his chest and burying his face in my hair. "Shit, I'm sorry. It's just...I think I know him. And I need to know if it's the same guy."

His tone and the distress he can't hide send waves of apprehension racing through me. "Am I in any danger?"

He pulls back and presses his lips to mine gently. The mingled taste of our releases from our most recent round dances across my tongue.

"I won't let anything happen to you. *Ever.*"

STONE

The heavy wooden door slams against the brick wall.

Dom doesn't even flinch. He just sits watching me from his

desk like he's been expecting me to barge into his office unannounced in a rage.

Fucking prick.

"Stone, I see you are finally done ignoring me. To what do I owe the pleasure?"

I want to punch that smug grin off his face, but I settle for slamming my palms down on the desk. It's been a few days since I last saw or spoke with him, but I couldn't put this off any longer. Not after my conversation with Nora last night.

"What the fuck were you thinking?" The words exit through gritted teeth. I can't ever remember being this angry. The only thing keeping me from leaping across this desk and bashing his face in is the fact that there are about ten men just outside that door who will kill me before I ever finish Dom off. That and I want some fucking answers.

"I haven't the slightest idea what you are talking about, Son."

Son.

The term used to make me feel wanted, loved, protected. Now, it just makes me clench my hands into fists and bile churn in my stomach.

"Dani...Savage...Gabe..."

The names hang in the silence between us.

He smirks and leans back in his chair. "I knew it was only a matter of time before they told you. There was no way they were going to abide by the agreement once you were back in town and working for me."

"Is that why you've been having them...and me...followed?"

Dom inclines his head toward me but doesn't offer any explanation or excuse for what he's been doing.

"What about Nora? I know you sent Robert to watch her. Why are you dragging her into this? She has nothing to do with anything."

With a devious chuckle, he leans forward and places his elbows on the desk. "Bullshit. She has *everything* to do with this."

Impossible.

He's just talking in fucking riddles again.

"What the fuck does that mean? What could she possibly have to do with the shit you've been up to?"

He rises to his feet, and I pull my hands up and take a step back from the desk still separating us.

His arms cross over his barrel chest and he frowns and shakes his head. "You want to know why I did what I did to Dani? Why I had to make that deal with Savage and Gabe?"

"Of course I do, why the hell else would I be here?"

His eyes narrow on me, and he leans forward, placing his palms flat on the desk.

Dom can be an intimidating guy. Most people would cower under the look he's giving me. But I can hold my own with him... with anyone...under *any* circumstances.

"Jesus, Stone, sometimes you can be so damn oblivious to what's really going on."

"Let's just cut to the fucking chase, Dom. Tell me what happened."

He pushes off the desk and strolls over to the bar in the corner. Of course, I could use a drink right now, but I'm not about to enjoy a nice Scotch with the man who not only tried to kill members of my family but who's also been having me and Nora followed.

The amber liquid fills his crystal tumbler, and he turns back to me.

"I did it for you."

What the fuck?

"For me? What does any of this have to do with me?"

"Everything. You don't know very much about your girlfriend or sister-in-law, do you?"

The question gives me pause. I guess I really don't. I've only had a dozen conversations with Dani since she and Savage got together. And Nora and I haven't been doing a whole lot of *talking*. Something that needs to change and I hope will once she fully opens up to me. But his insinuation grates me just the same. "Well enough."

He gives a low, amused chuckle and settles back in his chair. His drink lands on his desk, and he steeples his fingers over his mouth.

"Dani was digging, and not just into recent activities. She was going back as far as she could. I've had people on her for a long time, watching and keeping tabs on her investigations. I had hoped she would hit enough roadblocks that she'd eventually give up. Despite what you may think of me, I don't enjoy hurting innocent people. But Dani was getting too close, digging too deep. She would have found out."

I slam my fist against the desk again. "Find out *what?*"

"The one thing that could ruin *your* perfect little world."

He doesn't elaborate, and I'm reaching the end of my patience with his games. I straighten again, using my full height to hopefully display my lack of tolerance for any more of his bullshit. Dom is a big man, but I'm big and in shape and decades younger.

It must work, because he finally relents. "August 10th, 2002."

All the blood in my body instantly freezes, and I fist my hands at my sides. We don't talk about that day. We *never* talk about that day. Dom instructed me to *never* mention it to anyone, even him... ever. That day never happened. That day is nothing but a terrible dream.

So why the fuck is he bringing it up now?

"What about it?"

"I'm sure you remember it just as vividly as I do, Stone. But the difference is, I didn't just shove it away to the back of my mind and try to forget it after it happened. I found out as much as I could, so I could protect you. That's all that mattered to me then, and it's all that matters now. Whether you believe it or not, you are important to me, and I wanted to protect you."

I wait for him to continue. He's clearly going somewhere with all this, though I have no fucking clue where. There's no way anything that happened then matters anymore.

"Not everyone forgets as easily as you, Stone..."

As if I could ever forget that day...

"He didn't die in a bubble, Stone."

"What the hell does that mean?"

Dom takes a sip from his glass and twists it around in his hand, letting the light reflect off the glass and liquid inside.

"Actions have consequences. People are affected. He had a family...a wife..."

His dark eyes search mine expectantly.

"Two daughters."

A niggling feeling of dread creeps up my spine and settles deep in my brain.

"People who missed him. People who had to go on with their lives without him in it anymore. People who have been seeking closure for fifteen years. People who are tenacious and won't give up once they get a whiff of a story."

No.

I shake my head and move backward until I slam into the wall.

No. No. No. No. No.

It can't be.

28

AUGUST 10th, 2002

STONE

*T*his is the last place I want to be today. Why does Dom make me come to these places with him? I mean, this warehouse is a total dump. Why anyone would set foot in here, let alone run a business here, is beyond me. But Dom seems to have lots of places like this all over the city, and he's constantly dragging me along when Mom makes me spend the day with him.

I push off the desk, letting the old desk chair spin wildly until I crash into a file cabinet against the wall with a loud clang.

Muffled voices float through the closed office door. I don't know what's going on out in the warehouse, but I hope he's done soon. I've got stuff to do today. And he's left me waiting for what feels like an eternity already.

Savage and Gabe get to go fishing while I'm stuck tagging along with Dom. It's punishment. I know that much. Mom thinks she's going to get me to "straighten out" if I spend some time with him.

What a load of crap.

Everything's fine. So what, I got caught shoplifting and smoking a few times. It's not the end of the damn world. She's totally overreacting and treating me like a damn baby. The girls and Savage don't get forced into this stuff. Only me. It's so unfair.

The door pops open, and Dom sticks his head in. He examines me and the chair against the file cabinet and raises an eyebrow. "You still doing okay in here, son?"

I heave out a sigh. "Are you done? Can we go now? I want to head to the canal and meet Savage and Gabe."

He narrows his eyes at me and steps into the office. "I thought you didn't want to hang out with your brother anymore."

I sigh and slide off the chair to my feet. "I don't really, I just want to go fishing, and that's where they went." Savage is annoying, and I'd rather hang out with my own friends, but Mom said I can't see them for a while. She thinks they're a "bad influence." They were always my fishing partners. It's been a long time since I actually caught anything, and I heard there were a lot of fish in the canal since that storm came through last week.

A large hand claps me on the shoulder and urges me back around the desk. "I'll be done soon. We'll grab a bite to eat, and then I'll take you over there to see if they are still fishing, deal?" He grabs the chair and wheels it over to me.

With some reluctance, I slink back down into it. "Fine, I guess." It's not like I have any choice. I have no idea where we are and have no way to get out of here without Dom. Plus, I am hungry, so lunch would be good. Maybe he'll take me to that new burger place.

"There may be a book or something in the desk you can read

to entertain yourself." He motions toward the drawers before he disappears out the door again and closes it behind him.

Read a book? Come on...

This is summer vacation. No way in hell I'm reading anything. But maybe there's something else in here.

I yank open a drawer and freeze.

A shiny silver revolver lays on the pale wood inside.

Damn.

I've seen guns before, even handled one a couple times when Dom took me to the range shooting. He always said it was a good skill to have because you never knew when you were going to have to defend yourself. I'm a pretty good shot too, actually better than Dom.

Check to make sure a gun is unloaded before you handle it.

Dom's words echo in my head, and I glance at the door. I probably should leave it be, but checking it out won't hurt anyone.

My fingers tighten around the grip, and I lift it from the drawer, careful to keep it aimed down to the floor. I open the cylinder.

Loaded.

I should put it back, but it feels so good in my hand. The grip is perfect and the weight sits in my palm like it's meant to be there.

Maybe Dom will give it to me if I ask?

Yelling and loud pops of gunfire in the warehouse have me jerking my head up and my attention focusing on the door.

What the hell is going on?

My heart thunders in my chest as I race to the door and fling it open.

The two bodies on the floor several feet into the warehouse cause my blood to run cold. My fingers flex round the grip of the gun still in my hand.

I peek around a stack of boxes, and my breath catches in my chest.

Dom is halfway across the warehouse, facing me, with his arms raised in the air. A man stands with his back to me, gun raised at Dom's chest.

Shit.

The thought of calling the police from the office phone briefly crosses my mind, but the two bodies and the gun pointed at Dom assure me this is a situation that won't end well if I wait for the cops.

Dom and the man yell angrily at each other, but I can't make out their words. The whooshing of blood in my ears drowns out everything else.

Don't point your gun at someone unless you're prepared to use it.

He needs my help. I don't have a choice. Whoever that is, he came here intent to hurt Dom, that much is clear.

I raise the gun slowly and step out from behind the boxes. Dom's eyes widen when they land on me. He opens his mouth to say something.

The man facing him with the gun begins to turn toward me...

Bang.

The gun recoils.

I aim again.

Bang.

Bang.

Bang.

Bang.

Bang.

The empty gun clatters on the concrete floor.

~

P RESENT DAY

NORA

Something's very wrong.

Stone should have been here by now.

When he dropped me off for my shift, he told me he had to take care of something but would be back in a little while.

That was hours and five unanswered phone calls ago.

Where the heck is he?

I know it might be weird for him to watch me dance with other men around, but he seemed pretty intent on coming back for me and even catching one of my performances tonight. It's weird that he's not back yet and not answering. It's so unlike him.

It's slow tonight, which only makes it worse. If it were busy, I wouldn't have time to worry about him or what's going on. I wonder if it has to do with Robert? He acted really weird last night when I talked about him. And after he had me tell him everything I remembered about Robert from the times I've seen him, his anger was palpable. Whoever Robert is, he's someone Stone doesn't want anywhere near me. He told me that in no uncertain terms and ordered me to tell Gabe and Byron to keep him out of the club.

His reaction makes me more than uneasy. Who is Robert and why is he so dangerous? I trust Stone. Whatever it is, it's not just jealousy. So I told Byron when I got here that he should alert the bouncers and Gabe to keep Robert out. He wanted to know why, but all I could come up with was that he was giving me the creeps. Thankfully, that was enough.

Now, all I want to do is crawl back into bed with Stone and pick up where we left off.

But my gut tells me something isn't right.

And given the way Byron is eyeing me from the bar, my

distraction is showing. By the time I finish my dance and make it into the back, he's waiting for me.

"Go home."

I brush past him to my locker and tug it open. "What?"

He leans against the row of lockers and sighs. "We're slow, and you're so distracted, it's like watching a coked out junkie sway aimlessly around on the stage when you dance."

Jerk.

"You know, Gabe isn't the only one who has noticed you've been acting weird lately. And I couldn't help but note your sudden fondness for bracelets. If something is going on, you need to take care of it, or you won't have a job much longer, sister-in-law or not. Does this have to do with why you don't want Robert in here anymore?"

"No. This isn't about Robert." He's not wrong, though. I know I've been letting what's going on with Stone, and in my own head, get in the way of my work.

How ridiculous is that? I leave school because I can't hack it, and here I am, failing at being a dang stripper too because I think too much. How's that for irony?

"I swear, Byron. Things are fine. I've just had a lot happening."

He sighs and looks over my shoulder as one of the other girls enters. "Do you want to go back over to TWO for a little while? A change of pace might help. I know you didn't exactly love it last time, but it's still an option, at least until THREE opens."

I hadn't even thought about that. Once the third location opens, Savage and Gabe will be looking to fill spots over there. Maybe getting out of this building would help at least relieve some of the stress of the sneaking around with Stone situation.

"When does it look like that's going to happen?" I vaguely remember hearing Ben discussing it with everyone at the dinner table the other night, but frankly, my ability to comprehend and process any sort of information was greatly diminished by those gosh darn panties.

He shrugs and pushes himself off the lockers. "Looks like maybe a month or two. Ben and Caleb have been working on some interior stuff."

I nod and grab my things. "I'll think about going over to TWO again. I definitely am not ruling it out right now." I have other things to worry about, like where the heck Stone is. He's really starting to worry me now.

Byron's large hand lands on my shoulder. "You know we're just looking out for you, right?"

My heart swells with his concern. Byron is a really good guy. He's like a brother to all of us, taking care of us and watching our backs. "Of course, I know that. And I really do appreciate it. But I promise, I'm fine."

"Good." After a gentle squeeze, he disappears out toward the front of the club.

Scarlett eyes me from her place in front of the vanities. "What was that about?"

Sigh.

I love Scarlett, I really, really do, but I don't want to get dragged into a convo with her right now. I want to go try to find Stone.

"Oh, nothing. He was just letting me know the offer to go to TWO still stands."

Her eyebrow quirks up. "You going to go back? I thought you didn't really like it."

I offer her a non-committal shrug. "Maybe. And it's not that I didn't like it, it's just a different environment than here."

She chuckles and grabs her mascara. "I know what you mean. The clientele here is way better."

I don't want to insult the catty dancers from TWO, so I bite my tongue. "Yeah, for sure."

"Speaking of which..." She turns in her chair to face me. "Have you seen Stone around lately?"

His name from her ruby red lips sends ice water through my veins. Why is she asking about Stone? Does she know something is going on between us?

"Um, I saw him at the Hawke dinner on Sunday. Why?"

She shrugs and tries to look nonchalant, but a dreamy, longing look overtakes her green eyes. "Oh, just wondering. He used to come around a lot, and I figured now that he's back permanently, we'd be seeing him more. I haven't seen him much lately."

Because he's been spending all his time with me.

Her eyes flick down to the thick bracelets on my wrists, and she gives me a wry smile.

Holy crapballs.

The words from so many months ago come flooding back...

"Girl, you are missing out. You wouldn't believe what this man can do with some handcuffs and a little rope."

Jesus...

How did I never make the connection before? She had tried to hide it, when she started saying his name and changed it to Steve.

My skin heats, but not from embarrassment. It's anger.

But why does it bother me so much?

Of course Stone has been with other women. Probably lots of them. But it never even *once* crossed my mind that he might have slept with someone I know, someone I work with every day. For some reason, that makes it ten times worse.

My heart creeps up into my throat. I cough it away and move toward the door. "I'll tell him hi from you if I see him."

Lame, Nora, really lame.

She grins and chuckles. "You do that, honey."

I can't be mad at him about this, right? That would make me a possessive psycho. But still, my concern for him is quickly being replaced by jealousy and an anger I've never felt before.

Stone has a way of stirring up emotions in me best left dormant. Last night was amazing, and it was precisely what I needed. But now, the feelings swimming through me are not a good thing, at least not for my relationship with Stone. He and I need to talk.

29

STONE

I stumble into my house and slam the door shut behind me.

This can't be happening.

Either I'm having a really bad coke hallucination, or my world is falling apart at the fucking seams.

I never would have believed Dom, if he hadn't pulled out a newspaper article dated August 11, 2002 with the headline proving the truth of his words

Officer Killed on Duty

My eyes skimmed the article until they landed on the one name that could shatter my life—Fredrik Eriksson.

It didn't even register at first. I stared at it with blind eyes for what felt like an hour before Dom cleared his throat.

"Now you understand."

That's all he said before I fled from his office and made my way to the closest bar.

What the fuck am I supposed to do?

My phone rings as I step into my office.

Nora. Again.

I send it to voicemail for the third time in the last twenty minutes.

She's the last person I want to talk to right now. What would I even say? Sorry, I killed your father when I was a kid but it was an accident. I didn't know he was a cop?

"Fuck." I drop down into my office chair and tug open the middle drawer. This isn't some bad trip, but at least maybe I can dull my senses for a while with a good one. I haven't touched the stuff in weeks, but the booze isn't dulling the memories of Dom's screams, the blood pooling under the man in the warehouse, the chaos as I was rushed out of there...

It's all so crystal clear, as if it happened yesterday.

The pinnacle moment of my life. The turning point.

The single second in time when my fate was decided for me.

It sent me down the path I'm on today...

I just couldn't have known that path would lead straight to Nora, or how tangled this web would become.

My hand shakes removing the small vial from the drawer.

Shit. I'm a fucking mess.

I need some relief from the onslaught of images...the gut-wrenching pain...

But the ping of my phone momentarily distracts me from my mission.

A text from Nora.

> Where are you? I thought you were coming to the club? Is something wrong? <

I ignore her again and concentrate on arranging the lines of coke on my desktop.

My shaking hands make it hard to roll up the bill from my

drawer, and I have to pause for a moment to take a deep breath and steady myself.

A quick snort, and almost instantly, the rush hits my body, relaxing my tense muscles and momentarily clearing my mind from all the bullshit rattling around in there.

It's not enough to keep the image of Nora's father's blood pooling out under his body from flashing before my eyes, though. So I do another line. And another.

Fuck.

I recline back into the chair, close my eyes, and let the blissful high overtake me. But I can't sit still. The coke floods my veins and has my heart thumping wildly in my chest. I rise and pace through the house until I practically wear paths on the wood floors. The boxes I haven't yet unpacked sit in the corner of the dining room and call to me.

I tear into the one on the top. A picture of my father with the five of us before he died is the first thing my eyes land on.

Searing pain rips through my heart. Nora and Dani lost their father. Because of me.

The frame shatters against the floor, and I shove my hands back through my hair.

My high is already starting to wear off. And my head feels like it's being twisted in some sort of medieval torture device. I make my way back to the office and drop into my chair. The remaining lines on the desk top call to me.

A door slamming vaguely registers, but I can't manage to bring myself to care.

"Stone?"

Her footsteps echo across the wood floor and fade as she ascends the stairs. The thumping of her feet as she searches my room above me is like a banging drum in my ear, but I can't move. I'm physically and emotionally exhausted. And now that my high wore off, all I want to do is another line or sleep. I can't face Nora like this. I don't know how I'll *ever* face her.

"Stone?"

That damn voice...

It cuts through the anger and post-drug fog and goes straight to my cock. But it almost makes bile rise in my throat.

I can't tell her.

She would never understand. She could never forgive me.

The footsteps grow closer until she appears in the open doorway of the office.

Her eyes narrow in on me, then shift down to the desk. She takes two tentative steps in, her mouth pressed in a tight line.

"Stone, what are you doing?"

I raise a hand over my desk and let it flop back down on the armrest of my chair. "What does it look like I'm doing?"

"Something really stupid." She wanders around the desk, eyeing the two lines of coke still laid out on the wood. "Seriously, Stone, what the heck are you doing?"

What am I doing again? Oh yeah...

"Trying to forget."

She huffs and leans her ass against the desk, eyeing me with concern and anger.

"I don't know what's going on, and you clearly don't want to tell me. But I'll tell you this, Stone...drugs aren't the answer. And I can't be with you if you are using. That's a deal-breaker for me."

I scrub my hands over my face. "Nora, this is not the time for ultimatums. Really, you need to go."

She scowls at me.

Damn, how can that be so fucking hot with everything else going on right now?

Because she's fucking perfect. A literal angel brought into my life only to be ripped away by this joke of fate.

"I'll leave after you listen to me. You've been begging me for weeks to tell you why I dropped out of school. This," she waves her hand over the white lines, "is why."

What?

I heard her, but my brain isn't processing her words correctly. I swear she just said coke was the reason she dropped out of school.

She shakes her head. "Well, not *this* exactly. I was drowning in all the work—reading, studying, exams—and I was falling behind...way behind. I couldn't handle it. Then one of my roommates gave me one of her Adderall. She swore it was a miracle pill for concentration. I should have said no, but I wanted to succeed so badly."

Even as messed up as I am right now, I can already see this story is going nowhere good.

"It was fine for a while. I only used it when I had a big exam or some project to finish. But then, things got out of control, and my roommate couldn't give me any more of her prescription."

A deep breath puffs from her mouth, and she drops her head. *Fuck, I hate seeing her like this.*

It will only be worse if she learns the truth. And I can't lie to her forever. I could never do that to her. I need to end this.

"There was this guy...in one of my classes. Nick. He was nice, and not bad looking, and he had asked me out a couple times, but I always turned him down because I was so busy with school-work. Turns out, he was dealing Adderall, and some other things. When I found out, I asked him for some."

A tear trickles down her pale cheek. My fingers itch to wipe it away, but I can't move. Doing it would only confuse things more anyway.

"He agreed. But...crap..." She swipes at the tears now flowing rapidly and takes a deep breath. "I didn't have any money. I was at Tulane on scholarship. But I needed it. It felt like I couldn't function without it. So...dang...I didn't think it would be this hard to tell you..."

She doesn't even have to say it. Her reluctance speaks volumes. But being the dick I am, I remain silent and let her finish. I make her say it.

"So, I slept with him...to get the pills."

Motherfuckingcocksuckingshit.

Rage simmers in my veins, mingling with the after effects of the coke to create a potent and volatile combination.

"I felt like dirt and couldn't even look at myself in the mirror afterward. I couldn't concentrate on school. I couldn't do anything. So, I dropped out and started dancing. It was low stress and made me feel like I was in control. Now, I'm not so sure that was true."

I suck in a deep breath and gather my strength to do what needs to be done.

"What do you want me to say, Nora? You fucking prostituted yourself out for some pills."

Her wet eyes widen, and her bottom lip quivers.

"I can't pity you right now...I have...my own shit to deal with. It's over between us anyway. You would be out the door...if you knew the truth."

NORA

I don't have a clue what Stone is rambling on about. He's high or just coming down and not making any sense. But what's abundantly clear, is I've made a huge mistake in trusting him with my heart and with the truth about what happened in school.

He's taken it and thrown it back in my face. Knowing he's capable of that burns like acid down my throat as I swallow and search for the right words in response.

What am I supposed to say?

Sucking in deep breaths doesn't calm my racing heart or the ache in my chest. How could I have been so naïve? Everyone warned me about Stone. *I* warned me about Stone. But I didn't listen.

I let myself believe that deep down, he's a good guy with a great heart. And he's shown me he can be sweet, and loving, and thoughtful. He just can't let go of whatever anger and hostility he has boiling under his skin.

And I can't let myself be dragged under by him.

"I don't know what you're rambling on about, Stone. But I know I don't need this in my life."

I push off the desk and give him another once-over. His half-lidded, unfocused blue eyes search my face before they shutter closed.

"Just go, Nora."

"Goodbye, Stone."

Saying the words shatters my heart into a million pieces I know I'll never be able to puzzle back together. Anyone could have seen this coming from a mile away, but it still blindsided me. I *let* him do this to me.

Tears fall as I race from Stone's house to my car.

Dumb.

How could I be so dumb?

I'd give anything to be able to drive straight over to Dani's and collapse in a sobbing heap right now. But she's the last person I can go to. I promised her I would stay away from Stone, and at the time, I meant it. But it was out of my control. I was helpless once I was sucked into his orbit.

We circled around each other for far too long to let it go. There was bound to be a collision at some point. I just never imagined he could be so dang cold and heartless after everything we shared.

I can't go home to an empty apartment right now. But it's three a.m.

There are only so many options I have at this point.

I start my car and make a call. "Hey, sorry to call you so late. Do you mind if I come over? I really need to talk and don't have anyone else to talk to...okay...thanks...ten minutes, tops."

At least I won't be alone.

It won't ease the pain flooding me to my core right now, but maybe I can get some perspective.

By the time I pull up outside, the tears are flowing so fast, I can barely see the street.

I knock lightly on the door and wait for it to open. Two seconds later, Caroline has me in her arms, hugging me fiercely. "Tell me what's going on, hon."

She drags me into her apartment and deposits me on the couch. A bottle of Jack Daniels sits open on the coffee table with two glasses next to it.

Without prompting, she pours way too much and hands it to me.

"Drink that, then spill it."

It burns going down, but it's a good burn, the kind that promises some hazy relief soon.

When I have it half gone, I drop my head back against the couch and stare at the white popcorn ceiling. "I've been sleeping with Stone."

"What?" She grabs my shoulders and shakes me until I look at her. Her wide eyes meet mine. "Are you serious? For how long? Oh, my God...does Dani know? Holy fucking shit...does Savage know? What does—"

I halt her with a hand. "Stop. Give me a minute, and I'll explain everything."

She pulls back, but I can see the curiosity in her eager gaze.

"You have to promise not to tell anyone, especially Dani or Savage. Please."

Her mouth curls down into a frown. "I guess I can do that, if it's important to you."

I manage a nod.

"We danced around each other for a long time. He was coming to the club to watch me every time he was in town, but he hid in the shadows. I didn't realize it was him until I got dragged to a Hawke family dinner. He was flirting relentlessly, even in front of everyone, and I recognized his watch. I knew it had been him. It scared the crap out of me."

Caroline nods, and I down another couple swallows of Jack.

"I don't blame you, sweetie. Those Hawke boys, Gabe included, can be a little overwhelming."

"You have no idea."

I can't reveal all of Stone's quirks and kinks. That's not mine to tell. But to understand what's happened between us, she needs to know what he's really like.

"If you think Savage is a control freak, geez...Stone would blow your mind. I can't even put it into words. He just controls... everything. If he told me to stop breathing, I'd probably do it without even thinking."

Caroline presses her hand over her heart and sighs. "Damn, girl, that's the sexiest thing I've ever heard. I am so fucking jealous right now."

I understand why she would feel that way. There's something about a man who takes complete control that just ruins most women. But I never wanted someone to have that much power over me. I let the drugs take over my life and completely change my direction and focus, and I couldn't let that happen again. I never knew I wanted or needed that...until I met Stone.

"It was great, for a couple weeks, but..."

Criminey.

How can I tell her this without telling her *everything*?

"But what, honey?"

I bury my face in my hands and will the tears back. "Everything went to crap tonight. He was..." I suck in a breath and struggle for the right word. "Brutal. It's like he was intentionally trying to hurt me."

Caroline grabs my arm and tugs on it until I turn my face to her.

Anger flashes in her eyes. "Did that bastard lay a hand on

you? I swear to God, if he fucking touched you, I will rip off his nuts with my bare hands and shove them down his throat until he fucking chokes on them."

Well. That was graphic.

I shake my head and pat her arm. "No, not like that. He was just so cold and heartless with the things he said tonight. I never expected it from him, but maybe I should have. Everyone tried to warn me."

She laughs mirthlessly and tugs me into tight hug. "Oh, honey. The heart wants what it wants. And you can't control who you fall in love with. Everyone is somewhat blind to the faults of the person they love, that's just human nature. You can't blame yourself for him being a fucking prick."

The person they love?

Do I love Stone?

I care about him. Far more than I should. I can admit that. But love him? I sure as heck hope not. Because if I do, I am well and truly in a deep pile of S. H. I. T.

30

STONE

ow the fuck did I get to my bed?
I roll onto my back and stabbing knives assault my brain. The cotton dryness of my mouth and throat makes it hard to swallow.

Fuuuuccckkkkk...

Last night was a cluster fuck of epic proportions. The ache in my head echoes that in my heart. Those things I said to her...God. How could I be so damn cold after she opened up to me completely...after she revealed everything I've been asking of her since we got together? Since *before* we even got together.

She laid it all out, the worst thing she had ever done in her life, the thing that changed the entire *course* of her life, and I shoved it back in her face and kicked her out of my fucking house in tears.

What the hell is wrong with me?

My conversation with Dom returns to the front of my mind... and it's crystal clear again. Acid burns up my throat, and I lurch from bed to race to the bathroom and heave up the bile in my stomach.

Shit.

A few minutes on the cold tile calm my gag reflex enough for me to rise to my feet. The man staring back at me from the mirror is a fucking stranger, though.

Red, bloodshot eyes. Bags that make me look like I'm fifty-five instead of twenty-six. Splotchy, unshaven skin. But the thing that terrifies me most, the thing that almost has me lunging for the toilet again, is the emptiness in my stare. There's nothing there anymore. Everything is gone. All the joy and peace I found with Nora...gone in a fucking instant.

Christ. I'm a fucking wreck.

Even though I know I had to let her go. I had to get her away from me, what I said was just...unforgiveable. I scrub my hands over my face several times, trying to scrape away what happened last night.

It doesn't do any good.

That look in her eyes, the tears streaming down her face, that quivering lip...even all that coke can't erase those images from my head.

There's no way I can let things end with Nora like that. Even if I can't be with her, I need to at least apologize and make her understand what I said had *nothing* to do with her. That my words were meant to hurt, but they weren't true. They aren't how I really feel. I can't let her go on believing she's worthless.

I stagger back to bed and grab for my phone on the night-stand. When I open the messages, I toss out a silent prayer there's one from Nora.

Nothing.

Not even a "Bite me A-hole" or whatever non-sweary thing she could say to sum up what she feels.

It's never been a secret that I can be a real asshole, but last night went above and beyond douchecanoe and straight into doucheyacht territory.

She didn't deserve that. All she wanted to do was check on me and make sure I was okay, and I took her admission and threw it back in her fucking face.

You're a fucking prick, Stone.

I glance at the clock.

Shit.

I'm going to be late for court if I don't get my shit together. Nora will have to wait. Everything that needs to be said has to be said in person, I can't do it over the phone or a text.

It must to be done face to face, where she can't just turn off her phone to get rid of me, where she has to look me in the eye and see how sincerely sorry I am and hear the truth in my words when I tell her she is *everything* good in this world.

It's my only chance to get her to listen.

A quick shower and race to the courthouse later, I trudge into Judge Calhoun's courtroom, still feeling like ass and like a complete asshole.

"You're not looking so good, counselor. You feeling all right?"

I am most definitely not feeling all right, but I'm not about to tell the judge's clerk that. Instead, I plaster on my most charming smile and lean down over her desk. "I'm fine, Nancy, just a little over-worked...the usual." I force a chuckle to make sure she buys my line.

She looks down at her list of cases on the docket for the day. "You're here on Michael Figueroa? Looks like there's two cases ahead of you. I'll try to get you in as soon as I can, though."

This is why you have to be nice to clerks. A little flirting, an occasional box of chocolates, and treating them like human beings goes a long way. People who treat them like dirt end up spending their entire days waiting around for their cases to be called and waiting weeks to get on the docket. I make one call, and I can be in front of almost any judge the same day, if need be.

I shoot her a wink and a grin and wander over to the chairs where attorneys wait. Michael nods at me from his place in the benches at the back of the courtroom. After a quick greeting to the handful of other attorneys waiting for their cases, I pull out my cell phone.

A push notification from the local news channel's app immediately catches my attention.

EXPLOSION ROCKS WAREHOUSE

Shit.

My hand trembles as I swipe to open the article.

Just as I suspected. It's one of Dom's places. Probably retaliation for what he did to Castillo.

It's one more reason I can't have Nora anywhere near me. Even if she wants to be, after I tell her the truth, which I highly doubt, this life is too dangerous to have her wrapped up in it. I never should have been selfish enough to get involved with her in the first place. Hopefully, our relationship has slipped under the radar, and after what I said to her, it won't be an issue anymore anyway. I'll apologize and make sure she understands this is about me, not her, as fucking *lame* as that sounds. Then, I'll let her go.

There's still no messages from her, but there are five texts from Dom telling me he needs to talk to me immediately. No doubt about the fact one of his warehouses just went up in flames.

Motherfucker.

The last thing I want to think about right now is Dom, or what he told me last night, which would be inevitable if I go meet with him. I want this to go away again, even though I know that's impossible now.

It's not that I'm worried about going to jail. That ship sailed a long time ago. There's no way they could charge me with anything more than manslaughter for shooting Nora's father. I was twelve, and I didn't know he was a cop. I was protecting Dom from what I thought was a real threat. The statute of limitations requires they would have had to charge me within six years.

No, going to jail isn't my concern. The reaction of every single important person in my life is.

Dani and Nora deserve to know the truth about what happened to their father and my role in his death. I just don't know how the hell I'm supposed to do that. How do you look a woman you're falling in love with in the face and tell her you killed her father?

Shit. I'm falling in love with her.

But I'm not mentally prepared to tell them what happened. I need time to wrap my head around it. Time to form a plan. I'm going to have to try to explain what happened last night without revealing the true motivations for my actions. After what I said, there's a good chance she won't let me anywhere near her. It was heartless, and cruel, and downright fucking spiteful. If I were in her shoes, I would do a lot more than run the other way, I'd probably be looking for ways to inflict physical damage equivalent to the emotional damage perpetrated against me.

But Nora's a different animal. She's too sweet and forgiving for her own good.

That may play in my favor.

~

NORA

Kashmir has just reached its peak when I lift my head and my eyes meet the ones I hoped to never see for the rest of my life.

What is he doing here?

The last time those dark eyes looked into mine, I was making the biggest mistake of my life. My heart seizes in my chest, a cold sweat breaks out across my skin, and my head swims as panic sets in.

His momentary shock is quickly replaced by a giant smile spreading across his face.

Oh God. Oh crap.

He recognized me.

Son of an ever loving gun...

Someone whistles, and I realize I stopped moving, my concentration on my routine utterly destroyed by Nick's presence here.

I need to get my crap together or I'm not going to have a job anymore. Gabe and Byron are already worried about me, and Lord knows if they say anything to Savage, I'll be done soon.

And I don't have a dang clue what I would do without this job.

Somehow, despite fear making my limbs shake, I manage to regain my composure and get myself back on the pole for the rest of the song while avoiding looking in Nick's direction again.

But my stomach feels like it's climbed up into my throat, and the room is swirling around me like I'm drunk. When I stumble offstage, Dawn casts me a worried look. Her warm arm wraps around me, and she assists me over to a chair.

"You okay, honey? What happened?"

No, I'm not okay.

What the heck is Nick doing here? It's been almost two years, and I never expected to see him again. I hoped he had dropped off the face of the Earth. Maybe been arrested for dealing. Did he know I work here? Is he looking for me?

Oh God.

Oh God.

Oh God.

I drop my head into my hands. Dawn rubs my back gently.

"Honey, you're scaring me a little. Are you okay?"

It must look like I'm having a freaking mental breakdown so I pull myself together and raise my head up. "I'm all right, I just got a little dizzy on stage. I don't think I had enough water today. I'm a little dehydrated."

Good cover, Nora.

I practically roll my eyes at myself.

Dawn casts me a dubious look that tells me she's less than convinced. But she gets up and walks over to the cooler, grabs me a bottle of water, and returns to me with it. "Well, drink this. You got a while before you have to go back on again, right?"

I nod. "Yeah, another forty-five minutes or so."

"Okay, good. I'll check on you when I'm done. But if you aren't feeling good, you should tell Byron."

Not a lot Byron can do about why I feel like crap. Not a lot anyone can do. I put myself in this situation when I climbed into bed with Nick for a few dang pills. I did this to myself by selling my body to feed my success in school. I force a smile. "All right, thanks, love."

She disappears, and I pop the top of the water and guzzle half of it before my heart finally stops racing.

Maybe he didn't recognize me. Maybe I imagined the whole thing. I mean, I certainly don't look like I did when I was in school. My Cashmere personae and appearance is about as far from how I looked before as possible.

"Cashmere?" The male voice makes me jump before I look in the mirror and see it's only Rocky standing behind me in the doorway.

"Hey, what's up, Rocky?"

"You have a customer out here asking for you. He says he's an old friend of yours. Nick?"

Dang it.

I guess it wasn't my imagination. Of course he recognized me. We had class together for months before we ever slept together. I can't really say that I won't go talk to him. That would create a lot of questions I don't want to have to answer. I just need to get myself together enough to say a couple words to him and then I can come back here. I just need to maintain and be professional for two minutes. I can do it.

"I'll be out in a minute, okay?"

He nods and retreats back into the club.

How do I make it through a conversation with Nick?

He called several times after that night and left me messages wondering why I wasn't in class and asking if we could go out.

What an absolute moron to not understand what happened and why I've been avoiding him. I guess maybe in his world, it's normal for women to sleep with men for drugs, but it's not in mine. I'm sure he didn't think he was doing anything wrong and has no idea how what happened has crushed me.

I take a deep breath and walk on shaking legs out into the main club. My eyes meet his almost immediately, and he grins at me and approaches with his arms open.

"Cashmere!" He winks at me, and I hold out a hand to stop him from embracing me. Not only is it against the rules of the club, but I'm pretty sure I'd vomit if he puts his hands on me again.

"Sorry, Nick. I can't here." Or anywhere else, for that matter.

He drops his arms and nods his understanding while looking around. "Oh right, sorry. I guess I'm just excited to see you. I tried to get a hold of you. Where did you disappear to?'

I glance around the club and shrug. "Here."

Confusion flashes in his eyes. "Wait, so you dropped out of school to become a stripper? Not that there's anything wrong with that."

I'd love to be able to tell him exactly why I really quit school. I'd love to be able to scream at him and tell him how he took advantage of me when I was at my weakest point and that he's probably done it to scores of others and ruined their lives with the stuff he slings.

But I don't want to cause a scene here, and it won't change anything. It won't change where I am now.

It's clear he genuinely doesn't think he did anything wrong, and there's a problem with that, a very real one, but it's not one that I have the energy to correct right now.

"I had a lot going on back then, and school was just becoming too much with my personal stuff, so that's why I left."

Fair enough answer that should shut him up.

He runs his hand back to his sandy blond hair and offers me a tentative smile. "That sucks, I mean, I really hoped to hear from you after that night, you know."

What a moron.

"Yeah, I'm sorry I disappeared."

God, Nora, that sounded so lame. He's going to know something is wrong.

Thankfully, I don't have to struggle to recover because Byron catches my eye from across the room and mouths "*do you need help*?" I give him a slight nod that I hope Nick doesn't catch and wait for Byron to come to my rescue. He makes it to me in thirty seconds flat and wraps an arm around me.

"Hey Cashmere, I need your help with something. Can you spare a couple minutes?"

I try not to sigh audibly with relief. "Oh sure, Byron. Sorry, Nick, I've got to go, but it is nice to see you again."

The words are like acid coming from my mouth.

His eyes light up. "Oh yeah? It was nice to see you too. Maybe...can I give you my number?"

I shrug and show my empty hands. "No phone. And I'm kind of seeing someone."

Disappointment is evident in his gaze, and the interest is just as evident in Byron's. I have a feeling there are going to be some questions later. About a lot of things.

Byron always seems to know what's happening in the club,

and there's no doubt that after our last conversation, he's going to want me to spill.

Honestly, he's really easy to talk to and always has some pretty decent advice. So being able to tell him about Nick and Stone and everything that happened would probably be a huge weight off my shoulders, but frankly, I don't think I can keep myself together long enough to do that if I start talking.

With Byron's hand on my lower back, we walk to the changing room, and I drop into a chair.

"You ready to tell me what the hell is going on now? Is that the guy who has had you all messed up? Or is it the guy you are *seeing*?"

Uggg.

I might as well come clean. Something tells me, if I don't, things will only spiral more out of control.

"If I tell you, you can't tell anyone. I mean it. No running to Savage or Gabe. No one."

His eyes narrow. "As long as you aren't in any danger, I can do that."

"Well, danger is a relative term."

31

STONE

The unknown number flashes on my screen. It's the last thing I need right now. It could be anyone, including Dom, who I have no doubt will be sending someone to collect me in the near future. He may be cutting me some slack and giving me a little space to come to grips with everything, but it won't last. I know too much. There's no way he's going to let me flap in the wind for long.

"Hello?" My voice sounds shaky even to me. That's a really fucking bad sign. I've trained myself to never give off any signals of weakness. In front of a jury...or judge...that could mean catastrophe.

But the caustic mix of guilt, dread, love, and pain has burned me from the inside out and shattered the very core of who I am.

And that one word was a dead giveaway of my fucking frailty.

"Mr. Hawke?"

Castillo's voice is strong and unwavering...the exact opposite of mine.

Fuck.

I need to get my shit together. Immediately.

One sniff of weakness, and this man will devour me.

"Mr. Castillo, to what do I owe the pleasure?"

He chuckles. "Oh, Mr. Hawke, let's cut out the pleasantries. You know exactly why I'm calling."

The blown up building that used to be one of Dom's large warehouses immediately flashes into my mind. I do know exactly why he's calling. To issue a warning.

"I assume this is in regard to our mutual acquaintance?"

"Yes. I just wanted to make sure we are on the same page, given all that's occurred."

On the same page.

I drop down into my chair and try not to snap when I reply, "What page would that be?"

"The one where you understand you are to stay out of my way. And where you assure me our mutual acquaintance understands the same. If things don't get resolved, they could get *very* messy. And no one wants that. I think you agree on that front."

No argument there. But I'm not really in a position to make Dom understand anything. He's going to want to ensure the threat from Castillo is completely removed. And the only way that's happening is if Castillo himself is gone.

It's exactly what I had been trying to avoid when I had my sit-down with him. But he's bound and determined to take over.

"Look, I can talk until I'm blue in the face, it doesn't mean our mutual acquaintance will listen to me. And frankly, you started down this path knowing full-well the potential repercussions. My advice is to back off and hope our acquaintance forgives your transgressions."

There's momentary silence before Castillo lapses into an all-out fit of laughter. "Oh, Mr. Hawke, your naïveté is comical. It's time our friend realizes he is the past, and I am the future of the city. If he wants to get out of this in one piece, he will back off and maybe just retire in peace."

Unlikely.

"I'll have a talk with him. But you and I both know, I can only do so much."

"I appreciate your directness and honesty, Mr. Hawke. All I can ask is for you to make an attempt to keep things civil. I know you're a man of your word and will at least try. Let's just pray your words don't fall on deaf ears."

Click.

He hangs up without another word.

Well, motherfucking shit.

Just one more wrench to throw into an already convoluted clusterfuck of a situation.

The danger to everyone is ramping up, and I can't help but shake the feeling that things are going to come to a head very soon and not in a good way. What was I thinking working with Dom? Did I really think I would be able to keep my hands clean and stay out of the crosshairs? I might as well have a fucking bull's-eye on my back now that it's publicly known that I'm working for him.

Cock sucking son of a bitch.

All I want to do is fix things with Nora, but this just confirms that I can't have her and keep her safe at the same time.

I can't let her go though, not without apologizing before I say goodbye and she learns the truth and never wants to see my face again.

The very real desire to go snort a line tugs at me, and my knee bounces just thinking about it. But I don't want to touch the stuff right now, not after what happened with Nora.

A pounding at the door prevents me from having to make that decision.

What are the chances it's her?

Right now, I would welcome an enraged Nora. Nora in *any* capacity is better than the alternative.

But when I look out the peephole, it isn't Nora. It's just another fucking problem I don't need to be dealing with right now.

The moment I open the door, Skye barges in past me and storms into the living room where she tosses her purse on the couch in a huff. When she turns to look at me, her eyes are blazing, and she narrows them at me. "We need to talk."

"Skye, what the fuck is going on?"

She paces the room, frustration radiating off her. "Look, I don't want to have to do this, but you've reached a point here that I can't ignore anymore."

I love Skye to death. She's probably the only one in the family who truly gets me, but I haven't the foggiest fucking clue what she's talking about. I've barely even seen or talked to her since I've been back other than family dinners and an occasional text message here and there.

"I don't know what you're freaking the fuck out about."

She growls and fists her hands at her sides. "You've been avoiding me, and I know why."

This should be good.

"What makes you think I've been avoiding you?"

Her eyes roll up in her head, and she offers me a wry smile. "Because I'm the only person who calls you out on all your bullshit."

Well, she's not wrong about that, but I haven't been avoiding her, at least not intentionally. "What bullshit is that?"

She takes a deep breath. "Stone, I know you're using something. My guess is coke."

FUCK!

"I knew you were on something at the wedding, and I let it fly because that was a stressful situation for all of us, and frankly, you didn't seem like you were out of control with it or anything that was worrisome. But since then, things have definitely changed."

I step toward her and open my mouth to argue, but she stops me with a look and a raised hand.

"You look fucking haggard half the time, like you haven't slept in days. And looking back, there was other stuff, like you messing up at work and almost getting fired. You not wanting to come visit as much. And now that you're back, you're spending more and more time alone and with Dom."

"Wait a second, that's not true. I just had lunch with Mom the other day." And I didn't want to come back because of Nora, not because I was partying every fucking night in San Diego.

"Yeah, and she called me and asked me what's going on with you because she said you were acting weird and asking questions about Dom and just being...well, weird."

Was I acting weird with her? I don't think so.

"And it started long before Gabe and Savage told you what happened with Dom, so you can't blame it on that."

She's right, but she's also wrong. I've been using recreationally for a while and probably relying on it a little too much, but what's been happening and what Dom told me has affected me more than I care to admit. I wish I could tell her everything so she'd understand, but now isn't the time. Nora and Dani need to know first; I owe them that.

Skye needs to know I'm not out of control, and while I appreciate her concern, I need to set her straight, before this inquisition gets out of hand.

"Look, I'm not gonna lie and say that I don't enjoy a little pick me up when I'm partying or want to unwind or something. But it's not like I use every day. I'm a recreational user, I'm not a fucking addict."

She scoffs and crosses her arms over her chest. "Stone, don't be a fucking idiot, I'm a nurse, for Christ's sake. I understand what an addiction looks like, and maybe you're not a full-blown addict, but you're definitely using it as a crutch and we both know where that leads. You're too fucking smart for this shit, and you know that. Don't tell me you don't."

My desire to argue with her is quelled by remembering what I said to Nora. And the fuck ups at work. And the urge to do a line I had been feeling right before Skye got here.

Fucking shit.

I hate to admit Skye might be right. But there's definitely some evidence to support her concern.

"It's fine, Skye. I'm done." I made that decision the moment I realized what I had done to Nora.

She narrows her eyes at me again. "I'll believe it when I see it."

It may be easier said than done, especially with everything going on right now. But she needs reassurance. And I need a reminder that there's a very real reason to stay away from what's left in that vial in my desk. I should have fucking flushed it the moment Nora left.

"Don't worry, Skye. I got this."

Hopefully.

Setting aside everything else going on, it's going to take a fucking act of God for Nora to even speak with me. And that's all my fault. I can't even blame the drugs.

I guess I should be praying.

NORA

Saint appears at the door to the changing room and leans against the jamb. His immense shoulders practically reach to the other side of the frame and his head grazes the top.

Dude is seriously huge.

But having him here is comforting. There's no way Stone is getting back here if he shows up, no way Saint is even letting him in the building.

Not after the conversation I had with him when I got here.

He doesn't know everything, but he knows enough to keep Stone out.

I didn't think I would want to come back to TWO, but the thought of Nick or Stone waltzing into the main club had me begging Byron to let me work here tonight. Since I spilled my guts to him, he understood and called Vance to tell him I was heading over. Getting things off my chest to someone was an incredible relief. I didn't even realize how badly I needed to do that until my face was buried in Byron's shoulder and I was sobbing and pouring my heart out.

Tonight, I just needed to be somewhere there was a true buffer in case Stone tries anything, because Lord knows, he can waltz into the main club and do anything he wants. But not at TWO. Vance is in charge here, plus he has Saint backing him up.

And even Stone isn't arrogant enough to think he can take on that beast of a man.

His dark brown eyes meet mine, and he tilts his head toward the hallway, indicating I should follow him.

I'm not scheduled to go on for another half an hour, and I told Vance I didn't want to do any waitressing tonight. Sitting in the back with nothing but my thoughts and the other girls, who basically hate my guts, may not be the best idea, but I frankly don't think I can handle real interaction with any of the patrons tonight.

Saint backs into the hallway as I approach, and I follow him down a ways until we're out of earshot of the changing room and anything we say will be drowned out by the bass bumping from the main room.

"What's up?"

He leans back against the wall and crosses his massive arms over his chest. "A particular gentleman, who shall remain nameless, has requested entry into the club. Word is, he's already been to the main club looking for you and seems pretty intent on getting to you."

Jesus.

My stomach roils, and I step back until I hit the cool wall. Stone has some real nerve showing up here. How can he think I would see him after what he said, after what he did?

"Did you let him in?" The voice that asks the question barely sounds like my own.

Stone is turning me into a quivering ball of nerves. He's broken me more than anything else that's happened in my life. And I hate him for that.

No.

Fudge that.

I'm not going to let him do this to me. I will *not* let that man shatter the life I have. He keeps telling me how strong I am, and how I'm the one in control. It's time to prove it's true.

"Let him in."

Saint's dark brows arch, and he steps off the wall. "Are you sure, Cashmere? I haven't let him inside the building. He's stewing in the parking lot, and I can send him packing. I don't give a fuck if his brother owns the place. You are my priority."

I release a sigh and nod. "I know, Saint. And I really appreciate it. But I need to get this done and over with. Sending him away will only drag it out more."

He runs a large hand over his shaved head. "I don't really like letting him in, given how upset you were earlier. But if you're sure."

Am I?

Thinking about it too much will probably make me insane. I just need to go with my gut, which is telling me now's the time to tell Stone what I really think about him.

"Yes. I'm sure."

With a sigh, he turns back toward the main room. "I'm going to put him in the Diamond Room. And I'm going to stand outside that fucking door the entire time you are in there with him. That's not negotiable."

"Thank you, Saint."

He winks and flashes me a bright white smile. "You don't need to thank me, sweetheart. It's my job."

Crap. Crap. Double dang crap.

I pace the hallway for several minutes after he disappears, trying to figure out what I'm going to say to Stone. A million different words have flown through my head since the other night —stupid, arrogant, pompous, idiotic, self-centered, and a few four letter ones. But I still have no idea how I'm going to look him in the eye knowing what he knows and hearing those words over and over again in my head.

You fucking prostituted yourself out for some pills...I can't pity you right now.

Bile climbs up my throat, and I drop my hands into my face, taking long, deep breaths to try to gain any semblance of control.

Don't let him break you!

Renewed resolve fills my veins, and I storm down the hall, past Saint, and into the Diamond Room.

Where I stop dead in my tracks.

Stone looks like complete and utter crap. He's nothing like the man I saw two days ago. In fact, he may actually look worse than he did that night, which I never would have thought possible. He runs a shaking hand back through his disheveled hair, and his eyes meet mine. Red rims those baby blues, and every line on his face seems crater-deep.

"Nora..." A thousand things are said in just my name, but I refuse to allow myself to fall for whatever act he's going to put on tonight.

"Why are you here?"

He sighs and takes a step toward me. I stand my ground, refusing to give an inch to him even though everything in me screams for me to run away to somewhere safe.

"Because...I...shit...I need to explain...I need to apologize."

I shake my head, willing the tears burning in my eyes away. "There's nothing to explain or apologize for. You made yourself very clear the other night."

Another step brings him closer, and my heart thunders in my chest. Even now, his presence affects me physically in a way I wish I could simply push away.

"No, no I didn't. Shit, Nora, that was *not* me talking, that was a selfish prick who was drunk and high and angry and not thinking about anything but himself and his own problems. *That* had absolutely nothing to do with you or how I feel about you or who you are as a person. Christ..."

He runs that hand back through his hair again, and I notice how badly it's shaking. It might be withdrawals. I don't know how deep Stone is in this stuff, or what he's let it do to him. That alone terrifies me more than the hundred ways he has and can hurt me.

"What happened, Stone? To send you down that road the other night?"

His eyes meet mine, and he shakes his head. "I can't, Nora. At least, not right now. Right now, I need you to understand how fucking sorry I am for how I acted, how I treated you, what I fucking said. I can't...I can't even believe those words left my mouth."

There's no need for him to say what words he's referring to. We both know that.

"You have to know, I don't think that about you, I don't think *anything* negative about you. I wouldn't, I fucking couldn't ever think *anything* bad about you. You're the only good thing in my life, the one thing that keeps me grounded and able to function in this shitty world."

I raise an eyebrow. "Really? Because the other night, it seemed like coke was the most important thing in your life and the thing you were using to deal with whatever was going on."

"Shit, Nora." He closes the distance between us and reaches out, wrapping his fingers around my biceps. "The coke is nothing. I do it occasionally, and it's not a big deal. I *know* it's a big deal to you now, and I'll stop. You are way more important to me than the fucking coke."

Christ, Stone...

I want to believe him. I want to believe *in* him. So damn much. But the words he said cut deep, and I don't know if anything he can say or do now will ever heal those wounds.

"I'm so fucking proud of you, Nora. For opening up to me and telling me what happened. I abused your trust in me and failed you as a boyfriend, a Dom, and a man by throwing that back in your face, and I can never expect you to forgive me for that. But I need you to know, that *nothing* you did makes you a bad person. You have nothing to be ashamed of. It's just something that happened, it doesn't make you who you are or define you in any way. Please don't fucking let it. And definitely don't let something I said when I was buried under the weight of my own bullshit deter you from moving on with your fucking life and finding where you belong."

Every brain cell I have screams at me to pull away and never look back. But my heart is breaking at his words, the sincerity and meaning there. Stone is eloquent. There's no doubt about that, but this wasn't a speech to a jury, he really meant what he just said to me. There's no doubt in my mind he meant every single word.

For better or worse, Stone Hawke understands me and the situation I was in, and he doesn't judge me for what I did. I want to believe, with every fiber of my being, that he only acted the way he did and said the things he said because of whatever is going on with him. And hopefully, he'll open up to me and let me help him through whatever he's going through.

I have to at least try...

Right?

32

STONE

S omehow, I've managed the impossible. Nora is in my house, standing in my living room, and she isn't holding a gun or an axe or any other deadly weapon aimed at me.

Thank Christ.

I didn't think it would work, throwing myself at her feet and begging for her forgiveness. But she's here, and she doesn't even seem mad at me anymore. In fact, she's eyeing me like I'm some sick, abused puppy she's just rescued from the pound.

And I'm not entirely certain what to do with that. The Dom in me wants to tie her up and continue to apologize to her with every dirty trick I know, to show her how much she means to me, but the human in me, what little is left, knows after what's happened, I'll be lucky to get Nora to even climb into bed to snuggle with me tonight.

The fact she was even willing to come over after her shift is more than I ever expected or deserve.

"Are you sober?"

Her question comes out of left field, and it takes me a second to process it. "What? Yes, of course."

Why would she even ask that?

"Have you ever been high when we were together...physically?"

I shake my head and take her hands in mine, squeezing them gently. "No. Never. That's a line I would *never* cross. It wouldn't be safe, for either of us. I would never put you in that position. I told you, it was just an occasional thing. One that got a little too frequent lately, but I'm done."

She sucks her bottom lip between her teeth, and her eyes drop down to the floor momentarily before returning to mine. "Okay."

When she tugs her hands from mine, I'm expecting her to head for the door. Instead, she moves toward the stairs and pauses to look back at me.

"You coming?"

My heart may have just stopped in my chest. Maybe the snuggling isn't out of the question.

I follow her slowly and when we reach my bedroom, she stops in the center of the room and turns to face me. She tugs her shirt off over her head and tosses it on the floor behind her. Absolutely fucking perfect breasts sway gently with her movements.

No. Damn. Bra.

Any ability to form words has fled.

What is she doing?

The tiny shorts and itty bitty thong follow her shirt, leaving her naked before me. My cock stands at attention, but I'm still not sure what's happening here.

She came over after her shift, presumably to finish the conversation we started at TWO, but this, this is so far out of the realm of what I pictured happening, I'm not even sure what to do.

"Nora, what are you doing?"

Her shoulder raises in a slight shrug. "Giving you what you need."

Giving me what I need?

"I don't understand."

She steps toward me and cups my cheek in her palm. "Stone, you're a wreck. I don't know what's going on with you—"

I open my mouth to interrupt her, but she holds her hand up, silencing me. "And you don't need to tell me right now, okay. But whatever it is...it's eating you up inside, that much is obvious. You feel out of control. Maybe you are out of control, you certainly were the other night."

Ouch.

I cringe.

"Either way, what you need is to have some semblance of control back. So, I'm giving you what you need."

Well, shit.

Not only does Nora know me well enough to read me like a fucking book, she's also selfless enough to offer herself up to me like this even after everything I put her through.

"Christ, Nora." I drop my forehead against hers. "I don't fucking deserve you."

Her response is barely audible, just above a whisper. "I know."

But she doesn't.

She doesn't know.

She doesn't know the half of it.

My gut churns. Having to reveal the truth to her is going to be the hardest thing I've done in my life, even harder than trying to forget what I did to her father. But at least I have tonight...one last night with her. It may make me a dick to want her one last time, but no one ever said I was selfless. She can soothe my soul. I need it.

I'm going to make the most of it.

I kiss her firmly and squeeze her ass in my palms. "Are you sure you're ready for this?"

She answers me with a look of absolute determination. "Yes, sir."

I don't know how she can't see how strong and fucking determined she is. She's let one thing, one horrible choice, ruin her self-confidence so much, she can't even recognize her own strength.

If I were her, I'd be shaking in my fucking boots, or high heels as it were.

Her fingers trail across my cheek and down my neck, sending flutters of heat through my body. "What are you gonna do?"

What aren't I going to do?

I move behind her and tilt her chin up just like the first time she was in my room. "I'm going to put you up there." The eye hooks gleam in the moonlight streaming in the windows.

An audible gasp slips from her lips, making me chuckle against her warm neck. "Don't worry, baby girl, I know what I'm doing.

"I trust you." Her whispered words go straight to my cock. They're the sweetest words I could ever hear from her. Who the fuck knows why she trusts me. I really haven't given her much reason to, but I know she does, nonetheless. "What do I have to do?"

I grin and turn her head back so she can see me. "All you need to do is relax and continue to be the most fucking beautiful woman on the planet."

Her soft laughter makes her chest vibrate under my forearm currently pressed there.

"You don't have to sweet-talk me, Stone. I'm a foregone conclusion."

"I wasn't sweet-talking you, honey. That was just stating a fact." I smack her ass, relishing the way the tight globes jiggle in the faint light. "Now go stand in the middle of the room directly under the eye hooks."

She follows my command, and when she reaches the center of the room and pauses, she tosses a grin over her shoulder at me.

Fuck, this woman truly is perfect in every fucking way.

And I have to let her go.

The cabinet door creaks slightly as I open it. I study the lineup of ropes available but I don't really need to. I've known exactly what I was gonna use on her since the first time I saw her on that pole.

The pure white nylon ropes are exactly what I need for this binding. I grab them and walk over to stand in front of her. She eyes them but there's no trepidation in her gaze this time.

"I'm going to do a new binding on you. You need to let me know if it gets too uncomfortable. I can have you out of it in a few seconds. And you can always use your safe word."

"Yes, sir. I understand."

I kiss her gently and then brush my thumb over her wet lip. "Good girl. Put your arms behind your back, palms together, with your elbows pointed out."

She complies without hesitation, and I move behind her.

I hold her wrists together and bind them tightly. She flinches slightly when I jerk on them, but then she settles back, straightening her shoulders.

"Get as comfortable as you can. You won't be able to move your arms after this." After a slight shift of her shoulders, she nods, giving me the go-ahead to continue.

Over one arm and across to the other...

Back and forth...

Up and down...

Around her shoulders and across her chest in the front, creating a harness that will bear the weight when I suspend her.

Her breathing hitches when I tighten the chest harness; I

wrap my arms around her from behind and brush the back of her ear with my lips. "Just breathe."

She nods and a whispered, "yes, sir," floats through the air.

When the last tie has been made, I step back and examine my work.

Fuck.

The basket weave pattern resembles angel wings on her back...and it's precisely how I've always pictured it in my head.

"I'm going to loop another rope through this binding in the front and up through the eye hooks so I can suspend you."

A tiny gasp escapes from her mouth, but she remains silent.

"Did you hear me, Nora?"

"Yes, sir."

"Are you okay with this?"

I've been waiting fucking months to see her strung up like this, and my cock is so hard right now, I swear to God, I now fully understand the saying hard enough to pound nails.

"Yes, sir. Are you gonna...you know...when I'm up there?"

I chuckle behind her. She still can't bring herself to say *fuck.*

We'll change that tonight. I'd bet my car on that, and I fucking love that thing.

I reach up and loop the ropes to the eye hooks, ensuring they're secure before finally turning to face her. Pink tinges her cheeks, and her eyes are half-hooded already.

Christ, I bet she's even fucking wet.

And I don't have the will-power *not* to check.

Holding her eyes locked with mine, I slide my free hand down between her legs and cup her pussy. Wet. So damn fucking wet.

My cock jumps and throbs against my pants. I would strip, but I don't trust myself not to fuck her brains out right now instead of waiting to complete my masterpiece.

"Jesus, Nora. You are so ready for me, aren't you?"

She whimpers, and I run a single finger through her wet slit.

"Soon, love."

I press a quick kiss to her trembling lips and then loop the ropes through the chest harness.

"You ready, darling?"

"Yes, sir."

I pull on the rope, gently and slowly easing her up and taking the weight off her legs until her toes don't even brush the floor anymore. Her chest points toward the ceiling and her head and legs dangle down on either side of the harness. She sucks in a breath, and I pause. "Does that hurt?"

"No." She shakes her head. "Just...it just...feels weird, I guess."

Reassured she's fine, I resume raising her until she's finally suspended three feet off the floor by her chest. Her legs dangle below her, and her pseudo-wings splay back behind her as if she's ascending up to Heaven.

It couldn't be more fucking perfect.

Because Nora truly is my angel.

The one sure, clean, pure, untainted thing in my life.

I've been dreaming of this moment for so long, but actually seeing her like this...

Shit.

The image I created in my own mind didn't come close.

The ethereal look on her face, with her eyes closed and her mouth slightly parted, only adds to the vision before me.

I know I won't be able to leave her there for long like this, but I can't stop staring at her.

As much as I want to be inside her, I want to ingrain and burn this image into my head for the rest of my life even more.

This is gonna be the last time I see Nora Eriksson. Or at least, the last time I see her where she's going to talk to me...let alone let me touch her. I need to savor it while I can.

Because once she's gone, my whole world will go back to being a dark, empty, meaningless abyss.

NORA

Being suspended from Stone's ceiling is surreal. I thought it would hurt, but it doesn't. The pressure just reminds me of the intricate way Stone built the harness and bound me in what is no-doubt a beautiful piece of rope art. It hugs my body as if his arms were around me, securing me and assuring I'm safe.

The fact that he's standing back, admiring me, instead of banging me like the giant bulge in his pants assures me he wants to, speaks volumes.

Seeing this, taking it in, is more important to him right now than sex.

And for Stone Hawke, that's saying something.

I let myself drift in the weightlessness Stone's created. The only sensations breaking through my daze are the slight tugging of the ropes and cool air of the room against my naked skin.

After what feels like hours, but is likely only a few minutes, he steps up to me and takes my head in his hand, turning me to face him.

"You are divine." The words float through the foggy bliss and into my heart.

Well, dang...

I wasn't expecting that. I'm not even sure what it means really, but I'm pretty confident it's as close to saying he loves me as is possible for a guy like Stone.

He presses his lips to mine gently, and then briefly rests his forehead to mine before pushing away and moving to where the ropes are secured.

Slowly, I move downward until my feet brush the floor. I try to stand, but I wobble and strong arms wrap around me, holding me steady.

"I got you."

Yes, he most certainly does.

I sag into his arms, letting him support my weight.

"Let's get you out of this."

He sets me to my feet and waits until I'm able to somewhat support my own weight by leaning against him. Then he starts the tedious process of undoing the intricate work. Rope falls to the floor around me, and he bends down and lifts me up, holding me against his body closely.

The soft sheets feel like Heaven on my heated skin. The mattress dips, and I expect to feel Stone's warm body pressed against mine. But instead, he hovers over me, assessing me with dark, stormy eyes.

"Sleep. I've got something else planned, and you're going to need some energy."

Energy?

I should probably question it...ask what he has in mind. But frankly, I don't care. The exhaustion is suddenly too much to fight. Between our fight the other night, no sleep, my confrontation with Nick, work today, and the emotional drain of it all, I can barely keep my eyes open.

A soft kiss lands on my forehead before I sense him shift away from me and off the bed.

Mmm...

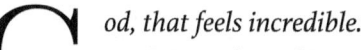

God, *that feels incredible.*

Warm lips skim across my skin. Hands grope and probe and my hips arch of their own accord.

"Mmm, Stone..."

"Yeah, baby. Sorry I had to wake you, but I can't wait any longer."

Wake me?

My eyes drift open slowly. The room is still dark, the only light a faint glow from the window. "I fell asleep?"

He nods and resumes his exploration with his mouth. "For two hours."

His hot breath across my sensitive skin makes me shiver.

"But it's time to get up now. I have something special planned."

The glint in his eyes sends a shiver through me. That's the look...the one that promises all kinds of debauched and depraved things...the one I tried so dang hard to ignore for so long.

He pulls back and slides off the edge of the bed. His naked skin glimmers in the moonlight, and his straining cock juts out at me. "Come on." His proffered hand hovers near mine, and as soon as I place mine in it, he tugs me up and off the bed.

That's when my eyes catch a flash of something metal sitting on the foot of the bed.

Holy mother of God...

It's the meat hook ball thingy, and it's attached to a rope, and lying next to another coil.

What the ever-loving heck is he planning on doing with that?

His warm breath tickles my ear, and his hand trails down until it's cupping my butt cheek. "I told you I had something planned." He squeezes it and chuckles against my skin before placing a gentle kiss behind my ear.

Good Lord, this...this is...just...

He pulls my hair back and secures it with something. "You're going to want this up."

A tug on my hand has me following him around the bed to center of the room again. I look up at the eye hooks.

Okay, Nora, you can do this.

When my eyes travel back down and meet his, he grins. "Don't worry, babe, you'll enjoy this."

Something tells me his definition of "enjoy" and mine are

quite different. But at this point, I'm willing to let him do whatever he needs to do to regain his sense of normalcy and control.

Even if it means sacrificing my poor behind's virginity.

I trust Stone...and so far I've never *not* enjoyed what he's done to me. When he was playing around back there before, I can't lie and say I didn't love it. He knows what I will like.

Worst case scenario, there's always *cupcake*.

Although, I kind of think that would break his heart right now and probably push him even deeper in on himself.

Which is the last thing I want.

Still...

Why does it have to be the butt?

A chuckle slips out at that thought, and Stone raises an eyebrow at me. "What's so funny?"

I press my lips together firmly, silencing myself. "Nothing, sir."

"Are you laughing at *me*, Nora?"

Oh, heck no!

I shake my head so vigorously, I almost make myself dizzy. "No, sir." He grabs my left hand and winds rope around it, then tugs it up above my head and loops the rope through the eye hook. He repeats the process on my other hand, raising it up over my head and securing it.

This isn't so bad, I'm not even suspended, my feet are still flat on the floor.

Which makes me confident something else is coming.

When he steps in front of me, the Lucifer hook is in his hand gleams the same way his eyes do.

"This is going in your ass, Nora. It will be uncomfortable working it in, but I promise, once it's there, you'll understand why I love this so much, and I think you will too."

Uncomfortable.

Right.

Having a metal ball shoved up my butt is going to be more than *uncomfortable.*

"Just remember to relax and breathe."

Easy for him to say.

He moves behind me and goes silent. The only sounds in the room are our mingled breaths. A wall of heat presses into my back. I sag into him, as much as the ropes will allow, which isn't much. Stone naked is a decadence I'll never get enough of. The feel of his hot, hard body against mine, anticipating what's coming next, makes my core clench in need and my clit throb.

His cock presses between my cheeks and up my lower back, assuring me it won't be long until I have him inside me, and I can help him forget whatever's been weighing on him so heavily.

Wet lips press against the back of my neck and work their way down my spine.

Kiss.

Lick.

Suck.

He pauses briefly at the spot right above the split of my cheeks and brushes his thumbs across my lower back.

"These little back dimples are sexy as fuck, you know that?"

His tongue slowly swirls around and over each one, sending a shudder up my spine. I shift and the ropes tug on my arms.

Any movement is going to leave marks. I'm sure that's exactly what he intends.

He drops even lower and spreads my cheeks with his hands.

A groan rumbles from his throat, vibrating against my skin where his lips are still pressed.

That sinful tongue hits the top of my crack, and I jerk.

No...he wouldn't.

He can't.

Oh...God...he's going to.

Lower, and lower, and lower...

Licking and sucking...

Until he reaches the place no man, or woman for that matter, has been before.

Another appreciative groan fills the air.

He loves this.

And I hate to admit...I do too.

My legs shake with every flick of his tongue and probing search in my most forbidden place.

"Holy he—"

I barely manage to catch myself from saying the word that *wants* to come out.

Stone is wicked, evil, depraved, shameless...he's everything good girls should avoid. But I haven't been a good girl for a while, and this feels so dang incredible.

Why is my clit throbbing so hard while he goes to town on my backside?

I am so going to burn for eternity for loving this.

But it will be so worth it.

His mouth leaves my skin, and I turn my head to try to see what he's doing. I instantly regret it when the ropes tug on my wrists.

It's forgotten when a wet finger probes and then pushes into my tight hole.

"Here we go, baby."

Ho. Ly. HELL!

I instinctively clamp down around it, and his free hand grabs my hip gently. He squeezes it. "Relax baby, it's okay. Let me in."

Let him in?

That ship sailed a long time ago. Stone has managed to work his way so deeply into me, I don't know if it will be possible to ever shake him.

I take a deep breath and do my best to relax every muscle in my body. He pushes further and then adds a second finger, slowly stretching and spreading me.

"Oh...God."

His hand leaves my hip and then something liquid hits my crack and drips between my thighs. I jerk forward against the ropes. Then something new meets my skin. Cold and wet...metal.

What the heck is that?

It rolls against my cheek and up next to where his fingers are probing me.

It's that damn Lucifer hook.

He removes his fingers and pushes the metal against my opening. "Lean forward slightly and relax, Nora."

Lips press gently against my butt cheeks while fingers work the ball against my tight opening. His free hand snakes around to the front and finds my slick slit. He drags through it then rolls circles around my clit as he works the ball into my tight butt.

My body wars with itself, desperate for him to keep touching me, but unable to relax into what he's doing behind me.

"Oh God...I don't know if I can do this."

Stone kisses my lower back. "It's okay, baby, just breathe."

I take a deep breath and try to concentrate on what his amazing fingers are doing to my clit. A second later, the ball slips all the way into me and my body closes around it.

A strangled moan falls from my lips, and Stone chuckles and then smacks my ass, sending the ball even deeper.

Sweet Christ!

His body wraps around mine from behind, and he kisses the side of my neck.

"I hope you're ready for this, baby, you better hang on."

33

STONE

*N*ora shudders against me, and I tug gently on the rope attached to the top of the anal hook.

She jerks. I'm sure she's forgotten all about the fact that it will be tied to the ceiling.

"Oh, you didn't think this through, did you?" I reach up and hook it through the eye hook above her then tug gently. She yelps and shifts up on the balls of her feet.

I tug again and again until she's inched up onto nothing more than her toes, little whines and whimpers coming from her with each movement of the rope.

It doesn't hurt. I know that. But the sensation is definitely overwhelming.

And it's about to get worse.

With a tug on the ropes attached to her wrists, I ensure she has very little room to move. She gasps.

"Oh, Jesus Christ..."

I laugh and secure the ropes. "Oh, I'm not Jesus, but I'm pretty sure you're gonna be calling me God by the end of tonight."

She growls. "You might be the most arrogant man I've ever met, Stone."

"That might be true, Nora. But sometimes, arrogance is warranted."

I smack her ass again, and she jerks forward, her butt clenching around the ball. She gasps and shifts uncomfortably on her toes.

She's just discovered the real joy of the anal hook. If she attempts to move or lower her feet in any way, even a centimeter, she's going to push it deeper into herself. Every slight shift is going to rub that ball in all the right places. By the time we're done tonight, she's going to be begging to have my cock up her ass.

God willing...

The double Wartenberg wheel gleams in the moonlight flooding in through the open window. It looks sinister, even to me, but I know what it does to the body, what it can do to Nora.

I move to stand in front of her, making eye contact with her the first time since I tied her up. Half-hooded eyes meet mine with a mix of lust and unease.

She's scared. Maybe she should be.

This is so far out of her wheelhouse. I'm so fucking proud of her.

"Don't forget your safe word, baby."

Her eyes widened slightly, and she nods. "Yes, sir. I remember."

Her skin is blazing when I touch my lips to her collarbone. I want to feel her reaction when the wheel hits her sensitive skin. The metal touches the taut expanse of her stomach, and she jerks, letting out a moan with the movement. The ball shifting deeper inside her is stimulating every sensitive nerve she didn't know she had. Combined with the prickling sensation of the wheel against her stomach, she can't stop herself from moving.

I work my way up and over her breast, intentionally avoiding her sensitive peaked nipple. She arches against me, straining for some sort of contact.

The fingers of my free hand grasp her nipple, and I twist. She gasps and tugs against the ropes.

I run the wheel up over her shoulders and around her back, relishing the shivers and moans it elicits. Her entire body will be so over-stimulated by the time I'm finally inside her, she'll go off like a rocket.

Her long, elegant spine arches and rolls in the light, beckoning me. I start at the base of her neck and roll it down slowly, then back up the other side. She tenses and undulates under it, pulling on the ropes.

My lips trail behind the wheel, covering every inch of her skin until she's vibrating with need and shaking, shifting the ball deeper and deeper inside herself.

"Stone..." My name comes out as a strangled groan, and I wonder how much more she can take.

I wonder how much more I can take.

My cock has never been this hard in my entire life. I feel like if her hand even brushes against it, I'm gonna come. Good thing those things are tied up high.

"You still with me, love?" My breath floating across her ear sends another full-body shudder rolling through her.

"Yes...sir..." comes out on a muffled groan.

"Good." I kiss the back of her neck then move over to the bed to grab a condom. My hands trembling as I roll it on is not a good sign for my control.

Keep it together, big guy.

When I move back and behind her, I grip her hands, still wrapped around the ropes, in mine. Her skin is on fire, and she curls her fingers into the ropes when I tighten my hold.

Slowly, I run my hands down the length of her arms, over her rib cage, and all the way down until they're grasping her hips. She rolls them back into me, pressing that luscious ass straight against my cock. The metal of the hook is chilly against my lower abdomen but the heat radiating from between her cheeks is fucking sinful.

"I'm going to fuck you now, Nora. And you're finally going to understand."

Understand me. Why I do this. Why I need this. Why she needs this.

I know what's gonna happen as soon as I shove my dick inside her. The combination of me spreading and filling her pussy and the ball rubbing against her from the inside is going to be overwhelming for her.

But in the best way possible.

I fully expect her to lose her shit in about three seconds, which is probably about as long as I'm gonna last too. I stroke my cock a few times.

Don't lose your shit, Stone. She needs to come first.

She's the important one here, not me.

I'm like a loaded gun with a hair trigger, but somehow, I need to find a way.

The searing heat of her pussy when I press the head of my cock against it makes me suck in a groan.

Fucking A...this woman...

I pause momentarily to collect myself. Then I grasp her hips and angle her back slightly. I push in slowly, letting her adjust to my size and the sensation of the ball moving inside her with my entrance.

"Holy shit!"

It takes me a second to process what she just said because, right now, my head is swimming with the feel of her pussy clasping around my cock and that ball rubbing against me with every slight shift of her body.

Holding myself steady, I lean forward and nip at the back of her neck. "Told you I'd get you to swear."

She mumbles an unintelligible response, and I watch her fingers close tightly around the ropes at her head.

It's not enough though.

I need her to completely let go and lose her shit. I won't be happy until fuck-bombs and unholy curses are screamed and echoing in this room.

Gripping her hips tightly for purchase, I pull back and slam into her...hard...driving her forward, the ropes creaking under the strain of her weight.

"Oh GOD!"

I piston in and out, in and out...giving her no reprieve from the sensations wracking her body. My hips slam against her ass. The drag and pull of the ball against my cock with every thrust, combined with her clasping pussy, is the most magnificent feeling on this planet.

She jerks and squeals with every shove of my dick, gasping and moaning.

I'm gonna come soon, and I need her to go over before me. I reach forward and find her clit, rolling it in time with my pumping hips.

"Jesus...*FUCK!*"

Two more hard, driving thrusts, and she explodes around my cock, screaming, gasping, tugging, moaning, and releasing a litany of curses the likes I haven't heard before, from anyone, let alone her.

Victory.

∾

NORA

There are men in this world...

Men women aren't supposed to fall in love with.

Men who are dangerous.

Men who are cocky and arrogant.

Men who believe they're in control of everyone and everything.

Men who think the world revolves around them.

Men who look at you like their dick is already buried inside you.

Men who own you with a single glance, word, or smile.

Men who will take your heart, smash it into a million pieces, and stomp all over it, just for the joy of hearing it crunch under their feet.

Stone Hawke is all of those things and then some.

Yet, somehow, I've managed to fall head over heels for him, breaking every dang rule in my book and shattering all my plans to get my life back on track.

That realization hit me about thirty seconds into him thrusting into me with that Lucifer hook shoved up my butt.

Good Lord, who comes up with that stuff, anyway?

What person said, *you know what would feel good? A giant ball shoved up a bum while you hang from the ceiling?*

But God, did it feel good. No, actually, good isn't the right word. It was...transcendent.

I don't know what happened while I was strung up like a side of beef, being hammered by Stone's huge dick. There really isn't any way to describe it to someone who hasn't experienced it themselves. It was like floating away from my body, yet still feeling every thrust and retreat, hearing every labored breath, experiencing the euphoria from another plane.

Stone said it's called sub-space. And I guess that's as good a name as any for it.

Because by the time he finally finished and released me, I was definitely in a different galaxy, maybe even universe.

Yeah, definitely universe.

Even now, laying in his arms and listening to his rhythmic breathing, I'm not sure I'm one hundred percent in my own body. Every single inch of my skin tingles and a hum thrums through every muscle and limb, centering at my core.

I shift and throw my leg over his, snuggling closer to him and inhaling the scent of Stone and his clean skin. The bath we took is only a hazy memory. All I remember was his hands on my skin and murmured words of reassurance that I'd done well.

His arm tightens around me, and he mumbles something unintelligible.

If I could have any superpower right now, it would be the ability to read minds because I've no idea what's going on inside Stone's head.

Whatever's been eating away at him, that drove him to that breaking point, is still very much real. Even though what we did tonight seems to have calmed him somewhat, I can still see it in his eyes every time he looks at me. There's something dark deep beneath the surface, something that wasn't there before a few nights ago.

Stone has always been dark. He's always been raunchy and reckless and a little bit crazy. But whatever this is, is so much more than that. This is something he's letting deeply affect the way he lives his life. He resorted to drugs to deal with it, and that's more than mildly concerning. He isn't the type to take bullshit from anyone or to let things get to him that are inconsequential. This is serious.

But just like he couldn't force me to tell him what happened and why I left school, I can't force him to tell me what's going on. If it has to do with his work for Dom, I guess I can understand his reluctance because knowing the things he knows probably puts him in danger. But it doesn't appease my need to ask why and ask what's happening every time I look at him.

Even now, as he sleeps next to me, the creases and worry lines on his face are deeper than I've ever seen them, and he shifts restlessly. Even in his sleep, he can't find relief from whatever is haunting him.

He mumbles something, and I bury my face against his chest, wanting to offer him what comfort I can. Almost as soon as I touch my lips to his pec, he jerks up and I pull back. His wide, frightened eyes meet mine, but he sees right through me, almost as if I'm not here, as if he's seeing something completely different than what's actually in front of his eyes.

"Stone, what's wrong?" He doesn't acknowledge my question, and I don't even think he heard me. I reach out and grab his shoulders and shake him. "Stone, what's wrong?"

His eyes finally focus on me for a moment before he closes them, shakes his head, and takes a deep breath. When he reopens them, he's here again.

"Shit, I'm sorry. It was just a dream."

"About what?"

He scrubs his hands over his face a couple times and shifts back slightly until his back is pressed to the headboard.

"About you."

"Me?"

That sure as heck looked like a nightmare. And he appears absolutely terrified.

My gut churns, and I sit back on my heels in front of him, bracing myself for whatever he's going to tell me.

The shrill ring of his phone prevents me from asking him to explain.

He leans over to the nightstand and grabs it. His eyes narrow when he sees the caller. "What the hell does he want?" He swipes to answer. "Savage? It's four in the morning, what's wrong?"

Those haunted eyes of his widen, and his hand closes on the phone so tightly, his knuckles turn white.

"Right now? Jesus fucking Christ. Are you going down there? Okay, I'm on my way."

He hangs up and immediately shifts to climb off the bed, tossing his phone back on the nightstand. "Savage's club is on fire."

"What?" I jump up and follow him to his closet, grabbing my clothes along the way. "Which one?"

"THREE. That's all I know. They're heading down there now."

How does a place catch on fire when it isn't even open yet?

Despite his attempt to appear calm, I can see the panic set in Stone's eyes. I tug on my shorts and shirt. "I'm going with you."

He glances over his shoulder at me as he pulls on a pair of jeans. "Of course you are."

No explanation is offered for his comment, and I'm not sure whether I should take that to mean of course I am because I'm his girlfriend or of course I am because it's my brother-in-law's business. Either way, I'm just happy he wants me to go.

Stone is already walking a razor-thin edge, and something like this could send him spiraling down again.

I just hope that this time, he lets me catch him before he falls.

34

NORA

Flames and smoke rise high above the city, visible from miles away as we race down to the club location. Stone's driving like a mad man, and I'm clinging to my seat and door, trying to keep myself from flying around inside the car every time he takes a corner way too fast for safety. Even my seatbelt can't keep me from sliding across the leather seat with each turn.

Holy cow. It's an inferno.

Fire trucks and ambulances litter the parking lot. Stone parks as close as we can and barely turns off the car before he's out and bolting toward the building.

"Stone! Wait!"

I run after him, stumbling on still-weak legs.

A fireman halts him, and I finally catch up. Even from here, the heat of the flames lick my skin. I reach out and take his hand in mine, giving it a reassuring squeeze. It's not his business, but he knows how much this place means to Savage, Gabe, Ben, and Storm, how much work they've all put into it.

Water streams from hoses, and firemen rush around, shouting orders.

"How did this happen?" It's a dumb question. Stone doesn't know what happened any more than I do, I just can't imagine how a fire like this could have started here. Ben runs a tight ship. From what I've heard, his worksites are always well-maintained, and he's a stickler for code.

"Stone!" We both turn toward his yelled name and see Savage and Gabe approaching with Dani and Skye hot on their heels. They all examine us suspiciously.

Dani narrows her eyes on me. "Nora, what are you doing here?"

Crap on a cracker.

I sigh and take a sleeping Kennedy from my sister. "This really isn't the time, is it?"

She scowls but drops her line of questioning, instead focusing her attention on the blaze while the boys talk heatedly in hushed tones.

"It has to be him..."

"...only thing that makes sense..."

"...isn't an accident..."

Their words don't make sense. How can they know it's not an accident? Who are they talking about?

Before I can ask for an explanation, a scream rents the night air.

"Noooo!" Storm sprints past us and toward the building.

Gabe catches her arm as she passes and yanks her back. "What are you doing?"

She sobs and struggles against his hold, trying to free herself. "Ben...he's in there! I tried to call him...he's not answering...he's... oh, God..."

Oh...oh no...

Gabe grabs her face, turning it until she's looking at him. "Storm, are you sure?"

Another sob falls before she manages to answer him. "Yes, he couldn't sleep...last couple nights...been coming down here with Caleb to...work out some plans. He was gone when I woke up. My phone was off. I saw your text about...fire...when I turned it on... tried to call..." She shakes her head and collapses against Gabe.

Stone takes off past the line the firemen have created, running toward the building. Dani and Skye pull Storm from Gabe's arms and embrace her, mumbling something unintelligible. Savage and Gabe take off after Stone, leaving me standing alone, watching the scene unfold.

Ben can't be dead...he can't...

The solemn look on Stone's face when he turns to look at me from where he stands talking to one of the fireman tells me everything I need to know.

It's true.

Ben is gone.

As the Hawke boys make their way back to us, Storm pulls her head from Skye's shoulder and releases a sob that rips the air around me.

She knows.

But Stone, Savage, and Gabe don't just look distraught. They look angry.

No, angry isn't the right word.

Rage.

That's what is burning in their eyes when they reach us.

Stone fists his hands at his sides, so tightly, his knuckles turn white. "This was no fucking accident, and we all know it."

"What?" Storm pushes out of Skye's hold and approaches him. "What do you mean?"

He paces the parking lot, running his hands through his hair and clenching the ends. "He can't fucking get away with this. Not this time. Not this fucking time."

"Who? What are you talking about?" Storm grabs at his shoulder to stop his movements, but he shoves her off.

"Not this time," he mumbles the phrase over and over.

Images of the night outside the club flash through my head. This is exactly how he was acting that night. I know what he's like when he's not thinking clearly, when he's in this state.

This won't end well.

I approach him and place a hand on his arm. He jerks away from me, his eyes wild and unfocused. This is bad. This is really, really bad.

Gabe steps up next to me. "Stone, whatever you're thinking, stop. You can't go after him half-cocked and upset like this. It will only make things worse."

"Who the fuck is him?" Storm's screech breaks my heart even more. She's just as confused as I am, but she also just lost her husband. I can't imagine how confused and angry she is right now. How devastated she must be. And what Stone is doing is only make things worse.

Savage joins us, leaving Dani and Skye hovering in the background. But they don't seem confused at all. If anything, they look just as angry as the boys.

What do they know that I don't?

"Will someone please tell me what's going on?" My question isn't directed at anyone in particular, but all three of them look to me and then their gazes shift over to Storm.

Stone is the one who finally answers. "Ben and Caleb were murdered. And I'm not going to let the motherfucker responsible get away with it."

Before I can question him further, he turns on his heels and storms off toward his car.

Crap.

Stone in this state is dangerous. I chase after him, Gabe and Savage's shouts to stop following in our wake.

But his long legs eat up the distance faster than I can run.

The car's engine revs as I reach his door. Without even glancing at me, he peels away from the curb, smoke rolling from the tires in his wake.

STONE

Déjà fucking vu.

Storming into Dom's office is unwise. But here I am, going off half-cocked with no damn plan...again.

There's no doubt in my mind Dom is behind the fire. The only other possibility is Castillo, and despite his disdain for Dom, and his recent attack on him, I don't believe for a second he would come after a business of one of my family members to prove a point. If he wanted to send me a personal message, it would have been *personal*—my house, my car, even Nora.

No, this has Dom written all over it, which is exactly what I told Savage and Gabe before I came here. We managed to get one of the firefighters to tell us Ben and Caleb were found in one of the interior upstairs rooms with large construction materials blocking the door from the outside. With no windows and the obvious accelerants used, they were doomed the moment the flames started.

The fucking bastard did this, I just know it...

I slow my walk when I spot three of Dom's goons sitting in the area outside his office. They nod at me as I pass. I'm not sure if it's a good sign or a bad one that he hasn't said something to them about keeping me out of the building. I would think by now, he would have to know I wouldn't be coming in bearing flowers even without this attack on Savage and Gabe's business.

As usual, he's seated at his desk, the fucking master of his domain. And he isn't surprised to see me in the least.

I step into the office and stop halfway to the desk. It's safer if there's some space between me and Dom right now. Otherwise, I'm liable to do something really fucking stupid.

"Why?"

A slight grin tugs at one corner of his mouth. "I needed to send a message to everyone to keep their mouths shut, including you, Stone. I didn't mean for Ben and the other man to die, but, in this business, collateral damage happens. They were in the wrong place at the wrong time."

"Collateral damage? He was my fucking brother-in-law! My fucking family!"

Dom raises a dark eyebrow at me. "I thought I was your family."

"Maybe you were at one time, but now, you're just a sick fuck."

Any hint of humor that may have existed is wiped from Dom's face in an instant. "Do you really think your family is going to stand with you after they find out what you did? Will Dani and Savage? Will *Nora*?"

Her name on his lips makes my blood roar in my ears and thrum through my veins.

"Don't fucking threaten me, Dom."

He raises his hands in a surrender motion. "It's not a threat, just a question based on my observations of the inner workings of the Hawke clan."

"You don't know shit. Stay the hell away from my family or you'll regret it."

Dom barks out a laugh. "Are you actually threatening me, Stone? Because that would be *very* unwise. I've been more than gracious with the way you've been acting lately. I could have ended this and you a long time ago. The only thing saving your ass has been my loyalty to your mother and my love for you. Neither seems as important to me as they once were."

The mention of my mother boils my blood even further. I don't care about myself. But my mother, she's everything to everyone. And she trusts him. She loves him. She has no fucking clue what a monster he is.

Complete fucking maniac.

Something has to give. It's time she knows the truth. Then maybe, just maybe, he'll back off and leave us all alone.

"I know that look, Stone. Don't do something stupid. Let this be the end of it."

I release a mirthless laugh. "The end of it? You fucking *killed* my brother-in-law, and one of Savage's employees tonight! You burned his business to the fucking ground! This isn't something I can walk away from Dom, and if you think Savage, or Gabe, or anyone else who knows the truth is going to either, you are sorely mistaken. You may have had the upper hand with Dani, but any fear they had has been replaced by a burning rage for vengeance. And that doesn't just go away."

"No," he shakes his head, "I suppose it doesn't."

That's it?

Where are the threats? The promises to end me and everyone else?

His easy acquiescence and calm response cause unease to crawl up my throat.

I'm missing something.

Fuck.

He anticipated this. His men knew I was coming. He already has a plan in motion, and I walked *right* into his castle where he has a damn firing squad.

A smug grin spreads across his face. "Given the panicked look in your eyes, I'm guessing you just realized your mistake in coming here tonight." His hand disappears behind the desk and emerges with a .45 Glock. He lays it on his desk with a blood-chilling thunk and watches me for a moment.

I'm well and truly screwed. I ran in here gun's blazing without an actual fucking gun.

Fucking moron.

"I really hate to have to do this, Stone. You were like a son to me, even more than my own flesh and blood one. But times change, people change. I can't let this vendetta you have against me get in the way anymore. There's enough to worry about without having to look over my shoulder all the time for you too."

"And what about when I'm gone? You going to do the same to Savage and Dani? What about Gabe? Skye? Might as well take care of Storm too, you've already ruined her life. And Mom...she won't have anyone left, you should put her out of her misery."

He chuckles. "Don't be so melodramatic. I'll do what needs to be done. And, as always, your mother will come to me as a shoulder to cry on when things go bad. In this case, very, very bad."

"You won't get away with it."

His satisfied smile has me taking a step back toward the door. He raises the gun and levels it at me, straight at my chest where my heart is beating wildly.

"You forget so easily, Stone...I always get away with it."

The finger wrapped around the trigger flexes and time stands still.

Every terrible thing I've ever done on Dom's behalf flashes before my eyes, sealing my fate. Karma is a bitch, and it's about time I pay up for my sins.

I let my eyes drift closed. If I'm going to die, I don't want to have to look the man who was my father in the eye while he does it.

When the *bang* finally hits my ears, it's much quieter than I anticipated. Not at all how I remembered the guns I've shot sounding, but I still expect to instantly feel pain, searing, soul-gutting pain.

Instead, a muffled grunt and moan fill my ears, and a hand grabs my elbow.

My eyes fly open.

Dom's body, slumped in his chair, a small red hole spreading in the center of his white shirt fills my vision. His glazed eyes meet mine, and he makes a pathetic attempt to grab for the gun that he dropped onto the desk.

Before he can make it two centimeters, four more shots ring out, jerking his body until he's still.

"Jesus Christ, Stone..."

I turn toward my brother's voice and find Savage and Gabe just inside the office door.

Gabe lowers his gun. The suppressor on the end of it registers briefly.

Savage just gapes at me. "He was going to kill you. What the hell were you thinking coming here by yourself? A minute later, you would be dead on the floor, and I'd be explaining to Mom that her best friend killed her son."

I retreat until the solid wood of the open door meets my back. Sliding down it, I drop my face in my hands and try in vain to make my lungs function properly.

He was going to kill me. Actually going to pull the fucking trigger.

"Stone." I look up at Gabe. He kneels in front of me and places a hand on my shoulder. "You all right?"

I manage a nod. But I am far from all right.

He inclines his head and rises to his feet. "I need to call the police. They're not going to be happy about another body count."

Body count?

Shit.

"Wait, where are Dom's men...they were out there. Did you kill them?"

Gabe shakes his head. "One. The other two were smart enough to surrender after they saw what I did to their buddy.

They met us out front, almost like they knew we would be coming."

Because they did.

Dom may not have intended to kill Ben or Caleb initially. I do believe that was a case of bad timing on their part. But he knew damn well that fire would draw me, and likely Savage and Gabe here. And he was right. We played right into his maniacal plans.

He just made the mistake of underestimating the Hawkes...again.

35

NORA

"That's all he said?" Mrs. Hawke's question is no doubt the same one running through all our heads right now.

I open the text from Stone again and read it out loud, word for word. "Everyone is fine. At police station. May be here a while."

Dani throws her hands up and rolls her eyes. "Seriously? That's it? Why aren't any of them answering their phones? Maybe we should go down to the police station."

That's a terrible idea.

As her sister, I feel like I should tell her that, but sitting here in the room full of Hawke women, including a grieving Storm and a very worried Dani and Skye, I'm playing it safe by keeping my mouth shut. The only thing that has kept them from bombarding me with questions about Stone is the fact that Ben is dead.

After Stone sped away from me, Gabe and Savage took off

after him, saying something about needing to stop him from doing something stupid.

Knowing looks had passed between Dani and Skye, but I don't really have a place to be asking questions. They don't know what's happened between Stone and me. As far as they are concerned, I'm the odd woman out in my sister's condo right now.

Mrs. Hawke shakes her head and rises from where she's been sitting with Storm on the couch. "No, that would only make things worse. Whatever's happening, trust that Stone can handle it. This is his forte, isn't it?"

Her eyes dart over to me, and a hot flush rises in my cheeks.

Talk about awkward.

Everyone in the room knows Stone and I are sleeping together. Once things settle, I'm in for a real inquisition.

Storm clears her throat, drawing everyone's attention to her. She's been relatively silent since we brought her here four hours ago. We waited for almost three hours, but the fire still wasn't out. The fireman who seemed to be directing things at the scene told us there was no reason for us to continue to stay there. They would start the investigation once things were safe, probably tomorrow, and Storm would be contacted by the coroner's office in the morning to make arrangements.

It was clear given the grim tone he used that he suspected foul play as much as the Hawke men seemed to.

Who could have done this?

And why?

"Why?" Storm voices my question, almost as if reading my mind. "Why would anyone want to hurt Ben? Or Savage and Gabe for that matter? I just don't get it." She shakes her head, a new wave of tears streaming down her reddened cheeks.

Skye moves over to the couch and embraces her older sister. "I have a feeling we'll have the answer to that when Stone, Savage, and Gabe get back here."

It better be soon. The tension mixed with the anguish in this room is doing a number on all of us. Seven hours and not a word from them except that text has turned this into a cauldron of antsy, angry, distraught women.

Thankfully, Angelina and Kennedy have slept through most of it. Storm's nanny brought Angelina over shortly after we arrived, and she crashed in the guest room almost immediately. She has no idea her father is gone.

Poor girl.

I know exactly what she's going to go through when she finds out. I was only a few years older when Dad died. And look where all that led me—prostituting myself for drugs and wrapping my naked self around a pole.

Only the door to the condo opening saves me from delving further into how losing him will likely destroy poor Angel's life.

"Savage!"

"Gabe!"

Dani and Skye fly across the room and practically launch themselves at their men. Stone trails behind them, deep bags under his eyes and a sullen look I've never seen before on his handsome face.

"Stone?" His eyes snap over to me and widen. I knew I shouldn't have come. He wasn't expecting me here. This is a family thing. I should leave.

"What the hell happened?"

"Why were you at the police station?"

"Where did you go?"

Questions fly at them from all sides. The only ones not bombarding them are me and Storm. Shock has settled in, and she appears completely lost to the world. I'm not even certain she realizes they're back. Her unfocused eyes stare at the fireplace, almost as if searching for the flames that aren't there.

Savage holds up his hands, silencing the room. "We'll explain everything. But everyone should really sit for this." He moves to the center of the room and waits for everyone to get settled. Gabe releases Skye from an embrace and joins Savage while she sits next to Storm and their mom on the couch.

I'm the only one who stays in the back, hovering near the stool under this side of the kitchen island.

Stone remains near the door, avoiding eye contact with everyone in the room and shifting uncomfortably, tension obvious in his stance.

What happened?

He looks terrible, and I didn't think it could get much worse than the other night.

Savage runs his hands back through his hair, a move so darn similar to Stone. They're more alike than they want to admit. "Mom, this isn't gonna be easy for you to hear, but I need you to listen. I know how much you care about Dom, and I understand where your loyalty to him comes from, but there's something that you need to know. You need to know the truth about what's been happening and what happened early this morning when we left the fire."

Mrs. Hawke freezes and glances between Savage and Gabe. "I don't understand what you're talking about."

"You will." Skye reaches over and wraps her arm around her mother shoulders, giving her a pat. "Just listen to them, Mom. It's important."

It's clear Skye already knows what's going on, or at least part of it. That much has been evident since we were at the fire.

But I'm still standing over here completely in the dark. And I don't like it.

Savage nods and glances at Gabe before starting again. "I guess it's best to start at the beginning. With Dani."

Dani sighs and reclines back on the couch. "I've been investigating Dom for years."

That doesn't surprise me. I knew Dani had some big story she'd been working for years and years, but she never let me in on what it was. Dom makes sense. She's always been hell-bent on taking down men like him. Something she inherited from Dad, no doubt.

"What? Why?" Mrs. Hawke's startled question almost makes me chuckle.

She can't be *that* naïve or blind to who and what Dom Abello is. Even I know he's dangerous, and I haven't known him his whole life.

Skye turns to her mother. "Because he's a criminal, Mother. He's a goddamn gangster. And don't try to argue that point with me right now because you'll soon realize that your trust and belief in him is misplaced." She looks to Savage and nods.

"Dani had been digging, just looking for anything she could pin on Dom to finally get him sent away. I, of course, knew nothing about this until it was almost too late. You remember when Dom's men were killed last year, and we told you Dani and I were at the scene because she was doing an article about it?" His mother nods. "Well, that's only sort of true. She was there because his men had lured her and her source to the abandoned market in order to kill them."

Mrs. Hawke's gasp matches mine and Storm's. Dani didn't tell. How could she keep this from me...from Mom?

"We barely got to her in time once we realized what was happening."

The matriarch of the Hawke family turns her eyes to Gabe. "You killed them." It isn't a question. Given Gabe's history, I guess it's an obvious assumption to make.

He nods. "I didn't have a choice. They had already killed her source, and the gun was aimed at her head. Thirty more seconds, she would have been dead."

Storm rises from her seat. "Dom planned that? Okayed it?"

A grim look passes between Savage and Gabe before he answers his sister. "Yes. We met with Dom and turned over a copy of what Dani found, including some very damaging evidence on Gabe's father."

Mrs. Hawke shifts forward in her seat. "Brian? Is that why he..." she trails off, her question doesn't need to be finished. Former Mayor Brian Dunne went out with a bang and left everyone wondering how such a successful and loved politician could fall so hard so fast.

Gabe shakes his head and runs a hand over his face. "I don't know for sure. But part of our deal with Dom was that he wouldn't touch me, Savage, or Dani, and he needed to get my father to retire from government service. In exchange, we agreed not to make anything Dani found public."

Storm approaches Gabe and Savage. "I don't understand. What does any of this have to do with you being at the police station today? Did they arrest Gabe for what happened? Why now? Wasn't that well over a year ago?"

"No, I was cleared a long time ago." Gabe takes her hand and pulls her against him.

She pushes away from him and looks to Savage and Stone, who has remained silent and lurking near the door. "Then why are you telling us this? What does what happened with Dani have to do with anything? Why does it matter now?"

Stone finally moves, stepping into the front of the room between his brother and Gabe. He closes his eyes and takes a deep breath, holding his head in his hands for a moment before raising his eyes and looking to everyone gathered in the room. His gaze lingers on me long enough for me to catch the true depth of the despair burning there.

Whatever this is, it's epically bad.

～

STONE

It takes me a few moments to work through the giant lump in my throat. I shouldn't have looked at Nora. That was a huge mistake. I'm going to break a lot of hearts with what I say, but hers is the only one that matters. She's all that's ever mattered.

Another deep breath helps me clear my head.

Can't put it off any longer.

"Because of something that I did a really long time ago."

Mom's mouth opens to ask a question, but I raise my hand. There's no way I'll get through this if I'm interrupted.

"Something happened when I was twelve...something I never could've imagined or anticipated...something I've tried to forget the last fifteen years."

Unsuccessfully.

"Stone, you're scaring me." Seeing Mom's lip quiver shatters my already broken heart. "Just tell me what happened."

I sigh and shove my hands through my hair. "It was one of those days when you sent me off with Dom to do whatever. The boys were fishing, and the girls and you were doing something girly. He brought me to a warehouse and said he had some business to take care of, that it wouldn't take long." I heave in a deep breath before I continue. "He set me up in the office there and told me to keep myself occupied for a few minutes until he was done. He said there might be a book or something to do in one of the drawers."

Breathe, Stone.

"So, I opened one and found a gun."

The looks from around the room tell me they can already anticipate what road this story is taking. Savage and Gabe have already heard it. I spilled everything at the police station. Telling strangers was hard enough. Seeing the reactions of my brothers was like being kicked in the balls again. Knowing what this will do to Dani and Nora though, I'm not sure how I'll survive it.

"Dom had taken me to the range numerous times. I knew how to handle it and to not do anything stupid. I just looked at the revolver to check to see if it was loaded, and I was just about to put it away when...Christ, this is harder than I thought it would be..."

I close my eyes. I can't look at any of them when I finish this. "There was shouting and the sound of gunfire, and I didn't know what was going on. I opened the door, and when I went into the warehouse, I found two of Dom's men shot to death."

Mom gasps, and I can't stop from opening my eyes to make sure she's okay. She holds her hand over her mouth. "Oh, my God, Stone. I'm so sorry you had to see that. I had no idea..."

The last thing I want is for Mom to feel guilty about what happened. She did what she thought was best for me by making me spend time with Dom. There's no way she could have known what would happen.

"Honestly, I didn't even have time to think about it. I was so worried about what might be happening, so I followed the sound of shouting and found Dom being held at gunpoint. I didn't know who the guy was, just that he had killed two of Dom's friends and now had a gun pointed at the man who was essentially my father. Dom taught me not to panic in situations like these, so I didn't. I watched. But the yelling got louder and louder, and the man shook his gun at Dom and screamed something I couldn't understand. It looked like he was about to shoot Dom, and then he turned toward me...so..."

Jesus, this is fucking hard.

"So, I shot him first. I emptied the gun, all six rounds. I barely even registered what had happened before Dom grabbed me and dragged me out of there. He told me never to mention it to anyone, not even him, and to pretend like it never happened. He said I had done the right thing but not everyone would see it that way. I believed him because what other choice did I have? I was twelve years old, and I was scared as hell, and the man I trusted more than anything was telling me that it would be okay if I just did what he said."

Tears stream down Mom's face, and I chance a look at Nora. She's frozen in place, her hand over her heart, as if trying to keep it inside her chest. I know what's coming. That heart will be decimated.

By me.

But she needs to know. They all need to know.

"I tried to push the whole thing out of my mind and forget about it. Of course, that's impossible, but I did my best, at least the best a twelve-year-old can. That was kind of a turning point in my life, thinking that I could go to prison for something really made me want to become a lawyer."

Mom rises and walks over to me, her lip trembling. "Stone, how come you never said anything to me?"

How do I answer that question?

"Because I packed it away with everything else, all my other feelings about everything that happened. I listened to him and moved on with my life."

She shakes her head and swipes at her tears. "What does any of this have to do with what happened with Dani? I don't get it."

Dani steps forward on shaky legs, tears shimmering down her cheeks. "When did this happen?"

The question is cold and direct.

She knows.

But that date wouldn't mean anything to anyone else in the room except her and Nora.

I close my eyes again and fight the urge to turn and run. But this isn't something I can run from. Running from what I did back then is what got us here in the first place.

"August 10, 2002."

Nora gasps and rises from the stool she's been perched on since I started talking. She shakes her head back-and-forth, taking a few steps forward. "No...no...that's impossible...you can't mean..."

I can't even begin to fathom what words to say to her right now. What can I say that will mean anything in this moment?

"I'm so sorry, Nora."

Dani stops in front of me, her fists clenched at her sides. "You killed my father?"

Gasps fill my ears, but I look at Nora, even as I answer Dani. "I'm so sorry. I didn't know he was a cop. I didn't know what was going on..." Dani lets me pass her, and I move toward Nora.

She holds her hands up, halting me from advancing further and shakes her head and takes a step back until she hits the stool behind her. She's never looked at me with so much fear in her eyes. Not with everything I've pushed her to experience.

"No...I can't...I don't..."

How did everything end up so fucked?

Six months ago, things were amazing. Life was exactly how I'd always imagined it. I had a great job, a great apartment, a great sex life, everything a man could ever want. Except I *don't* want that life anymore. I haven't since the moment I touched Nora.

Right now, I'm just dying to comfort her. I've never needed anything so much in my life as I need to take her in my arms and hold her right now.

I move toward her slowly.

A trembling raised hand stops me in my tracks. She shakes her head and takes another step back, flinching away from me. Her eyes meet mine, tears streaming down her face, and she says the one word that can shatter my entire fucking world...

"Cupcake."

EPILOGUE

THREE MONTHS LATER

STONE

*T*he coffee shop looks exactly the same as it did that morning so many months ago..

I shouldn't be here. I shouldn't even be back in New Orleans. I should have stayed in California, but I have to see her.

Even after three months of rehab and endless hours of therapy to try to deconstruct the spider web of lies, guilt, and pain, she's still the only thing I can think about. I can't just let her go.

No fucking way.

She's been the only thing good and light in my world for so long, I can't imagine living without her in it.

It's a real possibility she's going to walk away and refuse to even talk to me. And I can't really blame her for that. After everything I did to her family, and to her, it would be completely warranted. But I'm a fucking selfish prick, and I need for her to at least hear me out before I can attempt to reassemble my life again.

I knew I needed help. After that night when she found me coked out and spiraling down into the darkness, and then after what Skye said...

And it wasn't just about the coke.

Yes, I was using it as a crutch and letting it become my fall-back when shit got too heavy. But it all stemmed from the disorder in my head, stuff I had buried deep for so damn long, I hadn't even realized it existed.

Dealing with what happened with Nora and Dani's father, what I did...it needed to happen. And even though I may never be able to accept what occurred and my role in it, therapy at least helped me get a grip on it enough to keep me from reaching for blow.

But it can't stop me from craving Nora like fucking air. Or change the dreams I have of her every single night.

The familiar scent of coffee and baked goods fills my nose as I step into the shop.

My eyes find her instantly. She's like a goddamn beacon shining out to me across the dark water, drawing me to safety.

Christ, she's beautiful.

She's practically fucking glowing in the pale morning light filtering in from the bay of windows in front of her. The halo of light surrounding her and the white, gauzy shirt she's wearing make her appear ethereal. She's a fucking angel.

Images of her in the angel binding return to my head. That was the single best night of my life.

That then became the worst. She fucking safe-worded on me. And instead of staying and facing the fallout, I fled, like the fucking coward I am. I left NOLA, I left my family, I left the mess Dom's death left, I left a madman like Castillo unchecked, and I left Nora, broken and sobbing in the arms of Dani. Other than a phone call with Skye to tell her where I went and why, I completely cut off everyone. It was the only way I could wade through my own issues and hopefully find my way back. She told me Savage and Gabe explained to everyone what happened with the fire and how Dom died.

Her description was apt. She said it was the perfect bookend to the turmoil he created by just existing, and that the healing was just starting. Without me there. No amount of begging could convince me to return. I needed to leave. To give everyone time. To give myself time to get things in order.

I force myself to shake off the memories and concentrate on the here and now.

She's at *our* table.

Does she even realize it?

Maybe she did it intentionally. But it's more likely just a freak twist of fate designed to make this even harder for me.

I gather what little strength I have and move slowly toward her.

The laptop on the table occupies her focus, and her fingers fly over the keyboard. I don't think I've seen her so intent on something, other than maybe trying not to swear while I was fucking her.

A smile tugs at the corner of my mouth at that memory. One of the ones that kept me going through the last several months.

I stop next to the table, every word I had planned to say disappearing instantly.

Her fingers pause, hovering over the keyboard. Wide blue eyes lift to meet mine, and she sucks in a breath. Her hands fall to the table.

"Stone? What are you...I thought you were..."

I should have known Skye would tell her if she asked, if she even wanted to know. The fact that she did ask has to mean something. At least, my aching heart hopes so.

"I was, but I had to see you. Please, just give me five minutes."

The hesitance and apprehension in her gaze breaks what's left of my already demolished heart. But it beats the fear and hatred there the last time I saw her, when I left her standing in Savage and Dani's condo, sobbing and reeling from finally knowing the truth.

I accept her silence as reluctant acquiescence and plow forward.

"You have every damn right to hate me. I'm an asshole. I always have been, and I probably always will be. I can't even begin to apologize for everything that happened, everything I did...to you, and your family. I wouldn't know where to begin because no words can ever take back what happened or what I said."

Tears stream down her face, but she doesn't look away or try to interrupt me.

Strong girl.

"I've spent the last three months trying to work through my shit. And I finally realized something I already knew that night before the fire, I just wasn't able to accept it then."

My heart thunders in my chest. I take a deep breath and prepare to put everything on the fucking line. They're words I never imagined I would say to anyone, let alone in such a messed up situation as we find ourselves now. But they're true.

"You fucking own me. I can't live my life without you in it. I love you."

She shakes her head and fists her hands on the table. Anger and tears shimmer in her eyes. "They told you, didn't they?"

I don't have a fucking clue what she's talking about. "Told me what?"

She slams her palm on the table, rattling the dishes. Tears drip down her cheeks. "I begged them not to. How could they not understand?"

Understand what?

Her distress has my chest tightening. I want to comfort her, but I don't dare move closer. "Nora, what are you talking about?"

A man appears at her side and glares at me, but I barely spare him a glance. My entire focus is on her. "Everything okay, Nora?" When his hand lands on her shoulder, my gut seizes.

Holy shit. She's with someone.

I'd be lying if I said I didn't want to smash his fucking face in for touching her, but I want her to be happy. And she looked happy when I came in. She certainly doesn't anymore, and it's my fault, yet again.

She lays her hand on top of the douchebags and pats it. "I'm fine, Jamie. Really. It's okay."

Jamie? The owner?

I refocus on him and, sure enough, the familiar face from that fateful morning stares back at me. He eyes me again before nodding and disappearing behind the counter.

"Are you with him?" It's the same question I asked her that day. And I'm praying it's the same answer.

"What?" Her head jerks up, and those wide eyes meet mine. "No, of course not. I told you, he's just an old friend."

The relief that floods my system almost buckles my knees.

Thank fuck.

"Then what were you talking about? Who do you think told me what?"

A deep sigh slips from her lips, and she closes her eyes. She opens them again, flattens her palms against the table, and pushes her chair back.

Any semblance of control and restraint I've maintained since walking in here disappears the moment I see the slight swell of her belly.

"Jesus, you're pregnant?"

∾

NORA

This isn't the way I'd imagined him finding out. I thought I had made it pretty clear to everyone that they weren't to tell him anything about my pregnancy. At first, it was for selfish reasons, because I was so dang mad at him...for everything. But then, once I realized how dumb I was being, my primary concern was not interrupting Stone's treatment. He didn't need the extra stress of finding out he was going to be a dad.

I thought I had another week or two before I'd have to finally come clean. He was supposed to be in rehab until the end of the month. Him being here has blindsided me. It's something he's apparently an expert at.

I've spent these early months of my pregnancy with the Hawke family bringing me into their fold in a way I never could have anticipated. With everything that happened, all that we all lost, they didn't even question my place as one of them when I told them another little Hawke was coming.

My hands automatically drift down over my stomach and rest there. "Yes."

His wide eyes move up my body until they meet mine. "Is it mine?"

I scoff and nod. "Of course it is. I didn't want anyone to tell you because you needed to focus on yourself."

"I...I...shit..." He runs his hands back through his thick hair and shakes his head. "I swear I didn't know. I haven't spoken to *anyone* about *anything* since I left, other than telling Skye where I was heading."

Apparently not.

He stares at my stomach with a fascination I haven't seen there before. "How...when?

"Given my due date, I'm guessing it was our first night together, in the shower."

I see him running it over in his head. It was the *only* time we ever had sex without protection, and given how wrapped up we were in each other, I don't think either of us even thought about it. Pretty stupid, actually. I was on the pill, but I guess he has super sperm. It doesn't surprise me really. Everything about Stone is above and beyond the expected.

When he appeared beside me and said all those things...told me he loves me...I thought for sure he was doing it because he felt obligated when he found out I'm pregnant. Now, I'm just confused.

"If not because of the baby, then why are you here?"

He closes the distance between us and captures my face in his hands in a split-second. "Because every damn word I just said is true. I love you, Nora, and I need you in my life. I've been trying to get myself in the right frame of mind to come back to you. I had no idea if you would even talk to me after what happened, what I did—"

I know where he's going with this. It's the same conversation I've played over and over in my head a thousand ways since I learned what happened. And I can't lie. At first, the thought of ever speaking to Stone again, of being able to look him in the eye after finding out he's the reason my father was ripped from my life, was unfathomable.

Dani and I were reeling. And going to tell Mom felt like we were going to rip her heart out all over again. But she was the one who ultimately put it all into perspective, at least for me, after weeks of talking through it.

"You were a child, Stone. You didn't set out to kill anyone. You were doing what you thought was right to protect someone who was basically your father. I understand that now. It's time you do, too."

His forehead presses against mine, and his warm breath flutters over my lips. "I don't know how to do that...forget the guilt. Not just about your father, but about what I did to you."

Crap. This is...hard.

I should have prepared myself better for this conversation. It's not that I haven't gone over it a hundred times in my head, I just never knew what my response would be. Early on, it would have been *cupcake* again. It was the single hardest word I've ever spoken. But it was also right at the time. I never could have handled him touching me, him talking to me and trying to explain and apologize again and again...not back then.

Now, it's a different story.

"I forgive you, Stone."

Warm tears splash against my hands where they clutch the front of his shirt. They aren't just mine.

His emotion-choked voice fills the space between us. "Give us a chance. Please. I've always been hungry, Nora. For something—attention, power, money, love...I just never realized I'd been fucking starving until I tasted you."

My heart is screaming for me to say yes. But I don't know if I can. That dang logic keeps creeping in, telling me I'm only going to set myself up for disappointment if I let him back in. Stone is imperfect, as we all are. And he will make more mistakes, ones that will no doubt hurt me, even inadvertently. At the same time, he is the father of this baby, and I can't keep him from being a father, I would never do that, even after everything that happened. Even if *we* can't be together.

"You want to be involved with the baby?"

His head flies back, and he narrows his eyes on me. "What? Of course. It's my child, why wouldn't I want to be involved?"

I shake my head and try to pull back from him, but his hands on my face hold me in place. "My stripping days are done, Stone. I re-enrolled in school before I found out I was pregnant. I'm swamped with work and dealing with morning sickness, which is more like all day sickness, really. I'm not really sure how I'll be able to juggle things once the baby arrives."

I'm terrified of spiraling down the same hole to keep up.

Those words aren't spoken, but I know Stone will understand exactly what I'm saying even without them.

"Christ, Nora. I am so damn proud of you. Don't worry about anything. I'll take care of you and the baby. You follow your dreams. Let me carry the load."

The weight of the last several months of worry and despair lifts from my shoulders, and I bury my face in his chest. That familiar spicy scent envelops me as he wraps his arms around me and holds me tight. Despite all of Stone's flaws, this is it. This is where I'm meant to be. His arms offer safety. They offer love. They offer something I've never found anywhere else on this planet. Complete and total acceptance.

We stand like this long enough that I can feel eyes on us. He pulls back slightly and tips my chin up. Tears blur my vision, but the love in his watery eyes is clear. He meant what he said, all of it. And I believe him.

Stone will never let me down or let anything hurt me or this baby.

I love him.

He leans in and presses his mouth to mine. The familiar taste and heat has me sagging against him. His tongue swipes over my lips, and I open for him, tangling my tongue with his and pouring everything I can't say into the kiss.

When we finally come up for air, he grins at me. I grasp his hand and place it over my belly. "Your son."

His eyebrows raise, and a grin spreads across his face. "It's a boy?"

I nod and reach up to swipe away the tears trickling down his cheeks.

Seeing Stone Hawke cry destroys any remaining barrier I had erected around my heart.

He flexes his hand over my stomach and brushes his lips over mine again. "You have no idea how happy you've made me. I thought there was maybe a one percent chance you might *consider* giving me another shot. I never imagined you would say yes, and be offering me a real family."

My heart breaks at his words. "You already have a real family, Stone."

It's clear he wants to interrupt me to argue, but I press a finger over his lips to stop him.

"Everyone loves you. Dani struggled with what happened with our father for a while. Truthfully, she still does. I did too, but, it was easier for me. I barely knew him or remember him, I guess that's why. But she eventually realized the same thing I did. The actions of a child do not make the man. Do you remember when you told me that one action does not dictate or define who you are? You need to heed your own advice. You are a *good* man, Stone, whether you want to believe it or not. And I'll keep telling you that until the day I die."

That sly, devious grin that promises a hundred dirty, sensual things spreads across his face. "I'm good, huh?"

The flash in his eyes makes my core throb. Every single nasty thing he's ever done to me, or promised to do, races through my head.

Oh God...I'm in so much trouble.

He leans in, nuzzling the sensitive spot right behind my ear. "What if I want to be bad?"

I laugh, the first *real* laugh in what feels like forever, and slide my hands down over his ass. "That would most definitely be acceptable, too."

I hope you enjoyed *Stone Sober*! Click here to get an exclusive BONUS SCENE with Stone and Nora on New Year's Eve! https://BookHip.com/LLHXWNC

A NOTE FROM THE AUTHOR

For anyone interested in learning more about Dear Mistress and the BDSM lifestyle, please check out her blog on the Shameless Book Club's website, here:

http://shamelessbookclub.com/category/columnists/dear-mistress/

A special thank you to Christine and Angie from Shameless Book Club for allowing me to use Dear Mistress in *Stone Sober*, and for always providing amazing book recommendations and advice!

Gwyn McNamee is an attorney, writer, wife, and mother (to one human baby and two fur babies). Originally from the Midwest, Gwyn relocated to her husband's home town of Las Vegas in 2015 and is enjoying her respite from the cold and snow. Gwyn has been writing down her crazy stories and ideas for years and finally decided to share them with the world. She loves to write stories with a bit of suspense and action mingled with romance and heat.

When she isn't either writing or voraciously devouring any books she can get her hands on, Gwyn is busy adding to her tattoo collection, golfing, and stirring up trouble with her perfect mix of sweetness and sarcasm (usually while wearing heels).

Gwyn loves to hear from her readers.
Here is where you can find her:
Facebook:
https://www.facebook.com/AuthorGwynMcNamee/:
Twitter:
https://twitter.com/GwynMcNamee
Instagram:
https://www.instagram.com/gwynmcnamee
Bookbub:
https://www.bookbub.com/authors/gwyn-mcnamee
FB Reader Group:
https://www.facebook.com/groups/1667380963540655/
Website:
https://www.gwynmcnamee.com

OTHER WORKS BY GWYN MCNAMEE

Billionaires of New Orleans:

The Hawke Family Series

Savage Collision (**The Hawke Family - Book One**)

He's everything she didn't know she wanted. She's everything he thought he could never have.

The last thing I expect when I walk into The Hawkeye Club is to fall head over heels in lust. It's supposed to be a rescue mission. I have to get my baby sister off the pole, into some clothes, and out of the grasp of the pussy peddler who somehow manipulated her into stripping. But the moment I see Savage Hawke and verbally spar with him, my ability to remain rational flies out the window and my libido takes center stage. I've never wanted a relationship—my time is better spent focusing on taking down the scum running this city—but what I want and what I need are apparently two different things.

Danika Eriksson storms into my office in her high heels and on her high horse. Her holier-than-thou attitude and accusations should offend me, but instead, I can't get her out of my head or my heart. Her incomparable drive, take-no prisoners attitude, and blatant honesty captivate me and hold me prisoner. I should steer clear, but my self-preservation instinct is apparently dead—which is exactly what our relationship will be once she knows everything. It's only a matter of time.

The truth doesn't always set you free. Sometimes, it just royally screws you.

AVAILABLE AT ALL RETAILERS:

books2read.com/SavageCollision

Tortured Skye (The Hawke Family - Book Two)

She's always been off-limits. He's always just out of reach.

Falling in love with Gabe Anderson was as easy as breathing. Fighting my feelings for my brother's best friend was agonizingly hard. I never imagined giving in to my desire for him would cause such a destructive ripple effect. That kiss was my grasp at a lifeline—something, anything to hold me steady in my crumbling life. Now, I have to suffer with the fallout while trying to convince him it's all worth the consequences.

Guilt overwhelms me—over what I've done, the lives I've taken, and more than anything, over my feelings for Skye Hawke. Craving my best friend's little sister is insanely self-destructive. It never should have happened, but since the moment she kissed me, I haven't been able to get her out of my mind. If I take what I want, I risk losing everything. If I don't, I'll lose her and a piece of myself. The raging storm threatening to rain down on the city is nothing compared to the one that will come from my decision.

Love can be torture, but sometimes, love is the only thing that can save you.

AVAILABLE AT ALL RETAILERS:

Books2read.com/Tortured-Skye

Stone Sober (The Hawke Family - Book Three)

She's innocent and sweet. He's dark and depraved.

Stone Hawke is precisely the kind of man women are warned about—handsome, intelligent, arrogant, and intricately entangled with some dangerous people. I should stay away, but he manages to strip my soul bare with just a look and dominates my thoughts. Bad decisions are in my past. My life is (mostly) on track, even if it is no longer the one to medical school. I can't allow myself to cave to the fierce pull and ardent attraction I feel toward the youngest Hawke.

Nora Eriksson is off-limits, and not just because she's my brother's employee and sister-in-law. Despite the fact she's stripping at The Hawkeye Club, she has an innocent and pure heart. Normally, the only thing that appeals to me about innocence is the opportunity to taint it. But not when it comes to Nora. I can't expose her to the filth permeating my life. There are too many things I can't control, things completely out of my hands. She doesn't deserve any of it, but the power she holds over me is stronger than any addiction.

The hardest battles we fight are often with ourselves, but only through defeating our own demons can we find true peace.

AVAILABLE AT ALL RETAILERS:

books2read.com/StoneSober

Building Storm (The Hawke Family - Book Four)

She hasn't been living. He's looking for a way to forget it all.

My life went up in flames. All I'm left with is my daughter and ashes. The simple act of breathing is so excruciating, there are days I wish I could stop altogether. So I have no business being at the party, and I definitely shouldn't be in the arms of the handsome stranger. When his lips meet mine, he breathes life into me for the first time since the day the inferno disintegrated my world. But loving again isn't in the cards, and there are even greater dangers to face than trying to keep Landon McCabe out of my heart.

Running is my only option. I have to get away from Chicago and the betrayal that shattered my world. I need a new life-one without attachments. The vibrancy of New Orleans convinces me it's possible to start over. Yet in all the excitement of a new city, it's Storm Hawke's dark, sad beauty that draws me in. She isn't looking for love, and we both need a hot, sweaty release without feelings getting involved. But even the best laid plans fail, and life can leave you burned.

Love can build, and love can destroy. But in the end, love is what raises you from the ashes.

AVAILABLE AT ALL RETAILERS:

books2read.com/BuildingStorm

Tainted Saint (The Hawke Family - Book Five)

He's searching for absolution. She wants her happily ever after.

Solomon Clarke goes by Saint, though he's anything but. After lusting for him from afar, the masquerade party affords me the anonymity to pursue that attraction without worrying about the fall-out of hooking-up with the bouncer from the Hawkeye Club. From the second he lays his eyes and hands on me, I'm helpless to resist him. Even burying myself in a dangerous investigation can't erase the memory of our combustible connection and one night together. The only problem... he has no idea who I am.

Caroline Brooks thinks I don't see her watching me, the way her eyes rake over me with appreciation. But I've noticed, and the party is the perfect opportunity to unleash the desire I've kept reined in for so damn long. It also sets off a series of events no one sees coming. Events that leave those I love hurting because of my failures. While the guilt eats away at my soul, Caroline continues to weigh on my heart. That woman may be the death of me, but oh, what a way to go.

Life isn't always clean, and sometimes, it takes a saint to do the dirty work.

AVAILABLE AT ALL RETAILERS:

books2read.com/TaintedSaint

Steele Resolve (The Hawke Family - Book Six)

For one man, power is king. For the other, loyalty reigns.

Mob boss Luca "Steele" Abello isn't just dangerous—he's lethal. A master manipulator, liar, and user, no one should trust a word that comes out of his mouth. Yet, I can't get him out of my head. The time we spent together before I knew his true identity is seared into my brain. His touch. His voice. They haunt my every waking hour and occupy my dreams. So does my guilt. I'm literally sleeping with the enemy and betraying the only family I've ever had. When I come clean, it will be the end of me.

Byron Harris is a distraction I can't afford. I never should have let it go beyond that first night, but I couldn't stay away. Even when I learned who he was, when the *only* option was to end things, I kept going back, risking his life and mine to continue our indiscretion. The truth of what I am could get us both killed, but being with the man who's such an integral part of the Hawke family is even more terrifying. The only people I've ever cared about are on opposing sides, and I'm the rift that could end their friendship forever.

Love is a battlefield isn't just a saying. For some, it's a reality.

AVAILABLE AT ALL RETAILERS:

books2read.com/SteeleResolve

Then check out the Billionaires of New Orleans: The Hawke Family Second Generation Series to meet the children of the original characters!

www.ingramcontent.com/pod-product-compliance
Lightning Source LLC
Chambersburg PA
CBHW061513020726
47502CB00006B/2059